A GOOD TIME

O'LEARYS 2

SHANNYN SCHROEDER

DEDICATION

To Paly, you are a great critique partner.
Thanks for reading this more times than any person should
have to.

ACKNOWLEDGMENTS

This book was originally published by Kensington Books (eKensington) in 2013.

This book was definitely a labor of love. I wanted to tell Indy's story, but she is the hardest character I've written. That difficulty meant that this book was drafted and then rewritten multiple times. First, I want to thank Lani Diane Rich, who pointed out that the book didn't work because I kept breaking my character. I learned so much from her. Next, I want to thank my critique partners and beta readers. Paly, Cynthia, and Ryann, this book wouldn't be if you hadn't read through and given me awesome advice. To my agent, Fran, and my editor, Peter, thanks for loving my work. Finally, I want to thank my son for teaching me that there is more to video games than blowing things up and shooting.

CHAPTER 1

Tequila was not her friend. Indy Adams couldn't believe she'd forgotten that one simple rule last night. The drumbeat behind her eyeballs was a blatant reminder. When the guys at the bar offered her a shot after closing, she hadn't seen the harm.

Too many shots and a crappy night's sleep later, she regretted every sip. She got out of her car and raised a hand to shield her eyes from the sun's glare. If she'd planned better yesterday, she wouldn't have had to get up early to come to the office now.

She pulled open the door, and a waft of expensive perfume smacked her in the face and clogged her throat. Indy swallowed the gag and faced the exiting clients with a perfunctory smile. The woman clicked by in her Jimmy Choos, followed by her husband and Indy's colleague Susan, real estate superstar.

Indy ducked into the office hoping to avoid a conversation with Susan. The clock on the wall showed an hour until her meeting with Griffin. He'd finally decided to start his house hunt. Correction, his mansion hunt. The thought of selling a million-dollar house made her giddy. Her giddiness almost made her forget the hangover.

She knew Griffin had hired her only because his best friend, Ryan, was marrying her sister, but she'd take any connection she could. She'd met Griffin casually on several occasions, usually at Ryan's bar, but he'd put off the search and seeing houses for months.

"Indy," Susan said from behind her.

Shit, she really wanted to escape without this. Every conversation with Susan bordered on hostile.

"I hear your big client is finally ready to buy. I'd started to think you'd made the whole thing up."

After locating the codes she'd left tucked in her desk, Indy faced Susan and her usual pinched expression. "No, Susan, I don't have to make up clients."

"Well, after you gloated about how much money this one would bring in, you dropped off the map."

"Well, I'm here, and now I'm off to show houses." She waved the paper and turned to leave. She wouldn't admit she'd gone back to waitressing because she needed the money.

"You're not going to show a house to a millionaire looking like that, are you?"

Indy stalled in her tracks and turned cautiously.

"Haven't you ever wondered why you don't attract more affluent clients? You don't play the part. You have to act as though you belong in their world and you"—she paused and pointed at Indy's outfit from shoulder to hem—"clearly don't."

"What's wrong with the way I'm dressed?" Sure, she wasn't as buttoned up as Susan, but she wasn't dressed for clubbing either.

"You look a little trampy, ready to flirt with whomever comes your way."

Heat crept up Indy's neck and burned her ears. "I don't flirt with clients."

Susan arched an eyebrow.

"I'm friendly. You might want to try it sometime." Indy shoved through the door. Anger gnawed her nerves like fire ants. She didn't need to flirt to get the job done.

Once in her car, she studied her clothes. Would Griffin not take her seriously because of how she dressed? Her stomach gave a little squish. She couldn't honestly answer the question. Griffin had always flirted with her, but he flirted with everyone in social situations.

She checked the time. If she hurried, she could stop at home to change.

~

FORTY MINUTES LATER, racing to get to her appointment, Indy felt a little panicked.

"I hope the man who invented pantyhose died a slow and painful death," she cursed. It must've been a man, she thought as sweat snaked down her back and nylon suffocated her thighs. The damn air-conditioning in the car stopped working, and she hadn't planned to fix it yet since fall had supposedly arrived. Unfortunately, the Chicago weather didn't agree.

The remnants of her hangover made her regret the decision.

She whipped into the circle drive of the first mansion and saw Griffin's silver Jaguar already parked. Double damn. She parked behind him and got out. Her ten-year-old Taurus sagged sadly behind the Jaguar.

I am so out of my league.

She tugged at the collar of her blouse. Her skirt skimmed

the backs of her knees, reminding her of church clothes. At least she was ready if the heat really did kill her.

Griffin still sat in his car. The Winnetka house stood in front of her with a gorgeous, wide, pillared front porch. Selling a house in the wealthy Chicago suburb would be her first.

Looking back at the Jag, she couldn't quite reconcile the image of Griffin hanging out, drinking beer at his friend's neighborhood bar with the millionaire video-game developer. Indy threw back her shoulders and faked confidence as best she knew how.

She paused en route to his car. The door swung open and Griffin unfolded himself from behind the steering wheel. He wasn't just good-looking; he was drool-worthy.

His perfectly styled, dark hair slicked back from his face. His jaw was surprisingly smooth. He usually sported a dark five-o'clock shadow, and she'd figured it had been intentional.

He spoke into his phone for another moment, acknowledging her with a slight wave of his hand. His finely tailored suit revealed a fit body: broad shoulders and trim waist. He shed his suit coat and rolled his sleeves in concession to the heat, which should've made him look relaxed, but his face was solemn. She preferred him in jeans and a worn T-shirt, drinking a beer at O'Leary's.

Ending the call, he tucked his phone in his pocket before closing the door. Indy approached with her hand extended. "Mr. Walker, nice to see you again. I'm sorry I'm late."

He grasped her hand and tugged playfully. "Call me Griffin. I'm not looking for a dog and pony show, Indy."

She liked the way her name rolled off his tongue. "I'm simply greeting you the same way I'd greet any client."

He removed his sunglasses and made no attempt to hide his appraisal of her. She'd been scrutinized by worse. His expression held a hint of laughter. After raking his gaze over her, top to bottom, he smiled. Small lines fanned from eyes nearly as dark as his hair. The act removed the stiff business-man, and he became a drinking buddy. "I'm not *any* client. We've known each other for months. We're friends."

Her tense muscles relaxed a fraction. Their previous encounters had paved the way for a friendly acquaintance. He followed her to the house. Even in her two-and-a-half-inch heels, she had to look up to meet his eyes.

As she opened the door, chilly air brushed over her heated skin and caused a shiver. "Would you like a tour, or just want to wander?"

After she asked, she looked at the décor and cringed. The owners hadn't wanted photos of the interior posted online. Now she knew why. *Everything* was white.

Griffin's phone rang. He checked the screen and ignored it.

"You can take that if you need to," she offered. "I can wait." She wanted to have a few minutes to cool her body.

He stood in the middle of the foyer and turned in a slow circle. "No, I've seen enough. Where to next?"

Indy's stomach flipped. "You don't want to see other rooms?" she asked carefully.

His eyes locked on hers. "No."

"I realize the color scheme . . . or lack of one might be a turn-off, but that's paint and carpet."

"What else do you have?"

She fumbled with the clasp on her portfolio and pulled two listings from the pocket. "Here are the other two I told you about. We can go to whichever you like next."

"Let's try this one." He tapped the top page.

"Okay. Follow me." She exited the house. Excitement and optimism seeped from her pores like sweat. She'd hoped for a quick sale.

The next two showings went the same. Griffin walked in, looked briefly, and left. In the driveway of the third house, she said, "Maybe if you tell me a little more about what you do want, I won't waste your time looking at houses that don't work."

His broad, charming smile creased at the sides of his mouth and showed the hint of dimples. "You showed me exactly what I asked for. I'll know it when I see it."

"Okay. I'll keep you posted if I find other listings that might suit you." Disappointment gripped her.

"How about dinner?"

"Excuse me?"

"Can I take you out to dinner?"

She pulled her lips into a firm, businesslike smile. So much for friendly acquaintance. "I'm involved with someone, and I don't date clients."

So what if Richard had started out as a client. He'd bought before their first date.

He stepped closer, picked up her left hand, and looked pointedly at her ring finger. "We already covered that I'm more than a client; we're friends."

"We might be friends if you'd stop flirting with me."

"Flirting is something we both excel at. Besides, how serious could your involvement with your married boyfriend be?"

Quinn and her big mouth. She'd definitely have a talk with her little sister. She bit her tongue for a second and thought of Richard. "There's enough seriousness in life without me adding to it."

As soon as the words left her mouth, she feared she'd given him ample ammunition.

She tugged her hand from his grasp and twitched at his thumb's caress across her knuckles. Little jolts of pleasure shimmied up her arm. Damn, she hated the effect of charming men. No matter how hard she tried, she wasn't immune. He released her hand and moved to his car without another word. His phone rang as he drove off with his engine purring.

Kind of like her nerves.

Griffin had all the markings of a rich playboy. He was charming and arrogant, and women swooned at the sight of him. But she wanted only one thing from Griffin Walker: a big, fat commission.

A block from the last house, she pulled over. The itchy pantyhose drove her crazy. She opened the door and looked up and down the street. Not a soul in sight. Reaching under her skirt, she tugged the nylon from her body. Once she dragged it to her thighs, she sat on the edge of the driver's seat and rolled the pantyhose down. A slight breeze kissed her skin, and she sighed.

Just as she pulled them off and stood barefoot on the street, a revved engine caught her attention. The silver Jaguar pulled up beside her. *Could the day get any worse?*

"Everything okay?" Griffin asked through the open window.

"Yeah." She balled the nylons into her fist and stifled a laugh. She didn't care enough to be embarrassed, but she scrambled for an excuse.

"What are you doing?"

"Nothing. I pulled over to take a call."

"With no phone?" His gaze raked down her body again and stopped at her bare feet. "And no shoes?"

She sighed and held out her pantyhose. "You caught me. I couldn't wait to get out of my pantyhose. The heat was strangling me."

His laugh echoed on the empty street, and relief washed over her. Her own smile followed. If Richard had caught her stripping off her pantyhose on the street, he'd be mortified.

"Next time, leave them at home. Your legs are sexier without them."

"Flirting will get you nowhere," she said, and leaned against the door. Even to her own ears, her remark sounded hollow. The air-conditioning tickled her arms and she repressed a shiver.

One eyebrow rose above his sunglasses. "When something interests me, I go after it."

"Even if it's unattainable?"

"Nothing is unattainable."

She straightened. "We'll see."

He slid his glasses to the top of his head. Dark brown eyes bore into her and no longer held amusement. "Be warned. I always get my way."

He pulled away. She wanted to be pissed, tried to feel indignant and angry, but failed. She would do whatever was necessary to make Griffin Walker happy.

THE OFFICE DOOR FLEW OPEN. Griffin looked up from the file to meet his publicist's eyes. Kendra was one of few people who would enter his office unannounced. Some days she stopped in to say hi. Today she looked pissed.

"What's wrong now?" He settled back in his chair. Every time she had that look, he imagined lightning bolts shooting from her spiky blond hair.

"What's *wrong?* Didn't we spend hours talking about your image and how you appear in the press?"

"Yes." It had been the longest afternoon of his life. Almost as bad as the time Sister Mary Bridget lectured him about how resolving a problem didn't involve fists.

"Then what is this?" She slapped the society page of the newspaper on his desk. "A reporter? Not your smartest move, Walker. Especially with the mom brigade downstairs telling the world you're bad for their kids."

"Huh?" He'd already managed to avoid the rally point for whichever parent group hated him today. Every few months, a group showed up at his office building and picketed. He never thought creating video games would be so controversial.

He focused on the picture and smiled. "That's Moira O'Leary, Ryan's sister. She wasn't a date; she just wanted to get into the benefit."

"But now you're linked to a reporter, someone looking to make a name for herself." She slapped a second paper down. Kendra had a flair for the dramatic. The headline read THE BOSTWICK CHARITY: AN INSIDER'S VIEW.

Moira had gotten a byline in the *Times.* His chest filled with pride, as if she were his sister. "So? I got her in the door; then I left."

"You were photographed with her, and then she wrote the story. If that's not bad enough, they have another picture of you with a senator's daughter." She tapped a small photo on the bottom of the page.

"This is an old picture. I haven't seen Ashley in over a month." He pushed the paper toward Kendra.

Kendra growled. "You don't get it, do you? This is how people see you—different women at every turn. You can't commit, you're not loyal, you're not trustworthy." She drummed her fingers on the photos.

"That's bullshit." He flicked the paper away and stood to pace.

"We agreed absolutely no politicians."

"Who her father is shouldn't matter. She wanted a good time."

"Which is even worse. We talked about this. Given your history, we don't want anyone to dig. The story is going to come out sooner or later and we need to be prepared for it, but we don't want to offer up fuel. All we need is one person to link you to political families."

Griffin didn't respond. Kendra was right. His past would come back to bite him in the ass. Too bad he hadn't been smart enough to hire someone like Kendra ten years ago. "I never did anything wrong."

She inhaled a slow, deep breath. "Look, I know it's bull-shit. It doesn't matter if you were right or wrong. All that matters is how people perceive you. I know you, and I know what you want to accomplish. You're a good man, but it's not me you have to convince."

"So I'm supposed to give up my social life?"

Kendra laughed, the sound tinny and hollow. She excelled at her job, so he never knew when she was being genuine.

"Like that would happen. Discretion, Griffin. Don't date the flighty socialites who enjoy posing for the society page. Keep your *social life* out of the limelight. When people Google you, this is all they see. We need to change that perception."

He shoved his hands deep in his pockets. "Fine. I get it."

She moved to stand next to him. "That's what you said before. The idea for your foundation is fabulous. The program will make a huge difference in the lives of those kids. If the public doesn't trust you, you might as well keep throwing money in and nothing more."

"It needs to be more."

"I understand," she said, her voice soft. "It will be, but you have to believe in me. I know what I'm doing."

He thought of his own childhood and what a program like this could've done. Money alone couldn't make the differences he wanted.

"That's why I hired you." He pointed at the newspaper. "I

helped a friend, so I don't regret it, but I am sorry it threw a wrench into your plan."

"And Ashley?"

"Has moved on down the list of Chicago's most eligible bachelors. No hard feelings."

Kendra rolled her eyes. "Are there ever? I have a feeling you con these women into thinking they've left you broken-hearted."

He gave her a half shrug. "It's a gift." A skill he'd nurtured after the one and only time he'd fallen in love had ended in a spectacular fiasco.

She turned and went back to the desk. "Any luck finding a house so you can get rid of the bachelor pad?"

"No." Thoughts drifted to Indy and her bare legs.

"You know it's an integral part of the plan."

He nodded and returned to his chair. "The house will be a bachelor pad, too, since I won't be getting married."

She shook her head at him.

Waving the papers, she headed to the door. "I'm going to see what I can do about this."

Kendra was one of the best PR people he knew, but she was a pain in the ass. He'd listen to her, though, because she understood his goal.

He'd been working toward the creation of this foundation for years. Helping troubled teens gave him a purpose. If he could pass on his knowledge and skills, it could change their lives. He was finally in a position to make it happen.

As long as he didn't let his dick screw it up.

He looked over the notes he'd taken on each of the houses he'd visited with Indy. By pinpointing why they weren't the right ones, he should be able to find what would make it right.

He wanted the O'Leary house on a bigger scale. Ryan O'Leary had been his best friend since first grade when he'd punched Ryan in the nose. He'd spent more time at the O'Leary house than he had at home.

At the O'Leary's, loneliness was impossible. Six kids, two parents, and however many friends filled the house to bursting. They ate dinner together. Fought over the TV together. Shared victories and suffered defeats together. Home.

That's what he wanted in a house. He had no idea how to explain it to Indy.

His mind wandering to her bare legs didn't help. His mouth watered at the image.

She'd been stiff but professional throughout their meeting. Unlike the steal-the-spotlight woman he'd seen singing karaoke at Ryan's bar, Indy, the agent, was a different person. At least until he'd caught her stripping off her pantyhose.

When he saw that, he wanted to help her loosen the rest of her outfit, starting with her hair. She'd had it all pinned up and neat. He preferred the wild, long hair of Indy the singer. He'd been attracted to her from the first time he laid eyes on her, but she'd kept her distance. Being rejected, even subtly, stuck in his gut. He found himself wanting to press the issue to see if he could change her mind.

His secretary buzzed, interrupting his less-than-professional thoughts. "Mr. Walker, there's a Mr. Malcolm on line one. He wouldn't give a reason for his call. He said it was personal."

Malcolm. He knew only one person with that name. The back of his neck tingled.

"Mr. Walker?"

"Sorry. I'll take it." His finger hovered over the Hold button. He prayed that, for a change, his gut would be wrong. "Hello?"

"'Bout time. How do you like that Mr. Malcolm business? I know how much it bugs you to share my name." The pride in his cleverness sang across the line.

Griffin's shoulder muscles knotted. *Dad.* As if his life needed more complications. "What do you want?"

"Now, is that any way to talk to your old man when we haven't spoken in three years?"

"With you it's always the appropriate response." Griffin pinched the bridge of his nose, grasping for composure.

"I thought I'd stop by for a visit, but you have some crazy protesters in front of your building . . ."

Malcolm obviously wanted to make it clear that he was already in town. Griffin's mind raced. Everything with Malcolm led to one thing—money. "It would be better if you didn't come to my office. We have a lot going on right now." *And the last thing I need is questions about who the hell you are.* "Do you still have the address for my condo?"

"Of course."

"Meet me there later. Nine o'clock. Don't call me at work again."

After they hung up, Griffin paced his office. He wanted to throw something across the room and smash it, but he didn't want to draw attention. He'd actually thought his father was gone for good. Maybe even dead. No contact for three years. Before his mother had died.

If he knew Mom died, he would know he doesn't have a hold on me anymore. He wouldn't be back looking for more. Tonight Malcolm would learn. No more handouts. No more contact. No fake father–son bullshit.

Griffin pushed down the innate desire to have a real father. He'd prefer being a bastard than being Malcolm Walker's son. He'd get rid of his father one last time.

No one would know Malcolm Walker existed, just as it always had been.

CHAPTER 2

Griffin leaned hard against the drywall and screwed it into place. He wasn't sure how Ryan had suckered him into helping, but it actually felt good. He hadn't done much manual labor since college. Back then he'd worked any job he could to pay tuition. Today it felt like coming home, a nice escape before having to meet with Malcolm.

Ryan's drill whirred away on the opposite side of the room. The radio blared over the noise of their power tools. Kid Rock sang about being seventeen. Before slapping up the next sheet, he grabbed a beer from the cooler on the floor. Having a friend who owned a bar had its perks.

The room came together. Ryan and his brothers had spent many hours over the last month to get this first apartment above O'Leary's Pub fit for habitation.

After taking a long drink of beer, he hefted the next sheet of drywall into place. "So what's the rush with the wedding?"

Ryan answered over the sound of the drill. "When it's right, you know it. Besides, you know my mom."

Ryan's brother Michael crossed the room to the cooler.

"Don't listen to him, Griff. The old man wanted to beat me to the altar."

"Is the bathroom done?" Ryan asked.

"No, slave driver. It's hotter than a three-alarm fire in there."

"Being the big, bad fireman, you should be able to tough it out." He took the open beer from Michael's hand and drank.

Michael took another beer and disappeared back into the bathroom.

Ryan turned a bucket over and sat on it. "Quinn's pregnant," he said quietly.

Griffin stopped, holding the drill poised for driving in a screw. Then he finished the sheet and took a seat on the floor.

"You have nothing to say?"

Shit, he didn't know how to respond. "Congratulations?"

"Are you asking?"

"Seriously. I don't even get the marriage thing. Now you're talking about a kid." He didn't know if he could be faithful to only one woman for the rest of his life. But being a father was a forever thing. "How do you feel about it?"

He looked at Ryan. No one hid stress better.

Ryan took a deep breath. "I'm happy. Mostly I'm scared shitless. What do I know about being a dad?"

"You'll be fine. You had a great role model. If you're half the father your dad was, you'll already be better than most." The conversation brought Malcolm back to the forefront of his mind. And he couldn't tell his best friend.

No one could know about Malcolm and the secrets he brought.

"Thanks, but it doesn't make me feel better. What's been going on with you?"

Work. Always a safe topic. "Same old. Production's flying

on the new game to get it out for the holidays. Gamers are already buzzing about it."

"You don't sound too excited about making another million."

"I have some group bitching. It's evil, bad for kids, too violent. Same old crap." But the noise could impact the new phase of the foundation.

Ryan laughed. "Whenever you want to give up the corporate life, I've got plenty of work to do around here. Three more apartments after this one."

"Have you and Quinn decided where you're going to live?"

"We'll stay at the loft for now. She wants to sell it. Indy thinks she should rent it out. It's one of those places that'll retain value. Indy's looking for houses near Twilight for us."

Thinking about Indy proved to be a better distraction than anything for getting his father out of his head.

"I hear you're finally looking for a house."

"Yeah, but I'm not having any luck. The houses Indy's showing me are . . ." He searched for the right word. Pretentious? "Not right."

He finished his beer and pushed to his feet. Feeling the chalky dust on his hands gave him an idea about house hunting. He made a mental note to call Indy later. "Hey, grab me some more screws, wouldya?"

Ryan kicked a box across the floor.

"Thanks, *Dad*." He smirked at the thought of Ryan holding a screaming baby.

Ryan chucked a small piece of drywall and it bounced off Griffin's shoulder. "Not so loud. No one else knows. We're not saying anything until after the wedding."

Griffin snorted. "You don't think Quinn's already told Indy and Kate? Get real. I don't get the impression they have too many secrets."

"Keep your mouth shut."

～

GRIFFIN SCANNED his living room to make sure it held nothing of value his dear old dad could pocket on his way in or out. Small things lay around, none important. His dad couldn't take anything from him now.

Ten years ago, he'd thought he'd hit the jackpot. His life was going exactly as planned. He'd fought to be at the top of his field, one of the youngest to reach that kind of success. He had Selena in his life; then his father reappeared.

Even then, he'd held no expectations about some great relationship, but he figured he at least deserved some answers about why his father had left, to get his side. If nothing else, he could rub his success in his father's face. Show Malcolm he didn't need him.

But he didn't have the chance. Malcolm had gotten the better of him. He charmed his way into Griffin's life, talking about how he'd wanted to get in touch for years but didn't know how. How he'd felt ashamed to come back.

All part of his game.

Griffin swallowed the last of the whiskey in his glass. More than one before facing Malcolm and things would get uglier than he could afford. The doorbell buzzed at nine thirty. Just like Malcolm—keep everyone waiting.

Griffin answered the door, and the shock at seeing his father registered in his brain, like looking into a fun house mirror that instantly aged him.

Malcolm looked good. Thinner than Griffin remembered, and grayer, but the charming smile, so much like his own, was the same.

"Griffin." He entered the room with his arms spread.

Here came the deplorable exaggeration of affection.

Griffin stepped back to allow Malcolm plenty of room and to make his feelings clear. "Malcolm."

"I see you're still doing well for yourself."

Griffin closed the door, trying to hold back anger and resentment. He'd done well despite his father's absence. His mother had carried the load for both parents. He'd promised himself he'd stay calm and get rid of Malcolm for good. A business transaction. One last time.

He turned to the man who was the object of his disgust and watched Malcolm appraise the room the same way he had ten years earlier. As far as Griffin knew, Malcolm hadn't come back to town since then. Every transaction happened via phone and wire.

"I guess business is good, eh? I mean, all the kids are playing some kind of game or another, right?"

Griffin tucked his hands in his pockets and waited. Sometimes silence proved to be an effective tool.

"What, you got nothing to say?" Malcolm crossed his arms.

"I've already asked what you wanted and I never received an answer. That would be a good place to start." They continued to stare at each other across the room.

Malcolm broke first. The man wasn't much of a poker player or businessman. "I haven't seen you in ten years, unless you count what I read and see in the paper. I thought maybe we could get to know each other."

Griffin's chuckle of disbelief came out more as a growl. "Are you getting so old you can't remember which ploys you've already used? You tried that ten years ago. I guess you're here for your last check."

"It doesn't have to be this way."

"Mom's dead. More than two years ago. Did you know?"

Malcolm shook his head. Griffin couldn't read the expression in the older man's eyes.

"This will be the last time you ever contact me. You have nothing else over me. You can't hurt her anymore. You don't even deserve money now, but since you had the balls to actually show so I could say this to your face, I'll give you that." He crossed the room and opened a drawer to the side table. "How much this time? And remember, it has to last."

Now the wheels turned in his father's head. The realization that he couldn't get to Griffin through loved ones ruined his plans. First Selena, then Mom. Griffin made sure no one would ever get that close again. But Malcolm still knew about Selena, and Griffin would do anything to save her parents any more pain. Add in the damage to his reputation, and paying his father became worth it.

"You drive a hard bargain. You're a lot more like me than just looks. Keep it simple so no one can touch you. I tried to tell your mother so many times. She never understood."

The pen in Griffin's hand began to bend, so he released his grip. "Unless you want to get tossed out on your ass without a check, I suggest you shut up and give me a number."

"Fifty thousand." He smirked as if the number would shock Griffin.

Hell, he'd expected twice as much. "I'll cut you a check for ten. I'll wire the rest when you leave town."

Malcolm tilted his head, but then nodded. Griffin scribbled out the check and ripped it from the book. Handing it to Malcolm, he said, "Now get out."

With the check tucked safely into his pocket, Malcolm smiled broadly. "A pleasure doing business with you. We'd make quite a team. If we were together, there wouldn't be a safe heart in all of Chicagoland."

Griffin took one step forward and Malcolm jolted from his spot. He quickly left the condo. Griffin returned to his bottle of whiskey and wondered how much he'd need to make him forget where he came from.

INDY DRAGGED her feet toward her apartment. The bar had been slammed with business. The stack of singles shoved in her pocket made the sore feet and aching back worthwhile. Even though she wanted the money to go straight into her vacation fund, she had a feeling it would be poured into her car instead. The beast had begun making strange noises. Again.

She stopped in front of her neighbor's house, surprised to see Richard leaning against her porch. "Hi. What are you doing here?"

At the sound of her voice, he looked up and his back stiffened. "You said you had to work. I thought you were showing houses, not shaking your tits at a bunch of drunks."

She so did not need this right now. She'd had enough of Richard's jealousy. "I'm tired. It's been a long day."

"We need to talk."

She hated that sentence. Nothing good ever came from it. Already sore muscles clenched.

"About what?" she asked, trying to keep the irritation from her voice. She walked up the steps and unlocked the door.

Without turning around, she knew Richard scanned the street to check on his car. At least he didn't make his routine comments about the location of her apartment. She shook her head and went in alone.

Kicking off her shoes, she sank onto the couch. The cool leather stuck to her skin. She closed her eyes and relished in the quiet.

The familiar sound of crinkling cellophane had her gaze

shooting up to Richard's arms. He carried a huge bouquet of roses. He brought roses only when they'd been fighting. Usually because he tried to change her.

The thought came in a flash, but stuck.

Why was she still with him? Her best friend, Kate, and Quinn had both been asking her for months. She'd brushed the question aside, but now, as Richard approached her with a serious expression, the question reverberated in her brain. Their relationship was no longer fun.

He sat beside her and laid the flowers on her lap. "You know I don't like you working at that place. I've offered to help."

"I don't want your money. I can pay my own way."

He slid a small, black velvet box onto the table. He flipped the lid and a huge, sparkly diamond winked at her. She wanted to reach out and touch it, but shifted the flowers from her lap to the table beside the ring. Her heart raced and her stomach roiled.

Marriage had never entered even the remote recesses of her mind. Especially with Richard. He was a guy with money looking for a break, and she knew how to show him a good time. Good times tended to end when commitment came into the picture.

Someone always had to change.

"Marry me. You can quit that crappy job and leave this place." He handed her a key.

"What's this?"

"The divorce is done. I got the house."

He took the house from his ex-wife and kids? "What about your kids?"

"What about them? They've moved to a new house. We can start our own family together."

The snort burst from her before she thought. "I told you a

long time ago. I'm not looking for marriage. I'm not marriage material."

"Everyone is marriage material when it's the right person. You could stop working and stay home to take care of the baby." He leaned back and crossed his legs as if this was a done deal.

"Baby?" She laughed, and he jerked back. Startling him hadn't been her intention, but the man was clueless. "What's next? Dinner on the table every night at six?"

"That would be nice. It's one thing I do miss from my marriage to Marion."

Yeah, that's what every woman wanted during a proposal—to be compared to the ex-wife. "I can't do this, Richard."

"Do what?" He scooted forward on the couch.

"Marry you. I don't want to be with someone who doesn't get me."

"I get you, Indy. I love you." He grabbed her hand and held it to his chest.

She tugged free and tried not to laugh. "You love the idea of me, but not me. Not really. I'm the girl who leaves tawdry messages for you in the middle of the day. The girl who loves the ceramic cows in her kitchen. The girl who strips her pantyhose off in the middle of the street."

"Why would you do that?"

The question said it all. He would never understand her. He didn't know how.

"Because I can. I'm not the right woman for you because you can't imagine doing something ridiculous or silly."

"Don't do this."

"You need to move on, Richard. I was a nice distraction during your divorce, but now that it's over, you need to look for whatever will make you happy." She handed him the key and the ring. That part was hard. The price on the ring would pay her rent for months. She moved away from the couch.

"You make me happy."

"But I won't for long." She crossed her arms. "I can't give you what you're looking for."

Backing away from her, his hands balled into fists. "There's someone else, isn't there?"

"No." Priceless. So much for being nice and letting him down easy. Her phone rang. She pulled it from her pocket. Griffin. "I need to take this."

She turned away from Richard, hoping he'd take the hint and leave. "Hello."

"Hey. Sorry to call so late. I planned to leave a message."

His rough voice massaged her irritated nerves.

"It's fine. I just got home. What did you need?"

"I want to refine my search for a house. Are you free for lunch tomorrow? I have some things I want to talk about."

She paused, immediately thinking he was trying to make another date, but something in his voice convinced her otherwise.

"Sure. Text me the time and place." She paused again. "Are you okay?"

"Yeah, long day. See you tomorrow."

She hung up and turned back to Richard.

"There is someone else. Don't try to lie."

"That was a client."

The disgusted *humph* made her want to slap him.

"What kind of client calls after business hours?"

"The kind who happens to be a friend. Someone who wants to make plans. Someone who knows I don't mind late-night calls." She recrossed her arms. Time to end it. For good.

He stared at her with eyes burning. "I've felt it for months now. You've been pulling away, and I've been trying to hold on. I guess I'm too late."

His eyes darkened and new wrinkles spread around them. Indy's stomach fluttered and she clutched her phone in her hand. He'd never given her any reason to fear him. He was controlling and manipulative, but never violent.

"No one else can give you what I can. Be careful who you choose to be with." He snatched the bouquet of roses from the table. "And remember. I always take what's mine."

He stormed out the door, and she stood silently. What the hell was that? She inhaled deeply and locked the door. Good riddance.

I always take what's mine. What was he talking about? Would he want the gifts he'd given her? He could have the ugly-ass furniture he'd insisted on getting for the living room. She stripped her clothes off in the middle of the room and tossed her T-shirt on the white leather couch.

The move would've driven Richard crazy. *Everything has its place.* She laughed and threw her panties on the coffee table.

She hadn't felt so free in a really long time.

CHAPTER 3

After a long, hot shower, Indy called Quinn, and like a good sister, Quinn arrived quickly, carrying chocolate cake.

Cake. Not cookies. In their family, cookies made you feel better when things went wrong. They celebrated with cake. So much for sisterly commiseration.

Quinn rushed into the living room. "Are you okay? I didn't have any cookies at home and didn't think you'd want to wait for me to bake some."

Relief eased into Indy. Quinn did want to support her. Indy took the plate. "So you just happened to have chocolate cake lying around?"

"Well, you know how I get when I'm nervous. I tried a new recipe." Quinn tucked her short dark hair behind her ears.

"Nervous about what? The wedding?"

"Dinner with Dad. You forgot, didn't you?"

Indy rolled her eyes. "No, I didn't forget. I don't know what you're so worried about. He'll be thrilled that you're getting married to a nice, stable guy. Plus, I'll be there, so he'll have plenty of things to pick at."

Indy led the way to the kitchen, anxious to get away from Richard's furniture. "What do you want with cake? Wanna get drunk?"

"Uh … no. Just some water for me."

Something in Quinn's voice made Indy spin around. "We always drink at least a bottle of wine when we get rid of a boyfriend. What's up?"

Quinn's cheeks grew pink, and she fidgeted like she had when they were kids and she tried to lie.

Then the lightbulb went on. "You're pregnant, aren't you? The rushed wedding and now you're not drinking."

Quinn smiled, and her eyes became misty. "I've wanted to tell you, but we decided we were going to wait. But then Ryan spilled to Griffin."

"Griffin knows and I'm just hearing now?"

"He told him earlier today." Quinn pulled out a chair and sat. "Ryan proposed before we knew. He wants us married before the baby comes, and I don't want to be huge at my own wedding. So rushed it is."

"And you're worried Dad will figure it out?"

Fear filled Quinn's wide eyes. "I hadn't even thought of that. I'm worried he won't like Ryan."

"Everyone loves Ryan. You have nothing to worry about." Indy grabbed two glasses and filled them with milk. Then she grabbed two forks. No need to dirty plates when they would certainly finish the cake. "Congratulations. I'm happy for you."

Satisfaction filled Indy. She'd spent the summer trying to show Quinn that she could find love and even nudged Quinn into Ryan's arms. Hmm . . . maybe she could have a new career as a matchmaker. It would probably be more lucrative than the current real estate market.

Quinn bit her lip. "I'm sorry. Tonight is supposed to be about you. What happened with Richard?"

"He proposed."

Quinn choked on her milk. "What? I thought he was still married."

"The divorce finally went through. We celebrated last weekend because he was sure his wife would sign this week." She'd planned to spend all of Sunday in bed with Richard, but it didn't work. What should've been pure pleasure barely registered as so-so. Richard had been right; she had been pulling away from him. The relationship had become boring.

"So you celebrated and then what? What changed?"

"Sex with Richard was, I don't know . . . efficient."

Quinn barked out another laugh. "What, no foreplay?"

"It's not that. It was more like taking the shortest route to get from point A to point B. No journey, no adventure, no detours."

"Yeah, we all know how you like your detours."

"Anyway, he came over tonight with a ring and a key to his house. The house he shared with his wife and kids. I don't want to get married. Definitely not to him. I knew that going in, but he obviously didn't." Indy took a forkful of cake and shoved it in her mouth. She had never sent mixed signals about marriage, not to Richard or anyone else.

"How'd he take it?"

Indy swallowed the creamy, smooth cake and took a swig of milk. Cake was not making her feel better. "Not well. He accused me of having someone else."

Quinn raised an eyebrow in question.

"No. I haven't done anything with anyone, unless you count Griffin."

Quinn's mouth dropped open.

"I haven't *done* anything with him. Even though it's

tempting. He flirts with me all the time. He makes it hard to resist. But I remained monogamous. Then Richard . . ."

"What?"

Unease twisted through her. She poked at the cake. "He got weird. He took the flowers he brought me and said he always takes what's his."

"What did he mean by that?" Quinn took a small bite of cake and made a face. "I'm going back to my usual recipe."

Indy's mouth watered at the thought of Quinn's chocolate cake. "I have no idea what he meant. Maybe he wants all the stuff he bought me. Maybe he was spewing crap because I dumped him." She tasted another bite of cake. "You're right. The regular recipe is better. I don't know why you would mess with perfection."

Indy sighed. Her mind wandered over the months she'd wasted on Richard. How had she lost herself? "You know, I don't know why I let it go on for so long. I know better. He kept trying to change me."

"How?"

She thought back across the many times over the months. Which example to choose? "One time, he invited me to go to a business party, cocktails and dinner. He offered to buy me a new outfit to wear. After two department stores and one huge fight, I told him to find someone else to take. Every outfit he picked out looked like it came from the closet of the Queen of England."

Indy described the dresses Richard had chosen until Quinn laughed so hard, she had tears streaming down her face.

When Quinn quieted, Indy continued. "Afterward, he came over with a gift to apologize."

"What was it?"

"A string of perfectly lovely pearls."

"What's wrong with pearls?"

"Nothing. But he bought me pearls assuming that if I wore pearls to the dinner, I would have to wear an equally boring dress. It's like he wanted me to be a fifties wife." Indy shook her head. "Tonight he even suggested we have a baby and I stay home to raise it and make dinner every night."

Quinn broke out in another bout of laughter, and this time Indy joined her. The ridiculousness of the night beat her down. She had to laugh.

If she didn't laugh, she'd fall apart crying.

After Quinn left to go home to her fiancé, Indy dove into de-Richarding her house. All of the clothes and presents he'd given her she tossed in trash bags. If he wanted his crap back, he could have it. The process had been long and draining. She'd had good times with Richard, and going through all the stuff brought back memories.

By the time the sun came up, she was spent emotionally and finally went to bed.

When she woke hours later, gritty-eyed and exhausted, she saw Richard had called twice. His messages were kind and apologetic. Just like they had been when he'd blown off a date with her. She was done with his games.

After crawling out of bed, she checked her e-mail. She had nothing going on. If Griffin would buy something, she could quit working at the bar. Juggling two jobs to pay the bills was exhausting. Commission from that sale would give her time to find something else or build a better client base.

She went back to bed, thinking she'd rest for a while until she had to meet Griffin. Unfortunately, the fatigue from her long night dragged her under, and the next time she woke, she was running late.

Skipping a shower and showing up looking anything shy of professional was not an option. Her lightweight navy blazer and skirt paired well with the cream camisole she chose. No amount of makeup could fix the pasty complexion, so she primped and fussed at her hair, hoping it would be good camouflage.

Without thinking, she put on the sapphire earrings Richard had given her that went so well with the suit. She wore them so often, she'd almost forgotten they'd been a gift from him. His words caught in her mind. *I always take what's mine.* If returning his gifts would rid her of him and his possessive nature, she'd gladly agree. She pressed her lips together.

She wasn't even sure why she was so upset. Things hadn't been fabulous for a long time between her and Richard. Coming in second to his ex-wife never sat well with Indy. She could understand taking a backseat to his kids, but it had never been about them. Time to let go and move on.

She excelled at moving on.

Traffic at midday was almost nonexistent, so she made good time getting to the restaurant. She drove through the neighborhood, praying Griffin would be late. She pulled into the lot of the mom-and-pop diner. Her tire smacked into a crater of a pothole before easing into a spot. Griffin had already arrived.

Just my luck. Why can't he be like a regular businessman who gets hung up in meetings?

She hurried from her car with another apology on her lips. Griffin was leaning against his car, keenly focused on his phone. His posture gave the impression of a relaxed man, shoulders slightly slumped, legs crossed at the ankle, but his face belied the image. Jaw muscles tight, mouth straight, and a slight furrow between his eyes. Nice to know she wasn't the only one having a crappy day.

"I'm sorry I'm late. I have no excuse. I overslept."

"No problem," he said distractedly. "You're only a few minutes late. I got here early."

She shifted her bag higher on her shoulder, headed toward the entrance, and realized he didn't follow. "Griffin?"

"I'm coming," he answered. "Did you say you overslept for our one-thirty appointment?"

"Yes."

His gaze landed on her face, studying her more intently than he had any house she'd shown him. His brown eyes narrowed in concern. "Are you sick? You're not looking too well."

"I'm fine. Are you ready to eat?" She pointed toward the door.

"What happened?" He set his briefcase on the ground and tucked his hands into the pockets of his expensive, Italian tailor-made pants as if he had no intention of moving.

"I don't want to talk about it." On a good day, she had a hard time facing Griffin's constant scrutiny; on a day like today, she wanted to hide. She strode into the diner and waited for him.

Thick, greasy air assaulted her, and she looked at the ancient Formica tables and cracked red vinyl seats.

The bell above the door tinkled when Griffin decided to finally join her. He pointed to a table, and they sat.

"KD's Diner, huh? Eat here often?" she asked, looking around the simple restaurant.

"I haven't been in here in years."

She pulled out her notebook and pen. "So what changes do you want to make regarding the house hunt?"

"I'd like to find a big, old house in need of renovations. I'd be able to make it into whatever I want." He slid his phone into his pocket. Her pen froze.

"If you want something built-to-suit, we can look for land farther out west or north. I would think it'd be easier to hire an architect to design what you want."

"It would, I'm sure, but closer to the city is better. I also want something I can work on myself. I can't build a house from scratch, but I can tear one apart."

She didn't try to suppress the laughter. "What are you going to do, load lumber and drywall onto the roof of your Jag?"

Irritation stared back at her. "I like expensive toys." He reached out and flicked her earring. "You're not immune to trinkets either. That doesn't mean there's nothing more to you."

The reminder of Richard's pricey gift startled her. She pulled away from his reach and blinked rapidly. She would not let Griffin rattle her. "Excuse me."

She rushed to the bathroom to compose herself.

After splashing her face with cool water, she dabbed at it with the rough, brown paper towel. She regretted not having a full complement of makeup in her purse. She was able to fix her eyes but decided lipstick drew attention to her pale complexion.

She braced her palms against the sink. *What am I doing here? The last thing I need to do is hang out with Griffin.*

At least she knew where she stood with him. There was no pretense there.He didn't think much of her, which explained why they were eating lunch at a cheap diner. The man had more money than God, and he brought her to this.

He knew she belonged here, not some five-star restaurant.

She yanked the door, which stuck, the wood swollen. Griffin's back faced her. She took a deep breath and smoothed her skirt.

When she sat across from him, he asked, "I ordered coffee. Is that okay?"

"Yes, thank you. Where do you want me to look for the handyman-special homes? It'll be slim pickings." She picked up her pen, ready to write, to be the professional she professed to be.

"I'm open as far as location goes, but not too far from the city."

He took a drink of coffee, watching her over the rim.

She held her cup in both hands for the warmth. Between the air-conditioning and Griffin's steady gaze, she felt chilled. The coffee was cheap but good. The silence at the table, unsettling.

Griffin handed her a menu. She looked at her options, knowing she'd order only a salad. It gave her eyes somewhere to look besides at Griffin, a place for her mind to focus instead of on Richard.

"Hi. Need a few more minutes?" the waitress asked.

Indy looked up at the woman's name tag. Lily. Pretty name. "No. I'm ready. I'll have a garden salad, no dressing. Some lemons on the side, please."

"Anything else?"

"No. I'm good with the coffee."

Lily turned to Griffin. "How about you?"

His attention remained on Indy. "You need to eat more than a salad."

"No, I don't."

"You're worn out. A salad isn't enough."

Lily bounced her gaze back and forth, pen poised but not writing.

Griffin turned to her. "I'll have a cheeseburger and fries. So will she."

"No, *she* won't." How dare he think he could tell her what to eat. Richard never minded that she ate a lot of salad. He never tried to tell her what to eat. It was the one thing he hadn't tried to change about her.

Suddenly Indy realized she was doing exactly what Richard had last night: comparing someone to her ex. Which didn't even make sense since she and Griffin were nowhere near being a couple.

This time, his eyes stayed on Lily. "Two burgers. One salad."

Lily turned away, but Indy saw her bite her lip to conceal a smile.

"I'm not that hungry. Ordering a cheeseburger for me is a waste."

"When was the last time you ate?"

She wanted to ask him why he cared, but she pressed her lips together to stop the question. She answered coolly, "I had some chocolate cake last night."

"You're drained and you need something more substantial."

"Look. I didn't come here to fight." She couldn't handle a fight with him.

"So don't fight. Let's talk." He took a drink of coffee, and his phone bleeped. He took it from his pocket, checked the caller, and hesitated. He scored points for consideration.

"You can take that if you need to."

"Sure?"

"Yes. Business is business."

She zoned out for a few minutes while Griffin dealt with his call. She needed to organize a bridal shower for Quinn. She couldn't expect Kate to foot the bill by herself. If they held it at Quinn's loft, it would save a lot over using a banquet hall. They'd have to plan fast.

"Sorry."

Indy snapped her attention back to the table. "No problem."

"What were you thinking about?"

"Kate and I have to plan a shower for Quinn. I was thinking about how to save some money by having it at Quinn's." She took a sip of coffee, now cool. "Speaking of which, how is it you got the news about Quinn being pregnant before me?"

His broad shoulders rose. "I'm a good listener."

"Hmm-mmm."

Griffin placed his cup back on the saucer. "What do you think about it?"

"Quinn being pregnant? Not too surprised, really. It's all she's been talking about for months. Why? You have a problem with it?" A sensation pricked the back of her neck. She might not be up for a fight about herself, but she'd sure as hell defend Quinn.

He turned his cup in slow circles. "It's so fast. How well can they possibly know each other? Marriage is crazy enough, but to add in a kid . . ."

"Sometimes you just know, I guess. I wouldn't want to be in her shoes, but it suits them."

"That it does."

Lily breezed by, topped off their cups and let them know their food would be ready soon. Griffin stared at her coming and going.

The girl appeared barely old enough to drink. It didn't matter that this was a business lunch and not a date. It was rude to check out other women. "Isn't she a little young for you?"

"Yeah." He shook his head and turned his attention to Indy. "I know her, but it looks like she doesn't remember me."

"So many conquests, hard to keep track, I'm sure."

"I never slept with her."

His gaze tracked over Indy's shoulder to the counter. He shook his head again.

"I'll be back in a minute." He stood and walked to the bathroom.

Lily returned, loaded with plates. After placing the food, she smiled at Indy. "He hasn't figured it out yet, has he?"

"You *do* know him." Indy put her cup down.

"Yeah. Griffin and I go way back. He's a good guy." She walked away before Indy could ask any questions.

Griffin returned and pulled a napkin from the dispenser. Indy squeezed lemon over the plain iceberg lettuce.

She poked at her salad. Her stomach felt so empty it hurt. The coffee sloshed around like acid. "I thought you wanted to talk about houses. You haven't given me much to go on."

"We'll get there. I wanted a chance to get to know you better." He popped a fry into his mouth.

"What do you want to know?"

"Why are you dating a married man?"

She dropped her fork, and it clanged against her plate. "What does my personal life have to do with how well I perform my job?"

"In general, nothing." He settled back against the booth. "I know better than anyone that my personal life should have nothing to do with my professional one. Unfortunately, one leaves impressions on the other whether I want it to or not."

His straightforwardness surprised her. He didn't strike her as the kind of guy to lay all his cards on the table. "If my personal life bothers you, why not find another agent?"

"Why can't you answer my question?"

She sighed. She could tell him she broke up with Richard. That would lead to more questions, questions she didn't want to discuss. "Not everything is black and white. Legally, Richard was married when we met. They'd already separated and papers were filed, but it was one of those never-ending messy divorces."

"Oh."

He obviously hadn't expected that. "It never even

occurred to you to give me the benefit of the doubt, did it? You automatically assumed I played the part of a mistress."

He leaned forward, lips parted in an almost smile. "In my defense, one of the first times I saw you, you sang a karaoke song about being the other woman and you left Ryan's bar in tears."

Indy thought back. She and Richard had had a fight. He'd canceled a date with her because he was with his wife. "Sometimes I felt like the mistress. That doesn't make me one. I would never date a truly married man."

"Okay."

Indy thought he looked relieved somehow, which made no sense. Why would he care? He was supposed to be a client, nothing more. But Griffin was a good conversationalist—no, a good listener. Just like he'd said.

AFTER SWALLOWING A BITE OF BURGER, Griffin asked, "Why real estate?"

She stopped licking the salt left from a French fry off her finger, and he regretted interrupting. He shifted in his seat. Everything this woman did turned him on.

"I kind of fell into it. A girl I used to waitress with was studying for the exam. It sounded like fun. The other girl didn't pass, but I had Quinn, who helped me study." She scooped another fry and dragged it through a puddle of ketchup. "Why video games?"

"I discovered early on I had a knack for computers. I like to tinker with things. Then I found out I could actually get paid to play video games all day."

"Boys and their toys." She eased into a smile and stabbed at her salad.

"I'm an equal opportunity employer. I have a couple of

women working for me who happen to be two of the best hackers I've ever met."

Indy studied him as if evaluating what he'd said. He saw a lot going on behind her beautiful eyes.

"I actually want to show you something."

She tilted her head. "I am not playing a game of 'I'll show you mine if you show me yours.'"

He bit the inside of his cheek. While it came out wrong, he definitely wouldn't mind seeing hers. "Okay, that sounded like a proposition. I want to show you something that will help you understand what kind of house I'm looking for."

Her eyes narrowed, and she nibbled on her lip. "Fine, let's finish and go."

"We don't have to go anywhere." Her acquiescence came quicker than expected. He needed to make sure Indy was the right person to talk to about his foundation. He didn't want word being spread until he was ready. His small pilot program at a west side school drew no attention from anyone. He wanted to keep it that way.

It was the sole reason for meeting at KD's. No one here would care about his conversation. KD's had been a safe place for him as a kid. He still clung to that notion.

They finished their food and slid the plates near the edge of the table. He reached beside him and popped open his briefcase. He handed her the file with the information on the program and the foundation. A strange feeling fluttered in his stomach, one he hadn't felt since childhood. He squashed the nervousness down the way he would an opponent in the boardroom—quick and ruthless. She'd either get his vision or she wouldn't.

He wanted Indy to get it and to like it.

"What's this?"

"I've started a charitable foundation. I plan to work with inner-city kids and teach them computers."

"Okay." She flipped open the file.

"The program is intense. Better than they'd get most places."

"And?"

He was losing her. She didn't get it.

"No one cares about these kids. I'm targeting kids who are smart but who have had a hard time or been in trouble. If I can get them involved, where they can make a real future for themselves, I can change a lot of lives."

She looked up from the folder. "What does this have to do with me?"

"My house is part of the program. That's why I need so much space. I plan to run the foundation out of my house. Classes will be held where I live." He turned the pages in her hand to the sketch of what would be the workroom. "This is a rough sketch, since I don't have an actual room to base it on."

She took the drawing and studied it. "So you're going to take a bunch of inner-city kids and trust them in your mansion."

He snatched the file back. Irritation pinched his nerves. "Go ahead and laugh. I know what I'm doing."

"I'm not laughing. I'm trying to understand. Have you forgotten my sister has taught kids like these for years? I've heard her talk about kids whose lives have been changed once they were given a shot, a chance to believe in themselves. I get it." She reached across the table and curled her fingers over his fist. Her soft, smooth skin eased his tension.

He sighed and loosened his grip. He'd never considered Quinn would tell Indy about teaching in that neighborhood. Obviously Indy paid closer attention to her sister than anyone gave her credit for. "They need to know they're trusted. What better way to do it than to share my home with them?"

"So you need a house with space that can be divided without looking like it's been divided. You trust them to be in your home, but you still need your own space, away from kids, away from work."

The tension in his torso eased. She did get it. Kendra would be thrilled. Indy was about as normal as he could find. She'd never appeared on the society page, at least not according to Google. "Yes, but I want a separate wing. I need enough space for the kids to work as the foundation grows in size. I'll also need offices for staff."

Lily slid the green and white bill on the table and scooped up the dishes.

Indy leaned forward, her elbows propped on the Formica. "She knows you."

Wallet in hand, Griffin stopped. "How do you know?"

"She told me. Actually, she gloated about you not being able to figure it out. She said you go way back." Indy's sly smile was borderline flirtatious.

"What else did she say?"

She hesitated and pulled away from the table. "She said you're a good guy."

"Hmm. That's it?" His mind continued to search for any memory of Lily.

"In a nutshell." She pulled her wallet out and tilted her head to see the total.

"I said I'd buy you lunch."

"And I'll leave the tip." She pulled a ten out and tucked it under her cup.

"That's almost a forty percent tip."

"Lunch cost me nothing, and in a place like this, good tips are few and far between. I think Lily would appreciate it. And I enjoyed watching her make you squirm." She slid from the booth and waited by the door while he paid at the register.

Lily rang him out with a smile. "Have a nice day. Come back soon."

"I will."

She winked at him and went back to wiping down the counter.

Indy opened the door with her keys in hand. "Thanks again for lunch. I'll start a new search for you today. I'll let you know what I find."

He walked Indy to her run-down car. "You sure you're okay?"

"Yes."

"A piece of advice. Don't talk to him. When he calls, don't answer."

Her eyes widened, then she laughed. "What are you talking about?"

"You've been upset all afternoon. You look like you spent the night crying instead of sleeping. There are few reasons for a woman to do that. A man leads the list. Don't talk to him."

She stood at her open car door, looking vulnerable. "What makes you think he'll call?"

He'd be stupid not to. "You're an easy mark." Her head jerked as if he'd slapped her. "He'll be back. Don't be a yo-yo. You're better than that."

She said nothing before closing the door and starting the engine. He hadn't meant to piss her off or hurt her, but coming off a visit with his father made him edgy. Malcolm specialized in jerking women around. Hopefully this ass wasn't anything like Malcolm.

Griffin looked back at the diner. He tossed his keys in the air and then caught them. Memories flooded his brain. Good memories. Blond hair, near white, with soft curls framing the little girl's face. Big blue eyes staring up at him like he was a god.

When he reentered the diner, Lily was filling saltshakers at the counter. She turned at the sound of the door.

"Back so soon?"

He walked quickly to her. "Little Lily. Are you going to keep pretending you don't know me?"

"I wondered how long it would take." She smiled brightly.

He scooped her up in a hug, and she squealed in his ear. Some things never change. Sure, she'd grown taller, and her hair was longer, but the shriek hadn't changed.

"Who's out there, Lily?" a voice called from the kitchen.

Lily raised a finger to keep Griffin quiet while she answered. "There's a guy who says he really needs to talk to you, Mom."

The kitchen door swung open, and stout KD pushed through. She'd aged, of course, but she was the same. She looked up at him and smiled. "Well, it's about time you came to visit. You think you're too rich and uppity to hang out with us peons now?"

"Never, KD." He bent over and hugged her. "It has been too long."

At twelve, he walked through her door for the first time to apply for a job, determined to help his mother. Instead of laughing at him, KD hired him to do menial tasks. Later, she paid Griffin to babysit Lily when she needed a few hours. Her husband thought Griffin was weird, but KD trusted him.

Why had he stayed away so long?

KD eased onto one of the counter stools. "Hungry?"

"No, I just ate."

"Why didn't you come to the kitchen to say hi?"

He sat beside her while Lily continued to fill salt. "I didn't think you'd still be here. I figured you'd have hired someone else to do your grunt work."

"Ha! I won't leave this place till I keel over. How are things going with you?"

"Good. Busy."

"You married yet? Kids? I read the article about you in a magazine. I bet they were coming out of the woodwork. Chicago's most eligible bachelor."

"You know it. Not *the* most, I was one of fifty. No wife or kids. I'd never get married and not invite you, KD." He turned to look at Lily. "I've been waiting all these years for Lily to grow up and fall in love with me."

She blushed. "Not likely, Griffin. I couldn't compete with the women who trail after you. The one today was pretty."

KD smacked his arm. "You brought a woman here and didn't have the decency to introduce us?"

He rubbed the spot on his arm. "She's my real estate agent. And her sister is marrying Ryan O'Leary."

Lily's head whipped around. "One of the mighty O'Learys has fallen?"

Griffin nodded with a smile. "Two. Michael's engaged too."

"Wow." Lily plopped on a stool. "How about Liam?"

"Single as far as I know. He's thinking about opening his own restaurant. How do you know Liam?"

She waved her hand quickly. "The O'Leary boys are legendary. All troublemakers and all ladies' men. But the things they say about *you* almost put the O'Learys to shame."

"Wow. Didn't know you cared so much, Lily-pad."

"Don't call me that. I'm not three anymore."

He tugged at her ponytail. "I can see."

Lily poured coffee for all of them and he spent the next hour catching up on neighborhood gossip. It felt good to be home.

CHAPTER 4

$\mathcal{I}$ndy wanted to kill Quinn. If they weren't sisters, she'd probably have followed through. But then again, if they weren't sisters, she wouldn't be stuck going to a stupid family dinner after having to switch schedules at the bar.

She wasn't up for seeing their dad. There hadn't been enough time to mentally prepare for him. Especially on the heels of her breakup with Richard.

Walt Adams was not an easy man.

Indy rushed down the block from the bus stop, still in her uniform of spandex shorts and too-tight T-shirt. Her bag of clothes thumped against her side as she ran. She was determined to not only *not* be late but to beat her father to Quinn's. If her car hadn't been in the shop, she would've had plenty of time.

As she rounded the corner, her cell phone chirped. She sucked in a gulp of air. "Hello."

"He's here. Early. Please tell me you're almost here."

Shit. Shit. *Shit.* Her heart crashed against her ribs. Nerves or exertion? Instinct told her to run the opposite way, but she'd promised Quinn she'd be there. "I'm outside. I'll be up in a few minutes."

Indy tucked the phone back in her bag and leaned against the cool brick of the building to catch her breath and calm her heart. She thought of stripping and changing right there on the street. It would be less humiliating than facing her father. If she'd packed better, she could slip her clothes over her uniform, but the white blouse couldn't hide her uniform shirt.

A shadow blocked the sun, and she eased her eyes open. Great, Griffin.

"Problem?"

"I was trying to figure out how to change my clothes without going upstairs." Getting naked here was no longer an option. "Why are you here?"

"Your sister invited me so Ryan wouldn't be alone."

She straightened as his gaze glided over her body. His eyes stayed focused on the rise and fall of her chest.

"What are you wearing?"

"My uniform."

"I thought you were a real estate agent."

"I am. The market's slow. Plus, my biggest client can't decide what he wants, so I'm waitressing to pick up money." She smiled and then heaved a sigh of resignation. "And now I have to see my father like this."

"It's not that bad." The glint in his eye mimicked every other guy at the bar. He studied the words END ZONE stretched across her breasts.

She took a moment to look at him. He was dressed down today in pants and a dress shirt. No tie, no coat, shirt open at the collar. And the five o'clock shadow had returned. She wondered if it really happened daily.

She shook the thoughts from her mind and entered the

building. Griffin held the door open for her when Quinn buzzed them up.

"Where's your date?"

"What date?"

"I figured he would've made nice with you by now." He tucked his hands in his pockets.

"We broke up. Even if we were still together, I wouldn't subject him to this." But to see the look on her father's face when she introduced Richard might've been worth it.

When the elevator doors opened, inspiration struck. Indy moved to the back wall. "Stand in front and don't turn around."

"Why?"

"I told you, I need to change."

"You think you'll have enough time in the elevator ride?" He pressed the button for the fifth floor. "I could pull the emergency stop."

"No, the noise would cause drama. It sticks a little on the third floor." She dug her clothes out of her bag.

"So what happened?"

"With what?"

"Your boyfriend."

"He asked me to marry him."

She whipped off her T-shirt and turned to pull on the blouse. Of course it was tangled. She shook the blouse, hoping it would straighten. The elevator beeped passed the third floor. "Oh, shit."

Griffin turned to face her. "What?"

The doors slid open at the fifth floor. He spun back around at the sound of a throat clearing. Griffin blocked her view, but the smell of a cigar wafted toward her. *Dad. Double shit.* She pulled her T-shirt back on and walked around Griffin, who leaned on the open doors.

Quinn appeared in her doorway and Indy hugged her,

explaining, "I'm early. I brought clothes to change. Dad's just earlier. And he was in the hall." She pulled back.

Quinn took in her uniform. "I told him he couldn't smoke in the loft. I thought he went outside. Now my neighbors are going to be pissed at the smell." She waved her arm ineffectually in the air.

"Look at the bright side. He'll be so busy commenting on my appearance that it'll take the heat off you."

She pushed past Quinn, back straight, smile in place. "Hey, Ryan. Look what I picked up on the street."

All eyes in the room turned to her. She clutched the white blouse, no longer worried about wrinkles. She wasn't surprised to see Kate already here. Kate was superefficient—Indy's opposite. Indy always wondered how they'd become friends.

Lydia rushed over to give her a hug. "Oh, Indy. I'm so glad you're here. It's been too long."

Indy held Lydia's softness for a moment, hoping for a bit of extra strength. An old friend of her mother's, Lydia had stepped in to take care of Dad after both Indy and Quinn left town. Indy figured Lydia put up with Walt because she was half in love. Not that Indy could see the appeal.

Walt stood, watching her entrance. He'd combed his white hair neatly away from his face, which accentuated the blotchy redness that came from too much alcohol. He hadn't moved from his spot where he talked to Kate and Ryan, beer in hand.

No, he would never come to her.

She walked to him and kissed his cheek lightly. "Hi, Dad."

He glared at her uniform. "I thought you had a respectable job."

"I do. I sell houses during the day and waitress at night. I pay my bills without any handouts. That is respectable."

The statement would wound his pride even though the

only person outside the family who knew his daughters helped support him was Lydia. Indy struck first, knowing it wouldn't last.

"You're dressed like a floozy. Always wanting men's attention." He narrowed his eyes and looked over her shoulder. "And getting plenty of it on the elevator."

Her stomach rose to her throat and her ears burned. She firmed her jelly legs. She refused to feel like a child being scolded. "Your assumptions are wrong. I was trying to change my clothes so you wouldn't see this. Griffin was being a gentleman by covering me."

"How can working at a place like that make any kind of real money?"

"The money's real enough. Besides, I have a big-dollar client on the hook. Once he finally decides to buy a house, the commission will be enough to send me to Acapulco for Christmas."

"Going to the beach isn't what you need to be worrying about. You need to plan for the future."

"Christmas is months away. That is the future." She straightened her spine knowing she would never get her father's approval. She felt all eyes following as the silence of the room pushed her, so she swung her hips with emphasis during her retreat.

Griffin's voice broke the quiet to introduce himself to her father.

Indy ducked into Quinn's bathroom and changed quickly. *I'm an adult, damn it. I'm independent and I take care of myself. I don't need him.*

But Quinn did. She wanted him at her wedding to give her away.

Indy took one last deep breath, brushed her hair, and left the bathroom. She eased quietly into the kitchen in search of some alcohol.

Griffin stood leaning against the counter drinking a beer like he was waiting for her. He looked down at her gauzy white blouse and long black skirt.

Before he could comment, she swiped his beer and took a swig. Alcohol wasn't going to help, so she returned the bottle.

As she bent over to grab a bottle of water from the fridge, Griffin said, "The other outfit would've given me a much better view."

She spun around and leaned against the door. "If you like it so much, maybe I'll wear it next time I show you a house."

"I'd enjoy that."

Flirting with Griffin definitely took her mind off the guests in the other room. She opened the water and drank.

"So what's with the clothes? Those aren't really yours."

"Yes, they are. The General out there would throw a fit over most of my wardrobe. I'm keeping the peace for Quinn's sake." The cool water eased down her throat.

"So you pretend to be something you're not."

His statement shot through her—an arrow of truth—but she felt the need to defend herself. "I'm trying to prevent any ridiculous arguments. But he'll start. He'll bait me. I'll walk in there, and he'll say"—she lowered her voice in imitation baritone as she spoke—"Independence, that is more appropriate attire. If you acted more like your sister, you'd be married."

"Wait. Your name is Independence?" Deep dimples bracketed his broad smile.

She nodded, his smile contagious. "I figured you knew. I was supposed to be John, and child number two out there Quincy."

He choked on his beer. "You're not serious. John and Quincy Adams? You're making that up."

She peered over the breakfast counter into the living

room. "I wish. We ruined his grand plan for forming a family militia by being born with vaginas."

Luckily the beer hadn't made it back to his mouth or she would've been wearing it. He laughed so loud the din from the other room quieted.

"Now you did it. Our hiding place is ruined. Time to go play nice."

∾

INDY SWISHED past him with humor and bravado. Her spicy perfume followed in her wake. He hated the dowdy outfit she wore to please her father.

She masked the pain, and her humor was well played. He knew the damage fathers did to their children. More often than not, it lasted a lifetime.

Griffin followed Indy back to the small group. Ryan approached him, but Indy kept moving.

"Tense?" Griffin asked.

"Hell, yeah. I thought my family was nuts. At least we yell and scream and then it's over." He looked over to Indy. "From what I gather, with them it's small painful jabs and a shitload of resentment."

Griffin drank more beer. "Indy's uptight. If their father has that effect on them, why do they bother?"

"He's harder on Indy, but I don't know why." Ryan moved to Quinn's side.

Indy finished her conversation with Kate and moved toward Quinn as well. She and Ryan flanked Quinn with support against her own father.

Walt's voice boomed louder than necessary. "Much more appropriate choice, Independence."

She snuck a look over her shoulder and shot a flirty grin at Griffin. "Told you," she mouthed.

He returned the smile. The woman needed an ally more than Ryan did.

Kate sidled up to him. He'd only met her a couple of times, enough to know she and Indy had been friends since college. He'd spoken to her once over drinks about legal issues, but since she was married, he didn't take it any further.

"Hello."

"Hi, Kate. Where are the kids?"

"I left them at home with Mark. They don't need to witness this disaster." She sipped her drink. "So what's going on with you and Indy?"

"She's finding me a house."

"Yeah, houses are so funny. We heard your laughter from the kitchen."

"This is a loft with an open floor plan. Not hard to hear."

"And?" She sipped patiently.

"We're friends. At least friendly. We have to be with Quinn and Ryan getting married." He finished his beer. How should he respond? *I keep fantasizing about her?*

"If you say so."

"I do." Although Indy said she wasn't interested, her flirtation spoke volumes. And now she was single.

Quinn walked past them toward the kitchen. "Dinner's coming out. Go take your seats."

Kate turned. "What can I help with?"

Quinn lowered her voice. "Go entertain Dad. He loves you, and I don't know how much more Indy can take."

"No problem." Kate twirled off and slipped her arm around Walt's elbow. "Come on, Mr. Adams. Let's get you to the table and you can tell me what's going on in your life. We haven't seen each other in ages."

Indy followed Quinn, nudging Griffin on the way. "I called it."

"Yes, you did." Rather than going to the table, he followed Quinn and Indy.

Quinn thrust a huge bowl of salad at him. "Take this to the table and sit."

He did as he was told. Quinn and Indy each made two trips carrying bowls and plates of food.

Indy sat beside Griffin; her only other choice was to take the seat obviously meant for Quinn, between Ryan and Walt. Tension vibrated the air around her.

As Griffin passed Indy the plate of dinner rolls, he brushed his fingers against her hand. Her eyes rose to his, and he offered a smile of reassurance. When the food made its rounds, Walt began his inquisition.

"What do you do for a living, Ryan?"

"I'm a bar owner. Partial owner of the family bar, O'Leary's Pub, full owner of my own bar, Twilight," Ryan answered, smooth and steady.

Walt turned to Quinn. "Bar business is at night and you teach during the day. How are you going to be happy? When will you see each other long enough to start a family?"

Obviously, Walt didn't know she was already knocked up.

Quinn pressed her lips into a thin line. "We've been dating for a while, and we see each other quite a bit. I'm happy."

Walt looked past Quinn to Ryan.

"I have very good managers running both bars, so although I'm on site at both most days, I'm not there around the clock. Both are operating in the black."

"In the black enough you can support her and your children when she stops working to raise your family?" Walt pushed potatoes into his mouth after asking. Nothing wrong with his appetite.

"*Dad.*"

He raised his eyebrows at Quinn.

Ryan put his arm around Quinn's shoulder but leaned forward slightly. "We're buying a home together, Mr. Adams. My income is stable. Quinn can do whatever she'd like to do. If she wants to continue working after we have kids, it's her choice. If she wants to stay at home, I can provide."

"Fine then."

Lydia, who had been silent, now spoke. "Tell us about the house, Quinn."

Griffin wasn't quite sure how she fit into the family, but Quinn and Indy seemed to genuinely care for her.

Quinn talked about the house Indy had found for them. The excitement in her voice broke much of the tension at the table. Small talk took up the remainder of time until dinner ended.

Ryan and Lydia helped Quinn clear dishes. When they stepped into the kitchen, Walt propped his elbows on the table, ready to attack.

"You couldn't find a better deal for your sister? You're supposed to watch out for her."

Indy met his steely gaze. "It is a good deal for the house. And she loves it. Houses here cost more than they do in the south."

He leaned back. "For that kind of money, she could've had two houses by me."

"She wants to live here, Dad."

"But the savings would give them a nest egg."

Griffin leaned in. "Actually, sir, by the time you factor in two lost businesses for Ryan and the time and capital needed to start a new business, it would cost more than the initial savings."

From the corner of his eye he saw Indy's shoulders relax. "And that doesn't count the expense of traveling back and forth to visit family. Ryan has five siblings and a mother he checks in on."

Walt offered a small nod. Griffin leaned back and patted Indy's thigh. The thin material allowed him to feel the heat of her skin. He jerked his hand away like he'd been burned. What he really wanted was to feel that heat on bare skin.

Quinn returned carrying a huge chocolate cake, Lydia had the coffeepot, and Ryan held a bakery box.

"You made chocolate cake?" Indy asked eagerly.

"Did you have any doubt?"

Kate added, "I love you."

Ryan opened his box. "I have a regular coffee cake for anyone who doesn't want chocolate."

"I told him we wouldn't need it." Quinn began slicing the cake and passed the first piece to Indy. Griffin shook his head to decline. Although he never ate dessert, he felt tempted to try a piece to see what the excitement was about.

Indy put a forkful into her mouth and closed her eyes. A borderline sinful sound emanated from her throat. She rolled her tongue over her bottom lip to catch some stray frosting.

His pants tightened at the groin. He felt like a kid seeing his first porno. No self-control.

She thought her father's reaction to the uniform was bad? Had her dad ever seen her eat chocolate cake?

Watching her now did things to Griffin that her spandex shorts only attempted.

Indy opened her eyes to find him staring. "This is the best cake ever. If Quinn could mass-produce it, she'd be richer than you."

Griffin took a quick look around the table. He thought for sure that everyone had been watching Indy, entranced as he was. They were all eating dessert and carrying on their own conversations.

"You don't know what you're missing out on," Indy continued.

"It's cake."

She scooped a piece of her slice onto her fork. "Here. Try it. Then tell me it's just cake."

He opened his mouth.

"You have to close your eyes to get the full effect."

He started to lower his lids, but stopped. "The fork better make it into my mouth, not my face or my shirt."

She grinned. "That's childish. I'm being a grown-up today. And as tempting as it might be, I wouldn't waste this chocolate cake."

The rest of the world ceased to exist with her smile. With his eyes closed and mouth open, she slid the cake onto his tongue. Creamy, smooth, and sweet, the cake melted in his mouth startling his taste buds awake.

He popped his eyes open. He wouldn't moan over it, but he could appreciate why Indy had.

"See. I don't exaggerate."

He picked up his fork to take another bite and she slapped his hand. The moment of intimacy passed. "Get your own."

He took the piece anyway. "I'm helping you save your girlish figure."

"This coming from the man who force-fed me a cheeseburger and fries earlier this week." She didn't stop him from taking more.

When they finished the cake, Indy stood. "I'll do the dishes, Quinn."

"Not necessary. We'll get to them later."

Ryan looked at the dishes scattered on the table. "Hey, now. If we have a volunteer . . ."

Quinn shot him a look he ignored.

Kate stood. "I'll help."

Quinn aimed her cool stare at Kate. "Thank you."

The two women buzzed around the table collecting plates. Indy's waitressing experience showed. She maneuvered twice as many dishes as Kate.

As they were making their escape, Griffin grabbed the last of the cups from the table. They must've had a reason for wanting to get away. He piled the cups on the breakfast counter and saw Indy and Kate with their heads together over the sink. "Why are you hiding?"

They both jumped and turned.

"We're not hiding," Indy said innocently. "We're washing a mountain of dishes."

"That was a sudden, but I'm guessing well-timed, escape."

Indy bit her lower lip on a smile. "Quinn hasn't told my dad yet about the wedding ceremony. She has to tell him they're doing it in a Catholic church."

"That's fightworthy?"

"We were raised Baptist. Neither of us is a churchgoer or even religious. The Catholic thing is important to Ryan."

"Important to Eileen," Griffin corrected. "He's keeping his mom happy."

"How sweet," Kate said. "Who's going to get the rest of the dishes?"

Griffin pointed to the counter. "Got 'em. Give me a towel. I'll dry."

They joked and chatted over the dirty dishes. The conversation in the living room was strained but quiet.

Indy handed him the last dish. "You know, you didn't have to stay for this. You did your duty as best man. No one would blame you for leaving."

"I don't have any place to be."

Kate pulled the plug in the drain. "Well, I do. I'd like to see my kids before bed, so I'm heading out."

Indy kissed her cheek. "Lunch tomorrow to finalize the shower stuff?"

"Sure. Call me." Kate looked at Indy and then at Griffin, suspicion clouding her eyes.

He bent and kissed her cheek. "It was good to see you again."

"Mmm-mmm. You two be good."

"You didn't tell me what the two of you were huddled over the sink whispering about," Griffin said after Kate left.

"Kate accused me of having something going on with you and not telling her. I told her we'd become friends."

"Did she roll her eyes at you too?"

"Kate likes to think she's too mature for that, but I got the equivalent. Her response was, 'Quinn and Ryan were friends too.'"

Griffin thought of the months Quinn and Ryan danced around each other, claiming friendship when they were both in love.

"Do you know any reputable movers?" she asked.

Her question caught him off-guard. "Huh?"

"Movers—do you know any?"

"Offhand, no. Why?"

"Quinn and Ryan are closing on their house days before the wedding. I'm thinking about getting movers to do everything while they're on their honeymoon."

He reached in the fridge for a beer. He held a bottle out to Indy, but she shook her head.

"Let me ask around."

"Thanks, I appreciate it."

Quinn came into the kitchen and eyed them suspiciously. "What's going on?"

"Dishes." Griffin pointed to the towel on his shoulder.

"Did Ryan survive?" Indy asked.

"Yes, no thanks to the two of you. They're out there now talking about fishing."

"Ryan doesn't fish," Griffin told them. He gulped his beer and planned his exit.

"He told Dad he was thinking of taking it up as a hobby."

"You're marrying a smart man, sis. We should all get so lucky." Indy stretched and arched her back. "I'm beat. I'm going home."

"I'll walk you out," he offered. He finished his beer while Indy went to get her bag.

Quinn wrapped up sliced cake. "Here. Take some home."

"No, thanks. It was definitely the best cake I've ever had, but I don't eat dessert."

Indy returned. "I'll take his, since he ate half of mine. Besides, you can never have too much cake."

Quinn handed Indy a plate loaded with two chunks of cake. Griffin had the urge to sit and watch her eat it.

Indy held the plate in his direction. "Will you please carry this for a minute while say good-bye?"

Cake in hand, Griffin followed. He said a polite good-bye to Lydia, who then embraced Indy in a hard hug and whispered in her ear. He waited patiently for her to go to Walt.

"Good night, Dad. Have a safe trip home." Again she kissed his cheek.

"It's about time you were with a man who has a head on his shoulders. This one doesn't seem like a waste of time and life." He hitched his chin in Griffin's direction.

"Dad, Griffin's—"

Griffin reached around her to shake Walt's hand. "Good to meet you, Walt. We'll see you at the wedding."

In the elevator, Indy took the cake back. "You didn't have to do that. I never intended for my father to think we were a couple."

"No problem. It seemed to make him happy."

"Yeah, that'll last. He'll suddenly remember which daughter he was talking to." The corners of her mouth pulled down, and they got off the elevator.

He didn't know what to say. No words of comfort would erase the pain. "Why is he so hard on you?"

The low, humorless chuckle didn't fit her. "So many reasons. I was a wild teenager. Big surprise, right? Then I went to the city for college to get away from him. I'm not married with a pack of kids." She sighed. "But he'll never forgive me for taking Quinn away from him."

They walked out to the street. "She doesn't look like a hostage to me."

"She would've been. She was seventeen when our mom died. She spent the next year doing everything for Dad while he poured himself into a bottle. She'd already applied to college here and had scholarship money waiting. Quinn is scary smart, but she was going to walk away from that to take care of Dad. One day, I drove home, packed her stuff into my car, and brought her to Chicago."

"It's been what, twelve years?" He stepped closer to her.

"Dad's good at grudges."

"She could've gone back at any time."

"But it's *my* fault. If I had never shown her the world outside Hooperville, she would've been happy there forever."

"You think so?"

"No, but it's what he thinks. She would've grown old and bitter. Luckily we have Lydia to keep an eye on him, or he probably would've moved in with Quinn."

He looked up and down the street. "Where's your car?"

She sighed again. "In the shop. Something's wrong with the transmission."

"How are you getting home?"

"Same way I got here—public transportation."

"You're taking the bus?" Somehow, he couldn't picture her standing at a bus stop and clambering up the steps, pushing into the crowd.

"Yes, I'm taking the bus. What's so funny?"

"How many times on your trip did a guy try to pick you

up?" That he could imagine, especially with her bar uniform on.

She shrugged. "No more than when I'm at work. The unwashed masses are not as bad as you picture them."

"Come on, I'll give you a ride."

"Not necessary. I don't mind taking the bus, and my apartment is out of your way."

"Come on. By the time the bus shows, I'll have you halfway home."

They walked to his car in silence.

"What, no Jag tonight?" she asked, approaching the SUV.

"Sorry, I came from the office."

Indy opened the rear passenger door and carefully placed the cake on the floor. She closed the door and leaned against it. "Thank you for tonight. You were an excellent distraction."

She smiled up at him, golden eyes reflecting the street-lights. On impulse, he lowered his lips to hers. Her heady scent grabbed him, and he pressed her against the car.

She tasted even better than he imagined. He expected light and breezy but found her spicy and secretive. He braced his hands on the car behind her, trapping her with his body and preventing himself from grabbing her. His fingers wanted to tangle in her long hair.

He pulled back before he could want more.

"Wow. What was that for?" she asked with a smile.

"It'll keep your dad happy."

"That would make sense if he were watching, but we're down the block and around the corner. And they're on the fifth floor. He can't possibly see us."

He gave a careless glance over his shoulder. "Huh, I guess you're right."

She laughed lightly. "Thanks. It's been much too long since I've been kissed like that."

He raised his eyebrows. Her comment said a lot about her

previous lover. His eyes went back to her mouth. How could a man look at those lips and *not* want to taste? He opened the passenger door for her to get in before he forgot himself.

He drove to the expressway before speaking again. "Where to?"

"Get off at Division."

He bit back a comment about her living in a crappy neighborhood. According to the mayor, much of the area was being regentrified.

As he drove down the off-ramp, he checked out the area. It was crappy. They traveled south to Division, and then headed east. The neighborhood didn't look any better. Abandoned buildings tagged with graffiti, panhandlers on the corner. Her neighborhood could compete with the ones his students came from.

"Turn right at the light. Left at the first street."

The turn down the side street made a difference. The neighborhood consisted of mostly two- or three-flats, the buildings varying only in the color of brick. Each had a postage stamp–sized front lawn, neatly trimmed. Some went the extra step and planted flowers around trees and in decorative pots on porches.

"Not as bad as you thought, huh?" she asked as if she'd read his mind.

"No," he admitted. "But it's still surrounded by shit. You're not on an island. Gang tags are on buildings all over."

She ignored his comment as if he hadn't spoken. "That's me up on the right."

He parked in one of the few spots remaining on the narrow street. He'd never have guessed she'd live in a loud, cramped area in the city.

"Thanks for the ride. I appreciate it." She got out and took the cake from the back.

He cut the ignition. "I'll walk you in."

She laughed. "Believe it or not, I don't need an escort, and regardless of what my dad thought, this wasn't a date."

He got out of the car anyway and followed her up a narrow gangway between two red brick three-flats. Window air conditioners stuck out, whirring and dripping over their heads. Some windows were propped open with box fans circulating air.

Smells of food cooking on grills and sounds of people partying in backyards echoed between the buildings.

Indy opened the old chain link gate and pushed through to the backyard. No one was grilling there, but the yards to the left and to the right were filled with people enjoying what might be the last warm weekend before fall took over.

"Hey, Gringa. You want a beer?" a voice called over the fence before Griffin could see who spoke.

"No, thanks, Eddie. It's been a long day," Indy answered.

Griffin stepped around the corner. A tall, tanned Hispanic man stood over the grill next door. He tipped his beer toward Griffin and smiled.

"Are you coming?" she called.

He followed into the first-floor apartment. The back door entered into the kitchen. The room was outdated, with cracked Formica counters and a rickety dinette. On the counter sat a collection of cows, the kind found in a country kitchen. Cows in clothes, cows stretched into funny poses. They seemed completely out of character for Indy Adams, businesswoman, but fit Indy the bar waitress.

A long hall ran the length of the apartment, connecting the kitchen to the living room. Two doors opened on the left, one on the right.

Indy went into the first door on the left, so he followed. She'd turned a bedroom into a home office. A high-end computer sat on a cheap desk.

"As long as you're here, I have information on a couple of

houses, but they don't look too promising." She looked up at him and held out a few sheets of paper. "Did you want a tour?"

If he had a tour, it would lead to her bedroom. He took the pages from her. "No, thanks. I'll get out of your hair now."

He walked back to the kitchen and she took the lead to the door. Before she could open it, he turned her around and kissed her again. Slow and hot, his tongue tangled with hers. When he pulled away, the papers in his hand were crumpled and his dick was rock hard.

"Good night." She sounded as breathless as he felt.

He leaned in again. "Find me a house soon so we can continue this."

She smiled against his lips. "I'm trying."

"How about we worry about the house later? I want to get you out of these clothes."

She sucked in a sharp breath. "No."

He stepped back again, opening the door as he did, and raked his eyes over her. "Those are really ugly clothes."

Her laughter echoed across the yards.

"See you later, Indy."

"Bye."

Walking back to his car, he thought of the fun he could have with chocolate cake and Indy's naked body.

CHAPTER 5

*A*nother restless night was going to do her in. She didn't know which was worse, being emotionally drained or being so turned on that sleep escaped. After Griffin's steamy kisses last night, she had a hard time turning her brain and her hormones off. He moved way beyond flirting and she didn't know how to react. She needed to sell him a house.

She checked the clock on her dashboard as she parked beside the house. She was on time, even with getting her car from the shop, but Griffin was early. Again. Every time she tried to be extraprofessional, he ruined it.

He climbed from his car after she parked.

"Hi," she said, trying not to sound breathless. One look at him and her mind strayed back to his lips on hers. "Thanks for coming here. I know you said you wanted a remodel, but this house might work."

She hoped it would. Finding the perfect house for him was difficult enough. Finding one to renovate was near impossible. She strode up the front steps and opened the door.

"As you can see, the front door opens to a beautiful staircase leading to the second floor. To the right you have the den, to the left the formal dining room, and behind that the kitchen. Would you like to start up or down?"

He cocked his head to the side. "I'll wander around on my own."

"Fine." She leaned against the cherry banister and waited for him to walk toward the kitchen. She actually wanted to see this house. Since he started downstairs, she went up to investigate.

She'd always dreamed of living in a house like this when she was growing up. One of the bedrooms had a huge bay window with a built-in seat, begging for a teenage girl to curl up and write in her diary. The soft, cushiony carpet squished under her feet. She kicked off her heels and dug her toes into the shag.

Completely unprofessional, but it felt good.

The master bedroom had double doors and two closets—his and hers. The bathroom had two sinks made of flawless black marble. The tub looked big enough to swim in. She sighed, knowing she'd never be able to afford the luxuries this house offered.

Indy headed back toward the stairs, assuming Griffin would be on his way up. She paused at the top and peered over the rail. He leaned against the newel post, typing again. Her heart sank.

She liked this house. She'd hoped it'd be the one. Beyond the money it would bring in for her, she'd thought, far back in her mind, that if Griffin owned it, she'd be able to visit it on occasion.

She started down. "Not for you, huh?"

He looked up and over his shoulder with a sexy smile. "I don't think so."

Trying not to show her disappointment, she headed down the stairs.

"Why do you look sad?"

She shrugged. "I like this one. I know it's not exactly what you wanted, but part of me hoped . . ."

"Hoped what?"

"Nothing." She shook her head. "You sure you don't want to check out the bedrooms?"

He raised his eyebrows, and she realized it sounded like an invitation. She'd never had to worry about screening her words as much as she did with him. Maybe it was her subconscious telling her something.

"You know what I mean."

"Do I?" he asked, taking a step up and closer to her.

Her heart ticked up a notch. The scent of his soap or cologne tickled her senses. Her hormones responded like they had last night, which was supposed to be unacceptable. "Yes. We've been over this. I don't sleep with clients."

Not that she'd ever had a client who could turn her on like Griffin did.

"I know what your voice said, but the rest of your body told a different story." He leaned in, and she stepped back.

The wood rail bit into her spine. She couldn't lie. Her body reacted to him at every glance. She'd been fighting to keep it in check, but he kept pushing.

Griffin ran a finger down the pearl buttons of her blouse. "Not as bad as the clothes you wore yesterday during dinner, but not nearly as sexy as the barmaid outfit."

Her breath caught, and she halfway wanted him to flick the buttons open. She couldn't tell him to stop. Her voice wouldn't work. *Because I want this.*

"I seem to remember your promising to wear it next time you showed me a house."

"I . . . I forgot." She glanced to the side at the expanse of stairs. She could easily turn around. An image of gripping the rail while he lifted her skirt to have his way with her flashed in her head. Her blood raced hot.

He pressed his body to hers. His hard-on deliciously poked her, and she ground into him. He covered her mouth with his. He sucked on her lower lip, and she trembled. God, she wanted this so bad.

He kissed her neck and bit at her throbbing pulse. She threw her head back to give him better access and opened her eyes. She stared at the chandelier above her.

What the hell was she thinking? She was in someone else's house. Imagining fucking on their staircase. This was beyond unprofessional. If anyone found out, not only would she not get bigger clients, she'd be fired.

With a burst of resolve, she pushed Griffin away from her. He looked bewildered. Breath puffed heavily from his chest.

"We cannot do this." She scooted around him on the stairs and headed for the door. She held it open, waiting for him to leave.

As he walked by, she tried not to laugh at his discomfort. Serves him right. Now they were both hot and bothered.

"I don't suppose—"

"No." She cut him off. She didn't want him to finish the sentence because she would probably cave. He'd offer to take her somewhere to finish. She could see it in his eyes. The lustful pull in her belly urged her to accept, but for once she'd follow her brain. "I'll call you when I find something more suitable."

"Sure?"

Such a loaded question.

She nodded, not trusting herself. While he got into his car, she locked up the house. Griffin was going to be the most difficult client she'd ever worked with, especially if she couldn't learn to control her hormones.

~

INDY FED off the distraction of working at the bar. Another waitress quit, so Indy picked up extra shifts. She also got two new real estate clients via referral.

Griffin being the referral.

He probably felt sorry for her because she worked in a bar wearing a skimpy outfit. He was the type of guy who would think a service job was beneath him.

But his kisses hadn't felt like pity. That had been attraction. Lust.

She needed to find him a house. Once Griffin found a house, it wouldn't matter what happened between them. By the time Griffin figured out what he wanted, Quinn and Ryan's wedding would be over and her commission safely tucked away. Awkward social meetings would be rare.

What am I doing? Am I trying to talk myself into sleeping with Griffin?

She snorted. The thought was ridiculous, but someone had to be a rebound guy. It might as well be a sexy guy.

End Zone was busy for a weeknight. Nick worked the bar. She'd thought it might be weird working with her ex-brother-in-law, but it wasn't.

"Hey, Indy. You got some regulars already looking for you."

"Yeah?" She looked over her shoulder. "Good. Maybe I'll leave with a pocketful of money."

"They asked for the singing waitress."

She stopped fiddling with her small apron. "Huh?"

"They came in and asked which section the singing waitress would be working."

"Oh, hell." She vaguely remembered the guys. All too young to interest her, but they thought they were the best thing going.

Nick looked at her expectantly.

"Last weekend I served a table while that Carrie Underwood song 'Last Name' came on. I sang along, and they volunteered to take me home and not reveal their last names." She finished tying her apron.

"You want me to move them?"

"Nah, I'll be fine." She filled her apron pockets with an order pad and some pens. She didn't even recall what the guys looked like. She just remembered them calling her the singing waitress. They thought they were being funny.

At her first table, she glanced at faces. Nothing popped. "Hi, I'm Indy and I'll be your server tonight. Can I start you with some fresh drinks?"

At the second table, she hit pay dirt. She recognized two of the guys. The other two were new. After her introduction, she took their order and spun to leave.

"Indy?"

Shit. Almost free. "Yes."

"You probably don't remember me, but I was in here when you sang on Saturday."

She nodded, prompting him to go on.

"I wondered if you'd sing a song for my friend here. It's his birthday."

She applied her brightest friendly smile. "I'm not really a singer."

She loved to sing, but people always reminded her there was a time and a place. Singing in her house or car made her feel good. She hadn't been on a stage to sing since karaoke night with Quinn. Normally, the attention felt great. That night, she'd been too upset to enjoy the cheers and applause.

"You should be. Here's fifty bucks. You choose the song." He slapped a fifty on the table.

Instinct had her reaching for it, but she stopped herself. She was a barmaid, not entertainment. "I'll be right back with your drinks."

She tapped her foot at the bar while she waited for drinks. What harm could it do to sing one song? The fifty alone made it worth coming in to work tonight. After she gathered the drinks from the bar, she looked around for the boss. Nowhere in sight.

Indy scanned her brain for a song that would be fun and not too serious. One she knew all of the words to.

After delivering the drinks, she noted the fifty still sat at the edge of the table. She tucked it into her apron and went to the jukebox. She scrolled through to find a song. Country always came easiest for her. She decided on Kenny Chesney's "No Shoes, No Shirt, No Problems."

The jukebox blared so loud, she didn't think she could drown out Kenny with her own voice, so she didn't bother. It ended up sounding like a duet. She sang at the table, knowing the other customers watched. Being the center of attention never bothered her.

She put on her game face and performed. Fifty bucks for three and a half minutes was a good take. What she hadn't counted on was the performance taking on a life of its own. By the end of the night, she'd sung four more songs. Two at ten bucks each, two at twenty each. She didn't tell anyone they had to pay for a song, but she took the money they offered.

The hours on her feet flew by. An extra hundred dollars in her pocket made time irrelevant. If she could keep this up, she'd make it to Acapulco in December after all. The thought added an extra spring in her step. Relaxing on a white sand beach would cure her quicker than a rebound romance.

She cleared her tray of empty beer bottles and glasses and refilled for the next round for two of her tables. Back at her station, she stopped short when she saw Griffin sitting at a table by himself. He already had a beer. His sleeves were rolled to the elbow and his collar was open. He looked damn good. The five o'clock shadow gave him the ultimate bad-boy look. So delicious.

His eyes locked on hers and he smiled. The predatory smile made her heart thump in her chest. She delivered the drinks on her tray before going to him.

"Hi. How long have you been here?"

"Long enough to watch you sing."

Her cheeks warmed with embarrassment. How did he manage to do this to her? She was a good singer and had nothing to be ashamed of. "Can I get you another beer?"

He leaned forward bringing his elbows onto the table. "I love your voice. You should sing more often. It suits you more than selling beer."

"Thanks, I think. What can I get for you?"

His eyes roamed the length of her body. "How about a song?"

She laughed. He did not come into this bar to hear her sing. "Are you drunk?"

He lifted a shoulder. "Not quite."

She looked closer at his face. He looked as tired as she felt. "Something wrong?"

"Crappy day. I came here so I wouldn't get drunk alone in my office."

Indy made a point of looking around. "You're still drinking alone."

"I'm not alone. I'm with you."

"I'm working." She stiffened at his sigh. "It might not seem like much to you, but this is my job."

"I know." He lifted his body and pulled out his wallet. He put a fifty on the table. "I want to buy a song."

"Put your money away, Griffin." The crowd had cleared and tables were emptying.

"You took the other guy's money and sang for him."

"If some idiot is going to give me money to sing a song, damn right I'll take it." She turned and wiped down the empty table behind Griffin's.

"So call me an idiot and sing to me."

She wiped the next table and hesitated, because singing for strangers, for an audience, was easy because of the anonymity. Griffin knew her, and attraction sizzled between them. She also knew he wouldn't give up. "Fine. What do you want to hear?"

"You choose."

She slid the fifty into her apron and went back to the jukebox. She scanned her choices, skipping anything slow and about love or sex. Carrie Underwood was a safe bet.

Who didn't like to hear about a woman getting even for her boyfriend cheating? As the opening notes of "Before He Cheats" sounded, Indy growled out Carrie's words.

Griffin eased into a half smile and finished his beer while she sang. His eyes locked on her face. Even when she moved and wiggled with the music. Regardless of his comments about her uniform, he stared into her eyes.

That alone unnerved her. A man ogling her body she knew how to handle. With Griffin, it felt like more. In that moment, she knew they were never going to have a strictly professional relationship.

GRIFFIN WAS VAGUELY aware of the pool players who stopped their game to watch Indy. She was a performer. The words of the song didn't matter. The one she sang now had no sexy innuendo to it. She sang about taking a baseball bat to a man's car, but her voice got to him.

And that mouth.

He hadn't been able to get her mouth out of his mind for days.

She finished the song and turned to walk away. He caught up with her and asked, "When do you get off?"

"Closing. About an hour."

"Can you leave early? Or do I have to sit here and wait?"

"Wait for what?" She wiped down the next table in line and he followed.

"For you."

Her long blond ponytail bobbed and swooshed with each swipe. The bartender kept a close watch on him. Griffin stared back, but the bartender didn't budge.

"The bartender's throwing daggers this way. He your new boyfriend?" Griffin stepped back and tucked his hands in his pockets.

"Nick, God no. He probably thinks you're a creep hitting on me."

"I am." Why wouldn't she turn to look at him? He couldn't read her unless he could see her eyes. Even while she sang an angry song, he saw the banked desire in her hazel eyes.

She stopped midswipe, then continued saying, "I thought we agreed to be friends."

"That worked until you kissed me."

Indy slapped the rag against the table and spun. "I did not kiss you. You kissed me."

He smiled. "I know. I wanted you to look at me. I don't enjoy talking to the back of your head."

She heaved a sigh of impatience, and the rise of her chest in the too-tight T-shirt distracted him momentarily. She cocked a hip and leaned against the table. "What do you want to talk about?"

"I haven't been able to get your lips out of my head." He stepped closer, keeping his hands in his pockets. Lowering his head, he spoke close enough to feel her breath on his face. "I want to taste you."

She closed her eyes and swallowed. "We had an agreement."

"Name your price."

"What?" Her eyes flew open.

He suddenly realized the remark sounded like he was propositioning a hooker. He stepped back to think clearly. "Your commission. I'll write you a check right now. Then it won't matter."

"Sorry, no deal. I work for my commission. I'll get it when I find you a house." She pushed off the table, intent on leaving.

He stepped in her path. "Just a kiss." One that would surely lead to the bedroom. He never misread those signals.

"Not a good idea." She walked around him. "I'll call you tomorrow with ideas on houses."

"Leave with me now. I took a cab here and could use a ride home."

"I'm working."

"The bar is empty. How much more do you think you're going to make tonight? I'll cover it."

Anger flashed on her face. "Do you think you can buy whatever you want?"

"Pretty much."

"I'm not for sale. Go home, Griffin."

Damn. He hadn't meant for it to sound like that. "I'm not trying to buy you. I'm serious about the ride. I don't have one."

"So call a cab."

"Are you always so stubborn?" He never had to work this hard to get a woman alone. Deep in his gut, he knew she'd be worth it.

"No, that's usually Quinn's trait. I'm learning to appreciate it, though."

She walked to the bar, and the bartender handed her a glass. She gulped what looked like water quickly. The bartender spoke quietly and Indy shook her head.

Bringing her glass, she returned to Griffin. "I'll drive you home when my shift is over. I owe you for putting up with my dad and giving me a ride home. Sit at the bar and wait."

"Thank you." He sat at the bar and asked for water. He wanted to clear his system of the buzz he had.

"You know Indy?" the bartender asked.

Griffin drank from the glass. "Yeah."

"Where did you meet?"

"Her sister is marrying my friend."

He tilted his head. "I was married to her sister."

Griffin swallowed another drink of water. "You're Quinn's ex." He kept the surprise out of his voice.

"Yep, I'm Nick." He extended his hand across the bar.

"Griffin." They shook briefly. "Isn't it tough working with your ex-sister-in-law?"

"Nah. Indy's cool. She was pissed when me and Quinn split, but then again, she wasn't happy when we were together either." Nick shrugged and went back to washing glasses. His gaze continued to follow Indy's movements. His look revealed more than friendly interest.

But Griffin figured most men looked at her that way.

Two glasses of water, one trip to the washroom, and twenty minutes later, Indy pulled her apron off.

"We can go. Lisa will close for me, and it's dead now."

"I'm in no hurry," he lied. He wanted to get her alone. His

blood rushed watching her coo and smile and flirt with every man who entered her path.

He followed her out to her car. She pointed her remote and clicked the door unlocked. Griffin grabbed her waist and spun her. His mouth captured hers when it opened in shock.

Indy yielded slightly as he savored her. Blood beat in his ears, and his hands gripped her hips.

She eased away from him, eyes wide.

"A mouth like yours should be illegal." His fingers tightened their grip, intent on pulling her into him.

Her breathing was uneven and her hazel eyes darkened. Her tongue darted out and ran along her upper lip.

He couldn't tell who moved first, but their bodies collided and mouths followed. Indy wasn't pliant and yielding. She took as much from him as he did her.

She pressed into him. His hard-on pressed against her, and her nipples stood erect through thin cotton.

Griffin kissed her neck, and she shivered.

"How far do you live?" she asked in a whisper.

"Hmm?"

She shoved his head. "Where do you live?"

"Close." He attacked her neck again.

"Then get in the car. Sex in public is one thing, but I have to work here tomorrow."

His brain clouded. Did she imply public sex was okay?

She tore away from him quickly. "Get in."

He sat uncomfortably in the passenger seat, his pants tightening across his crotch. He gave her the address and basic directions.

Her breathing slowed and regulated during the drive. He leaned over the console. He wasn't about to lose momentum.

Not now. Not this close.

He stroked her inner thigh. She jerked the steering wheel, and the car swerved slightly.

"Take it easy," he whispered. The shorts were tight and he couldn't slip his fingers under, so he brushed his hand over the top of the fabric and tongued her ear.

Her breathing became ragged again. "We're here. Parking?"

"Around the corner. Underground garage." He moved back to his own seat and fished out his parking pass. As Indy pulled up to the gate, a guard poked his head out of the shack.

Griffin leaned across Indy. She pressed her back farther in her seat, but not so far that he couldn't feel the rapid rise and fall of her chest.

"Hey, Jim. My friend gave me a ride. We'll be parked in my spot."

"Sure, Mr. Walker, no problem."

Indy giggled and drove past the gate.

"What?"

She deepened her voice. "Sure, Mr. Walker." Another giggle. "I was picturing whether he'd still be all businesslike and respectful if he saw your hand in my crotch."

"He would. It's a discreet building." He pointed to his parking slot.

Indy cut the engine and removed the keys but didn't open her door.

"Having second thoughts?"

"Yes. No. I need a minute."

He got out and walked around. Opening her door, he held out his hand. She accepted it and stepped out, but paused.

"Look, obviously we have some major attraction going on here."

"I'll say." He leaned in to kiss her again, but her hand on his chest stopped him.

"I don't do this."

"Okay." He leaned in again.

Again with the slap to his chest.

"I'm serious. I don't want you to think that because we're screwing means this is how I get clients."

So beautiful and smart, but she thought so little of herself. "The thought never crossed my mind."

"Okay."

"And I promise not to treat you any differently when we're looking at houses. Strictly professional then. After hours, though . . ." This time he did make it all the way to her neck and tasted the salty skin. He pulled the band from her hair, and the blond mess tickled his face as it bounced down past her shoulders.

"Who says there will be more than tonight?"

Moving up her neck to her ear, he whispered, "Once won't be enough for either of us."

She shivered a little and pulled his hips into her.

He groaned and stepped back. "We need to go upstairs, or we'll be doing this for an audience."

She rolled her lower lip into her mouth and wiggled her eyebrows. This woman would be the death of him.

"Not this time."

They walked to the elevator holding hands. The moment the doors closed and he pressed the button for his floor, Indy pushed him against the rail with her body. She kissed the V of his open collar and unbuttoned the next button, following with her tongue. Her knee nudged its way between his legs, and she rubbed her body against him like a cat in heat.

"You might want to stop." He felt her lips curve against his skin.

"Why?"

"We're not alone." When her eyes rose, he pointed. "Security cameras."

She looked over her shoulder and winked at the camera. She returned to stroking his body.

"I have to ride this elevator every day."

"So?"

Ding. The doors slid open and he walked her into the hall. She continued to unbutton his shirt while walking backward.

He wrapped his left arm around her waist while his right hand unlocked the door. Bodies together, they entered his condo. Griffin barely managed to kick the door shut before tugging her tight shirt off.

Her skin was hot under his hands. He pushed her shorts down her long legs. She stepped out of them while unhooking his pants. Her mouth, with those incredible lips, hungrily pressed against his. She crouched and pushed his pants down to his ankles.

Then she promptly lost her balance and brought him down hard to the floor, his pants still wound around his feet.

"Are you okay?" he asked, worried he might've landed on her. He propped himself up on his elbows, their bodies touching from chests to calves.

She burst into a raucous laugh, and it was such a great sound, he wanted to hear it more.

"I'll take that as a yes."

Her hand flew to her mouth. "I'm sorry," she said from behind her fingers. "It's not funny."

Something flashed in her eyes telling him she worried about his reaction. He smoothed a hand over her hair. "I'm fine. A little tangled right now, but okay. No worries."

A smile eased back onto her face and she pushed at his boxers. "God, I want you so bad."

His dick jumped in her hand. She shifted and rubbed herself against him. The expensive, normally comfortable carpet dug into his elbows. "The bedroom's this way."

He kicked the pants off his legs and yanked her to her feet. In nothing more than plain white bra and underwear, she was still incredibly sexy. He led the way into the bedroom and flicked on the light. He wanted to watch every move she made and enjoy her lack of inhibition.

Indy turned and looked around the room. "Oh, my God. This is amazing." She dropped his hand and took a running leap onto his bed, finishing in a somersault. Then she bounced up on her knees.

"What? Are you just going to stand there and stare?"

"You make quite the image."

The laugh returned. A bold statement that was Indy. He rushed at her and tackled her gently to the mattress. Her laugh died as his mouth covered hers and his hand found her wet heat. The moan was at least as powerful as her laugh, and he questioned how long he'd last.

He'd had plenty of beautiful women, but none so full of life.

He stroked her and she came before he had a chance to remove her underwear.

"Wow," she whispered, breathing heavily. Her flirty grin returned. "That was a damn good beginning."

She flipped him over and her mouth began doing the most amazing things to his body. Yeah, he'd been right about her mouth.

It should definitely be illegal.

CHAPTER 6

*I*ndy sat up quickly. Griffin snored beside her. She'd fallen asleep in Griffin's bed.

She brushed her hair away from her face. One look at Griffin's naked body and her nerves began to hum. Vivid pictures of what he could do to her slid across her mind. She suppressed the deep pull of desire and ignored the urge to climb on top of him.

Getting out of bed, she realized she didn't know where any of her clothes had landed. She scanned the dark room and couldn't find anything.

She slipped through the bedroom door and found the trail of clothes. She picked up everything, folding Griffin's and stacking them on the dark leather couch. Her shorts and shirt were easy to find, but her bra and panties were nowhere in sight. She slunk through the condo to find a bathroom. She freshened up and redressed in the clothes she did find.

She glanced toward the bedroom and then looked around the living room. Even in the moonlight, she saw the luxury and expense in the room. Leather furniture that made the stuff Richard bought look like it came from a garage sale. Marble counters, chrome finishes, a view of downtown. She didn't belong here.

Tiptoeing back to the bedroom, she stole a last peek for her bra and underwear. Nothing. They were probably tangled in something else. She spied a sweatshirt draped over a chair. Since she didn't have a jacket, she snagged it.

Indy pulled a slip of paper from her purse and left a quick note telling Griffin she'd taken his sweatshirt.

Then she snuck out the front door. She didn't want any awkward morning after.

The streets were quiet on the drive through the city. Every muscle in her body was relaxed. The chilly night air caused goose bumps to rise on her legs despite the warmth of Griffin's sweatshirt.

In her neighborhood, most people were already home for the night, so parking was scarce. She parked around the corner and walked down the block with her keys in hand.

She went through the front, careful to close the heavy door quietly to keep her neighbors undisturbed. She dropped her keys, kicked off her shoes, and crawled straight into bed. Griffin's scent coaxed her into sleep.

INDY JOLTED awake and looked at the clock. She'd only been asleep a couple of hours. Dawn had barely crept into the sky. Her phone rang. Is that what woke her? "Hello?"

"Answer your fucking door."

"Griffin?"

He disconnected, so she stumbled out of bed and looked out her front window. No one. She went to the back door and met Griffin's scowl.

She opened the door, still groggy. "What are you doing here?"

He pushed past her into the kitchen. He paced the length of the hall and back.

"Why are you here?" she asked again.

"I rolled over in bed, expecting to find a warm, naked body, and found nothing. When you didn't pop out of the bathroom, I went to look for you and found this." He tossed her crumpled note on the kitchen table.

She shook her head to clear it. "You're pissed because I borrowed a sweatshirt?" How petty was this guy? She stripped it off and threw it at him. He dropped it on the chair.

Indy moved to push past him, but he caught her arm.

"I'm pissed because you snuck out of my house. You just left."

She yanked her arm back. "I didn't see the point in waking you. What do you want, a big, fat thank-you?"

He deserved at least that much. It had been some of the best damn sex she'd ever had. Not that she would admit it right now.

"I want to know why you left."

She didn't know how to answer. *I don't belong in your world?* He wouldn't buy it, even though it rang true. She took a deep breath, stared at the floor, and lied. "I can't sleep in a strange place."

She'd felt too comfortable in his bed and knew it was a bad thing. Sex was sex, but sleeping together changed things.

His voice softened. "You fell asleep before I did."

She shrugged, hoping he wouldn't try to bust her on her lie. He moved closer and ran a hand over her hair. She wanted nothing more than to snuggle her face into his hand, but held back.

"Fine. I thought you might want these back." From his pocket he produced her panties.

She looked at the material dangling from his finger. The tense moment passed and she smiled. "No bra?"

His eyes wandered to her chest and her hard nipples. "I didn't know you left it."

"I couldn't find my panties or bra."

"I'll look for it." He took a step closer and she backed into the wall. "Next time, I won't let you off so easy."

She tilted her chin up, her heart already racing. "Who says there will be a next time?"

"You," he whispered against her lips, and kissed her.

Her mind floated back into a haze. The sleepy, lazy kiss held just enough heat to make her want more. Maybe she should've spent the night at his place.

He pulled back. "I have to get ready for work."

"Uh-huh."

"I'll call you later."

"I'm working tonight and I have Quinn's shower this weekend." She straightened from the wall.

"Then call me when you're free."

"Okay."

"Call me, or I'll show up in the middle of the night."

"I will." A surprise visit might be fun, though. She imagined him sneaking into her bedroom while she slept.

He grabbed her again and planted a hard kiss on her mouth, then turned to leave.

"Your sweatshirt."

"Keep it," he tossed over his shoulder as he walked through the door.

Indy picked up the sweatshirt and wrapped it around herself again. She crawled back into bed, thinking of her schedule and where she could pencil Griffin in.

He was worth making time for.

She sighed. Kate's disappointed voice echoed in her head. Kate had always been her Jiminy Cricket, letting her know when she screwed up. Her business was important. She couldn't let great sex cloud that.

But Griffin was more than a client.

Personal relationships already muddied everything. They couldn't deny their attraction. They'd have fun for a while, then it would cool down to a casual acquaintance.

Griffin was the perfect rebound guy.

GRIFFIN SAT at O'Leary's waiting for Ryan, nursing his beer. Irritation crawled over him because Indy hadn't called. He never waited for a woman, yet he waited for her. That fueled the irritation more than the lack of communication.

A slap on the shoulder told him Ryan had arrived.

He looked at his friend. "How was the girly party?"

"I couldn't wait to escape. After spending hours looking at paint chips and samples to keep the party a surprise, the roomful of women cooing over towels made my brain hurt."

"You asked for it." He took a long pull on his beer.

"No, I asked for Quinn. I got stuck with the rest." He walked around the bar and opened a beer for himself. "I'm glad you called. I needed to get out of there. They've included Moira in whatever girl gossip they've got going on while cleaning."

Ryan ranted for a while about the useless gifts, and Griffin's mind wandered back to Indy. The party ended and still no call.

"You and Indy, huh?" Ryan's question broke into his thoughts.

"She's already talking."

"To Kate and Quinn. And Moira."

"Great. I'm not responsible for your sister's corruption."

Ryan drank his beer. "You know Indy just got out of a crappy relationship."

"Shit. Is this you going all big brother on me?"

"This is me telling you that if you fuck with her, I'll pay for it because I'm marrying her sister."

"Guilt by association." Griffin finished his beer. "Indy's a big girl. She makes her own choices. We're having a good time. No expectations."

"Do you ever have any?"

"I avoid disappointment."

But he had expected her to call.

"Watch your step."

"I always do." They talked sports and family, but Griffin became restless with the late hour. He stood, said his good-byes, and left.

Instead of driving deeper into the city, he drove to Indy's. Unlike her, he followed through with his promises.

He squeezed into a tight spot a few houses down and looked at her apartment. The lights were off. He pulled his phone from his pocket as he walked up the front steps.

He rang the bell and waited, prepared to call her like last time. The porch light flicked on and Indy peered past the sheer white curtain. Her face was soft and sleepy.

She opened the door. "Hello."

"You said you'd call."

"I planned to . . ." She stepped clear of the door, allowing him to enter.

He walked into the living room to see an immaculate, almost sterile space. Two clear glass tables flanked a white leather sofa. Beige lamps stood on the tables. Not at all how he expected her living room to look.

Indy stepped around him and went to the kitchen. He didn't wait for further invitation. She drank a glass of water while standing at the sink.

"I'm not in the habit of waiting for a woman."

"You made that perfectly clear." The ice in her voice could've chilled the glass she held. She continued to drink as if she made total sense.

"What's that supposed to mean?"

"Quinn told me you're bringing a date to the wedding."

He stiffened at the implication, understanding her earlier jab.

Before he could rebut, she plowed on. "I know we only slept together once. It was sex. I'm okay with a casual relationship. I am on the rebound, after all. I don't expect a lifelong commitment, but I don't share."

He snorted. "Your last lover was married."

"Separated, and they weren't sleeping together."

"According to the adulterer, who is such an honest guy you believed him."

Her face reddened and her eyes blazed. "He was getting a divorce!"

His anger bubbled at being put in the same box with her ex. "I am not him. I don't sleep with a woman one night and look for her replacement the next unless that's the arrangement."

"Yet you're bringing a date to my sister's wedding." Her arms flailed and water sloshed out of her glass.

Women. Forever jumping to conclusions. "Why didn't you call me and ask? If you did, you would've found out she's not a real date."

Indy inhaled deeply and closed her eyes.

"Remember Lily from the diner when we had lunch?"

Her eyes opened wide. "You're bringing the child waitress to the wedding?"

He sighed. His anger dissipated as he explained. He knew how this looked. If roles had reversed, his reaction would've been worse. "She's twenty-five, not a child. After you left, I went back and caught up with her."

Indy pursed her lips and crossed her arms. Points for her for not asking his history with Lily.

"I used to babysit her. Turns out she has a thing for Ryan's brother Liam, so I offered to get her into the wedding."

"Fine." No shame or regret showed on her face.

"That's it? What about an apology?"

"For what?"

"Jumping to conclusions about me."

"I think my conclusions are dead-on about you." She turned and put her glass in the sink.

He stuck his hands in his pockets and rocked back on his heels. "I doubt it."

"Where does this leave things between us?"

He stepped closer, staring at her mouth. "Where do you want it?"

She laughed. "Such a loaded question." She took a step, their bodies nearly touched. "Casual works for me. I only ask that when you want someone else, you tell me first."

"Agreed." At the moment he couldn't imagine wanting anyone more than he wanted her. He lowered his head to taste her lips. The slow, lazy kiss stirred his blood more than the anger and yelling. "What time do you have to work tomorrow?"

"Afternoon. Why?"

He smiled against her lips. "That might give me enough time."

"You're pretty arrogant."

"Not if I can deliver." He ran his tongue down the side of her neck, and her pulse pounded.

They walked back to her bedroom. He looked around. *This is Indy.* The room was frilly and feminine. Her spicy scent clung to the air.

"I know it's not what you're used to," she said quietly.

"It's perfect. It's you."

She looked up at him and even in the dark, he saw a spark in her eyes.

TANGLED TOGETHER IN HER BED, Indy fought the urge to run her hands over Griffin's body. They were both still panting and slicked with sweat. She pressed against him, seeking his warmth, his solid presence.

"You keep rubbing against me like that and you won't be getting any sleep."

She nipped his shoulder. "Promise?"

When he rolled over and covered her body with his, she sucked in a sharp breath. Richard had never even considered twice in a night. *I guess fifteen years makes quite a difference.*

She was doing it again. Comparing Griffin to Richard wasn't fair. She had to stop.

SHE LAY spread-eagle on her bed, chilled but satisfied. Her nerves tingled. Griffin returned from the bathroom and slid next to her.

Goose bumps rose on her flesh. He held a glass of water above her face.

"Want some?"

She took the glass, propped herself on an elbow, and gulped greedily. When half the glass was gone, she passed it back and collapsed against the bed. She heard the clink of the glass on the nightstand.

Griffin's face filled her vision. "Still think I'm arrogant?"

"Yeah, but you can definitely deliver."

He pulled her close to his body before covering them

both with the blanket. He kissed her shoulder and curled his body against hers.

Indy's heart kicked. Did he plan to stay?

"Are you free for lunch Tuesday?"

She heard the question, but was too busy enjoying his arms around her to answer.

"Indy?"

"I heard. I can probably make myself free."

"Good. Put me on your schedule."

She immediately thought of a nooner, and it warmed her blood. "Meet you here?"

"I have reservations at RL."

"Ralph Lauren's restaurant? Are you kidding?" She turned in the circle of his arms to see his face.

"There's a guy I'm trying to hire, a software engineer from California."

"Why would you want me there for a business lunch? I know nothing about what you do. What am I, arm candy?"

A quiet laugh rumbled in his chest.

"You are some damn fine arm candy, but he's bringing his wife. She's concerned about uprooting their family to a new city. I figured if anyone knows the city it's you."

She inched up so they were almost nose to nose. Her breasts brushed against the smattering of hair on his chest. "A business lunch about real estate I can do. Let me know what information they need and I'll have it ready."

The idea of going to RL intrigued her. It was *the* place to be seen. Being seen with Griffin could help her tap a lot of potential clients with deep pockets.

He suddenly pulled back from her. "It's a business lunch, but I want you there as my date, not as my real estate agent."

She blinked slowly at the irritation in his voice. She hadn't considered that. They'd agreed to be casual. "Oh."

He studied her face. "What did you think we were doing?"

"Uh." Her heart crashed in her chest. Had she misunderstood their conversation? She sat up and stared at the shadows on the wall. She began slowly. "I assumed casual meant we enjoy each other's company. Here. Like this." She pointed to the bed.

He pulled himself up and took her chin in his hand. "You thought I'd come here to fuck you, but I wouldn't want to be seen in public with you?"

She winced and pulled away from his hand. "When you put it like that it sounds bad, but I guess that's what it boils down to. Isn't that what casual means?"

He sighed. The muscle in his jaw twitched. "Casual means we enjoy our time together without expectations for the future."

She shrugged. "I guess we should've shared definitions earlier."

"Hey, if all you want is a fuck buddy, I could probably suffer through." He stretched out on the bed again with a smug smile on his lips.

She smacked him with her pillow. "Your idea of casual might be more fun. Care to show me the ropes?"

He pulled her back until her head nestled in the crook of his shoulder. "First, sleep. Lunch Tuesday. We'll figure out the rest as we go."

She heard Griffin's breathing slow, and Indy settled into his warmth. Giddiness danced across her nerves. Griffin wanted to spend time with her out of bed. He was taking her to an expensive restaurant to meet a potential employee.

He trusted her not to screw it up or embarrass him.

The thought created a hard pressure in her chest. In one fell swoop her rebound guy had given her more than Richard ever had.

Don't get carried away. Casual was best.

We'll figure it out as we go.

It was the most promise she'd felt in a long time.

~

THE MORNING SUN streamed through the narrow window facing the neighbors' building. The sheets next to her were cool. So he hadn't spent the night. But she smelled coffee.

She flipped off the covers and pulled on an oversized T-shirt. The sight in her kitchen caused a hitch in her stride. Griffin stood in his underwear, staring out her back windows.

He had stayed.

The lines of his muscles were relaxed. Raising coffee to his lips caused the tattoo on the back of his shoulder to take life. The blue monster with claws and wings eyed her fiercely.

Griffin turned and looked at her. "Morning."

"I thought you left."

He met her at the counter while she poured her coffee. "Unlike *some* people, I don't sneak off."

He said it without animosity, but with enough bite to cause a ping of guilt in her chest.

"I apologized."

"With a bullshit excuse."

There had been no way to explain that she wouldn't be the way she'd been with Richard. She wouldn't stay in his expensive condo while he never came to her. But Griffin had come to her. He'd spent the night. She shrugged. "Want breakfast?"

She bent and pulled eggs from the fridge.

"Now I know why your neighbor Eddie looks at you like you're naked."

She straightened and nudged him out of the way to grab a

bowl and fork to scramble eggs. "Eddie has never seen me naked."

"You sure?"

"Look," she said, jabbing the fork in the air at him.

He cut her off. "No, you look. Your kitchen window lines up with his. We had a companionable nod over a cup of coffee earlier."

She'd never considered it. She'd never seen Eddie in the window looking at her. "I rarely stroll around naked."

She cracked eggs into the bowl.

His gaze wandered over the shirt that skimmed her thighs. "Barely dressed is almost worse than naked. Fuels the imagination."

"Whatever." She picked up her cow salt and pepper shakers and sprinkled the eggs.

Griffin eased away from the stove as she set the pan on the flame. He lowered the blinds on the window. "What's with the cows?"

"Do not give me hard time about the cows." Her voice came out sharper than she had intended. She popped bread in the toaster and put butter and jelly on the table while eggs sizzled in the pan.

Griffin sat silently, waiting for breakfast. He checked something on his phone while she plated food.

She set the plates down and took the seat across from him. He picked up his fork, then set it back down. "I wasn't giving you a hard time about your damn cows. It's a weird collection and I was making conversation."

She blew on some eggs before putting them in her mouth. "I know. I didn't mean to snap at you."

He took a bite of eggs, but she pushed her plate away. "Richard hated the cows."

Griffin's fork clanged against his plate. "I told you before, I'm not him."

Indy softened her voice. "I know. It's like I've suddenly realized I spent months trying to live up to the expectation of being something I'm not."

She paused. She enjoyed acknowledging the feeling.

It felt so good, she continued. "The living room furniture? Richard picked it out. He wanted one room where he could feel comfortable on the rare occation he came over." She got up from the table and words rushed out.

"I used to hide the cows. Or at least push them back so they were less visible. Which was ridiculous because he never came into the kitchen. He never used the back door."

Her eyes locked on Griffin's. "He never spent the night."

Griffin stood and wrapped his arms around her. She didn't cry. She didn't even want to. Anger ran through her.

"You're not crying, are you?"

Her cheek rested against his hard chest, his steady heartbeat soothing her. She smiled. "No, I'm fine. I'm frustrated with myself. Eat your eggs before they get totally cold."

He returned to the chair and she topped off both cups of coffee. She sat, feeling better after venting. "The collection was an accident. After my mom died, and I picked up Quinn, I grabbed the three cows my mom kept in the kitchen. I thought Quinn would want them."

She took a bite of eggs, now cold, and washed them down with hot coffee. "Quinn laughed when I tried to give them to her. She thinks they're ugly. So I kept them. Then friends bought more as gag gifts. Now it's a collection."

Griffin finished his eggs and toast without comment. "Thank you."

"You're welcome." She stood and reached for his plate.

"Not for breakfast. For telling me about your cows."

She put the dishes in the sink. "I figured I owed you for letting me rant about my ex-boyfriend. Most men would've walked away."

He stood and kissed the side of her neck. "He means nothing. His loss, my gain."

In a moment, she was breathless again, hoping her jelly legs would hold her. His almost beard rubbed roughly against her skin, burning pleasure through her. "Don't you have to work?"

His hands were all over her, warming her skin. "I'm the boss."

He picked her up and set her on the edge of the table. Making his intentions clear, he pushed his underwear down and ripped open a condom. Where the hell had he hidden that? "I don't think this table is strong enough. It might collapse."

"I'll buy you a new one," he whispered against her flesh as he nipped and sucked.

CHAPTER 7

Tuesday morning, Griffin received a text from Indy saying she'd meet him at the restaurant. Indy was always late, so he'd offered to pick her up, but she declined.

He arrived at the restaurant a few minutes early and waited for his prospective employee Rob and his wife, Michelle. And Indy. Before he could pull out his phone to check the time, the door opened and Indy stepped through. Her royal blue suit exuded professionalism, but being Indy, she wore a deep-cut silk blouse as a nod to her femininity.

"Hi." She smiled.

"You're not late."

Her smiled broadened and she raised a brow. "No 'Hi, Indy. How's your day?'"

He returned her smile and mocked, "Hi, Indy. How's your day?"

"It doesn't count if I have to prompt you. And I'm not *always* late."

He stepped closer and kissed her cheek, knowing if he touched her lips, he wouldn't be able to stop. "You look gorgeous."

"Thank you," she answered coolly.

The compliment meant nothing to her. Men probably said similar things to her all the time. He didn't know how to explain what she did to him. Any attempt would sound like a lame come-on. He'd never wanted a woman as much as she made him want her.

The hostess seated them near the center of the room. He pulled Indy's chair out for her. She shot a grin at him over her shoulder.

People noticed her. It happened when she walked into any room. The problem lay in the fact that many people knew him, if only by name or face. The whispering began.

As he took his seat beside Indy, she whispered, "Am I fodder for gossip columnists by being seen with you?"

He sighed. He hadn't wanted her to be. "Probably."

"Good."

His gaze shot to hers. "Good?"

"I don't think I've ever been in a newspaper before." She waved a hand near her face. "Makeup?"

"Flawless." He found her eagerness disarming. The novelty of the spotlight would fade. She wasn't part of this world. She wasn't one of the flighty socialites who craved the publicity. At least he hadn't thought so.

A couple approached the table, and Griffin recognized Rob.

"Mr. Walker?"

Griffin stood. "Griffin, please." He shook Rob's hand. "You must be Michelle."

"Yes." She extended her hand.

Griffin looked at Indy by his side. "Rob, Michelle, this is Indy Adams." They exchanged quick greetings and returned to their seats.

The couple was obviously uncomfortable. Griffin asked about projects Rob developed, and Indy nudged him.

"Don't interview the man over lunch." She turned to Michelle. "Have you had a chance to enjoy much of the city?"

Michelle's face relaxed, and the women talked about museums. Griffin changed the subject to sports and the various Chicago-based teams. During the main course, Griffin broached the topic that was the purpose of the lunch.

"What can I do to get you to relocate to Chicago and work for me?" He directed the question at the couple. The job itself would draw Rob, but Michelle had higher expectations.

"The job offer is fabulous," Rob began.

Michelle continued, "But we have two children. We need to make sure the move will benefit them as well."

Griffin didn't know what to say. He knew his offer would give Rob a huge pay hike. They could give their kids whatever they wanted.

Michelle looked flustered. "The money is great, but I've never been outside California. What I've experienced of Chicago over the last couple of days has been fascinating. But what about schools and neighborhoods and sports and friends for our kids?"

Indy placed a hand on Griffin's thigh under the table. The touch short-circuited his brain for a moment, and Indy jumped in. "I know what you mean, Michelle. I came to Chicago from a small town for college. It was a scary move. Now I'm a real estate agent. I know this city. Tell me about your neighborhood."

Michelle launched into great detail about the offerings of their little corner of the world. Indy listened and Griffin saw her developing a plan.

He took the time to talk about job responsibilities and the benefits package. Rob looked anxious to start something fresh.

A phone rang and Indy held hers up. "I'm sorry. I need to take this."

She stood and scooted out of sight. Moments later, Griffin's phone signaled a text. "Sorry," he said to Rob, and picked up the phone. A text from Indy? He checked the urge to look over his shoulder.

Can I take her out of here?

He responded with a quick yes. If Indy occupied Michelle, he could continue his hard sell on Rob.

Indy returned. "Sorry. What I was thinking, before we were interrupted, was that I could take you through some neighborhoods, Michelle."

Michelle's forehead furrowed, and Griffin thought they lost the moment.

"No pressure," Indy explained. "I think it will be impossible for you to make an informed decision without really looking at the city. Based on what you've told me about your neighborhood, I have some in mind that might be comparable."

Michelle looked at Rob, who shrugged.

Griffin interrupted. "Rob and I can go back to the office and have a tour."

Michelle looked at Rob and back at Indy. "You're sure you don't mind?"

"Not at all."

"I need to get my bag out of the car. I'd like to take notes." She stood. "Griffin, it was nice to meet you."

Indy said, "I'll meet you by the front door in five minutes."

Rob stood with his wife. "I'll walk you out." The couple left, murmuring to each other.

Indy stood and slung her purse over her shoulder.

Griffin slid his arm around her waist, pulled her to him, and planted a kiss. He knew heads were turning again.

She pulled away. "What was that for?"

"I would say your brilliance, but truth is, it's what you do to me every time I see you."

Her eyes widened and her mouth eased open. He hit his mark. He wanted her to know she was much more than excellent arm candy. She'd gone out of her way to help him without expecting anything in return. He'd only ever experienced that with the O'Learys.

"Thank you." The words were completely inadequate.

"No problem. My afternoon was free anyway."

He pushed her hair behind her shoulder, brushing her neck with his fingers. "I'll call you later."

INDY SPENT two hours driving through various neighborhoods with Michelle. She hoped Griffin knew how much he owed her for this. She'd figured a tour of the city would loosen Michelle up and give Griffin some time alone with Rob. The woman was extremely picky, though. Like Chicago could never compare to California. No matter what Indy showed her, she found fault.

As Indy drove back to the hotel, Michelle said, "Thanks for doing this. I really appreciate it. Mr. Walker certainly knows how to sell."

"What do you mean?" Indy stole a look at the woman beside her.

"I'm not dumb. I know he brought you to lunch to convince me to move here. He knows I'm the only thing standing between my husband and this job. I did my research. He's not the kind of man who likes to lose."

Talk about an understatement. "No, he's not, but my offer to take you around was not planned."

"It wouldn't have surprised or upset me if it had been.

Like I said, I did my research. Mr. Walker isn't a man who cares about kids. Mine are my life."

Anger tensed Indy's shoulders. What could this woman know about Griffin? She wanted to tell her all about the work he did with his kids in the foundation, but she knew Griffin didn't want it public knowledge yet. "Why would you say that?"

She felt Michelle's eyes on her, so she turned to catch a glimpse.

"Are the two of you serious?"

What a loaded question. It probably wouldn't go over well if she told Michelle Griffin was her rebound guy and she was in it only for the sex. "We haven't been together long enough to think like that."

From the corner of her eye, she saw Michelle shake her head. "I've researched both Mr. Walker and his company. The company is solid. The usual complaints about violence in video games. But personally, I don't think he's a man I would want to spend too much time with. He has a revolving door of women."

Defensiveness pricked her nerves. Griffin had never made her feel like part of the revolving door. But she supposed she was. Then she wondered what Michelle would say if she'd been able to research Indy.

"So he's not looking to settle down. It doesn't make him a bad person."

"Ten years ago, he got a woman pregnant, then denied everything. The woman was so crushed, she committed suicide. They buried the story, but I dug and found it."

Indy was grateful they'd arrived at the hotel. She stepped on the brakes and put the car in park. Turning to Michelle, she tried to figure out what to say. "You can't believe everything you read online."

Michelle shook her head again. "I don't want to ruin

whatever you have going with him, but he's not who I want to associate with. I do appreciate all of your help today. If we decide to move, I'd like to give you call. Do you have a card?"

"Sure." Indy pulled a card from her purse. "It was nice talking to you. Give me a call if you have any other questions." Indy felt very adult. She'd wanted to toss the woman from her car for being a gossip, but if Michelle wanted to become a client, Indy would take it.

Michelle slid from the car and walked into the hotel.

On the drive back home, she thought about what Michelle had said.

Did Griffin's past matter? They'd agreed to keep it casual.

Hell, anything that happened ten years ago should stay in the past. Everyone had baggage. She had skeletons of her own.

Of course, hers didn't involve anyone killing himself over her.

THE FOLLOWING MORNING, Griffin's office door swung open and the excitement of having Rob almost signed dropped. He knew Kendra was here to ream him again.

"There was nothing I could do about it," he said, preempting her yell.

As she had done for months, she slapped the newspaper on his desk. He'd already seen the online version.

Hands on her hips, Kendra started. "You were well behaved for a while there. Who is this one? She's not part of your usual crowd."

"You told me to find a regular woman. I listened."

"I also told you to stay out of the spotlight."

"I have. This was yesterday at lunch. She's my real estate agent."

"Oh, God. You couldn't have taken her to Chili's or Applebee's? It had to be RL, where someone is always snapping a picture?" Kendra began to pace.

"I brought Indy to keep lunch casual with a prospective employee and his wife. Because of Indy, he's getting ready to sign a contract with us." Griffin leaned back in his chair. He'd have to get a thank-you gift for Indy. "Chili's isn't exactly where you go to woo a hotshot programmer."

Kendra's nostrils flared. "When I said a regular woman, I meant a nobody. Dating your real estate agent is not a good idea. She can easily leak information about your plans to every newspaper and magazine. You didn't even make her sign a confidentiality agreement, did you?"

Griffin chuckled. "I don't need one. Indy's not calling anyone."

"No pillow talk?"

He stood. "Indy and I are friends. I told her about the foundation before we slept together. I'm not sure she totally gets it. I think she chalks it up to me being rich."

Kendra shook her head. "A woman scorned can do a lot of damage, Griffin. More damage than I'd be able to repair. Tread lightly."

"We're having a good time. It's casual. We enjoy each other's company."

She shook her head and walked briskly out of the office, leaving the paper behind. Two shots of him and Indy appeared in the article. One with her shaking Rob's hand, and then below the fold, Griffin kissing her good-bye. He wondered if Indy had seen it.

He dialed Indy's number while holding the paper in his hands. God, she was a beautiful woman. Natural and unassuming.

"Hi."

"Hi. Have you by chance seen today's paper?"

"No. Why?"

"Pictures were taken of us at lunch yesterday."

"Really? I'm in the paper?"

She sounded more excited than he thought she would be. Maybe Kendra was right. "Your picture is in the paper, but they didn't identify you."

"Oh. That's not really the same, but I'll take it."

"I have to ask you a question."

"Shoot."

"Have you told anyone you're my real estate agent?"

"Besides Quinn and Kate? No, I don't think so. Wait, the secretary at the office knows too, so technically my boss does. Why?"

"My PR person is worried about information being leaked to the press about where I buy a house."

She laughed lightly, and the sound tickled his ear. "Why would anyone care where you live?"

"Hell if I know."

"I have to go get ready for work. I'll talk to you later."

Griffin hung up. Kendra had been wrong. Indy had no connections to the newspaper. She enjoyed being in the spotlight because it was a novelty. She didn't seek it out like the socialites. He had nothing to worry about.

Indy walked into End Zone for her third shift that week. The bartender, Jane, greeted her and said, "There's a suit here looking for you. Must be nice to be so popular. He looks like money."

Indy smiled. "That's me—Miss Congeniality." She tied her apron on and turned to seek out the only suit who'd look for her: Griffin. She searched the crowd but couldn't find him. Her blood warmed at the prospect of seeing him tonight, but she didn't know how she'd make it all the way to closing.

She stopped at her first table and took the drink order, still scanning the area for Griffin. Customers crowded the room for some game on TV, and bodies blocked the view of all her tables. Squeezing between the sports fans, she moved to her next table to take the order. Everyone else looked settled, so she turned to head back to the bar to pick up the drinks.

Suddenly a warm hand wrapped around her wrist. Excitement welled in her chest. Griffin? She turned to the booth to see Richard, and she deflated like a forgotten birthday balloon. His fingers stroked the skin on the inside of her wrist. She yanked her arm away.

"What are you doing here?" He hated bars.

"I came to see you."

"Well, this isn't my station. I'll find your waitress for you," she lied. She'd ask Lisa to cover the table. She scooted quickly away.

She filled her tray with drinks to deliver and waited to find Lisa. Moments later, Lisa called out her drink order and Indy asked her to take Richard's table.

"Why? Are you trying to pass a perv on to me?"

"No. He's my ex. I don't want to deal with him."

"Sure. No problem. Want me to slip some Visine into his drink?"

Indy giggled at the image of Richard cramping with the runs. "No. Just take his order. He'll leave soon. This isn't his kind of place."

She turned back to her station and emptied her tray to each of her customers. A few asked her to sing, but she didn't want to compete with the game and shouts of the other patrons.

Unfortunately, Richard had chosen the one table she'd

have to pass repeatedly. She ignored his calls the first two times, but she was afraid he'd cause a scene. She couldn't afford to lose this job. On her next pass, he stood in her path.

"Give me a minute." He stroked her arm. "Please."

She sighed and inched out of his reach. "What do you want? I'm working."

"I miss you. You won't return any of my calls. My divorce is done. All the papers are signed. We're free to be together."

She took another step back. "I don't want to be together. I've moved on. You need to too."

"What do you mean, you've moved on? You're fucking someone else already?"

Her muscles tensed. "What I do with my life is none of your concern."

He grabbed her arm and squeezed. "Who? Who could you have possibly found who could give you more than I could?"

She jerked her arm free, knowing it would leave a mark. "Someone richer, sexier, and *younger*. A better man than you by a stretch. Don't call me and don't come here again. We're done."

"Don't do this, Indy. We're good together. You're mine. I changed my whole life for you."

"No, you didn't. You always live your life your way and expect the rest of the world to conform to it. I don't fit into your world. Find someone who does."

She walked away feeling unsteady on her feet. Richard wasn't a bad guy. She wanted to believe that. He didn't know what to do when he couldn't control things. Hopefully now he'd get it. She could never be what he wanted. Why couldn't he see that?

The rest of her night remained quiet. Richard had left after their conversation. When her phone bleeped, she cringed, afraid it might be him, but it was Griffin. "Hello?"

"When are you off?"

"Soon. Shouldn't you be asleep? Moguls like you get up early to stomp out the competition, right?"

"Some things are worth waiting up for. I have a surprise for you."

Her heart thumped and her nerves sang at the promise in his voice. "What is it?"

"It wouldn't be much of a surprise if I told you."

"Hmm," she purred. "How about a little hint?"

He answered in a whisper, "It's not so little."

Closing couldn't come fast enough.

HE DIDN'T NEED this crap. Griffin threw the newspaper across the room and barely suppressed a growl. Another parent group was crying foul over his video games. Parental rating existed for a reason. It wasn't his fault kids didn't follow the rules. They were well into production of *Night Beasts* and couldn't afford the bad publicity now. This kind of press wouldn't help with the foundation either. His phone rang and he hoped it was Indy. He'd gladly welcome her distraction.

Unfortunately, it wasn't his day.

"Griffin, you better come to the school right away." Mike sounded worried. He'd hired Mike for the sole purpose of working with the kids during the pilot program. Although Griffin tried to be there most days, sometimes his schedule wouldn't permit it.

Mike would offer them consistency. He didn't seem like the kind of guy to ruffle easily, so something extreme must've happened.

"What's going on?"

"I don't have the whole story. Kids are upset. Marisol is

crying. Something about Duane being suspended. I can't leave them in the lab unattended, so I can't find out."

"Damn. I'll be there in twenty." What could Duane possibly have done? They'd made progress, and Griffin had been sure Duane had accepted the rules of the program. Get in trouble in school and you get dropped from the program.

He sped to the school while making calls to cancel or postpone meetings. His day had been jammed, which was why he had Mike teaching solo today. Griffin rarely missed a session with the kids. He made them a priority. They needed to know they could count on him.

He hoped the problem could be resolved quickly. Principal Harris disliked a few of Griffin's kids, Duane in particular. Once in the school, Griffin went to the computer lab. He preferred to hear the kids' version first. Before he reached the door, Marisol accosted him in the hall. She was still crying, which made her Spanglish impossible to understand. The only two words he understood were "Duane" and "hacking."

"Marisol, you have to calm down. I can't understand what you're saying." As she took deep breaths, Griffin considered the situation. The girl's emotions ran wild for Duane being just a fellow classmate. He wouldn't have pegged Marisol as Duane's type. She tended to be shy and quiet. He imagined Duane with someone a little more brash, like him.

"Mr. Griffin, he didn't do it."

"Didn't do what, Marisol? What did Duane get into trouble for?"

"They say he hacked into the school's system."

Griffin ground his teeth until his jaw muscles ached. Principal Harris had been waiting for something like this. He could close the pilot program within the school. He didn't have to allow Griffin's foundation to use school property.

"He didn't do it."

"How do you know?"

She sniffed and lifted her chin. "Because it was me."

Damn it. "What? Why did you do that?"

"I didn't mean to, not at first. I was practicing the commands you gave us and I kind of—what's the word—tripped on it."

"You mean stumbled on it."

"Yeah. I didn't think it would work. I guessed the password. It was too easy. I didn't do anything. I just checked around."

"I need to go see Mr. Harris."

She twisted a ratty tissue. "Please, Mr. Griffin. I tried to tell him it wasn't Duane, but he wouldn't listen."

"I'll see what I can do. Go back into the lab." He peeked into the lab to see that Mike had gotten the rest of the kids to calm down and begin work. He'd love to trade places. Walking down the hall made him feel fifteen again, palms clammy, waiting to see if he'd get suspended. How he'd dreaded every visit. The phone call to his mother alone made him miserable. She couldn't afford the time off work to hear him get yelled at. He didn't envy Duane.

Griffin knocked on Harris's door. "Come in."

"Mr. Harris." Griffin nodded as he entered the office.

"Mr. Walker, I've been expecting you. I suppose you've heard about Duane Wilson hacking into the system. Have a seat." Harris gestured to a chair half the size of his own leather monstrosity. Griffin refused to fall for the intimidation.

"No, thanks. I'll stand. I have part of the story." *Like the truth.* "I'd like to hear what you know."

"Our tech supervisor found a discrenpancy when I was supposedly logged on here while I attended a conference. He traced it back to a computer in the lab during the time you work with your *group*." His distaste of the program hung in the air like the smell of greasy onions.

"How exactly did that lead you to Duane?"

Harris offered a cocky look that said an idiot could've figured it out. "He was the last one logged on."

"I can see how that would look to you, but the kids don't have assigned seats during lab work, and they often move around."

Harris pursed his lips. "Either way, someone from your group did this. I knew this would happen. It took longer than I imagined, but I knew."

Griffin moved two steps closer to the desk. He knew what to expect, and his muscles flexed.

"It's not your fault, not totally, Mr. Walker. I tried to convince you when you selected those students that they were not the right caliber."

"What more could I ask for in students? They show up for every class. They work on projects whenever they can get their hands on a computer, which for some of them is difficult. They're interested and motivated and put in more effort than you imagined." He was damn proud of what they'd learned in such a short time.

"I know you've worked hard for this, but I'm afraid I have to shut it down."

Griffin had anticipated the blow but still wasn't prepared. His heart thumped in his chest and he sucked in his anger. "You can't arbitrarily decide to shut us down. We have board approval for this program."

"But I decide what happens within the walls of this school. I'm not heartless. I understand what you're trying to accomplish, but I have to put the entire student body and this school first. Today's your last day." Harris leaned back in his chair and propped his elbows on the armrests.

Griffin crossed his arms on his chest. "There's no compromising on this?"

Harris shook his head. "I'm sorry."

"Fine. We'll find somewhere else, but you need to allow Duane back in school. He's innocent."

"How could you possibly know—"

"Because the person who actually did the supposed hacking confessed to me. Nothing was tampered with, no harm done. If you don't allow Duane back, I will personally hire a lawyer to sue you and the school."

"If he's truly innocent, tell me who the real culprit is."

"No."

"Someone needs to be held accountable."

"How about you? This student guessed your oversimplified password and got into the system. You should thank my kids for identifying the problem before someone else did this and caused real trouble." He left the room without another word. The last thing these kids needed was someone else telling them they weren't good enough. He'd break the news to them, but they'd be okay.

CHAPTER 8

Indy rushed into the boutique just in time to see Quinn turn in her wedding gown. "Oh, my God. You're glowing."

Quinn rested her fists on her hips. "You're late but forgiven because of the compliment."

"It's fact. That dress is perfection." Indy stepped up on the platform to stand next to her sister. "You're beautiful."

Quinn's eyes began to tear. "I feel beautiful." Her hand rested on her belly.

Indy stared for a moment. *Right now, all is right and perfect in the world.*

Kate came from behind a fitting room door barking orders. "Chop, chop. Get your dress on."

"Hi, Kate. Do you ever leave mom mode?"

"No. Now get your dress on." She turned to Quinn. "I spoke with Moira. She's going to get her final fitting with Maggie when she gets in. Assuming the measurements Maggie sent were on target, we shouldn't have any problems."

Indy entered the small fitting room and stripped. She

took the burgundy dress off the hanger. The dress wasn't fitted, thank God. She'd been feeling bloated for the last few days. When was her period due?

She inched the zipper up her back. Kate pounded on the door. "Out. We need to see."

Indy opened the door. She and Kate were built similarly, or at least they had been until Kate had kids. Kate's hips were wider now, her figure more shapely.

But the simple dress draped over their bodies in equal beauty. Kate definitely had an eye for such things.

Quinn bunched her dress and stepped down from the platform. "Okay, ladies. Let's see how they fit." Quinn eased into a chair and watched the seamstress check her handiwork.

"How are things going with Griffin?" Kate asked.

"They're . . . good." A smile spread slowly across her face.

"Just good?" Quinn wanted to know.

"No. Better than good." Indy talked about their lunch at RL, Griffin's expression of gratitude when Rob accepted the job offer, and their nights together.

Kate narrowed her eyes at Indy and tapped her toes.

"What? You wanted details." Indy hiked her dress and went to change. Kate followed.

"Yeah, the dirty details of great rebound sex. You know, exorcising Richard from your system."

Indy laughed and rehung the dress. "I think he's been adequately exorcised."

Quinn opened the door and pushed her back toward Indy. "Undo me."

As Indy worked at buttons, Kate responded. "This is more than sex. You're falling for him."

Indy looked up from Quinn's back. "No, I'm not. We're having a good time, enjoying each other. No expectations."

"Uh-huh," Quinn said.

"What do you know?" Indy asked Quinn. "You spend so much time in la-la land, you want to see the rest of us there." She held the dress while Quinn stepped out.

"If it was rebound sex, you'd be telling us about a couple of nights of hot, sweaty sex. Some booty calls," Kate called from her dressing room.

"I did." Indy dressed quickly, becoming uncomfortable with the direction of the conversation.

"You also talked about a business lunch and romantic dinner."

"People have to eat."

Quinn tilted her head.

"Okay. It's more than sex, but we talked. We're dating and having fun. Still no expectations."

Kate finished dressing and hugged Indy. "I'm glad you're happy."

The simple sentiment filled Indy with peace. Her relationship with Richard had caused a rift between her and Kate. She couldn't believe she let a man do that.

"I am pretty happy." She picked up her purse. "I have some house hunting to do. I'll talk to you guys later."

Thinking about her relationship with Kate had reminded Indy of an excursion they took while in college. They had both broken up with boyfriends. Instead of ripping on the imperfections of their exes, they created a list describing the perfect man. They drove around on a glorious spring day eating ice cream.

Their conversation developed into Kate describing her perfect life: successful law practice, husband, kids, house. Kate had reached her goals.

The house sparked Indy's memory. They'd driven through Oak Park, and Kate pointed out all of the fabulous old houses there.

On a whim, Indy drove to the historic suburb that clung to the edge of the city. Even if a house wasn't on the market, it wouldn't hurt to poke around.

She drove down Chicago Avenue past the cold concrete and broken buildings. In a matter of blocks she crossed into suburbia. The dilapidated neighborhood hunched behind her as she drove through a tunnel of foliage.

The aging trees were so big on each side of the wide street that their boughs arched and met in the middle of the thoroughfare. The fall colors dappled in the afternoon sun. In her rearview mirror, she was hard-pressed to find even a patch of green.

She wound through the charming neighborhood with the feel of a small town. The downtown area bustled with independent shops—a market, coffee shop, bookstore. It reflected a settled but lively community.

Then she saw it.

Tucked back on a large piece of land, a sad house stared at her. The lawn was ragged, the first indicator the house would be in disrepair. She'd forgotten that Oak Park didn't allow For Sale signs, but she had a hunch about this house.

She inched her car forward and parked at the curb. The wraparound porch sagged. The paint job on the house chipped and flaked, but the remnants showed light green and a pukey salmon color. It desperately needed a paint job. A fairy-tale tower stood tall on the corner.

A willow arched and bowed majestically in the side yard. Tall and wide with low-hanging branches. She envisioned a tire swing swaying in the vast shade.

Perfection.

This was the house for Griffin. He could renovate and restore it. He'd use it for a while until something else snagged his interest. Then he could sell it to a young family.

This house required a family.

~

GRIFFIN'S PHONE bleeped with a text message while he sat at his desk.

Call me ASAP.

He dialed Indy's number. When she answered, he said, "You know, you can actually dial my number to talk to me."

"I'm aware, but I never know where you are or who you're with. A text is less disruptive if you're in a meeting."

"Your disruption would be welcome. What's up?"

"I found your house. It's exactly what you're looking for. The renovation will be pretty extensive, but so worth it." Her excitement sang across the line.

She hadn't had a reaction like this to any other house she'd shown him.

"Slow down."

"You can't. It just went on the market and it won't last. You need to see it."

He flipped through his desk calendar. He was booked. "Can I get in tonight?"

She blew out a heavy breath. "Let me see what I can do. What time?"

"Any time after five-thirty."

"I'll get back to you in a little bit."

They disconnected. She'd told him she had to work at the bar tonight. He hadn't planned on seeing her. His afternoon took a turn for the better.

~

HOURS later he pulled up behind Indy's car. She still sat behind the wheel, so he opened the door for her.

She wore her bar uniform. She probably planned to head in after showing him the house. Indy stepped from the car and flourished her hand down the length of her body. "As promised."

"What?"

"I told you I'd wear my uniform to the next house I showed you." She smiled and closed her door. "I switched shifts and didn't have time to go home to change."

"Surprisingly, I don't mind."

He recognized the sweatshirt she pulled on. "You look good in my clothes."

"Thanks. Come on," she said, tugging his hand. "You have to see this house. It's perfect."

"Perfect, huh?" He looked up at the shadowed form looming in front of him. The color was indiscernible in the dark.

"I have the keys. The neighbor is keeping them. The old man died and the kids need to sell. They all live out of state. It'll move fast." She carried a flashlight and laid a path of light for them to follow.

The porch creaked and rotten boards squished beneath their feet. Indy swung the door open into the black. She found a switch and illuminated the front hall.

"They've left the utilities on, so you can check everything. By my estimation, you'll want to redo the electric and plumbing to bring it up to code. Which means you'll have to knock out the old plaster walls." She moved from room to room flicking on lights. "But the woodwork is phenomenal and probably salvageable."

"You've already gone through?"

"I had to make sure. I had a gut feeling when I pulled up and saw it yesterday. A walk-through sold me. I also did some checking. The house isn't historical, so you're bound only by regular building codes."

Her cheeks were pink from the cold, but her excitement swirled through the air. He began his tour alone. He needed to look beyond her excitement.

He needed to feel it.

By the time he reached the den after looking at the formal living and dining rooms, he knew. He saw past the peeling paper and chipped plaster. He saw the inherent potential. In the back beyond the kitchen was a separate hallway that led to what was probably once servants' quarters. The space would work perfectly for the kids.

He went upstairs. The master bedroom sat above the den. It had its own fireplace. The bathroom had a claw-foot tub he hoped could be restored.

Indy knew what she was talking about. After demo, electric and plumbing would be the next order of business. It would be a shitload of work.

And it was perfect.

He descended the stairs and found Indy leaning against the newel post. She straightened at the sound of his footsteps.

A knowing smile crossed her face. "Want to check around outside?"

"No. Land is land."

"So, what do you think?"

"You're right. It's perfect. I want it."

She jumped and danced in the middle of the front hall. "I knew it. It's the best feeling in the world to match someone with the right house."

He grabbed her and kissed her. Her eyes darkened with passion. "I hope you don't dance for all your clients."

She shook her head. "No. That would be unprofessional."

"Good." He lowered his head again to taste her incredible lips. Would he ever get enough of this woman?

She pushed away, breathless. "We can't stay here. I have to make sure the lights are off."

They broke apart and turned off lights, plunging the house into darkness. Indy turned her flashlight on.

The absurdity of her carrying a flashlight struck him. He'd never pegged her to be so prepared.

She locked up, and they eased down the rickety steps.

"What now?"

"You call and make an offer."

He held her hand as they walked. "Isn't that your job?"

"That's the catch." She stopped. "It's For Sale by Owner. They won't work with an agent. I had my office call and check. I have to bow out. I'll gather information on the area for a market analysis so you have an idea of what you can offer, but you have to do your own negotiations."

He stared at her in the shadows. "Why would you show me a house you're not making commission on?"

"I stumbled onto it, and it was right."

"Then I guess I at least owe you dinner."

"At least." She jogged across the lawn to the neighbor's house to return the key.

He remembered the elegant mansion she'd shown him a week ago. She'd looked like she belonged there. Or so he'd thought. Now, seeing her in the ruins of this Queen Anne house, he knew his image of her was mistaken.

His chest swelled at the sight of her running back to him. He shook his head. He needed to stop imagining Indy in his house.

"If you want, we can pick up pizza and go to my place. I can gather the information you need."

"Not much of a celebratory dinner."

She pointed to her clothes again. "I'm not dressed for dinner."

"Pizza it is, I guess." He wasn't in the mood to have other men ogling her anyway.

~

OVER DINNER, Indy combed through listings for a market analysis. The prospect of Griffin getting this house excited her. Not getting the commission she'd been counting on sucked, but this house was right.

She ran the numbers with him and they discussed ballpark figures for repair. Although the house was being sold "as is," the renovation costs had to be considered.

She watched him in his sleek suit, jacket off, sleeves rolled, eating pizza. Kate had accused her of falling for him. How could she not? He was smart, employed, and sexy as all get-out. Her blood raced every time she thought about him.

But he's my rebound guy. I can't get in too deep. It defeats the purpose of rebound.

"What does the rest of your week look like?" he asked.

"More of the same. Why?"

"I have to go out of town next week."

She plopped her pizza back on her plate. "The wedding's next week."

"I'll be back in time for the wedding. I want to see you before I leave." He wiped his hands on a paper napkin.

"Saturday?"

"Bachelor party," he answered. "Friday?"

"Bachelorette party."

"Shouldn't they be scheduled on the same night?"

Indy shrugged. "We had to plan around work schedules. Speaking of which, before you ask, I'm working Sunday."

He slid closer to her on the couch. "You could call in sick."

His hand slid up her thigh and he kissed her neck. Her brain went fuzzy. "No, I can't. I still need this job."

She moved away from him and picked up the pizza. He followed her with the dishes. Maybe it was good their schedules didn't match. They would get a little distance and cool off.

After she put the pizza away, Griffin grabbed her and spun her around. He pressed her back against the fridge and kissed her. "You expect me to go a week without this?"

"There's always phone sex."

As he nipped at her ear, she questioned why she wanted to cool off. She always felt so good with him.

"Tonight's all I get?" he whispered against her collarbone.

"It'll have to do." Her fingers quickly worked the buttons of his shirt. She needed to feel his flesh.

With his shirt off, he grabbed her wrists and held them. His eyes burned into hers with desire. She tugged her arms, but he held fast.

"If I only have tonight, I'm going to make it last. The kitchen table won't do." He released her arms. Before she could make a move, he hoisted her to wrap her legs around him and he carried her to the bedroom.

"I'd have come willingly," she said, wiggling herself against his erection.

"I know, but I like the feel of you wrapped around me. I love the way you smell when I bury my nose in your neck."

She stopped kissing his shoulder, and he tossed her unceremoniously on the bed. A small laugh escaped her lips as she bounced. She reached for the hem of her shirt to pull it over her head, but he stopped her hands.

He stretched her arms over her head and held them with one hand while his other hand roamed her body. The heat of his hand seared her through the thin cotton she wore. Her breasts filled with want. She needed him to touch her, skin on skin. He tugged her shirt up with his teeth, his hot breath grazing her skin.

Her legs wrapped around him, pulling him in. He pushed away from her, finally releasing her wrists. Before he could reclaim anything, she whipped off her shirt and bra. When she lay back down, he smiled wickedly before bringing his mouth to her breast. His beard stubble rasped against sensitive skin. She ran her fingers across his shoulders as he feasted.

Never had her breasts been so sensitive. He sucked and nibbled and had her writhing in minutes. His belt buckle dug into her thigh, reminding her that they still had way too many clothes on. She shifted her weight, afraid to have him stop but needing to wiggle out of her shorts. She tugged the shorts and raised her hips a little to shove them down.

The skin of his torso was cool against the heat of her thighs. As much as she didn't want him to stop sucking her nipples, she wanted, no *needed*, more. He trailed kisses down her ribs to her hip. So close.

She shifted again, inching herself nearer. His breath puffed out and fanned over her heat, and she felt like she would explode.

Her hips bucked and she pushed his head. "Please, Griffin, I need this."

His laugh was a quiet whisper, adding more heat to her already-explosive body. He swiped his tongue over her mound. "This?"

"God, yes." She threw her leg over his shoulder to give him better access.

But then he left her wanting. He pushed her thigh back and grabbed her wrists again. "What's your hurry? We have all night."

They were nose to nose, and his dick throbbed against her. She knew he wanted this as much as she did. "I'm ready now."

"All I get is tonight, so it's going to be slow, Indy. When I'm done, you won't have the energy to think about anything else until I get back."

She bit back a moan when Griffin's mouth covered hers. Didn't he know? He'd already accomplished that.

CHAPTER 9

The week swept by with Indy's thoughts consumed by the calendar. It didn't matter how many times she flipped the pages or did the math. She hadn't gotten her period. She couldn't even clearly remember the last one. The stress from breaking up with Richard and all the extra hours spent working could easily have caused a missed period.

All the excuses in the world didn't change the fact that it hadn't come.

She stood in the back of the church for the rehearsal and watched Kate's kids chase each other up and down the hall. Moira and Maggie were already at the front with their brothers. Griffin was nowhere in sight.

Quinn tapped her shoulder. "Griffin called. His flight was delayed, but he'll be in late tonight. He said he hadn't been able to reach you all week."

Kate began her walk down the aisle.

"I've been busy. My little sister's wedding didn't just happen on its own."

"Is everything okay?"

"Yeah. It's my turn to walk." How could she tell Quinn?

She walked down the aisle thinking about Griffin. Surely by now he'd be pissed. He'd called a bunch of times while he was gone. She couldn't talk to him. Her missing period occupied her every thought. She finally texted him saying wedding stuff kept her busy and she'd see him when he returned. Luckily, he was late. Now she only had to make it through the wedding before breaking up with him. She didn't want to string him along knowing Richard's baby could be growing in her.

Quinn's day wouldn't be ruined because of her stupidity.

Anticipating Griffin's anger, Indy had already arranged to spend the night at Quinn's under the pretext of helping her get ready. Griffin would arrive tonight and he wouldn't know where to find her. She couldn't face him yet. Twenty-four hours. Then she would end it with him and he could hate her.

But Quinn's wedding will be perfect.

Later that night, Indy turned her phone off and then she crawled into Quinn's bed. They pretended to be twelve having a sleepover. Head sunk into squishy pillows, Indy faced her sister and they talked about boys.

"Tell me what's going on with you and Griffin."

Indy's heart sank. She'd been able to put it all aside for the evening. She'd hoped to continue through the next day. "Nothing. He's my rebound guy. I think I'm done rebounding."

Quinn sat suddenly. "What do you mean, you're done?"

"How long did you think it would take for me to rebound?" Indy tried to keep her voice light. "You know I like to keep moving."

Quinn returned to her pillow. "You've been so happy. What did he say?"

"He doesn't know yet. I'm going to talk to him after the

wedding. After you leave for your honeymoon. I promised not to do anything to ruin your wedding, and I won't."

"You sure about this?"

Indy sighed. Lying to Quinn never came easy. Her chest tightened every time she thought about telling Griffin. He always saw right through her. He didn't need this kind of drama.

Quinn dropped it. "You were nice to Dad tonight. I appreciate it."

"Even I can put on a good act. Tomorrow will be perfect."

WEDDING DAY WAS HECTIC. Kate spent the time finalizing details and bossing people around. Indy focused on keeping Quinn calm.

The limo arrived to take them to the church. Maggie, Ryan's youngest sister, was giddy with excitement.

"I've never been in a limo before. Do we have time for a ride before we go to the church?"

Kate looked at her watch. "Let's get Quinn to the church and then you can take a ride if you want."

Moira interjected, "I'll go with you to make sure you get back on time. How about you, Indy? Care for a ride?"

Indy shook her head. "No, I'll stay with Quinn."

They piled into the limo, carrying bright bouquets. The chatter of excitement continued as they pulled up in front of the church. St. Matthews was an old church with huge stained-glass windows high above the ground. Indy never went to church anymore. She'd given it up mostly when she left for college. She stopped going even on holidays after her mom died.

Kate stepped out of the car first. "Wait here. I'll make sure the guys are out of sight. They should be with the photographer."

She scurried in her heels across the concrete to the open church doors. Moments later she emerged and waved them in. Indy slid out of the car and held Quinn's hand to help her. The beautiful autumn weather signaled a perfect day to get married. The sun was warm and the breeze cool.

Kate ushered them into a small room in the back of the church.

Moira gave Quinn a quick squeeze and said, "We'll be back in a little bit. We have plenty of time before we start."

"Have fun."

As soon as Maggie and Moira left, Quinn began to pace. "What am I doing?"

"You're getting married." Since when had it become Indy's job to be the voice of reason? That was Quinn's role.

Quinn's hands settled on her stomach. "I think I'm going to be sick. I told you I didn't want to eat."

Indy walked to Quinn's side. With her arm around Quinn's shoulder, she guided her to the padded seat and ottoman. "If you didn't eat, you'd pass out before you got down the aisle."

"I feel queasy."

Kate stood next to her. "Have you had any morning sickness?

"No." Quinn leaned forward, holding her stomach and taking deep breaths.

"Hold on. We'll get you something." Kate went to the door and looked out. "Hey, Griffin."

Shit. Don't let him in here. I can't do this now.

His voice boomed in the hall. "Yes, Kate. I told you the groom is pacing at the other end of the church, and I have the rings."

"I know. Come here." Kate held the door open only wide

enough to wedge her body in the opening. "Go down the street and get a Diet Coke."

"Now?"

"I have a queasy bride in here. Go."

Indy couldn't hear his response, but Kate moved away from the door, leaving it open a crack. "Pop will settle your stomach. It's nerves."

Quinn stood and paced. After fifteen minutes of silence, Indy had had enough. She took Quinn's hands and led her back to the chair.

Indy squatted in front of her, still holding her hands. "What's wrong?"

Quinn looked over her shoulder. Kate guarded the door. She turned back to Indy. "What if this is a mistake?"

"It's not."

Quinn stared at their joined hands. "How do you know? Look at what happened last time I rushed into a marriage."

"This isn't the same."

"How am I supposed to be sure?"

"Because you're different with Ryan. We all see it." She squeezed Quinn's hands to get her to look up. When Quinn's eyes met hers, she continued, "Do you love him?"

"More than anything."

"Then that's all that matters. You'll fight and make up and drive each other crazy, then unite to torment your kids. You'll get through it because you love each other."

Quinn's gaze steadied and she grabbed Indy in a hug. A voice cleared behind Kate.

Kate mumbled a few words and shut the door. She held a cup of Diet Coke in one hand and a stack of saltines in the other. "Stand up to drink so we don't drip on your dress."

Quinn followed directions. Bending at the waist, she leaned over to sip through the straw.

"Griffin sweet-talked the girl at the drive-thru to get

some crackers. He thought they might help." Kate handed Indy the crackers and looked at her watch. "I'm going to make sure Moira and Maggie are back. We start in five."

Indy waited until Kate left. "I know you're nervous. But this is good. When you get out there, don't look at anything but Ryan. He'll be the one at the front with the goofy grin."

Quinn laughed, and Indy gave her one more quick hug. She eased out the door. Their father headed toward her.

"She ready?" Walt asked.

Indy nodded and went to take her place in line. She couldn't stop the smile when she saw Griffin. The sight of him in the tux with his hair slicked back made her mouth water. "All I need to hear is a fake British accent and I'll have my very own James Bond."

He grabbed her arm and pulled her to the side. His eyes smoldered as he cornered her. "I don't fake anything."

They stared at each other. He broke the silence with, "We need to talk."

This time, the sentence didn't make her cringe because it was true. She kept her voice cool and remote. "After the reception."

Kate's voice sounded behind them. "What are you doing back here? You belong with Ryan. Hurry up. Go."

Griffin backed away and walked down the side aisle of the church.

Indy inhaled a steadying breath and went to wrangle Kate's kids to stand quietly behind her.

As the members of the bridal party began their march down the aisle, Indy caught a glimpse of Quinn entering the hall.

She was steady and smiling.

Indy straightened for her own march. With her eyes locked on Griffin, she thought *Quinn's day will be perfect.*

~

GRIFFIN COULDN'T WAIT to get to the reception. After posing for a hundred photos, he needed a beer. After holding Indy in his arms for a picture, he needed a shot of whiskey.

Indy had smiled and joked, keeping everyone at ease while Kate barked orders. But it was all superficial.

He didn't know what had happened over the last week, but she'd pulled back. Luckily, he sat next to Ryan at the head table. If he'd been seated next to Indy, he wouldn't have been able to hold his tongue.

After the meal, he stood to toast the happy couple. With his glass in hand, he waited for the attention of the crowd. "As best man, I prepared the typical speech. I planned to embarrass Ryan with tales of our youth and exploits with women, many of whom tried to get him to this point."

The O'Leary brothers all laughed.

"But I overheard something at the church that I think sums up everything."

Indy looked up and their eyes met.

"The maid of honor asked Quinn if she loved Ryan. Simple question. Quinn answered without hesitation, 'More than anything.'"

Indy's mouth opened. He winked at her and turned his attention to Ryan and Quinn. He lifted his glass. "I couldn't ask for a better response, because really, that's all that matters. If he doesn't treat you right, I'll have to kick his ass."

More laughter ensued, and some jostling from the brothers.

"Congratulations." He drank from his champagne, gave Ryan a hug, and kissed Quinn's teary-eyed face.

The dancing began, and every time he thought he'd catch Indy, she slipped through his fingers. Her avoidance pissed him off.

She had excellent evasion tactics. On the occasions he found her, they were never alone. She refused to take a walk. She wouldn't dance with him.

He hadn't seen her in a week, and watching her mingle and socialize while ignoring him was like being in a desert and seeing a mirage. He'd missed her so much, he had a hard time focusing. His need to touch her clouded his thoughts.

Now her avoidance gave him something to focus on. He found Quinn and pulled her to the dance floor.

"You look beautiful," he said once he had Quinn in his arms.

"Thank you."

"What's going on with Indy?"

Quinn stiffened. She wasn't much of a poker player. "What do you mean?"

"I left a week ago and things were hot and heavy. Now she's a freezer. She won't be alone with me."

"I don't know." Her gaze focused on his shoulder since she couldn't see past him.

"You're lying."

"I don't know the whole story. She hasn't told me." Quinn turned to look up at him. "I do know she's falling for you and she didn't plan to."

"Neither did I."

His words sank in, and a slow grin spread across her face. When the song ended, his gaze sought Indy. When he found her, he turned and caught Maggie's attention.

"Wanna dance, studly?"

"I need a favor. Give this to the deejay and tell him the next song has to be a slow country one." He pushed a fifty into her palm.

Her eyes crinkled. "The guy is paid to be here. You know this, right?"

"Yeah, but I need him to play the song now." He shot a look over his shoulder to make sure Indy hadn't moved.

"Ah, so if I get him to do it for less, I get to keep the change?"

"Whatever you want, sweetheart." He winked at her and knew she'd smile at the deejay and he'd melt. Griffin didn't know why he hadn't thought of this earlier.

He edged around the tables, taking a slow perimeter to Indy's position, stalking her. She swayed to the beat of music, and her burgundy dress swished around her like wine in a glass. This time she wouldn't get away. The first few notes of the song played and he reached for her elbow. "Excuse me, you owe me a dance."

"I'm in the middle of a conversation." She tilted her head toward one of Ryan's uncles.

"Oh, no. Go right ahead," the man said, almost shooing her away. "Young people should dance."

Griffin nodded and propelled her toward the dance floor.

"It's not nice to sneak up on people."

"I wouldn't have had to if you weren't avoiding me."

"I'm not—"

"Don't." The single word silenced her. The vocals started and he pulled her close. Her scent tickled his senses. "What is it with you girls and the country music?"

"We grew up listening to country."

"Who is this?"

She laid her head on his shoulder. "Toby Keith. 'You Shouldn't Kiss Me Like This.'"

He held her to his body and listened to the words. Having her in his arms satisfied a need he didn't recognize. As the last notes sang, he released her. His hands cupped her face and he kissed her, pouring every need and emotion into it. He released everything he'd held in all night. All week.

When they separated, he realized there was commotion

all around them. Quinn stood by the deejay, ready to throw the bouquet.

Indy turned and ran. The mob of single women rushed forward, scrambling to catch the bouquet. He fought against the crowd of onlookers to find Indy.

Near the hall he found Kate. She said nothing, but pointed to the washroom. He pushed the door open.

"Indy, come out."

"No."

"Then I'm coming in." He heard no response or squeals from other women, so he entered. She'd locked herself in a stall. He'd never been in the women's bathroom of O'Leary's. He took in the green paint and signs offering help to women who had too much to drink.

"Go away, Griffin."

"No." He leaned against the door where he saw her shoes peeking out. "What the hell was that?"

"Why don't you tell me? It was no 'I want to fuck you' kiss. It wasn't casual."

"No, I guess not."

"I can't do this. Not now."

"You don't have a choice. I'm not leaving." The lock turned and he straightened.

"Not here. Take me home."

Her skin looked pale and tight under the harsh fluorescent lights. She'd curled her long hair in a halo around her face, giving her a look of innocence. He fought the urge to hold her and solve whatever problems lie between them.

Instead, they left the bathroom and told Kate they were leaving. They'd already missed Quinn and Ryan's departure. Chances were good no one would notice they left.

He led Indy outside and she shivered in the cold evening air. Her crossed arms would do little to warm her exposed skin. He removed his tux jacket and draped it over her shoulders.

～

INDY SAT in the car and absorbed every ounce of warmth she could from Griffin's jacket. When she broke up with him, she wouldn't get any more of his warmth. Her chest tightened and she forced air into her lungs.

He drove in silence, and she was grateful. She hadn't thought about how to do this or what to say.

"Are you going to tell me what's going on?"

"I think I might be pregnant." The truth slipped out before she could formulate an adequate lie. She preferred the silence.

He whipped a corner with squealing tires. "What?"

The anger in his voice bounced off the closed windows. She looked up from her clasped hands.

His face filled with rage, and it dawned on her what her words sounded like. A chill crept down her back. "Oh, God. Not you. It's not yours."

She closed her eyes and leaned her head back on the headrest.

"How do you know?"

"You were Mr. Condom-at-the-Ready. *Every time.* I said it's not your problem. Please take me home." Weariness pulled her down. The effort of holding it together for Quinn's wedding had taken its toll. She kept her eyes closed, and Griffin began driving.

She hadn't planned to dump this on him. She didn't know why she did. All she had to do was break up with him. The car lurched to a stop, and she opened her eyes.

Griffin climbed out before she could ask why they

stopped. She looked up at the glowing 7-Eleven sign. Now was not the time for a Slurpee.

Moments later he returned and tossed a plastic bag in her lap. She opened it as he pulled out of the lot. Two pregnancy tests, different brands.

He shot her a look from the corners of his eyes. "I think we both have a right to know for sure. No mights or maybes."

What the hell was she supposed to do with this guy? Why couldn't he be normal? She'd expected him to dump her and run off.

They drove down her block and saw no parking. "You can pull over and let me out."

He glared at her and turned the corner. He found a spot near the alley.

"Thanks for the ride." Not bad for a brush-off of a breakup. "And the tests."

"You weren't going to tell me, were you?" His voice held an unusual tone. Like maybe he was hurt that she hadn't plan to share her problems.

With her hand on the door, she answered, "No. What's the point?"

She pushed out of his car, clutching her purse in one hand and the plastic bag in the other. She almost reached the corner before she realized she still wore his jacket.

The jacket slid from her shoulders, and she turned around. Griffin stood at the car, watching her. She folded the jacket over her arm and headed back.

His gaze softened, and he met her halfway. He replaced the jacket on her shoulders, keeping it in place with his arm. They walked together to her apartment.

In the living room she stepped out of her heels and sat on the couch. She pulled both boxes from the bag and examined them.

"I didn't know if one was better." His tie was long gone, but now he rolled his sleeves while he paced.

Indy read both boxes. Pee on the stick, cover, and wait. Seemed simple enough.

She took both boxes with her. Stopping in front of Griffin, she turned and said, "Will you unzip me, please?"

She could've pulled the zipper herself. She'd gotten it up. But she had the urge to feel his touch. His fingers brushed her neck as he moved her hair aside. The zipper hissed open.

The energy between them crackled. His breath seared her skin. She took an abrupt step forward and mumbled a thank-you.

Instead of Griffin's lips, cool air kissed her bare back. She slipped into the bathroom and out of the dress.

She stared at her reflection in the mirror. Other than the stress lines around her eyes, she looked the same. That was a good sign, right? Pregnant women looked different. They glowed.

Enough procrastinating. She opened the directions and read through the steps. The tests looked identical, so she peed on both. She set the tests on the edge of the sink and washed her hands.

Almost immediately a pink line appeared, and her legs weakened. She couldn't catch her breath. Her vision blurred. She blinked rapidly to clear it.

She grabbed the directions and saw the picture. Her heartbeat slowed. One pink line showed that the test worked. She had to wait three minutes. A second line meant pregnancy.

She inhaled deeply and tried to calm her nerves. The paper shook in her hand. She didn't wear a watch so she began counting. One Mississippi, two Mississippi . . .

She closed her eyes and heard the sheet of directions flutter to the floor.

Five Mississippi, six Mississippi . . .

She opened her eyes and stared at the sticks on the sink. Eight Mississippi, nine—

Four clear pink lines.

Two on each stick.

It couldn't be. Three minutes hadn't passed.

She couldn't be pregnant.

Her heart didn't pound. Her knees didn't buckle. Her stomach didn't roil.

Her body went numb.

She picked up the tests and tilted them in the light. No change. Still two lines.

She sank to the floor and leaned against the tub. The tub was cold, the tile floor colder. Some feeling remained if she could detect cold.

She preferred numb.

WHAT WAS WRONG WITH HIM? Even now Griffin still wanted her. Knowing she might be pregnant, he wanted to grab her and have her right now. He wanted to offer the only comfort he knew he could give.

He paced some more. He should've dropped her off and left. It was what she'd expected. But he had to know.

It's not mine. She said so herself. We used a condom every time.

Minutes ticked by. He grabbed a beer from the fridge and gulped it quickly. The alcohol wasn't strong enough to dull the pain.

He paced the hall again, pausing at the bathroom door. He raised his hand to knock and stopped. He walked back to the living room, looked at the ugly impersonal setting and returned to the kitchen.

The test shouldn't take so long. She should've been out to

tell him the results. Back at the bathroom door, he knocked softly. No response. "Indy."

Nothing.

He tried the handle—locked.

His fingers curled into a fist and he pounded. "Indy, let me in."

She answered faintly, "Go away."

He pounded again. "Let me in, or I'll break the damn door."

She didn't answer.

He tested the knob again, but the old push button lock held. He wanted to knock the door off its hinges, but he grabbed a paper clip from her office instead.

With the clip straightened, he popped the lock and swung the door open. Boxes and directions lay haphazardly on the floor.

Indy sat with her legs pulled to her chest, her head on her knees. She wore only her bra and panties and clutched both pregnancy tests in her hand.

He squatted beside her and touched her hair.

"I told you to leave."

"I'm not good at following orders." He took the tests from her hand. Both had two clear lines staring out.

Indy was pregnant.

He tossed them in the trash and fought the urge to run. Staying would be complicated. He didn't like complications.

Was that how his own father had felt?

"Indy."

She pulled farther into herself. Quinn had already left for her honeymoon. He could call Kate. Kate would take over.

Kate would tell Indy exactly what to do.

He sighed and slid his arm under her knees and the other behind her back. Lifting her from the floor, he rapped his elbow on the small pedestal sink. He bit back the curse that rose to his lips and carried her out.

She snuggled into his neck and whispered, "I don't know how I fucked up again. I promised myself this would never happen."

He paused in his journey. Her words stumbled across his brain. *Again?*

Rather than laying her on the bed, he sat and held her on his lap. She tucked her head under his chin and inhaled deeply. Likewise, he smelled her hair.

When had scent become a comfort?

"I'm sorry I snapped at you in the car. Years ago a woman said she was pregnant with my baby."

Indy pulled away quickly, knocking her head into his chin.

"She lied," he added.

Tears swam in her eyes. "You thought I'd get myself pregnant so I could trap you and steal your money."

The hurt rang deep in her voice. He'd effectively backed himself into a corner. How could he convince her that he hadn't meant to accuse her without dredging up the past? He wasn't even sure he could talk about it. The mess with Selena and his father still hurt. "There are a lot of gold diggers out there."

She slid her body from his lap. "I'm not one."

She pulled a T-shirt from the chair in the corner and put it on. The hot-pink shirt had a Care Bear on the front. One with a rainbow in its stomach.

"I didn't say you were." He stood in front of her.

"But you thought it. Thanks for making things clear." She pushed past him and went into the kitchen.

How much fucking up could he do in one night? He knew none of it applied to her, but it came out anyway. He followed her and watched as she set a kettle of water on a burner.

"You can go. You wanted to know, and now you do. I'm pregnant with Richard's baby." She busied herself with getting a mug and tea bag.

"Are you sure?"

She snorted. "I think I managed to pee on the stick correctly. Two solid lines. Yeah, I'm sure."

"No. Are you sure it's his?"

She wheeled around and ran into him with her arms extended. The shove caught him off guard, and he stumbled. "Get the fuck out of my house."

"What?"

She came at him again, but he braced for the blow. "I'm sick of your stupid accusations. I don't care what you think of me. But know this. You're the only man I've slept with in the last year besides Richard."

What the hell was she talking about? She'd gone completely crazy and he couldn't follow. He replayed the conversation in his head. What did he say wrong?

"Get. Out," she snapped.

"Wait." Every thought he had came out of his mouth jumbled, the meaning unclear. He took a deep breath and tried again. "Let me rephrase: Could it be mine?"

Indy's face had gone red with rage. Her muscles trembled with anger. "We've already established that. You wore condoms."

"You have your own stash of condoms, so I'm guessing you used them with Richard too."

She froze. The kettle whistled, and she turned away from him. "I already missed a period by the time we slept together, so I'm sure I was already pregnant."

He leaned against the doorway. "What are you going to do?"

She bobbled the kettle as she poured. "I don't know. Go to the doctor, see how far along I am, and then make a decision."

With her mug in hand, she turned to him, face and voice calm. "You're off the hook. You should go."

"I want to stay." He didn't even know why, but every cell in his body urged him to hold her.

"I don't want you here. It's over."

Her words slapped him hard. The ice in her eyes sliced through him. He turned and walked through the living room to get his jacket. If she was done with him, he sure as hell was done with her.

CHAPTER 10

*I*ndy's hands shook so badly, she had to put her cup back on the counter. The pain in her chest gripped so tight she couldn't cry. The weight pressed down on her, and she thought she'd suffocate. She had wanted Griffin to hold her more than anything, but she couldn't lean on him. Not now. Even she couldn't take advantage of him like that. He didn't know what he was offering. She needed to figure out what she was going to do.

She eased her way to the table and sat on a chair. What would Quinn do? Indy rolled her eyes. Quinn would be skipping and yelping in happiness. This was Quinn's dream. Indy dropped that dream at seventeen. She wasn't motherhood material.

The swarm of thoughts and emotions became too much. Nothing could be done at midnight on a Saturday. She should call Richard. He had a right to know. On Monday, she'd call the doctor.

She could handle this logically. In the meantime, she'd focus on other things. After a good night's sleep she'd make a plan. She had work at the bar. She'd keep busy.

God, I wish I could talk to Quinn. She'd make me cookies and a list of pros and cons. She's the queen of practicality.

Quinn would be back in a week. Seven days wasn't too long.

THE NEXT MORNING, Indy woke feeling better. Or so she told herself. She tried to believe in the power of positive thinking.

She needed a distraction and time to think. Quinn's house would give her both. She planned to paint the nursery as a surprise for Quinn and Ryan. She showered and dressed quickly. She packed some fruit and bottled water and headed out. The excitement of her newly formed plan consumed her.

At the home improvement store, she chose the perfect shade of bright yellow. Not too sunny, not too pastel. She dumped rollers, brushes, tape, and pans into her cart. With her back seat loaded with her purchases, she drove to Quinn's house.

She'd already walked through with Quinn. The split level was empty and fairly clean. Indy carried her supplies up to the room Quinn had picked for the nursery and plugged in the radio she brought from home.

With the windows open and a mask on, she got to work. Within two hours she had the room primed and ready for paint. While the primer dried, she walked through the other rooms. They were all a clean off-white, devoid of personality.

Indy decided if the nursery went well, she'd tackle some of the other rooms too. She knew that Quinn had chosen yellow for the nursery. It was the one color from their childhood home that Quinn loved. She also knew Quinn would want cool, subtle colors for the rest of the house. She'd live with the white, but she'd prefer something more inviting. Nothing too splashy or overwhelming. Something that said *family.*

Indy had all day to spend alone thinking, and Quinn would be gone the week. She could paint. Productivity might help her thought process. It couldn't hurt.

～

GRIFFIN HAD CALLED Indy three times. He'd never wasted this much time on a woman, but he wasn't ready to let go. Not yet anyway. He didn't even know what she planned. If she decided not to have the baby, they could continue on as they were. Nothing had to change.

What if she did plan to have the baby?

He shook his head. He had no control over that. Did it matter to him? The baby wasn't his. Maybe she'd go back to her ex. The thought burned in his gut. The relationship wasn't serious. Not with the ex, not with him. A baby made it serious.

How had his life gotten so complicated?

Strangely, the only thing lacking complications was buying a house. Using the research Indy had provided, he'd made an offer on the house she'd shown him. The house was perfect: near enough to the city for the kids and spacious enough for him to have privacy. He couldn't wait to get his hands on remodeling it. He'd already interviewed general contractors and planned for permits.

Not only did he want to get the program back on track, but he also worried about losing kids. If he didn't get them back together soon, they would drop out of sight. Maybe he could put Kendra on building some quality field trips for them. She had to know of some businesses that would allow them access. He made notes to talk to Kendra.

His phone rang, and he futilely hoped Indy wanted to distract him. A number he didn't recognize flashed, and he debated answering it. "Hello?"

"Griffin, it's Duane. I need your help."

"What is it?" He straightened in his chair. Of all the kids, he worried about Duane the most.

"I got arrested."

Griffin bolted from his chair. "What?"

"I didn't do it, but no one will believe me. You're my phone call. I know we had a deal, and if you don't want to help me, I get it, but could you please call my grandma for me?"

He grabbed his keys. "Where are you?"

"Seventeenth precinct." There was some shuffling and a very quiet, "Thank you."

In his car, Griffin raced to the police station while talking to his lawyer. The man didn't handle criminal cases, but he could offer advice and give him the name of a lawyer who could help.

Two hours later, Duane was free. The official charge ended up being criminal damage to property, basic vandalism. Griffin hoped they could beat it in court since there was no real proof Duane had painted the graffiti. His friends, however, had been charged with drug possession. Griffin was worried.

The boy sat silently on the drive until they pulled up on his house. "Are you gonna tell my grandma?"

"Do I need to?"

He shook his head.

"This goes beyond our deal to be in the program, Duane. This is about what you want out of life. You won't get anywhere running with that crowd."

"I know. But I had nothing else going on." He shot Griffin a look full of blame.

Griffin ached for the boy. He was failing him. The entire group. "I'm working on it. I know I need to hold up my end of the deal. Stay out of trouble and we'll get something going soon. I promise."

Duane opened the door and stepped out. Before closing it, he said, "I know you try, but promises from some rich white guy don't mean much around here."

Griffin watched him run up the front steps and go through the door. He would make sure his promises held up. Losing these kids wasn't an option.

He needed a stiff drink and a good time. He drove out of the depressed neighborhood and to the one place he figured he could get both: End Zone to find Indy.

THREE NIGHTS back to back at the bar proved to be too much for Indy. Spending her days painting Quinn's house added to the exhaustion. She enjoyed the mindless work of painting. No one needed her attention and she didn't have to remember anything. She could think.

The bar gave her time so she didn't have to think. She couldn't recall a time she'd ever felt so overwhelmed by life. Griffin had called and left brief messages. She couldn't deal with him right now.

She grabbed her keys and headed for the door to work her last shift for the next two days when the bell rang. She swung the door open and saw Richard.

"Hi. I got your message. Can I come in?"

She wanted to slam the door on his impossibly huge grin, but she widened the opening. "You can't stay long; I'm on my way to work."

"You're pregnant. For sure?"

She nodded. Why the hell was he so happy?

"I knew it. I knew it would work. This is good. Perfect." He wrapped his arms around her and squeezed.

Indy froze. "What would work?"

"I knew the thought of getting married and having a baby would freak you out some, but I knew, just knew, that if you were pregnant, you'd be happy." He rocked a little, side to side.

She shoved him away. "What are you talking about? What did you do?"

"Come on now, Indy. Don't get like this. I did it for us. We belong together." He reached for her hand.

Fury bubbled in her chest. "What. Did. You. Do?"

He sighed and shook his head slightly. "I poked holes in the condoms. It wasn't surefire, but this proves it was meant to be."

"You intentionally got me pregnant. Without my permission or knowledge." Her breaths came hard and fast. How could he do this? Why? She bent over and put her hands on her thighs.

He began to rub her back. "Are you okay?"

She stood abruptly, feeling slightly dizzy. "Okay? Okay? No, I'm not okay. How stupid can you be? What did I ever do to make you think I wanted a baby?"

"It's nature. Every woman wants to be a mother. You're genetically predisposed to want it. Even the women who claim not to are lying to themselves."

"No. You're wrong. I don't want a baby. I want my life. I can leave when I want. I can go to Acapulco at Christmas because no one needs me. If I get bored with my job, I can quit because no one is depending on me. When I get bored with a man, I can find someone else to fuck. I don't want to be tied to anyone forever." Her chest tightened and breathing became difficult.

"Indy, that's your hormones talking. Relax and think about this. We belong together. We can be a great couple."

"We're not a couple. We won't be a couple again. Get the

fuck out of my house and don't come back." Her brain clouded with anger. She couldn't think of anything except for how he had tricked her. How he knew so little about her that only what he wanted mattered.

"Indy."

"No. We're done. Get out."

"You can't do this." His face was slack with shock.

"I can and I am. Get out. If you're not gone in thirty seconds, I'm calling the cops."

His hands clenched in fist. "You can't do this. I won't let you. I have a right to my baby."

"Wrong. This is my body. I can do whatever the hell I want and you don't have a say."

"No." He grabbed her shoulders.

She fumbled for her phone and began to dial. "Think about it, Richard. It won't look good for you to be arrested."

His hands dropped. He turned toward the door. "I'm not giving up on us."

"There is no us."

He moved through the door without another word. She gulped air in an attempt to calm the anger pulsing through her. Blood beat in her ears. She looked around the living room that carried Richard's mark. She grabbed a table lamp and hurled it against the wall. Hearing the shatter soothed her nerves, so she repeated the action with its mate.

Looking for more satisfaction, she shoved the cocktail table but realized it was too heavy to throw. Glass littered the leather couch, making her feel better. She grabbed the big chunks of glass to clean up, and one dug into her hand. The gash immediately bled, a line of crimson running down her arm.

Shit. Now she'd be late for work. She hurriedly cleaned and wrapped the cut and headed out the door, leaving the rest of the mess for later. What was one more thing on her plate?

She needed a distraction, something to make her forget all her problems. Griffin came to mind. But she couldn't go to him. He'd want answers and she still didn't have any. In fact, she was even more confused now.

Richard had gotten her pregnant intentionally because he thought he'd be able to keep her. How delusional could one man be?

The anger left, but a sickening feeling settled in her stomach. The bar was crowded and she hoped the busyness would keep Richard off her mind.

She placed beer in front of her waiting customers. The after-work crowd sought the same distraction she did. Smile in place, she did her best to relax and flirt.

"Hey, how about a song?"

"Sorry, guys, not right now. Maybe a little later." She turned to the next table to take an order.

She should sing. The extra money came in handy, but she was so tired. When not facing customers, her body moved sluggishly.

Fingers wrapped around her wrist and tugged for her attention. Taking a deep breath, she reined in her anger so she could tell Richard to fuck off without hitting him. She shifted her body and saw Griffin.

Her shoulders sagged, but the anger lifted. She didn't want to see him, but happiness filled her. The emotional tug-of-war increased her fatigue.

"I've been calling."

"I know. I've been busy." He still held her wrist, and his thumb stroked her pulse. She didn't pull away from the comforting touch.

"Too busy to return a call?"

She closed her eyes. She wanted to lie to him. "No. I

avoided you. I have a lot on my mind, and I don't know what to do with you."

But seeing him now, in the flesh, gave her body plenty of ideas.

"Hey, Indy, we need another beer," a guy called from the booth behind her.

Indy tugged her arm free and looked over her shoulder with a smile. "Be right there." Returning to Griffin she asked, "Can I get you a beer?"

"Sure."

After grabbing the bottles at the bar, she intentionally dropped Griffin's off first, so she had an excuse to leave. With the second bottle of beer, she walked over to the table of office drones.

These three came in once or twice a week, every week, for a few beers. Since she'd been dubbed "the singing waitress," they almost always asked her to sing. At least one of them had a crush on her. She wondered if they knew she was almost ten years older than them.

"How about a song now?"

"I'm really tired tonight, guys. I don't think I'm up for singing." She took the three dollars for the beer and tucked it into her apron pocket.

The guy on the end moved over and patted the seat beside him. His blue eyes sparkled like a mischievous toddler. "Take a load off. Hang with us for a few minutes."

God, it was tempting. But if she sat, chances were good she wouldn't finish her shift. "Wish I could, but I have to work."

She stepped back. Griffin's eyes were on her. She didn't have to turn—she felt it. Not the distraction she needed. If he showed up on her doorstep to fuck her senseless, that would be a quality distraction.

But the kiss at Quinn's wedding had thrown her. She'd

been falling for him, and that kiss confirmed it was mutual. He'd complicate her life more.

She moved from table to table, taking and delivering orders. Griffin nursed his beer. He didn't try to touch her again, which made it easier to focus.

The office trio called her over again to order another round. They were pleasantly buzzed.

"Hey, Indy," the blue-eyed troublemaker said. He seemed to enjoy saying her name. "What would a guy have to do to land a hot woman like you?"

She held in a chuckle. "It's not so much what a man does as who he is. Smart, funny, adventurous."

"Blah, blah, blah. Every woman says that. We want the real scoop."

Indy set her tray on the table and thought. Images of Griffin washed over her. "You have to look at a woman like she's the only woman in the room. And that look tells her you want her naked and tangled with you all night long."

Two of the three hooted and shoved each other. Blue Eyes stayed focused on her. "And then?"

"If she returns the look, you follow through. You show her she is the only woman, even if it's only for the night. And if you want to keep her, respect her enough to let her be who she is." That last part was the single most important thing she had learned from her time with Richard. She picked up her tray and turned.

Blue Eyes grabbed her hand. From the corner of her eye, she saw Griffin stand.

"Since you haven't returned my look, sing to me." He stuck a twenty in her apron, his fingers lingering as if he had a shot of turning her on.

"What song?" Giving in to a song would be easier than dealing with a brawl.

"You pick."

"Sure. I'll be back in a minute." She went to the jukebox, dropped in her quarters, and punched in the selection for "Call Me Maybe."

While she waited for the song, she visited her other customers to make sure they wouldn't need her during her three- or four-minute performance. She swung by the bar for a quick drink of water.

She had less than an hour until her shift ended. Then she had two days off. Two days she desperately needed. The opening notes blared from the jukebox, and she walked back to the trio waiting for their song.

The rhythm and beat filled her will energy. She'd almost forgotten the powerful effect of music. The words flowed effortlessly. The music and lyrics were a flirtation of their own, and Blue Eyes stood and pulled her close to dance. Over Blue Eyes's shoulder, she saw Griffin edge from his seat again and she held up a hand to stop him.

The song was almost over and this guy was harmless. He might want to cop a feel, and he'd surely take her home if she offered, but he didn't frighten her. Regardless, Griffin had no right to interfere. They had a bouncer who looked in her direction, waiting for a signal.

She finished singing and pulled away. Blue Eyes tugged again. "Are you sure you're not interested?"

"Thanks for the offer, but no."

He released her and returned to his seat.

Griffin's gaze caressed her skin, following her every move, heating her blood, turning her on. He said nothing and continued to sip the same bottle of beer.

Blue Eyes and his friends left. Tables began to fill again, and Indy longed for Lisa to arrive to take over. She filled orders for new customers and kept an eye out. Lisa preferred the later shift so Indy often dealt with the after-work crowd.

Lisa's brown ponytail bobbed and swung as she rushed

through the door. Indy stopped at Griffin's table. "I'm done for the night. Can I get you anything else?"

The look he raked over her body made her stomach jump.

"Did you need another ride?" she asked, her voice low and husky. She felt some satisfaction in watching him shift uncomfortably. It was only fair for him to be as equally turned on.

He stood, the sudden movement putting his body within inches of hers. Sure that he would kiss her, she lifted her jaw, wanting his lips on hers. His breath whispered across her lips.

"I'll follow you home."

Then he was gone.

Indy couldn't move fast enough. She emptied her pockets and removed the apron. She dared a glance from her position by the bar. Griffin stood outside the door, his breath coming out in little puffs in the cool night air. He wasn't the arrogant, rich asshole she'd pegged him to be when they'd first met.

He was pushy and aggressive, and she liked a confident man. But he hadn't smiled tonight. While his eyes were filled with lust, he'd lost the playfulness. He sat watching her with the same grim expression he had now, standing in the cold. Getting rid of him made the most sense. How could she start, or continue, a relationship while pregnant with Richard's baby?

Plus, she really needed a man who liked to laugh.

She pulled her sweatshirt on and headed to the door. Halfway there, she noticed the sweatshirt she wore was Griffin's. She'd taken to wearing it often. The material was soft and warm and durable.

It felt like him.

Don't think like that. Tonight he'd be the distraction she needed. For tonight her body could be fulfilled while her mind and heart could be empty. Indy pulled the door open and cold air stung her cheeks.

He said nothing but held her hand. When he touched the gauze stretched across her palm, he looked at her. She shook her head slightly. She couldn't talk about it, not now, not with him. When they got to the parking lot, she saw his SUV parked beside her car. They stood sandwiched between the two vehicles, breathing heavier than normal people should.

"Indy—"

She couldn't bear to hear what he might say. She needed contact now. Needed something more than words. She pushed him against his car and leaned up into a hungry kiss to tell him what she wanted.

His hands tugged at her shirt, exposing her skin to the cold night air. The heat from his fingers against her cool skin made her feel alive. He was hard, and she rubbed her body against him.

"Here?" he asked, the single word rasping out.

She nodded and he opened the back door to the SUV. The tinted windows would offer some protection, but if someone put his face against the glass, he'd see them. She didn't care. She needed this.

They sprawled on the backseat and he pushed her shirt up. His mouth found her breast. She sucked in a sharp breath.

"Are you okay?"

She nodded, unable to speak. She wanted him so much she couldn't believe it. She'd missed his touch. Her breath released in short pants while she tugged at the buttons of his shirt.

Indy yanked at his pants. Her skin became so hot, she thought she'd combust. She shimmied out of her tight shorts and watched him roll on a condom, his pants pushed down on his hips.

Every sensation overwhelmed her like she hadn't been touched in forever. Griffin moved torturously slow. His fingers and hands explored as if memorizing her every cell. Her desire twisted into burning need.

She didn't need care and kindness. She sought mindlessness, and his body would be the perfect vehicle. She pushed him back into the seat and impaled herself on him. She stretched as he filled her, and she shuddered.

He let her take charge of pace. She rode him fast and hard, her nerves and mind in a race to oblivion.

Griffin said nothing, but he continued to watch her as she took what she needed. He knew how to touch her and move to enhance each sensation, take her to the next level.

On the verge of orgasm, her muscles contracted. Her nerves became so taut she'd thought they'd shatter. Griffin gave her the first sign that he too was losing his grip on self-control when his fingers dug into her hips, pulling her closer to completion, to fulfillment, to him.

CHAPTER 11

$\mathcal{I}$ndy lay boneless against him. They'd rushed this reunion. He'd wanted to go slower, savor her body and everything he'd missed about it, but Indy wasn't inclined to move slowly tonight. She wanted fast, out of breath, heart racing, mind numb, so he obliged. She wanted to lose herself for a short while. He could relate.

Now he held her, unsure of his next move. They certainly couldn't stay in his car in the parking lot all night. But he wasn't ready to let go.

They needed to talk. Figure things out.

While his mind fumbled for a plan, she pushed off his chest and slid back into her shorts. After she'd straightened her shirt and sweatshirt, the one she'd taken from him, she finally made eye contact. Without saying a word, she slid away from him and out the door.

He uncomfortably shoved himself back into his pants and flung his door open. No way was she running out on him again. He caught up with her as she opened her car door. "Wait."

She shook her head, still refusing to speak.

"Dammit, Indy. Stop."

"Go home, Griffin. I can't do this."

He moved to block her from getting in her car. "I beg to differ. We've already done this. At least you've done me."

"Leave."

"No."

"Don't tell me no. My life is a mess you don't want to be involved in. I can't do casual right now. I can't do anything."

He rubbed his knuckles across her cheek. "We're already passed casual and we both know it. I want to talk. Be an adult and talk to me."

She leaned forward and laid her forehead on his chest.

"Why were you so upset tonight?" He stroked her hair and hoped she'd answer.

"Richard came to my apartment. He's thrilled that I'm pregnant and wants to get back together."

Whoa. He hadn't expected that. His fingers left her hair, and he stepped back to look at her face. "Then what's the problem?"

"He did it on purpose. He fucked up the condoms to get me pregnant so he could keep me. He already has kids he doesn't care about, but he thought adding one more to the mix would be a good idea."

A single tear streamed down her face. He brushed it away with his thumb. Her skin was still warm, but she shivered. "Let's go back to your place."

This time she didn't protest. She nodded and turned away from him.

Griffin got back into his car and followed her out of the lot. He drove through Indy's neighborhood looking for a parking spot. The frustration of the last couple of weeks lodged in his muscles. Worry about Duane and the other kids filled his head in the few moments he hadn't been thinking about Indy. He hadn't planned to kiss her, much less have sex, but he couldn't resist her. Not when she was needy, or any other time for that matter. But he needed answers.

After his third circle, he found a spot. He cut the engine and looked at his overnight bag. Bring it in now, or wait to see what happened? The debate ended with his fingers curled around the handle. He'd always been an all-or-nothing kind of guy.

She'd left the front door open for him. Seriously unsafe in this neighborhood. He closed and locked the door behind him. "Why would you leave the door open?"

He turned to face the living room and took in the disaster in front of him. Glass lay everywhere. Panic gripped him as he rushed through the apartment. "Indy?"

The bathroom door opened and he skidded to a halt. "What?"

"What the hell happened to your living room?"

"I was pissed off when Richard left." She led the way back down the hall. "I want him gone. Out of my life. Including this ugly shit." She kicked the couch. "I'd rather sit on plastic milk crates."

He grabbed her hand and kissed the palm covered by a bandage. "I'll get it all out of here tomorrow."

Burning it in Richard's yard appealed to him.

"I can't stay in here."

"Let's go to my place."

She shook her head. "No, he won't drive me out of my own house any more than I'll let him dictate what I do."

Griffin followed her into the kitchen and watched her move around the room, filling the kettle and putting it on the stove.

"When you said you swore you wouldn't let it happen again, what did you mean?" Of all the questions he had, he didn't know why this one came out first.

Her shoulders curled inward. She didn't turn, but

answered while watching the kettle. "When I was seventeen I fell in love with a boy and got pregnant. We screwed up, but I wanted the baby. He would've married me and we'd still be in Hooperville, living a miserable life."

"What happened?"

"I told my mom. She wanted me to have an abortion. We stopped talking to each other for weeks. My father couldn't even look at me. Then I miscarried. I graduated from high school and went away to college like my mom wanted me to." Her arms tightened around her waist. "I swore I would never put myself in that position again. To love someone so much . . ."

The baby or the boyfriend?

The kettle whistled. Indy stared at it. Griffin reached around her and turned off the flame. He took her by the shoulders and maneuvered her to a kitchen chair. He pulled out a cup and tea bag and poured the hot water.

The process brought back his own childhood. He'd made tea for his mother after every broken heart. Every time she met a man, thinking he would be the one to love them both. By the time he'd turned ten, he knew better than to cling to his mother's hope.

If you held no expectations, you couldn't be disappointed.

He turned and placed the tea in front of Indy. Her hands cradled the cup. Her face was drawn and hollow. She needed sleep. She looked like she hadn't had any in a week.

Griffin pulled a chair close to her and sat. He put a hand on her arm and asked the most important question. "Do you want to have this baby?"

DID SHE? Indy nodded before any thought entered her mind. The word followed feebly. "Yes."

"Then have it."

She was afraid to meet his eyes. Afraid of what she'd see. Disgust? Anger? Pity? Bringing the cup to her face, the steam from the tea tickled her nose. Her eyes closed against the sensations.

I want this baby. She rolled the words over in her mind. For all the thinking she'd done over the days, she hadn't once stopped and listened to her gut. She had tried to be practical like Quinn, logical like Kate. It was her nature to run on instinct.

She needed to listen to her instincts. Following them might not be the best choice, but at least it would feel right. Indy reopened her eyes. Griffin still sat there, eyes locked on her face. She stood. "I'm going to take a shower."

He didn't respond. Her time in the bathroom would give him the opportunity to leave. He had his answers. What more could he want?

The hot water beat against her skin and eased her tight muscles. Her hands ran over her body. It didn't feel any different. The curve of her breasts, the flare of her hips. It would all change. It would no longer be her body.

When she felt relaxed from the steam and heat, she wrapped herself in a fluffy towel and combed her hair. Rather than drying it, which could take forever, she began the arduous task of braiding it. The apartment was silent around her, except for the toilet running continuously because she'd forgotten to jiggle the handle.

By the time the braid trailed down her back, her arms were tired. She rehung the towel and put on the robe she kept on a hook. Steam billowed into the hall when she opened the door. The overhead light glared in the living room. She reached to hit the switch and noticed the broken lamps were gone. Griffin had cleaned up.

It was a sweet thing for him to have done. She'd call him

in the morning to thank him. Her body jolted when she entered the kitchen. He stood leaning against the counter, phone in one hand, a bottle of beer in the other.

He looked up from the tiny screen. "Feel better?"

"Much. Uh, thanks for cleaning up the mess in the living room. You didn't have to do that." She dumped her cold tea in the sink and rinsed the cup. She filled a glass with water and took a long drink. She remembered Quinn and Kate talking about pregnancy symptoms. At least she didn't have morning sickness. That would suck.

Griffin studied her with his head cocked to the side. His phone no longer held his attention.

"What?" she asked after another gulp of water.

"You thought I left."

She shrugged.

"I told you before I don't sneak out."

She lifted one shoulder. "I thought you got the answers you wanted. There was no reason for you to stay. I'm not your problem."

He tossed his phone on the counter and set the beer down with a louder-than-necessary clank. He inched closer. "You are my problem. I can't get you out of my head."

His gaze dropped to her mouth. He would kiss her again and then she wouldn't be able to think. She stepped away.

"Are you crazy? I want this baby. Assuming I decide to have it, what do you think is going to happen?" She waited a beat. She saw nothing in his eyes except desire. "What do you expect to happen between us?"

"I don't have any expectations. I want you. You want me. I care about you. Why muddle something so simple by having expectations?"

He closed in on her again. His left palm cupped her jaw and he leaned down. His argument was simple and effective. Why couldn't they stay the way they were? This felt good.

But something bothered him. She saw shadows in his eyes. "Why did you come into the bar tonight?"

"I wanted company."

She tilted her head to get a better look at his face and waited.

"I was upset. One of my kids got arrested."

"For what?"

"It doesn't matter. He's out now, but I'm failing them. We lost the use of school property and they're back to their usual lives . . ."

His muscles were taut with tension. She hadn't been the only one looking for escape tonight. No wonder he'd let her take what she needed from him. She brushed hair away from his forehead. Grim lines creased at his eyes.

No, he wouldn't be a smiling man who would laugh with her, but she could return the favor and give him the escape he needed.

She laced her fingers through his and led him to the bedroom.

THE DARK NIGHT blanketed Griffin as Indy pulled him toward her bed. It looked like the time for talking ended. She slowly undid the buttons on his shirt and slid it from his body. She draped it neatly over a chair as if he'd be worried about wrinkles.

He kicked off his shoes before reaching for the belt on her robe. A hint of light filtered through the open door, enough to allow him to see her milky skin as the robe opened. She shook it from her shoulders until it dropped to the floor and then stood for him to look.

Griffin pulled her body to his, wanting to hold her and touch her. She said nothing, but as his hands found all her tender spots, she sighed and her breath hitched. He didn't need any more urging. He laid her on the bed and covered her body with his.

Moments later, when he buried himself inside her, he found comfort in being surrounded by her scent, her body, her.

They made love, slow and quiet, and then she cuddled close. It didn't bother him or make him feel claustrophobic. He toyed with her braid and the locks that had escaped.

"You know, I'm gonna get fat."

"Huh?"

"I'm going to get huge."

"You're pregnant. You're supposed to."

"But I might never look like this again. I'm thirty-five. My body probably won't bounce back."

"So?" What was she getting at? She didn't even look pregnant yet.

She pushed up on an elbow. "Are you still going to want to sleep with me if I have a belly out to here?" Her hand moved from her torso and smacked into his side.

He shrugged. He hadn't thought about having sex with a pregnant woman. Strange. His only thought had been that he wasn't ready for Indy to leave his life.

Indy pulled away. "That's what I figured."

Words fumbled through his head. He knew the wrong words would do damage. "It's not that. I hadn't thought about it. I know you'll grow, but I haven't actually pictured it."

"Yeah, no expectations."

"Are you okay with this? Playing it by ear?" Deep down he prayed for a yes. He didn't know how to offer more.

"Sure. It's what I do best. Quinn's the planner, not me."

She didn't sound any more convinced than he was. She

settled back against him. Her breath skimmed his chest. "What happened with the house in Oak Park?"

"I guess I forgot to tell you. I was a little preoccupied." He stroked his fingers on her back. "I got it. We close at the end of the week."

"Good. It's a perfect house, but it's too much for one guy."

"I like big." *So different from how I grew up,* he thought. "Besides, I'll have the kids in my program there." A chance to get them back on track.

Silence cradled the room and he thought she'd fallen asleep. His own eyes drifted closed.

"It seems like a waste."

"Hmm?"

"The house. It needs a family. With kids. And a tire swing on the willow in the side yard."

Sleep pulled at him. "It will," he mumbled.

WHEN THE EARLY morning sun squeezed through the gangway to peek into the bedroom window, Griffin eased away from Indy. She needed sleep, but he had furniture to move. After a quick cup of coffee, he saw movement next door. He left Indy's apartment door open and propped the exterior door by bunching up the hall carpet.

He rang what he hoped was Eddie's bell. Eddie answered the door in boxers and a white tank top.

"Hey," Eddie said, scratching his stomach.

"Would you be interested in a white leather couch?"

"What?"

"Indy needs to get rid of her living room furniture. It's yours if you help me move it now."

Eddie's dark brows rose. "She's getting rid of that sweet setup?"

Bingo. Griffin nodded. "But it needs to go right now."

Eddie opened his arms. "Let's go."

Griffin looked down at the boxers.

"Oh. I'll get some pants." Eddie disappeared into the apartment.

Griffin went back to Indy's, closed the bedroom door, and hauled one of the end tables over to Eddie's. He banged it a couple of times on the journey. It weighed a ton.

The couch would be a bitch.

Eddie met him at the door and held the screen open for him. They went back to Indy's for the other tables. In Eddie's living room, furniture crowded the space.

"What are you going to do with your couch?" Griffin asked.

"I have a cousin who'll take it. I'll keep it in the extra bedroom until he comes to get it."

"Okay. Let's go." Griffin moved to grab an end.

Eddie looked startled at the offer. "Oh, okay. Thanks for the help, man."

After they had the old couch settled in the equally crowded bedroom alongside a shrine to the Madonna, Eddie gave him a long look. "You're not like the old dude."

"Who?"

"The old guy Indy was going with. He looked at me like I was a cockroach. You look at me like competition."

Griffin didn't respond. The reason he offered the couch to Eddie, besides expediency, was to ensure that Indy wouldn't want to hang out at Eddie's house. It made him feel a little juvenile, but he didn't care.

The leather couch required a lot of grunting and swearing, but they got it moved without waking Indy. Sweat coated his skin by the time they were done. He checked on Indy and went to shower.

∿

INDY WOKE to the smell of fresh coffee. She stretched and smiled, knowing Griffin had spent the night.

What am I doing?

She spread her fingers on her flat abdomen. *This won't last, but I can enjoy time with Griffin until he bolts.* And he would. After that, she'd be alone. In her gut she knew this would be her last fling or relationship for a good, long while.

For now, she'd take what she could. If all she got was good sex and quality sleep, she'd survive. Griffin had already given her more than she'd gotten from Richard.

In the kitchen, Griffin drank coffee, looking crisp and clean. "Where'd the clothes come from?"

He turned away from the window. "I brought a bag."

"So you expected to spend the night."

"I prepared for the possibility."

She poured a cup of coffee, took a sip, and stopped.

"Something wrong with the coffee?"

"No." She set the cup down. "I don't know if it's okay to drink it."

"Too bad." His evil little grin told her the coffee was good. He took a gulp from his cup, and she wanted to hit him. She needed caffeine to function in the morning.

"I don't think one cup will hurt." She picked up her cup again and sat at the table. She pointed to the small, white box in front of her. "What's this?"

"A present I picked up while I was out of town."

Her fingers twitched to open it. She loved presents, but she wanted to avoid the slippery slope. It had been one way Richard had drawn her in. She slid the box toward him. "Thanks, but I don't want you buying me presents."

"You'll like this." He nudged the box back.

"I'm sure I would, but I don't want presents." She'd loved

everything Richard had given her. The presents never made up for him not being there in the morning.

He sighed as if somehow she was being intolerable. He opened the box himself and withdrew a ceramic cow. The gorgeous cow wore a business suit and heels. "It's a business card holder. It reminded me of you."

"A cow?" She tried not to be offended.

"The first time you showed me a house, you wore a business suit and stopped on the side of the road to strip off your pantyhose. She's bare-legged. I thought she'd go well with your collection."

He bought me a cow. Tears pricked the back of her eyes, and she bit down on the inside of her cheek. *God, do not cry over a cow.*

"Well, do you like it?"

Indy forced a smile to push back the tears. "She's beautiful."

Griffin handed her the cow. A ceramic cow couldn't cost much. An inexpensive gift would be okay. She let him buy her dinner, right?

He'd thought of her while he traveled. But that was before.

"Thank you." She rose and put the cow on her desk. Maybe she'd take it into the office for her desk there.

"What are your plans for the day?" he called from the kitchen.

"I'm going back to Quinn's to finish painting."

"What painting?"

"I'm painting their house for them."

"Why?"

"Because I needed time to think. I started with the nursery, but I've had a lot to think about, so I branched into other rooms."

He rinsed his coffee cup, and she knew he was getting

ready to leave. "What if they hate the colors?"

"They won't, but if they do, it's just a couple of coats of paint. We'll redo it."

He laughed and shook his head. "I'd go crazy if you let yourself into my house and started changing things."

Her stomach dropped. She hadn't thought about Ryan. Quinn wouldn't mind, but Ryan . . . "Shit. Will Ryan be pissed? I didn't even think about it being his house too."

"Ryan will probably be very grateful. His hands are full with the apartments above the bar."

The knot in her stomach eased. "What's his favorite color?"

"How should I know? Men don't discuss those things."

"How about a color he hates? It'd be my luck to paint the bedroom a color he despises."

"I don't know, orange?"

"You're a big help. I'll stop by O'Leary's. Colin should know."

He stepped closer so they were nearly touching. "Not likely. Colin will be more focused on hitting on you than answering paint questions."

She tapped his cheek. "I know Colin. He's never hit on me."

"How about at the wedding?" He moved closer still, backing her into the wall.

Her mind scrambled back over memories of the wedding. The day had been a blur.

"Every time I tried to get you alone, Colin was hanging all over you. It being Ryan's wedding was the only thing that saved him from being pummeled."

She remembered dancing with Colin, at a respectable distance. They talked quite a bit, but she didn't remember flirting. Certainly no direct come-on.

Griffin lowered his head, and his whisper brushed her

lips. "The wedding's over and I'll kick his ass if he doesn't keep his hands off."

His mouth covered hers, and words of protest disintegrated. His anger seared her tongue as he invaded her mouth. She tried to muster her own anger at his assumption that she'd be drawn in by Colin. The anger didn't mount.

Griffin cared enough to be jealous. That's what this was, right?

He pulled back and stared into her eyes.

A smile tugged at her lips. Yes, he was jealous, and she enjoyed it. "I'm capable of having a conversation with a man without falling into bed with him. I'll talk to Colin."

He stepped away, easing his expression. "Eileen would know more. Moms notice that kind of stuff. Go visit her."

"I'll think about it."

"I have to go to the office. How about dinner?"

"Sure. I'll be at Quinn's all day, so call me when you're done with work." She turned to go to the bathroom for a shower and froze.

Her living room was empty.

She felt Griffin standing behind her. He kissed the top of her head and tried to squeeze past. "I'll call you."

"Where's the furniture?"

He dropped the black bag he carried. "You said you wanted it gone. Did you change your mind?"

"No, but how?"

"I got rid of it."

"Where? How?"

He held her arms. "Do you really want to know?"

She shook her head and wrapped her arms around his waist. Her cheek rested on his chest.

The empty room filled her with contentment. Freedom. It held so much possibility.

"Thank you. I owe you one."

He stepped out of her embrace so she would look up at him. "Stay away from Colin and we'll call it even."

"Done."

He walked through the house, his footsteps echoing his departure.

She needed new furniture. Too bad she couldn't afford it.

CHAPTER 12

Griffin's day had sucked. He'd spent at least half his time fielding questions from his PR people about the rabid parents trying to block production of the *Night Beasts* video game. He finally gave up the idea of accomplishing anything and left the office early. He went home to change clothes and called Indy. She didn't answer.

A quiet night with her sounded perfect. He hoped she didn't want to go out.

After his shower he called her again. Still no answer. He drove out to Ryan and Quinn's house on the assumption she'd still be there. Sure enough, her car sat in the driveway.

He knocked on the front door but got no answer. He dialed her phone again. Nothing.

He walked around the back of the house. He knocked and waited. When Indy still didn't answer, he peered through the glass in the door.

No movement inside, but he heard loud music. Then he saw her bare feet in the living room. The kitchen wall obscured the view of the rest of her, but her body obviously lay on the floor.

His fist pounded on the door and he called her name. Panic crawled up his throat. He looked around for something to break the glass and kicked a decorative patio brick free.

As he lifted the brick and turned to swing it, the door opened. Indy stood staring at him, all sleepy softness. He dropped the brick and grabbed her shoulders.

"Are you okay? What happened? I've been calling and knocking." He could barely hear his voice over the sound of the radio blasting in the house.

Her eyebrows drew together. "I was tired so I lay down. I must've fallen asleep." She turned, walked back into the house, and flicked off the radio.

"You didn't hear your phone or me pounding on the door?"

She shrugged. "I guess not. What time is it anyway?"

He resisted the urge to scream at her when he saw the shades of purple under her eyes. He stepped through the doorway and drew her close. Her lips were warm and soft with sleep. He barely repressed the shudder of relief her gentle mouth released in him. "Almost six."

When she stepped back, her eyes were wide. "Well, maybe I should let you wake me from a nap more often."

He followed her through the kitchen. "Not like that. I looked through the window and saw your feet sticking through the doorway. I thought you fell or . . ."

The thought dropped off as he entered the living room and saw the freshly painted walls. A warm gold color glowed in the evening light. Even without furniture, the room had a homey feel. "Wow."

"What?"

"This room looks great." He turned and saw the blush rise on her cheeks.

"Thanks."

Griffin went upstairs. Two of the three bedrooms were

finished. The job looked professional. He came back to the kitchen to find Indy chugging a bottle of water and tapping her foot nervously. "Well?" she asked.

"Well, what?"

"Is he going to hate it?"

Where had her confidence gone? Her cavalier attitude about paint color had disappeared. "They'll love it. It looks good."

She smiled easily. "I'll have to tell my dad I finally put the interior design classes to use."

"Interior design?"

"One of many majors I toyed with during my stint in college."

"What else?"

"Architecture, philosophy, art." She looked up at the ceiling. "I think that's it. I bore easily."

"I'll keep that in mind. Ready for dinner?"

She looked down at her paint-smudged pants and T-shirt. "Where do you want to go?"

"I'd like to eat in if it's okay with you. I feel as beat as you look."

"Okay. Your place or mine?"

"Mine. The restaurants are better in my neighborhood." She needed to get more comfortable in his space. She had no reason not to spend the night at his house.

She quickly ran through the house closing and locking windows and turning off lights.

He waited in the kitchen and found notes scribbled on a pad next to her cell phone. When she came into the room, he held up the pad. "What's this?"

"Moving companies. Quinn comes back on Sunday so I wanted to get their stuff moved on Saturday." She took the pad and shoved it into her purse. "I have a few more calls to make. I hope I can find someone cheaper, but I waited until the last minute."

She turned off the kitchen light and held the back door open for him.

"I'll take care of the truck."

"You don't have to do that. I wasn't looking for a handout. My idea, my sister."

"My friend."

A small sigh escaped her lips. "Fine. Let's split it then."

"Okay."

She followed him back to his condo. She didn't stop at her apartment and he didn't think she kept a bag of clothes in her car. He'd have to find a way to get her to spend the night.

He wanted her in his bed come morning. Griffin pulled into the garage and got a parking pass for Indy's car, but she hadn't followed him in. He dialed her number. "Where are you?"

"Looking for a spot to park."

His sigh came out harsher than he wanted. "Pull into the garage. There are visitor spots."

"How would I know? I'm not a regular visitor in places like this."

He shook his head. "Just pull in. I'm waiting for you."

Moments later she pulled in and he waved to the security guard. He climbed into the passenger seat and clipped the cardboard pass to her mirror. "Drive down and around the corner. There's a bank of visitor slots."

She followed his directions, parked, and looked around.

"What are you looking for?" he asked, climbing out of her car.

"Some kind of sign or something. I'll never find my car otherwise."

"I'll get you back to your car." Pulling her close, he added, "At least I know you won't be sneaking out."

∼

INDY SAT in the exam room nervously tapping her feet. A paper sheet covered her lower half. She sagged with exhaustion, but Quinn's house was done. By tomorrow afternoon, Indy would have Quinn's stuff moved. She imagined how to arrange the furniture and where to place the dishes. Anything to avoid thinking about the doctor.

She'd already peed in a cup for the official pregnancy test. Goose bumps pimpled her bare legs. *You'd think they'd turn the heat up knowing I'm waiting in here half naked.*

A light rap on the door and then it swung open. Dr. Rollins entered, holding a thick file. She'd been Indy's doctor for more than ten years.

"Hi, Indy. How are you doing?"

"Why don't you tell me?"

"Well, you're definitely pregnant." She waited, letting the words sink in.

Indy scrubbed a hand over her eyes. "Can you tell me how far along I am?"

"Without knowing the start of your last period, no. You seem vague on that."

Indy inched straighter on the exam table, hating the rustle of the paper on her lap. "It's stress. My period hasn't been normal in months. I've missed one, maybe two periods."

Dr. Rollins made notes in the file and pushed her glasses farther up on the bridge of her nose. "We'll schedule an ultrasound. It'll give us more accurate information. Then you'll know what your options are."

Options. She still had choices. She'd told Griffin she wanted this baby, but could she, should she have it?

The doctor patted her knee, and Indy lay on the crinkly papered exam table. With her feet up in stirrups, she tried to imagine herself pregnant. Or holding a screaming baby. She couldn't develop the picture.

She wasn't mother material. She knew that. But the possibility curled deep inside her with a flutter. This might be her only chance.

"Indy?"

The doctor's voice pulled her back. "I'm sorry. I zoned out."

"Everything looks fine. Are you experiencing any problems?"

"I'm tired. All the time."

"That's normal. No morning sickness?"

Indy shook her head.

"Stop at the reception desk on your way out. They'll set you up with an ultrasound appointment, an information packet, and prenatal vitamins."

She threw exam gloves into the trashcan and turned back. "You know, depending on how far along you are will limit how much time you have to decide whether or not to terminate the pregnancy."

Indy nodded. Terminate. Such a clinical word.

Her doctor stood near the door, not yet opening it. "I can recommend someone if you need to talk."

Indy shook her head and swallowed past the lump in her throat. "No, thanks. My sister will be back from her honeymoon on Sunday. I have people to talk to."

She dressed, made an appointment for the following week for the ultrasound, and accepted a folder of information. On the drive home, the folder glared at her. She didn't want to read about being pregnant.

Indy drove to Quinn's loft to make sure Quinn had everything packed. Her sister was the only person she knew who could work full-time, plan a wedding, and pack for a move simultaneously. All while being pregnant. Indy started in the bedroom. It would be one thing to need the movers to pack books, but Quinn would be mortified if strangers rifled through her panties.

In her usual preparedness, Quinn had only the barest essentials still out. Boxes clearly marked stood open and waiting for the remaining contents of the room. Indy emptied drawers and tried to be as methodical as Quinn would've been.

$\sim$

HOURS AFTER SIGNING and initialing and finalizing the contract, Griffin sat in his car outside his house.

His run-down, falling-apart, decrepit house. What the fuck had he done?

After dragging the six-pack from the passenger seat, he walked across the overgrown lawn. He sat on the sagging steps and appreciated the hideous view of his property. Indy hadn't returned his calls. He even went to End Zone to see if he had gotten the days mixed up.

As he popped the top on his first beer he remembered the day. Friday. He chucked the bottle cap into the bushes and pulled out his phone.

Indy'd had her doctor's appointment. She shrugged off his offer to go. She acted like it was no big deal, but he knew she was nervous or anxious. Now he couldn't reach her.

Did something happen? Had the tests been wrong?

He dialed her number again. "Hey, Indy, I wanted to see how things went with the doctor." He paused, searching for the right words. "Call me if you want to talk or get together. If not, I guess I'll see you at Quinn's in the morning for moving day."

Griffin disconnected and chugged his beer. He held the phone, hoping it would ring. Being in a holding pattern with

Indy until she figured things out didn't sit well. It was time to change the rules. He'd make her an offer she couldn't refuse.

MOVING day went better than expected. Griffin had arrived early in the morning with Ryan's brothers and a rented truck. The O'Leary men were as smooth as they were hard-working. They joked and talked with Indy and wouldn't let her carry anything heavy. She wondered if Griffin had warned them. Before she knew it, they had the truck empty at Quinn's house and it was only three-thirty. She'd get her nap in after all.

She thanked the O'Learys for all of their help and hard work. They climbed into the truck and rumbled down the street, leaving her with Griffin. "Can you take me back to Quinn's to get my car? I'd like to lie down for a nap before I go into work tonight."

He sighed. "Come on, I'll take you home."

"I need my car."

"It'll be faster if you go straight home. I'll take you to your car before work."

"Fine. Thanks." Indy propped her elbow on the window frame and laid the side of her head against her fist.

"What happened at the doctor yesterday? I called, but you didn't answer."

"There's nothing to tell. I'm pregnant. Because my period has been messed up, they can't give me a due date. I have to have an ultrasound to see how far along I am."

"Okay." He started the car but waited before pulling into traffic.

"I can't make any decisions until I find out how far along I am."

"Decisions?"

"Whether I want to keep it or . . . terminate."

"Oh. I thought you'd already decided."

"I don't know. I can't think right now."

He reached out and placed his right hand on her thigh. She covered his hand with hers, squeezed, and closed her eyes. Having the baby meant losing whatever they had going. She wasn't ready to face that either.

Her muscles sang with strain and exhaustion. She had done too much this week. The painting would've been enough of a gift for Quinn, but Indy was glad they had the moving done. Now Quinn could focus on unpacking before going back to work.

Before Indy knew it, Griffin parked near her apartment.

"You're coming in?"

He held his door open. "Is that a problem?"

"When I said I wanted a nap before I went to work, it wasn't code for sex."

His playful grin shot straight to her stomach. She calculated whether she'd have time for a nap and sex.

"I know. I'll find a game to watch on TV while you nap and then I'll take you to your car."

"Okay, but I hope you like sitting on the floor. You got rid of my living room furniture, remember?"

"I forgot." He locked up his car and put an arm around her shoulder as they walked up the front steps. "I'll make do."

She didn't have it in her to play the good hostess. She dropped her purse near the front door and called over her shoulder, "Wake me in an hour. I don't want to be late for work."

"Why don't you call in sick and take the night off? You look beat."

"We've been over this. I need the job."

"Fine, have a god nap."

She slithered straight into her bed, not moving covers or

disrobing.

~

INDY SAT UP, startled to find her room shadowed in black. She looked at the clock. "Shit."

She bolted from the bed and scrambled to flip on the light. Griffin rolled over on her bed with a groan.

"Hey." She nudged him in the ribs. "You were supposed to wake me in an hour."

"Tried. You wouldn't budge." His words were little more than a murmur, and he kept his eyes closed against the glare of the overhead light.

Indy yanked her uniform from her dresser and quickly stripped. He must have been exhausted; he didn't even peek. "You have to get up and take me to my car. I'm going to be late for work."

"Call in sick." He reached out and caught her wrist. "Come back to bed."

She pulled away. "No. Get up or I'm taking your car."

He huffed, but sat up. "Fine." He scrubbed his hands over his face and then stood.

She watched him in her mirror while she pulled her hair into a high ponytail. He was definitely a fine hunk of man. His offer to return to bed tempted her, but her empty bank account called louder. He eased behind her and softly kissed her neck. How bad would it be to call in sick? The adult part of her brain overruled the hormonal part, and she stepped away from Griffin, even though she really wanted to lean into him. "Let's go."

Inside the car, Indy applied make up. Dark shadows marked her eyes and she touched them with powder.

"Covering it up doesn't change the fact that you're exhausted. You're working too much."

She closed the mirror on the visor. "I'm doing what I need to do."

He pulled into Quinn's lot beside Indy's car. "Come to my place when you get off."

He pressed a parking pass and key into her hand. Her heart thumped uncomfortably. The pass was one thing, but the key . . . maybe for convenience. She got off work late. If she had a key, he didn't have to wait up for her.

"What time do you get off?"

"One."

"I'll wait up."

She eyed the key in her palm. Not just a convenience. She held the key out. "Why don't I call you when I get to the garage?"

"Keep it."

Her breathing wobbled unevenly. No one handed out keys. Certainly no man she'd ever known. Definitely not one with no expectations. She tucked the key into her pocket and opened the car door. "Thanks for the ride."

When she leaned over to give him a quick kiss good-bye, he cupped the back of her head and drew her in. The slow, wet kiss made her nerves tingle.

His hand released her head, but his breath still mingled with hers when he pulled back. "We'll talk later. Come straight to my house."

She blinked to clear her vision and her thoughts. "One in the morning isn't prime conversation time. There are better things we can do. Talking can wait."

"I have to go out of town again on Monday."

"See you later, then." Indy forced her feet nervously from his car. Confusion struck her. Griffin's behavior was far from casual.

What had she gotten herself into? She stuck her key in the ignition and watched Griffin pull back out onto the street.

Her phone rang. *Quinn.* "Hey. Shouldn't you be enjoying the end of your honeymoon?"

"Indy . . ." Quinn's voice shook.

"What? What happened?"

"It's Dad. Lydia called."

Anger replaced fear. "What'd he do now?"

"It's serious, Indy. He smashed the car. Totaled it."

"How'd he get the keys? I thought we took them all."

"He took Lydia's."

Indy swallowed the disgust rising in her throat. "So he stole keys, drove drunk, and smashed the car."

"He's in the hospital," Quinn choked out.

Indy laid her forehead against the steering wheel. She could fight a lot of things, but not Quinn's tears.

"I tried to get an earlier flight. I can't. Please drive down there. I don't want him to be alone."

"Lydia's there."

"It's not the same."

Indy bumped her head against the steering wheel a couple of times, looking for an answer. None came. Did Quinn have any idea what she was asking? She sighed. Of course Quinn understood.

"Please. You know I'd go if I could."

Quinn always ran to their father's rescue. "Fine. But if he's an asshole and tells me to leave, I will."

"Thank you. Call me as soon as you know anything." Quinn's relief washed over the phone line.

Indy looked at the clock. "I probably won't know anything until morning, so don't panic if you don't hear from me until then."

"Thanks, love you."

They disconnected, and Indy's brain scrambled to formulate a plan. Call work. Pack clothes. Map route.

The key in her pocket poked her. She'd have to call Griffin. Their rendezvous/talk would have to wait. Part of her felt relieved, but she'd trade a talk with Griffin over one with her father any day.

～

GRIFFIN PACED in his living room. This decision felt right. He had plenty of space and Indy owned little. If she moved in with him, she could quit working at the bar.

And quit singing for men who only wanted to see her naked.

He hadn't lived with anyone since college. Sweaty palms reminded him this was a huge step. They hadn't known each other long. Neither had Quinn and Ryan, and they were happy. Married, but happy.

He enjoyed spending time with Indy. They were comfortable. More time together would give them a chance to figure things out. They'd enter this new territory together.

One-thirty and she still hadn't arrived. He called her cell, but it went to voice mail. She must've gotten hung up at work.

After another twenty minutes of pacing, he called the bar.

"End Zone, Nick speaking."

"Hi. May I speak with Indy?"

"She's not here."

"When did she leave?"

"She didn't come in tonight. She called saying she had a family emergency."

Griffin hung up and called Indy's cell again, and it still went to voice mail. As worry settled in, his cell rang. "Hello."

"Hey, it's me," Indy said.

"Where the hell are you?"

"The middle of nowhere."

"What?"

"Right after you left, Quinn called. My dad was in an accident, if that's what you can call it. I'm driving home to check on him."

"It's the middle of the night. Why didn't you call me?"

"I'm sorry. I packed and planned my route and . . . I'm stressed. I forgot to call. I meant to." Her voice was strained, like she couldn't possibly take one more hit.

"I would've gone with you."

Her laugh was quiet and tired. "I wouldn't subject you to this torture."

"But you'll do it alone."

"Not much of a choice. Quinn tried unsuccessfully to get an earlier flight. But she's always taken care of Dad. She doesn't need this crap now. She's pregnant."

Silence settled on the line and he spoke quietly. "So are you."

She didn't respond, but she didn't hang up either. Her quiet breathing whispered in his ear.

"How long will it take you to get there?"

"About another hour," she answered.

"Going straight to the hospital?"

"God, no. Those places are creepy at night. I already called. He's stable but out for the night. I'll go first thing in the morning."

"Good. Get some sleep. Take care of yourself first."

"I'm good at that."

"I'm serious. I'm here if you need to talk."

"Thanks. I'm sorry about our evening. Believe me, I'd much rather be sprawled on your couch than on my way to Hooperville."

"Yeah, me too." The admission was more than either of them had ever offered. He wanted her in his bed all the time. They didn't have to be Ryan and Quinn. They could figure out what would work for them.

Indy interrupted his thoughts. "How long will you be on your trip?"

"I'm not sure. It could be awhile." He'd been counting on having Indy to come home to, in his house.

"Okay. I guess I'll see you when I see you. Have a safe trip."

"You too."

They both lingered, and silence weighed heavily before he hung up. Griffin grabbed his overnight bag and quickly tossed clothes in. Indy might not have asked him to come, but she would need him. Griffin had the feeling her father would continue to jab at her unless he remained unconscious. She already had enough stress.

He drove through the night and pulled over at a truck stop to sleep for a couple of hours in the morning. By the time he arrived at the hospital, he felt crappy enough to be a patient.

The automatic doors slid open, releasing the hushed gloom of the hospital. The antiseptic smell assaulted him. He swallowed, afraid bile might rise. His feet became bricks as the memories of his mother's last days swam in his mind. The useless pacing, the horrible coffee, the quiet that wasn't really quiet.

He reminded himself that his mother's misery was over and he had nothing to fear. Pushing on, he went to the nurse's station to ask for Walt's room.

Indy was there all right. Her voice easily carried into the hall. "Don't you think I know the date? I know it's Mom's birthday. You're not the only one who lost her. You don't see the rest of us running out on a bender and driving drunk."

Griffin paused with his hand on the door. He waited instead of pushing it open.

"I loved her." Walt's weak voice croaked, so unlike the booming quality he'd had at Quinn's dinner party.

Indy snorted. "You loved her so much you trapped her in a life she hated."

"What are you talking about? I tried to give her everything she wanted."

"A life in this crappy little town is what she wanted?"

Walt sighed, and Griffin heard the mechanics of the bed whirring. Griffin removed his hand from the door and backed up a step, remaining silent. Guilt crept into his chest. He shouldn't listen to the private moment, but he couldn't leave.

"When I met your mother, I fell head over heels immediately. I loved everything about her. Two months after our first date, she told me she was pregnant. I didn't even know if it was mine."

"You're sinking pretty damn low calling Mom a slut."

"Don't you talk to me like that. I've never said any such thing about your mother. She wanted the baby more than anything, so I married her. I'd have done anything to make her happy."

A chunk of ice-cold fear plummeted into Griffin's stomach. Married? Is that what Indy would want? What the baby would need? He eased away from the door. Marriage wasn't an option for him.

He vowed he would never hurt a woman the way his father had crushed his mother.

He wouldn't make promises he couldn't keep.

Not after what had happened with Selena.

Griffin turned away from the room and stopped at the nurse's station. He forced his charming-do-me-a-favor smile "Hi. When Walt Adams's daughter comes out, could you tell her I'm outside?"

"You can go in to visit if you'd like."

"No. I think they need some time. I'll wait. Thanks."

ndy fisted her hands to control her rage. "That's a lie. You were married for three years before you had me."

"There was another baby. She lost him. Our son. All she wanted was a family. Babies." His red-rimmed eyes filled with tears.

It certainly explained a lot. "That's why you can't stand the sight of me. It's not that I wasn't born a boy. I lived. I lived, but your son didn't. And you hate me for it."

The anger and hurt burned through the tears streaming down her face. She turned away from her father. The one man she'd always sought attention from. The only one she wanted to love her. At least now she understood the futility of her attempts.

"Independence."

She couldn't face him.

"I've never hated you. I've always loved you too much."

Indy spun around. "Funny way of showing it. Everyone knows Quinn's your favorite. That doesn't even bother me.

What kills me is the look of disgust I've seen on your face for most of my life."

As the words left her mouth, Indy's mind spun back in time. He hadn't *always* looked at her like that. Deep in her memory, a flash of his loving eyes held her. The crush of the memory forced more tears.

"By the time you were a teenager, all I saw in you was your mother. I was afraid of losing you. You were wild and couldn't wait to get away from here. Then your mother died. Every time I look at you, I still see her. It hurts too much."

Her father cried. The only time he'd ever shed tears had been at her mother's funeral.

He cleared his throat and brushed away the tears. "I always pushed myself to give Quinn more attention because I didn't want her to know you were my favorite."

Indy laughed. Her voice bounced off the tastefully decorated, bland walls while the tears continued to streak her face.

"That's her right there. My Alice. Turn emotion on a dime and laugh like there's no tomorrow. I miss her laugh most of all."

Hearing him say her mother's name eased some tension. Indy sat on the edge of the bed and took Walt's hand. "I wish you'd talk about her more. It would've made the last fourteen years a whole lot easier."

"I can't."

"You just did."

"And look what it did to me." He rubbed his face again.

Indy sighed and stood, afraid she'd get no more out of him. She walked to the window and looked at the cars below. The colors and shapes of the vehicles looked like a child-created mosaic. "If Mom was so happy here, why did she always push me and Quinn out? She harped on us almost daily about going away to college."

"She wanted you to get as much out of life as you could. She wanted you to find your own happiness."

She sat with him until he fell back asleep. Unlike most people, Walt didn't look peaceful in his sleep. His craggy, bruised face still held sorrow. Indy went to the bathroom and splashed cool water on her face to smooth the ruddiness in her cheeks.

A walk in the fresh air would do her good. She reapplied her makeup. It would be just her luck to run into an old boyfriend when she looked like crap. She made sure Walt was still asleep and then she eased out the door. Everything she believed—no, assumed—about her mother had been wrong. *If Dad's telling the truth now. God, I wish Mom were here.* Why would he marry her without a paternity test? He trapped them both by being nice, doing the upright thing. She couldn't wrap her mind around the insanity.

She moved silently, afraid to make noise, knowing it made no sense. The patients were awake and doctors and nurses bustled around, but she still couldn't stop her steps from being quiet.

A rock sat in the pit of her stomach, grinding at already-frayed nerves. She knew she'd always been like her mother, but now the similarities were spooky. Pregnant and unmarried. What were the chances? She even had a guy who'd proposed. Although the father of the baby, he was a total ass.

"Ms. Adams," a nurse called.

Indy turned to face her. The younger woman beamed at her with a friendly smile. "Yes?"

"A friend of yours asked me to tell you he's outside."

"Did he give his name?"

"No." Her smile broadened and she lowered her voice, as if to reveal a secret. "Very good-looking with a killer smile. He came in some time ago, so I don't know if he's still out there."

"Thanks." Indy walked to the elevator and rode down. No one knew she was in town except Griffin. Good-looking and killer smile definitely described him. But why would he come here?

The elevator doors parted at the lobby. The exterior doors mimicked the motion. The glare of the sun made her squint. She felt his presence before she saw him. A tingling awareness tickled her nerves.

He leaned against the building, watching her. A smile tugged at her lips that she couldn't stop. Her heart swelled, and she tried to push it back. She wasn't supposed to feel this way about him. "Hi."

Griffin reached out and pulled her into his arms. "How are you?"

She took a moment to soak up the strength surrounding her. "I'm okay."

He kissed the top of her head and held her close.

"What are you doing here?" she asked, the sound muffled by his shirt.

"I thought you'd need a hug."

She laughed and stepped back from the embrace. "Awful long way to go to deliver a hug, but I appreciate it."

"How's your dad?" Griffin gestured to a bench.

"He'll be fine." Indy sat on the cool metal. "I don't want to talk about him. Tell me about your upcoming trip."

Keep the conversation neutral. Casual. She was the queen of casual.

"That won't make for interesting conversation."

"I don't care." She settled into the corner of the bench, keeping distance between them.

"I have to go play nice with some parent group who is making my life hell. I'm evil because I've created a video game kids want. It's rated for mature audiences, and parents are in an uproar because kids are asking for it."

"So what are you going to do?"

"I have no idea. We're counting on strong sales from this new game for the holidays."

"What kind of game?"

"It's called *Night Beasts*. You're a human and you choose what kind of hunter you want to be: vampire, demon, or werewolf. Then you hunt the creatures down."

"That doesn't sound too scary."

"The deaths are pretty bloody. I wouldn't want my ten-year-old playing it."

She tilted her head up. "You have a kid I don't know about?"

"An expression." A grim look clouded his face, but he covered it with a half-assed grin.

His face said more than his words. He didn't want a kid. She took that in. What the hell was she doing? She was pregnant and he didn't want kids. She remembered his reaction to Quinn's pregnancy, and she caught a glimpse of what Michelle had warned her about last month. At least Richard wanted a baby with her. Her brain felt like it would split.

Escape.

Safe ground. Talk about the game. "Why not make a kid-friendly version where the hunter . . . I don't know . . . shoots out a net to catch the creature. Offer it free on the Internet before the holidays. Moms like free and nonviolent."

His body stilled. Her idea was stupid and he didn't know how to tell her. She knew nothing about his business or video games. She should've kept her mouth shut. His face remained blank as he stared out into nothing. "Griffin?"

"That might be it. We've been racking our brains trying to figure out how to offer another version simultaneously. We didn't consider a free web-based version. You're brilliant."

"Okay." She didn't feel brilliant. She still felt like he was so completely out of her league.

"I'm going to have to go." He paused, turned to face her. "Look, I wanted to see you before I left because I might be gone for a while. I wanted you to have this."

He put a check in her hand. "What's this?" she asked, trying not to drool over the big number.

"You didn't get a commission on my house. I closed the other day. Without the information you gave me, my negotiation wouldn't have gone so well. You deserve the commission."

Indy swallowed hard. "Even if I got a commission, it wouldn't have been this big."

"Six percent is the going rate."

"I never would've gotten all six percent. One, one and a half maybe."

He closed her hand around the check. "This is for you. You need it and you worked for it."

He touched her cheek, and she looked up into his eyes.

"This is for you. Not him," he added with a tilt of his chin toward the hospital.

"What do you mean?"

"I know you help support him. This is for you, so you can stop working at the bar."

"Thanks. It's way more than I expected." Why now? Why offer money now?

He stood and she followed. He raised his hand as if to touch her, but thought twice. He'd never hesitated touching her. Then she realized why he pulled away. He was going out of town and he'd handed her a big check. He wanted out but didn't want to seem like a dick breaking up with the pregnant girl. She didn't know what had changed between last night and this morning, but he was different. They both seemed to be at a loss.

She reached deep into her pocket where she'd slid his key last night. "Here. You should probably take this back."

He stared at the key.

"You said you weren't sure how long you were going to be gone. I might stay here for a while to deal with my dad."

His stony face sank. She couldn't read the expression, but it didn't look like relief.

"You can hold on to it."

She swallowed hard. Why hold on to something she wasn't meant to have? "That's probably not a good idea. You're really busy and my life is still messed up."

"Will I see you when I get back?"

"I'm sure Quinn and Ryan will have us over for dinner and the holidays and stuff." Keep it simple and friendly. A civilized breakup.

"So that's it?"

"It's probably for the best, don't you think? I mean, we both keep saying no expectations, no strings, but here you are three hundred miles from home."

His mouth lifted on one side. "But you didn't expect it, did you?"

She bit her lip and forced a smile. "Have a safe trip. I better get back to Dad."

He kissed her quickly on the cheek, and she backed away before it could become more.

She strode back through the swooshing doors without a glance over her shoulder. She had prepared herself for this. She'd known it wouldn't last. Griffin had been her rebound guy and she'd gotten much more than she'd bargained for: a good time and a fat check. She walked through the lobby and tried not to think about the quiet house on a tree-lined street with the willow in the yard, but the image of a child on a tire swing squeezed her heart.

She almost made it to the elevator before she felt like passing out. Her chest tightened and her breaths exited as short gasps. She sat on a bench and closed her eyes. She didn't have panic attacks. Anxiety was foreign. Breaking up with a guy never had this effect.

Indy straightened her spine and inhaled deeply. Taking the check out, she thought of the baby growing inside of her. Griffin's money gave her a chance for a fresh start. The question became, what did she want to do with her life?

Rule One: No more useless men. I've wasted enough time having fun that went nowhere. Which might mean no men at all.

She stood and tucked the check safely in her pocket. She had a lot to consider and plan but no idea where to start. This new territory of being a planner sent shivers up her arm.

GRIFFIN COULDN'T BELIEVE she pushed him away again. To think he planned to ask her to move in with him. He'd dodged that bullet. If she wanted to run away, far be it from him to stop her. She wouldn't marry the baby's father, she wouldn't live with him, and now she intended to stay in Small Town, USA. As if this town could handle someone like her. She'd never be happy here.

Griffin drove back the way he came. At least all the hours in the car hadn't been a total waste. He had a solid idea to satisfy the parent group. They probably wouldn't be happy, but they could at least stop complaining. He made the calls to get production in motion, but his mind traveled back to Indy and how beat she looked.

He couldn't do anything about it. She wanted him out of her life. Her breakup method mirrored his—clean and smooth. Being on the receiving end felt strange. He wasn't angry. How could he be? If she called him next week and wanted to get together, he would. They always had a good time. But she wouldn't call. Of that much he was sure.

By the time he reached Chicago and headed for the airport, he'd just about had himself convinced that life without Indy would be an improvement. He shielded his heart with logic. He didn't need the complications she would bring. The press catching sight of her pregnant would certainly cause problems. Kendra would have a fit.

Yes, it was better all around that they ended before either of them got in too deep. His work projects and the foundation would keep him busy. She was pregnant with another man's baby. They were better off.

IT HAD TAKEN a lot of talk, but Indy had been able to convince Quinn to stay in Chicago. Indy managed to get a lawyer for her father and spend a day shopping for a used car for Lydia.

Responsibility was exhausting.

She'd quit her job at End Zone because she hadn't known how long she was going to be out of town. Now she returned home not knowing what to do for work. She'd called the real estate office to check in, but the owner seemed stiff.

She still hadn't told anyone she was pregnant. The debate raged in her head. The ultrasound appointment loomed over her. She didn't want to go alone. Call Quinn and have unyielding support, or call Kate and have reality slapped at her?

Indy imagined Quinn would be excited by the thought of having their children be the same age. Cousins growing up together.

She wasn't ready for excitement. She questioned her ability to do this. After cautioning Quinn about the hardships of single parenting, why did she think she could succeed?

She drove to Kate's house. Her husband, Mark, would be at work, so they'd be able to talk. Kate opened the door with a look of surprise. "Hi. What are you doing here?"

"I need to talk." Indy followed Kate through the house.

"It's not your dad, is it? Quinn said he was fine."

"He is."

"Let's go to the kitchen. I have coffee on. *Sesame Street* will keep the kids busy."

Kate quickly poured two cups of coffee and sat across from Indy at the table. "What's going on?"

"I'm pregnant."

Kate bobbled her mug, and coffee sloshed over her hand. "Shit." She jumped up and grabbed a napkin. "Did you say pregnant?"

Indy nodded.

"Do you know whose it is?"

Indy rolled her eyes. "Richard's. I'm not such a slut that I can't keep track of who I sleep with."

Kate shook her head. "I didn't mean it like that. I don't know how far along you are and thought maybe it was Griffin's."

The thought sent shivers dancing down her back.

"Does he know?"

"Richard planned it. He screwed with the condoms to get me pregnant on purpose."

"What an ass. What are you going to do?"

Indy cradled the warm cup in her hands. "I don't know. That's why I'm here."

"How far along are you?"

"Don't know that either. I'm having an ultrasound tomorrow to find out." She took a gulp of coffee. "Will you come with me?"

"Of course. I'll call my mother to watch the kids."

A long, steadying breath calmed Indy. "Thanks."

"What do you think you want to do?"

Indy lifted her shoulders a fraction. She couldn't even commit to being confused. "I think I want this baby, but I'm scared. I have no idea what I'm doing."

"Does Quinn know?"

"No. Griffin's the only person I told."

Kate's eyebrows shot up.

"He bought the pregnancy test and stayed while I peed on the stick."

"Really?" Kate drew the word out like she'd heard some astonishingly interesting piece of news.

"Don't do that. We had our fun, but we're over. He has his house. I have my commission. Plus, he's out of town indefinitely for work."

"Too bad."

"It's for the best." That's what she'd been telling herself for days.

"You have to tell Quinn."

"I know. I'm waiting until after the ultrasound." Hopefully by then she'd be struck by a bolt of wisdom leading her to the right decision.

THE FOLLOWING DAY, Indy and Kate waited for an ultrasound tech in a dimly lit exam room.

"Did you sleep at all?" Kate asked.

"Not much. A lot on my mind."

"It'll be okay." Kate reached out and held Indy's hand. "You're not alone."

The warmth and strength of Kate's touch loosened tight nerves. The technician entered and introduced herself. Indy couldn't concentrate on anything. Her brain filled with white noise.

"Lay back and ease the top of your pants down a bit."

The tech tucked crinkly paper into the waistband of Indy's open jeans and then squirted clear gel onto Indy's abdomen. The warm slime slid across her skin.

Indy closed her eyes and waited, unsure of what to expect. Kate patted her hand in reassurance.

"Here you go," the tech said.

Indy opened her eyes. The computer monitor faced her. A small blob appeared on the screen.

"That's your baby."

Indy's heart rate increased. Small flickers on the screen indicated a heartbeat. Her grip on Kate's hand tightened. *That's my baby*. The reality hit her, and in that moment, she was lost. She couldn't go back or consider abortion. Her baby was a real, live *person* inside her.

The tech turned the monitor back and said, "I need to take some measurements and then the doctor will be in to talk to you."

Kate leaned over and kissed Indy's forehead.

A little while later, the tech finished, wiped excess gel from Indy's stomach, and printed some papers. She left and the doctor came in, so Indy sat up.

"Hi, Indy. How are you doing?"

"I'm good. This is my friend Kate."

Kate squeezed her hand. "I'll wait outside."

"No, stay." Indy tugged her back.

The doctor nodded. "According to the measurements we've taken, you're seven-and-a-half weeks along."

"Huh?"

"You have time to decide what you want to do. There's no immediate rush, but the sooner, the better."

"Are you sure?"

"It's not an exact science, but we're usually pretty close."

"I've decided to have the baby. My baby."

The doctor made notes in Indy's file. "Okay. Congratulations, Mom. Take your prenatal vitamins daily and make a regular appointment for next month. Call if you have any problems."

They shook hands, and the doctor left to see other patients. Indy buttoned and zipped her pants. Kate pulled her into a hug. "Are you sure about this?"

"Hell no." She laughed, and tears streamed down her face. "I've never been so scared in my life."

"Good. You're supposed to be scared. What now?"

"I have no idea."

They walked back to the car and Indy's phone rang. Griffin again. She wanted to answer it. Wanted to tell him about her baby on the screen. The beautiful blob that was all hers.

Instead she hit IGNORE.

She had no right to burden him. They went their separate ways. Now she needed a plan.

LATER THAT EVENING, she stroked the filmy paper showing her baby's first picture. The date of conception felt off. She stared at the little white numbers and finally grabbed her calendar. She counted back seven weeks. Three days more. Four. She counted days instead of weeks and arrived at the same destination.

She had somehow gotten pregnant the one week she didn't have sex with anyone.

A week and a half earlier, Richard. A week later, Griffin.

The doctor had said it wasn't an exact science. But what if?

She shook her head. Richard compromised the condoms.

Griffin always had his own. It was probably a glitch in timing. She carefully put the picture in her purse.

In bed later, she rubbed her belly and wondered if her baby knew how scared she was. She wondered if she'd be a good mom.

The more she thought and wondered, the more she realized she needed to figure out her life.

~

"You can't do this." Quinn's voice practically squealed.

"Why not? I have nothing here." Indy grabbed a shirt, studied it, and tossed it in the Goodwill pile.

"Oh, thanks. Now I'm nothing."

Indy sighed. "You're not nothing. But you have your own new life as Mrs. O'Leary. You don't need me. Dad and Lydia can use some help."

"You're running away again."

"I'm not running away. I'm taking time to figure out my life. And what do you mean again?" She folded the last of the clothes she intended to take with her. The rest of her belongings were either headed into storage or being given away.

"Every time life gets too serious, you run."

She sighed and sat next to her sister on the bed. "The difference is, this time I need to get serious. I can live rent free with Dad. I won't have to blow any of the money I got from Griffin, which is a good thing, since I'm now jobless."

"I still think you should be able to sue them."

"It's not worth the fight. The agency accused me of sleeping with a client, which I did. Besides, the market's slow and they suspected I helped Griffin find the house. Wouldn't you be upset if someone cost you that kind of money? If I make an issue of it, I could cause myself more problems." She stood and closed the suitcase.

"When are you coming back?"

"I'm not sure. I don't want to have this baby in Hooperville. I'll take a break and figure out what I'm going to do. Then I'll be back." *Maybe by then I'll be over Griffin.* At least Quinn had the presence of mind not to mention him.

"Should I tell Griffin? He asks about you."

So much for the presence of mind. "No."

"I don't understand why you won't talk to him." Quinn gathered her coat and purse.

The sickening feeling curled in her stomach again. *It hurts too much to think about him. I miss him every day.* "He doesn't need to know my plans. We broke up. He should move on."

She desperately wanted to ask where he was and how things worked out with the video game, but she knew if Quinn saw any sign of interest, she'd be all over it.

"Can I at least tell him you're keeping the baby?"

"Why would he care?"

"Sometimes I wonder too, but he does."

She hugged Quinn. "I'll see you soon. Take care of yourself."

"You too."

Indy blinked back tears. This would be the first time she hadn't lived near Quinn since she brought Quinn to Chicago for college. Although walking away was hard, Indy needed a place where she could clear her head. There were no distractions in Hooperville. And maybe she'd even be able to repair some kind of relationship with her father. She walked Quinn out to the porch and gave her one more hug.

She went back inside, but before she closed the door, the bell rang. She swung around to see Richard standing on her porch. She hadn't spoken to him since before her dad's accident. She thought she'd escaped his craziness.

Learning from her previous mistakes, rather than letting him in she grabbed a sweatshirt and went out to meet him.

"What do you want, Richard? I thought I was pretty clear when I said I want to have nothing to do with you."

"I think I have a right to know if you're having my baby."

"I'm having the baby."

"I knew you'd make the right choice. Come back to me, Indy. We can be happy together."

Her stomach turned again. She remembered his words from their last visit: *I have a right to my baby.*

The last thing she wanted was for her baby to be one of the ignored status symbols he collected.

"I don't want to be with you." She hugged herself against the cold.

He ran his hands up and down her arms. "Can we go inside and talk? I want to be this baby's father." His voice got tight. "I have rights."

She might not be the best mother, but at least she'd try. She had no doubt Richard wouldn't be a good father. She'd known him to ignore calls from his kids so he could get laid. He missed recitals and games with lame excuses.

"You don't have a job. How are you going to support yourself?"

"How do you know I don't have a job?" She feared the answer. The same sinking suspicion crept through her.

"I just know. I make it my business to know what happens in your life."

Even without proof, she knew he'd done it. He told her boss she slept with a client. He'd gotten her fired in the hope of getting her back.

"I'm sorry, Richard. We're done."

"We'll never be done, not really. Not as long as we have a child. And if you fight me, I'll fight back."

A little light went off in her head. An exit. Safety. "You're not the father."

He stumbled back. "What?"

"You're not the father."

"You're lying."

She shook her head. "Hold on a minute."

She quickly ran inside and grabbed the ultrasound from her purse, praying this would work. Being tied to Richard forever was unimaginable. His trying to take her baby even worse.

Back on the porch, she handed him the ultrasound. "Do you know what this is?"

"Of course. I'm not that out of touch."

"Then look in the corner. At the date of conception." She waited. He continued to stare blankly. "Do the math. The date is a full week and a half after the last time we slept together. You're not the father."

He handed her the ultrasound back and sputtered for a minute. "How?"

She shrugged. "I have no idea. I think you should leave now. I'm busy."

He took a half step away. His face crumpled with something beyond sadness. "Good-bye."

She should feel guilty for lying. She knew she should, but she didn't. Maybe a little for making Richard sad, but not really. Her baby's health and well-being had to come first. Richard was not in her baby's best interest.

She watched Richard walk down the block to his car. She waved to Eddie, who had come out to watch her interaction with Richard. The moving truck pulled up, signaling the start to her new life.

CHAPTER 14

*G*riffin kicked at the sand in front of the villa while the phone rang in his ear. When Ryan answered, he said, "Merry Christmas."

"Hey, Griff. How are you?" He sounded tired, abnormal.

"Good. How are you?"

A shaky breath whistled in his ear. "Okay."

"Liar. What's wrong?"

Silence answered. He could see Ryan pacing, his only expression of worry.

"Do I have to call your mom and get her on your ass?"

A slow, quiet chuckle. Progress. "I'm stressed. Quinn's had some complications. The doctor put her on bed rest. I've been running like crazy with the bars, trying to keep busy with her out of work."

"Shit, is there anything I can do?"

"No. Indy's here to help out."

Indy. The name burned through the center of his chest. He wanted to ask about her, what she was doing, if she planned to keep the baby. But he knew better. Over the past months, Ryan had told him they couldn't talk about Indy.

"Ry, I know we don't ever talk about it, but you know if you need money . . ."

"No, we're good."

More silence.

"Griff, I'm scared shitless. I've never felt so completely incompetent. There's nothing I can do. What if we lose the baby?"

Griffin knew his friend had been holding in the stress so he wouldn't burden his family. Always the rock, that one. "You won't."

In the background, he heard Quinn's voice. "It's Griffin," Ryan told her.

"So, how's the beach?"

And just like that, the serious conversation ended. Griffin hoped his reassurance, although baseless, helped. "Hot. Sexy women in string bikinis. How's the snow?"

"Same as it is every year. Quinn wants to know when you're coming home."

"A couple more weeks."

"It's been a long vacation, especially by your standards. I'm surprised you've trusted both your business and your new house to be run by other people."

"Yeah, well, sometimes stepping back can give you a healthy perspective. Being out of the spotlight has actually been good for my image. Kendra is in heaven. The only publicity about me is what she's put out." He paced in the sand.

"That's good. Look, sorry to cut this off, but the family's on their way over. We're hosting Christmas dinner."

"Wow. You better go then. Give your beautiful wife a kiss for me. Tell the family I said hi."

"They're gonna wonder why you're not here."

"Tell them I needed a vacation." He'd only admitted to Ryan that he'd left because of Indy.

They disconnected, and Griffin imagined the noise and chaos of an O'Leary family holiday. He missed them. He smiled at the thought of Quinn dealing with all of them running over her house. Indy would love the instant party.

He walked out on the beach to let the water lap at his feet. Maybe he should go find a date for dinner. The quickest way to forget about a woman was to get a new one. It had always worked in the past.

He hadn't found anyone who sparked his interest for months. More good news for Kendra, not so much for him.

THREE MONTHS HAD PASSED since Griffin left Chicago. He stepped out of his car into the blustery cold wind. He hadn't missed the winter.

Indy was a different story.

He hadn't heard from her since they'd spoken outside the hospital. She wouldn't return any of his calls, so he'd quit calling. He hadn't expected her to call either. Avoidance was more difficult in person.

Looking up and down her street, he didn't see her car. He rang the front bell. She didn't answer, so he walked down the dark gangway to the back. A small light shone in the kitchen. He peered through the window. The room looked different. Then it hit him.

Her cows were gone.

He didn't want to call her cell. She probably wouldn't take his call. In person would be better. Griffin went next door to see if Eddie had any information.

When Eddie opened the door, he looked at Griffin for a moment. "Yeah?"

"Hey, Eddie. It's Griffin. Indy's friend. Do you know where she is?"

"She moved back home. She said she needed to hang with her pop for a while. If you're still *friends*, you shoulda known that."

"You're right. Thanks." Griffin turned back toward his car. She stayed in Hooperville? It didn't make any sense. Ryan had said she was here at Christmas. Maybe she and her father made amends, but it didn't seem plausible. Especially since she was pregnant. Somehow, he didn't think Walt would like the idea.

Unless she wasn't.

He hadn't given the idea any real consideration. Indy wanted to have the baby. Regardless of what she said about options, in her heart, she wanted to keep the baby. Griffin had assumed she was still pregnant. He'd even researched what she would look like.

Shit. He didn't have it in him to drive to Hooperville. Even if he did, what would be the point?

Hey, Indy, I know it's been three months and I can't make any promises, but I want you to move back to Chicago.

He didn't know what to say to her. He'd hoped for inspiration. The way things had ended between them had left him unsettled.

He'd thought about her daily. He avoided Chicago during the holidays and went to Aruba instead. Nothing worked. His time on the beach had been filled with images of Indy in a bikini. Instead of lapping water and rushing waves, he heard her laughter.

He drove to O'Leary's. Ryan would know where to find her. Although Ryan had been under orders from Quinn not to talk about Indy, he had to tell Griffin something. He wasn't some crazed stalker; he just wanted to talk to her.

The lot was crowded but not packed. When the bar door opened, music drifted out. He pushed through the crowd, the music washing over him, louder than usual.

Then he heard her voice. A freight train rattled in his chest. Indy. He plowed through the people between him and the source of music.

Indy stood behind the bar, wearing an O'Leary's T-shirt, with a microphone in her hand, belting out "I Got You Babe." Customers were two deep at the bar. She flipped her hair over her shoulder, imitating Cher. Her radiant smile shot through him, warming him in a way the sun had failed to all winter.

An off-key male voice joined hers. Griffin angled his body to see the other half of the duet. Colin.

He should've guessed. They sang into a shared microphone, looking like they shared a private joke. Old jealousies clawed up his back.

I'll kill him. Ryan's brother or not, he's gone too far.

Griffin swallowed hard. He had no business having those thoughts about Indy. They'd been apart for months. The song ended and the crowd thinned. Indy and Colin poured drinks. When space allowed, Griffin moved forward.

She must've felt him staring because she turned and searched the crowd. Her eyes widened in shock when she caught sight of him. Griffin tried to ease the murderous look he'd directed at Colin.

When he got to the bar, her shock melted into a gorgeous, warm smile. Her voice remained light, like she'd address any regular customer. "Hey, stranger. Long time, no see."

"Too long, I think." His gaze was drawn to hers, searching for anything, but she wouldn't maintain eye contact.

"Beer?"

He cleared his throat. "Yeah."

She turned to grab a bottle, and her profile shocked him. She was still pregnant. It looked like she had a mini-basketball pushing against her shirt. He'd thought she would've been bigger. Ryan had sent him a picture of Quinn, and they were due only a few weeks apart.

Indy put the beer in front of him. "Ryan's in his office. I'm sure he'd want you to go back. He's missed you."

She busied herself wiping down the bar.

What about you? He wanted to ask. Words froze in his throat. Other than the friendly smile, she didn't acknowledge him.

"I'll be back," he said, and went to see his friend.

Fuck. Of all nights for him to show up here, why tonight? Indy rubbed the bulge under her shirt, hoping the movement would have a calming effect.

Colin met her halfway down the bar. "Are you okay? You look like you've seen a ghost."

"I'm fine. Griffin's here."

"Hmm-mmm." He crossed his arms. "Need a break?"

"I said I'm fine." She gripped the rag in her hand.

"Were you expecting him?"

"Why would I? We haven't spoken in months." She pushed past him to continue wiping the counter.

"You guys were pretty hot and heavy."

She paused midswipe and wondered what Griffin had said to Colin. "What would you know? We had a casual fling and we went our separate ways."

A new crowd came up to the bar and a waitress needed an order filled, relieving Indy of any more of Colin's questions. She wasn't sure how she felt about Griffin.

She shouldn't feel anything. Casual didn't cross over the line to emotional. Seeing him, though, stirred something in her she hadn't thought about in months. Or at least she'd tried not to. The kiss they'd shared at Quinn's wedding hadn't been casual. She remembered the look on Griffin's face when she'd accused him of changing the parameters of their agreement. Casual wasn't on his mind. The kiss had been possessive.

But that had happened before they knew about the pregnancy. Before she decided to keep the baby.

She lied to herself with the thought that it had been only the one kiss at the wedding. After the pregnancy tests, the whole next week, they were together as a couple. He drove across the state to give her comfort when she had to deal with her father.

Still not casual.

Griffin came back. She could handle this. Even with his being Ryan's best friend, their paths wouldn't cross too often.

She had too much on her plate right now to even consider a relationship, casual or not. Classes started in a week, she needed to find a new place to live, and she needed a new job.

Indy served customers on autopilot, engaging in friendly banter, hoping to make the night move along. When her shift ended and Griffin hadn't returned, she assumed he'd slipped out the back. So much for being right back. She didn't know if she should feel relieved or irritated.

She drove to Quinn's house with the radio blaring to block out her thoughts. Inside, she found Quinn sitting on the couch. "Why are you up?"

Quinn's face brightened. "I'm bored. It's about time you got home." She clicked off the TV. "Tell me something interesting."

"How interesting do you think the bar is on an average night?"

"Anything is good when you've been stuck in bed for over a month."

It had been five weeks since Ryan called Indy in a panic.

Something had been wrong with Quinn and the baby. For the second time in a few short months, Indy had driven through Illinois in the middle of the night.

Everything's fine now. Quinn rubbed her belly. Indy stopped herself from mimicking the gesture. The unfairness struck her again. Quinn shouldn't be saddled with complications. Being a mother was her dream.

"Griffin came in tonight," Indy said with her body half in the closet hanging up her coat.

"What?"

Indy turned and sat beside her little sister, who wasn't looking so little. "Griffin came in."

"He's back? He didn't bother to call or anything."

Indy shrugged. "I figured Ryan knew."

"Not that he mentioned."

He wouldn't have said anything to Quinn if he thought it had the slightest chance of upsetting her. Indy knew Ryan tiptoed around the topic of Griffin. No one ever even mentioned his name.

"Well?" Quinn asked.

"Well, what? That was the highlight of the evening. Unless you count Colin trying to sing like Sonny Bono."

"What happened with Griffin?"

"Nothing. We said hi, I got him a beer, and he went to visit Ryan."

"That's it?"

"Yes. I was working." *I could hardly breathe at the sight of him.*

Quinn stood. "I'm going to make some tea. How do you feel about Griffin being back?"

"What do you mean?"

Quinn shuffled toward the kitchen. "Well, you've avoided any mention of him and refused to let us talk to him about you."

Not really. She often Googled him to get tidbits of information. She'd never admit it, though. It made her sound like a lunatic who couldn't let go. She broke up with him. Kind of. "It's fine. It's not like we'll see each other often. We rarely did before we slept together."

"What are you going to do?"

Indy inhaled deeply. "The same thing I've been doing. Since you're okay now, I'm going to find my own place to live and get a new job."

"You don't have to leave." Quinn pulled cups from the cabinet.

"Yes, I do. You don't need me anymore. The doctor said you can get back to your life."

"I'll always need you."

Indy began to tear up. Quinn never needed her. Damn hormones made her cry over everything.

"I'm moving back to the city. This house isn't big enough for all of us." Indy patted her belly. "Besides, I think Ryan's overwhelmed by the amount of estrogen surrounding him."

The kettle whistled, and Quinn filled their cups. "He wanted you to move in here."

"He asked out of desperation and fear. He wanted you and the baby to be okay."

"At least keep the job at O'Leary's. I feel better knowing family is keeping an eye on you."

Indy sipped from her cup. She'd taken the job at O'Leary's out of necessity, but she knew Ryan had offered the job out of guilt. "We'll see."

Quinn smiled. "You won't find a more accommodating boss."

Sure, but working there made avoiding Griffin more difficult.

The soft knock surprised both Quinn and Indy. Indy answered the front door to come face-to-face with Griffin.

"Hi." Her body stiffened, but her smile came easily.

"Hi. You left the bar before I came back," he said softly.

"My shift ended."

"Who is it, Indy?" Quinn called from the kitchen.

Indy opened the door wider and swung her arm to invite him in. She stepped back for him to enter, and her body responded to his nearness. Her heart beat faster and a low sexual pull tugged at her.

"Griffin." Quinn rushed forward and stood on tiptoe to wrap her arms around his neck. "It's good to see you. We missed you at Christmas."

"I missed being here."

Indy closed the door and skirted around them.

"Sorry to drop by so late, but there are few women I know I'd better visit immediately when I get to town. Eileen would already be in bed."

"No problem. We were just chatting." Quinn hooked her arm through his and led him into the living room.

Indy settled herself at the breakfast counter in the kitchen. She had some online coursework to finish, and thanks to thrumming nerves and hormones keeping her awake, she might even get around to searching for a new apartment. The low rumble of Griffin's voice provided a soothing background noise for her work. She listened as he shared details of his trip to Aruba, but he didn't sound very enthusiastic.

After about a half an hour, Quinn announced, "Whew. I'm tired. I think I'll head to bed. Sorry to rush out on you. Feel free to stay as long as you want. Ryan shouldn't be too late tonight."

Real subtle, Quinn. Indy counted her heartbeats. Ten. Then she felt Griffin enter the room. Her back was to him, but she knew the second he approached.

"Hey."

She spun in her chair. "Hey, yourself. How did *Night Beasts* do?"

The question bought her time to think. She already knew the answer because she'd followed it closely.

"Very well. It's a huge hit. Still selling well. Thanks to your free Internet idea, the parent group is mostly off my ass. I owe you a huge thank-you." He walked around the counter and stood beside her.

"You don't owe me anything. Your team of übergeeks would've come up with the idea."

"Maybe." He reached out and pushed a lock of her hair back over her shoulder. "You moved."

"Yeah, I did."

"Eddie seemed to think I should've known."

Her fingers froze on the keyboard. "Where did you see Eddie?"

"I went to visit him when I realized you no longer lived in your apartment."

"Oh." *Oh, shit. He'd gone to see me first? Before Ryan. Before Eileen.* He stood close, but she kept her eyes trained on her screen.

"Why are you living with Quinn and Ryan? Surely you couldn't have already burned through the commission I gave you."

His near-accusation rankled her nerves. She slammed the computer shut. "How dare you question how I spend my money? You said I earned it. I'm entitled to spend it however I want."

Her rant startled him and his eyes widened.

Her skin warmed, and she took a deep breath before continuing. "Not that I owe you an explanation, but Quinn had complications and I moved in to help her while she was on bed rest. Her doctor has given her the okay, so I'm moving out."

He raised his arms. "I'm sorry. Take a breath."

She did.

He continued, "That came out wrong. I didn't expect so much to be different after three months."

"Stuff happens. Life goes on even while you're out of town on vacation." The muscles of her abdomen constricted. She rubbed the bump of her belly and sat back down.

"Everything okay?"

"Yeah. He doesn't like it when I get upset."

Griffin's eyes lit. "He? You know you're having a boy?"

Indy shook her head. "No. I just think saying 'it' is creepy. I want to be surprised."

She kicked the chair out next to her. "Have a seat."

He scooted the stool close enough that the heat of his body reached out and touched her.

"Tell me what else I've missed. You're working at O'Leary's. With Colin. Living here. What else is new?"

She smiled broadly, but she tried to contain her excitement. "I'm going back to school."

"WHAT?" Had he heard her right? She's pregnant, still working at a bar, and now she's adding school? Images of his overworked mother slammed into his brain.

"Well, right now I'm finishing an online certification program. But I'm taking a couple of classes when the semester starts next week."

"For what?"

She blushed, emphasizing the importance if her revelation.

"I had a blast redecorating the house for Quinn. It was the most fun I've had while working in a long time. Singing at the bar is the only thing that has come close."

His neck muscles tightened. Remembering her singing and dancing with drunks at End Zone caused his jaw to twitch.

"I figured there had to be a way to make money doing it. I mean, if I can make money singing along with the jukebox, anything is possible, right?" She spoke animatedly, arms waving for effect.

He nodded, not wanting to interrupt her flow. He'd missed the sound of her voice. It held the same excitement it had when she'd called him about his house.

"I looked into finishing my degree in Interior Design, but it's not what I want. I might go back for a degree after I establish my business and the baby's a little older." She rubbed her belly again. "I don't want to be away from him too much."

He heard the love in her voice that matched the sweetness of her smile. "Business?"

"Yeah. I want to decorate, but not run-of-the-mill stuff. I plan to specialize for a specific market. The real estate market, to be exact."

Griffin leaned back in his chair and crossed his arms. This wasn't some crazy whim. "Go on."

"Remember the first house I showed you? The one with—"

"The gleaming white everywhere. How could I forget?" The place looked more like a hospital than a home.

Indy chuckled. "That house is the perfect example. You were immediately turned off because of the décor. If I redecorated it, you might've at least given it a chance.

"A lot of people watch the decorating shows on TV and think they can copy what they see. They have no sense of color or space. Small changes, big impact. That's my tagline." Her smile broadened like a child holding a report card full of As.

"Sounds like you have a plan. When are you going to start?"

She stood and refilled her teacup. Then she pulled a bottle of water from the fridge and handed it to him. "Like I said, I'm finishing my certification. I should be done by the end of the month. I'm taking two classes I think will benefit me, and they work toward a degree if I need them to."

She tucked her hair back again and fidgeted. "I'd like to get a client or two this spring to build my portfolio. Then I'll start advertising more this summer after I have the baby."

"It's a huge undertaking. Starting a business as a sole proprietor while being a new mom will be difficult." He hoped to open her eyes to the reality, but he wanted to rescue her.

For a moment she deflated, and he began to reach out to her. Then a gleam rose in her eyes. "I don't back down from a challenge, and I'm not afraid of hard work. This has the potential of being phenomenal for me and the baby. Thanks for the words of caution, but I know what I'm doing."

"I didn't mean it like that." Why did his words keep twisting? He was more articulate than this. "Have you heard from Richard?"

Her eyebrows furrowed. "No. What does he have to do with the conversation?"

"If he paid child support like he should, you'd have some cushion."

"I don't want his money. I don't want him to have anything to do with my child." Her hand rubbed her belly rhythmically.

His hand covered hers. "I don't want to upset you. This is his responsibility too. He owes you that much."

"He owes me nothing. I'll take care of myself." The strength in her voice matched the hardness in her eyes.

Griffin wished he had the words to express the difficulty

of single parenting. His mother never got ahead. Their daily routine drained her. Fun had become a foreign concept. Any day he saw his mother's smile qualified as a good day. He didn't want the light in Indy's eyes to disappear, extinguished by the monotony of solitude.

"Did I ever tell you about my mom?" Silly question. He never talked about her.

Indy shook her head, and he removed his hand from hers.

He stood and walked across the small kitchen. "She married a chronic cheater. I don't know what she saw in him, but he didn't know how to be faithful. He left before I turned three. When I got older, my mom told me he left to be with one of his girlfriends. He popped back into our lives, for the next three or four year, begging forgiveness, giving my mom hope every time. Then he disappeared for good."

"I'm sorry," she whispered.

He shrugged. He didn't talk about it. The past stayed in the past. "I'm not telling you this so you feel sorry for me. My mother struggled every day just to make ends meet. She spent more hours out of the house than in it, including sleep. She would never admit it, but she was never happy."

"I think you're wrong." She stood and looked deep into his eyes. "If you had told me that story last summer, I might've believed it. But now, I'm starting to get the whole 'mom' thing, and I can't even hold my baby yet. *You* were your mother's happiness. Your first steps, the first time you explained processing speed to her, when you started your own company . . . those gave her happiness."

"You're missing my point. If my father had ever gotten off his ass and given her any kind of financial support, her life would've been easier. She would've spent more time smiling instead of worrying." The familiar churn of emotions ran through him. Anger. Sadness. Regret.

She touched his hand briefly and then pulled away. "Money can't buy happiness."

"No, but it makes life easier."

"I can't argue that." A huge yawn forced her mouth open. "Sorry."

"No. It's time for me to leave. Get some sleep." He paused and smoothed his hand down her hair. "It's good to see you again."

"You too."

He stepped away before he got careless. He wanted to tangle his hands in her hair and kiss her blind, but he had no right. The time for casual had run out and he didn't know how to be more.

CHAPTER 15

*G*riffin's footsteps echoed in the empty foyer. The plans and permits for construction were in place. Work had already commenced. This should've been his first stop after arriving in town. Instead he wasted time looking for Indy, only to find her at O'Leary's.

He flipped on light switches to check the work. Bare bulbs dangled from the high ceiling. Fresh drywall waited to be taped. The fireplace brickwork had been demolished.

The kitchen was gutted. He tried to envision the finished product, but the picture couldn't form in his mind. The willow outside the window drew his attention. What had Indy said about the tree? Something about a tire swing.

This would be his home. It's what he'd searched for, but it still felt empty. Retracing his footsteps, he turned off lights and walked back outside. A few flakes fell from the sky and swirled around his head.

He hated winter. He could live anywhere, but he kept coming back here. This was home. The good and bad, these were his roots. Other than a shitty beginning, what did he really have?

His mother was dead and he'd gotten rid of his father. The O'Learys accepted him as one of them. As close to family as he'd ever get. But now he had his foundation and the program to reach kids. He thought of Duane and Marisol and knew the reason for returning to Chicago.

Then there was Indy.

Talking with Ryan earlier had been informative. Indy left out many details during their conversation. Sure, she'd moved in with Ryan and Quinn to help out, and prior to that she had been living in Hooperville. She didn't go back to hang out with Dad, though. She quit at End Zone, and after she returned, the real estate agency asked her to leave. Indy suspected they found out she had found Griffin's house and they lost their commission.

No job, no apartment, and she hadn't approached her ex for any money.

Griffin knew he had no claim on Indy, but if he could do something to change the path her life was on, he'd do it. He cared about her more than he wanted to, and he feared she'd turn into his mother.

HE HADN'T SLEPT NEARLY ENOUGH. Three cups of coffee forced him awake, and he found himself in front of the O'Leary house. He rang the bell since no one expected him.

Eileen opened the door. She had her purse in one hand and her coat in the other. "Griffin, what are you doing here?"

"I thought you might want a ride to church."

"Thank you. You look like you could use some sleep."

That was Eileen. She pulled no punches. He took her coat and held it open.

She slid her arms into the sleeves and locked the door

behind her. She patted his arm. "After mass you'll take me to breakfast and tell me your troubles."

His smile came easily. "What troubles? I lead a charmed life."

"Griffin Walker, you know better than to lie to me. You only come around to see me without Ryan when there's trouble. And today you're volunteering to go to mass."

She had him. She'd always known him as well as her own children.

Griffin drove back to St. Matthews. A few short months ago, he stood in this church and witnessed his best friend getting married. Indy had walked down the aisle like she owned it. Looking back, he realized what a good actress she was. It felt like half a lifetime had passed since.

He sat through the mass, enjoying the routine of it. The words, the gestures, they were constant. It didn't matter that he was lapsed. Years of Catholic training afforded him the ability to slide into any mass and blend.

After church, Griffin drove Eileen to KD's for more childhood comfort. They settled into a booth, and a waitress poured them coffee.

"Lily's not working today?" he asked. He hadn't seen her since the wedding either. She'd ditched him the moment they'd entered the reception.

"No, she's off." The waitress left menus on the table and made her rounds, filling cups.

"The young girl you brought to Ryan's wedding?" Eileen laid her napkin across her lap.

Griffin nodded. "She wasn't really my date. She wanted to go to the wedding to see Liam."

"My Liam?"

"The one and only."

"Hmm." Eileen thought briefly and seemed to tuck the

information away. Then she prompted, "Tell me what's wrong."

Griffin looked into the pale blue of her eyes. "It's complicated."

"If it were simple, it wouldn't be much of a problem."

Their waitress returned and they fumbled through placing an order.

Alone again, he dove in. "Before the wedding, I dated someone casually. Nothing serious, but we had the start of something special."

She folded her hands primly on the table. "Having a woman's never been a problem for you."

"She's pregnant and it's not mine. She got pregnant before we got together."

"And?" Eileen's face became stony. Her protective mother streak showed.

"She broke it off right after the wedding. That's why I stayed away for so long."

"Maybe she's gone back to the baby's father."

"No. She doesn't want to have anything to do with him. I've seen her. She's still alone." He didn't even know what he expected from Eileen. Guidance? Permission?

Eileen shook her head in disappointment. "Do I know this girl?" she asked suspiciously.

He nodded again and forced the name out. "Indy. Quinn's sister."

"What have you gotten yourself into?" The lines on her face seemed to deepen with disapproval.

"She's a good person. She's smart and beautiful." He sighed. "There's something just under the surface. A fragile vulnerability." Where had that come from?

Eileen raised her eyebrows and her mouth smoothed.

The waitress delivered their food.

"You're in love with her." It wasn't a question.

"I don't know."

Eileen shook her head. "You've never brought a woman to me. You've never talked about your feelings for one. If she's what you want, God help me, fight for her."

She spread orange marmalade generously on her toast. The sticky sweetness turned his stomach.

Fight for Indy? Fight for what? "I don't know what I'd be fighting for. We weren't serious. We were playing it by ear. No expectations."

"And you'd both be lying to yourselves. Everyone has expectations. You say you don't, but you don't mean it."

He lowered his voice. "She's pregnant with another man's child."

Eileen dropped her toast. "Are you telling me, Griffin, you couldn't love someone else's child?"

Heat crawled up his neck.

She spoke rapidly and her brogue lashed out in anger. "Patrick loved you as one of his own boys. It never mattered who gave you life or your name. You were his." She reached out and grasped his hand. "You're mine, and blood has nothing to do with it."

She shamed him with her words. He hadn't thought about fatherhood. At least no further than to know he wasn't cut out for it. Could he look at another man's child and not think of Indy being with another man? What if he could and then things didn't work between him and Indy? Then he'd lose a lover and a child.

A late-morning breakfast should've been relaxing, easy-going. He couldn't make life-altering decisions over scrambled eggs and bacon. He boxed it up to think about later. "How's Maggie doing? I didn't get to speak to her much at the wedding."

"So I guess that's the end of the conversation. Maggie's been having the time of her life traveling through Europe.

She's meeting people and making friends. I haven't seen her this happy since before."

Griffin knew Eileen wouldn't talk about Maggie's rape more than three years ago. The crime had crushed the family, and they'd had a hard time moving past it. Now it looked like they'd made progress.

They finished their breakfast talking of the mundane. His mind, however, remained on Indy.

GRIFFIN WAITED in the foyer as Indy parked her car. When she got out, she assessed the property. He wondered what her thoughts were. She pushed away from her car, her smile warm, even as the wind whipped her hair around her head.

When she walked up the steps, she paused to look at the new porch. "I'm glad you kept the same style. It looks good."

He grabbed her hand and pulled her through the doorway. The excitement of having her in his house overwhelmed him. Her fingers were warm despite the bitter cold outside. Desire coursed through him, and he wanted to taste her cold lips to see if he could detect a difference with the passing of months and seasons.

Her hand squeezed his to draw his attention. "So why am I here?"

"I wanted to show you my house. We've made a lot of progress." He needed to slow down so she could envision what he did.

"Oh. Okay."

"Something wrong?"

"You made it seem important, not a tour of a construction site."

"We'll get to the important part later. You need the tour first."

He started on the main floor since it still had the most work to be done. They'd nearly finished the upstairs, so he wanted to end there.

That's where her work would begin.

The kitchen, living room, and dining room were only partially drywalled, so Indy was quickly bored. He rounded back to the stairs and started up, but Indy didn't follow.

The lab grabbed her attention and he lost her.

"Indy?"

"You skipped this room."

He followed her into the expansive room. An entire crew of men spread out across the space, installing trim and running wire to accommodate the electronics.

"What the heck is this room for?"

"A workroom."

"For what? Your entire office?"

"The kids."

As she spoke, work in the room slowed. Eyes followed her, as they did whenever she entered a room. No one approached her, but they ogled. Griffin grabbed her elbow. "The upstairs is almost done. That's what I wanted you to see." He circled her back around to the stairs. "Wait until you see it."

"Okay," she answered, sounding unsure.

At the top of the stairs, he released her elbow and she walked away to explore the five bedrooms and media room. He followed silently, waiting for her comments.

She said nothing.

She walked through each room, occasionally running a finger across a piece of trim. Finally she stopped and leaned against a wall near a huge bay window. "Why am I here, Griffin?"

"I wanted you to see the house because I'd like to hire

you." He stayed near the doorway, saws buzzing and drills whining behind him.

Her faced filled with confusion. "For what?"

"To decorate, of course. I know you said you wanted to specialize in houses on the market—"

She huffed and shook her head. "Please don't throw money at me out of pity. I thought we were past that."

His hands flexed into fists of frustration. "I need my house ready to move into by spring."

"Remember when I painted Quinn and Ryan's? You said you'd hate for someone to redecorate."

"No, I'd hate for someone to do it without my knowledge. I expect you to draw up a full proposal for my approval before you start."

She moved away from the window and paced, no, stalked toward him. "Why me? Your money can buy the best."

"I like what you did at Ryan's. I know you and can trust you not to leak information about my home to the press."

It must've been the right answer, because a smile brightened her face. "You're sure?"

"Yes."

THE GIDDINESS ROSE UP in Indy's chest until she felt like she'd explode. She threw herself at him, wrapping her arms around his neck. "Thank you. You won't regret this."

His arms wrapped around her and held her close. Being in the strength of his arms, pressed against his solid mass, was the most comfortable she'd been in months. She wanted to rest her cheek against his chest; instead she gave him a peck on the cheek and pulled away.

Blinking her misty eyes, she asked, "When do you want to start?"

"What's wrong?" He reached out for her arm, but she busied her hands tying her hair back.

"Nothing." She flashed a toothy smile. "I'm excited. This is a huge opportunity." She dabbed at her eyes. "This is pregnancy hormones."

"I want to start immediately."

"Okay." Her mind raced to what she'd need to start: photos, floor plan, sketch pad. She'd need to talk to Griffin about what he wanted. "Should I call your secretary to set up an appointment to talk about what style you're going for?"

"My secretary? Call me." Anger shaded his puzzlement. "Business or not, you can always call me."

Her stomach fluttered. She didn't want to read anything into his comment. They were just words. "I didn't want to assume I'd get preferential treatment because . . ." *We slept together, had a rockin' good time, started to fall in love.* ". . . of our past."

"You get preferential treatment because I care about you."

"Thanks." It felt weird to thank him for caring, but she was at a loss.

"I think you know me well enough to understand my tastes. I'd like to stick with the original feel of the house, but updated."

Did she know him well enough? "I'll need to come back with my camera." Which she hadn't bought yet.

"What kind of down payment do you need?"

She thought of the money he'd given her as a commission. "None. I'll do my proposal and then we'll talk price."

She extended her hand to shake, to close the deal on her first client.

"You're starting your own business. You need capital."

Dropping her hand, she said, "I'm fine. I have most of the money from my commission on this house and I've been working at the bar."

He reached out and pulled her hair loose from the ponytail. Running his fingers through it, he sighed. "Let me help you."

"You're giving me a huge break by hiring me." She tried to ignore the calming gesture of his hands in her hair.

"You shouldn't have to work at the bar."

"I like O'Leary's. I have to do everything I can now. I'm apartment hunting, so every penny counts."

He turned away from her. Frustration tensed his shoulders. "That's what I'm talking about. Trying to do everything on your own."

She laughed, and he faced her again. "I have help. Quinn and Ryan have been great, but it's time for me to take care of myself and do it responsibly." Indy touched his forearm. "Give me until the end of the week and I should have some ideas for the bedrooms."

She walked down the stairs and took her coat from the post where she'd left it at the beginning of the tour. Before leaving, she went to the back of the house to peek once again at the enormous workroom. It looked big enough to house a basketball court. He'd removed at least one wall to create this space.

He hadn't said anything about the room other than to say it was for the kids. Shaking her head, she left the house to go shopping. She'd return tomorrow to take measurements and photos. Her mind catalogued everything this job entailed, and her heart beat faster. How could she handle this huge job —her first—while taking classes? Maybe she should drop one of the classes. But if she didn't take them now, she might never get back to them.

Indy thought of her mother, who always thought she'd go back to school. She hadn't gotten past taking a couple of courses at the community college. Indy already followed in her mother's footsteps more than she liked.

~

THE FOLLOWING DAY, Griffin brushed drywall dust off his hands on his way out of the kitchen. He wanted to check on the progress in the computer lab. Kendra had said he wouldn't be able to bring kids here until they finished the house, but he might be able to convince her otherwise if the workspace, bathroom, and kitchen were done.

He got to the hall and heard it. Over the sound of tools, the laugh shot through his system. *Indy's here.* He turned the corner and saw her smiling up at Kevin, his foreman and project manager. They both held identical cups of coffee.

Jealousy heated his blood. He glared at the carpenters and electricians who slowed their pace with similar cups of coffee and the chance to stare at Indy. When he reached Kevin and Indy, productivity picked up throughout the room.

He touched Indy's arm, leaving a white smudge of dust. "Hey, can I talk to you?"

Kevin took the hint and went to supervise his men.

Indy eyed him up and down, stopping at the toolbelt slung on his hips. "You weren't kidding about working on this house."

"Nope." He turned and left the room, expecting her to follow. She did.

"What's up?"

"You were supposed to call me when you were coming back."

"No, I'm supposed to call you when I have ideas to discuss. I needed to get measurements and photos. I knew I could get in, so I had no need to call you." Her hazel eyes widened, waiting for an explanation of the problem.

"You can't come into a job site to have coffee and flirt. I need to stay on schedule." His muscles tensed.

"I'm not flirting. I brought Kevin a cup of coffee because he answered questions I had about the blueprint. Now, if you'll excuse me, I have pictures to take." She brushed past him to grab a notebook off the table. She looked around the room and called, "Thanks for the help, Kevin."

Griffin wanted to hit something. She had no right to dismiss him. He took a slow breath. With his jaw clenched, he stepped into her path before she could escape up the stairs. "Don't walk away from me when we're talking."

Indy tilted her head and he saw her hazel eyes blaze green. "We weren't talking. You were yelling at me for no reason."

"No reason? I walked into the room to find you joking with my foreman and half of his employees staring at you. Work stops around you."

"How is that my fault? What do you want me to do, put a bag over my head?"

The image made him smile. A bag wouldn't help. They'd stare at her ass or breasts instead. "No." He sighed, knowing his anger was unjustified.

"I don't think doing a pregnant woman leads the list of things men fantasize about."

She had no idea.

"Do me a favor and stay away from the guys."

She bit her lip but couldn't stifle the smile. "There are men working in almost every room. I can't avoid them all, but don't worry. I won't be here often, not until they're almost done."

His nerves jittered. Not around? He'd hired her so he would have a reason to have her around. "I thought you'd start soon."

"I will. After I draw up the proposal and you agree to it. But I can't paint until the construction's done." She turned and went up the stairs.

He was tempted to follow, but she needed to take her pictures and he had a kitchen to finish. Plenty of frustration to work out. The kitchen would be the perfect outlet.

He didn't know what to do about Indy. He'd missed her. Unable to erase her from his system, he brought her back into his life. The problem was, he didn't know what to do next.

They'd split up with no hard feelings. They remained friends, but every touch still sizzled. He knew she felt it too, but she kept pulling away. He couldn't blame her. He offered no commitment and she tried not to have expectations, but she was having a baby.

Now he had to prove he wanted her back. He didn't even know what that meant. All he knew for sure was that he couldn't walk away from Indy Adams.

But he also couldn't marry her and be the kind of husband her father would expect.

Where did that leave them?

More importantly, would it be enough for Indy?

The questions poured through his mind with each sheet of drywall he slung into place. Hours passed and his muscles screamed.

Damn. It's time to get back to the gym and the racquetball court when a few hours of labor make me sore.

Twilight had fallen outside, but that was little indicator of time in the middle of winter. He checked his watch. Almost dinner time. He dropped his toolbelt in the corner of the room.

In the computer lab, Kevin stopped him for a brief update. The wiring would be complete by the end of the week. The small crew would work for another hour or so and head out.

Griffin looked out the front window and saw Indy's car still at the curb. He'd thought she'd left. He climbed the steps two at a time. He checked the master bedroom and the one next to it. No sign of her. "Indy?"

"In here," she answered.

He followed her voice down the hall and found her sitting cross-legged on the floor with her notebook on her lap, sketching furiously. He'd never encountered such an intense expression on her face. He walked closer until he stood above her. "Come on. Let's go have dinner."

"Huh?" She squinted up at him and then over her shoulder out the window. "Damn. What time is it?"

"Almost five." He held out a hand to help her up.

She placed her hand in his and he pulled her to her feet, putting her body within inches of his. "What do you want to eat?" he asked quietly. He only had a taste for her.

Her gaze landed on his lips and she licked her own. "I have work to do."

"You've worked enough today. I want to take you out." He leaned forward to take her mouth.

She abruptly stepped back, breaking the moment. "You're not dressed for dinner. You're covered in dust."

"I'll go home and change. Then we can order in or go out."

"I don't think that's a good idea."

He stepped forward again, closing the gap. "Why not?"

She moved and bumped into the window, losing her balance and dropping her notebook. He caught her arm and steadied her. Indy was nervous. The thought brought a smile. He'd seen the woman bring a crowded bar to its feet to cheer for her and handle a business lunch with finesse. Being close to him, however, made her breathe heavy.

Indy jerked out of his grasp. "This isn't a good idea."

He answered with raised eyebrows.

"We're in a good spot. We're friends. I'm working for you, which is something I appreciate. Let's not ruin this." She stared into his eyes. Her face showed determination, but her eyes said something different and he couldn't quite read them.

"It's dinner. You have to eat. I have to eat. Let's do it together." He stepped forward again but stopped the odd dance when her hands fisted.

"It's not just dinner. There's too much stuff between us."

"I know. I want to get into that stuff."

Her shoulders straightened. "I don't. I can't. I have about four million things going on right now. School, a new career, my first big job, moving to a new apartment. And I'm pregnant."

Like he could forget. That was the sticking point.

"I get it. I'm asking you to dinner."

"No, you're not." She shook her head to emphasize her response.

"Fine. You caught me. I planned to talk to you at dinner or after, but if it's got to be now . . ." He rolled his shoulders and stepped back to put more distance between them. He needed to be able to think clearly. "I'm sorry I hurt you when I left. You said we were over."

"You don't have anything to apologize for. We had a casual fling and it ended. You were my rebound guy."

Her rebound guy? "It might've started out as a casual thing, but we both know it didn't stay that way. We had something more. We still do."

"You're wrong, Griffin. We're still attracted to each other. Great sex has that effect on people. That's all it is."

His anger returned. "We have more than sex. I know you feel it too."

"Stop it. We had phenomenal sex. We barely even know each other. At least, I barely know you. How close can two people be if they don't know each other?" She turned and headed for the door. "There are no more flings for me. I have something more important to think about than having a good time."

So that was it. He couldn't offer her enough. His gut screamed at him to go after her, but he froze in place. At his feet, her notebook of sketches stared up at him. He'd have another chance.

Tears welled in Indy's eyes. She tore down the stairs and grabbed her coat. She didn't even get her arms into it before she flung open the door. Wind stung her eyes while she fumbled with her jacket. She needed to get away from here, this house, Griffin. Her teeth chattered as she started her car.

She did the right thing. Making a life for herself and her child had to be her priority. It was the responsible thing.

Being responsible sucks.

The man in that house wanted her. Shit, he cared about her even though she was pregnant, and she'd pushed him away. He wanted to be with her, wanted to explore what they had. What did running away say about her?

Nothing is wrong with me. I can't have another fling. I deserve more and so does the baby. More? More what?

She'd never thought about anything but having a good time. Living in the moment used to work, but now she had a future, someone who counted on her for the long haul.

Her palms got sweaty and her breaths shallow. Having a baby was a forever kind of thing. She laid her forehead on the steering wheel and slowed her breathing to normal. The heat finally rattled on and she turned the blowers to face her. She looked up and saw Griffin's silhouette in the bedroom upstairs. Throwing the car into gear, she pulled away.

She'd felt this trapped months ago when he'd hired her to find the house in the first place. He'd done it again, but this time was so much worse. Then, she'd dismissed him as a rich playboy. Now she knew he had more depth. She'd spoken the truth, though. She knew little about Griffin Walker. A good man, a kind man, a great lover, but she knew next to nothing about his life.

She wanted more than a feel-good, shallow relationship. Her baby needed more. They both needed depth and longevity. Indy knew next to nothing about those too.

Quinn could help. No, Kate would be the better choice. Kate would lay it on her. She'd tell Indy if she was screwing up more than usual, so she drove straight to Kate's house.

She grabbed her purse and held her coat closed against the wind. She rang the bell and stomped her feet against the cold. Kate answered, wiping her hands on a dishtowel.

"Hi. What are you doing here?" she asked, swinging the screen door open.

Indy mumbled a greeting, unsure where to start.

After getting the kids settled in front of the TV, Kate returned to the kitchen. "So what's up?"

"I need help. My life is a mess and I have no idea what I'm doing. I can't even think straight."

Standing at the stove, Kate loaded a plate with meatloaf and mashed potatoes. She placed it in front of Indy. "Not being able to think straight is a pregnant thing. As for the rest, I don't know how I can help."

"Tell me what to do." Indy sank her fork into the slab of meat and ate. "Mmm. This is good. I don't remember the last time I ate homemade meatloaf."

"Thanks." Kate poured a cup of coffee and sat across from Indy. "Tell you what to do about . . . ?"

"Griffin."

"Quinn told me he was back. About time. So what's up with him?"

The meatloaf turned to stone in her stomach. "He hired me to decorate his new house."

"Congratulations." Kate's sigh detracted from the verbal pat on the back.

"He asked me to dinner tonight."

"I'm guessing you declined since you devoured my meatloaf."

"Yeah. I told him it wouldn't be a good idea. That I was done having flings because the baby and I need more."

Kate said, "Okay."

"But I'm a mess. Every time he gets close, I lose control of my body. I barely escaped throwing myself at him."

Kate laughed and shook her head.

"This isn't funny."

"It's hormones. You've had a sexual relationship with him and your body recognizes him. Your hormones are in overdrive."

They'd shared more than lust. Every time she looked into his eyes, she felt it in her heart. She'd convinced herself she was over him, but the lie wouldn't take hold.

"Oh, God. You fell for him. Do you love him?"

Indy dropped her head into her hands. "I don't know. I ache whenever I think about him. But like I told him tonight, I hardly know him. My life is so fucked."

"Does he feel the same?"

Indy shrugged, afraid to consider it. "At the wedding, I would've said yes. We had so much there, at least the beginning of something, but then I broke up with him. And he left. Gone for three months."

"He never called?"

"All the time."

"Did you talk to him?"

Indy shook her head. "He was my rebound guy. He was supposed to be meaningless."

Kate chuckled, and Indy raised her head. "Again, not funny."

"Sure it is. Mark was my rebound guy ten years ago."

Indy laughed. She laughed so hard, tears streamed down her cheeks. Ten years with a rebound guy? Indy couldn't believe she'd forgotten. She blotted her eyes against a napkin. "Thanks. I needed to laugh."

"You need to be honest with him."

"I know," Indy whispered. "I'm scared."

"Of what?"

"Everything. That he might want to pick up where we left off. That he might want to be part of my life."

Kate stood and refilled her coffee. "It's not a bad thing."

"It is if I screw it up like I always do. Then I'm left with a broken heart and a baby all alone."

"You sound like a woman in love." Kate cleared Indy's dish and loaded the dishwasher in silence.

It was unlike Kate. She usually filled the silence with something, even talk about the kids. "Something wrong?"

"No, not really."

"You're full of shit." Indy stood and leaned against the counter. "How are things with Mark?"

Kate closed her eyes and leaned heavily against the sink. "I think I'm done rebounding."

"Oh, shit." Indy pulled Kate into a hug. Things had been rough for Kate for months, but she'd never hinted at being ready to give up. "What did he do?"

Kate pulled away and blinked rapidly. "I'm not ready to talk."

Indy held her hand. "Doesn't seem fair. I unloaded a mess on you. You should do the same."

"I need to get the kids ready for bed." She stepped back.

"I'll wait."

Kate shook her head. "Mark will be home soon, and I'm not ready to get into it."

"Sure?" Indy's heart felt heavy. She wished she could be half the friend Kate had been over the years.

"I'll call when I'm ready."

"I'll be here." She hugged Kate tightly.

Kate whispered in her ear, "Talk to Griffin."

Indy left and drove aimlessly before heading home. Talk to Griffin. Crappy advice. Talk to him how? Tell him what? *I know we agreed to no expectations, but I fell in love with you. I know you left, but now you're back so it's all okay.*

It was all bullshit.

None of it was okay.

Maybe she could wait until she finished decorating. She should be done within two months. He'd said his deadline was spring. She could work on his house and see how things progressed. Maybe they would lose steam. Maybe he'd find someone else.

Someone who wasn't pregnant.

They'd have two months to get reacquainted. Not sexually.

Definitely no sex.

No matter how good it would be. She sighed as lustful images stormed her brain. Griffin looked hot in a toolbelt. She imagined his muscles flexing while using tools. Then those same muscles flexing over her naked body.

She rolled down her window and let the cold winter wind chill her fevered skin.

Definitely no sex.

Fantasies made her incapable of coherent thought. The real thing would render her useless.

She pulled into Quinn's driveway and gathered her things. Her notebook was missing. She couldn't find it in her bag or on the floor. Damn. The book had hours' worth of research and ideas in it.

She walked up the front steps, surprised no lights shone through the front windows. A note fluttered on the door. "We went out to dinner. Don't wait up. Q." The thought of having the house to herself without interruption increased Indy's energy. She hadn't had much alone time over the past couple of months.

While her computer booted up, she turned on the radio. Being alone allowed her to crank the volume to vibration level. She hoped the neighbors wouldn't notice. It'd be just her luck to have the cops show up.

She pulled up the research on Queen Anne houses she'd saved on her computer. After rereading, she knew she was wasting her time. She needed to do, not plan, and she worked best when she went with her gut. Flipping open her color deck, she imagined herself in Griffin's bedroom.

Bad idea.

With thoughts of the shape and feel of the second bedroom, she went to work.

HER CAR SAT in the driveway, but Indy didn't answer her phone. Griffin cut the ignition and stepped out into the cold with his peace offering. He'd get Indy to listen to him no matter what, but a bribe of chocolate couldn't hurt.

He heard the music before he reached the front stairs. Déjà vu. He climbed the steps and saw no sign of her through the front windows. Knowing he wouldn't get an answer, he knocked. The tip of his nose numbed in the cold before he walked around the house. At the back door he stopped.

On the other side of the glass, Indy bobbed and wiggled, dancing to the beat he could feel outside. The intensity of her concentration fascinated him. She studied sheets of paper spread on the table and across the counter.

He knocked with a fist, and she jumped.

Eyes wide, she turned to face him. Irritation replaced the surprise. She held up a hand and walked away.

The abrupt silence cut through the air, and Indy returned to the door. She opened it wide but hesitated. "Quinn and Ryan are out."

"I came to see you."

"Oh." She stepped back.

The smell of Indy's perfume did more to defrost his frozen extremities than the warmth of the house. He reached into the bag and extracted her notebook.

She reached for it, relief taking the tension from her shoulders. "Thank you. I thought I lost this."

"You dropped it at the house. You left in a hurry."

Her eyes shifted and her cheeks grew pink. He enjoyed her nervousness. "I'm here with a peace offering. I'm sorry I spooked you."

"You didn't spook me. What's in the bag?" She shifted farther away, but her tone was playful.

"Chocolate. The biggest brownie I could find."

Her lips eased into a smile. He loved those lips.

"Walnuts?"

He slid the small bakery box from the bag. "No. I thought you preferred your chocolate unadulterated."

Her voice became husky. "I do."

The admission slipped from her incredible mouth like an invitation, and his dick became half hard. His face must've revealed his lust because she took another step back.

"I've never known you to be skittish."

"I'm not skittish. I'm making tea to go with the brownie."

As she turned toward the stove, he stalked her, brownie in hand. He reached his arm around her to place the box on the counter. The motion put his body mere inches from her back. The sexual tension crackled. Only one thing would douse it, and he didn't think she'd get naked.

Although he enjoyed the sexual charge, he stepped away and moved to the other side of the kitchen. He'd be able to think clearly if he kept his distance.

With the kettle on the burner, she turned to face him.

He'd lay it out quickly. "I'm sorry I left."

"What do you mean?"

"I have a confession to make." He paced the kitchen and the adjoining dining area. He'd go insane if he had to live in such a small space. There was nowhere to move.

"Is this tabloid worthy?" she joked.

"No, sorry, you won't get rich off this one."

She snapped her fingers. "Too bad. I planned to use my profit to buy a villa on a tropical island."

If he thought it would make her happy, he'd buy it for her. "Remember when I showed up at the hospital?"

"Yeah."

"I overheard you and your dad talking. At first I waited outside the door, listening to you yell at him. I was proud of you for tossing some of his own shit back at him. But then he started talking about your mom."

Indy's face dropped. She moved silently to a stool and sat.

He fought the urge to hold her. "I realized you were in the same situation your mother had been in."

"You figured I was part of some twisted family cycle—"

"No." He grabbed her hand. "No. I heard your dad say he married your mom because of the baby."

Indy's gaze met his.

"It scared me to think you'd want the same."

She yanked her hand back. Golden eyes blazed. "When have I ever mentioned marriage? Now we're back to me being a tramp who would try to trap you for your money."

Frustration clawed at him. "Would you shut up and listen?" His sharp tone caused her jaw to snap shut. He softened his voice. "Please let me finish."

She said nothing but raised her eyebrows for him to continue.

"I thought you might want to get married, and that's the one thing I can't give you. You made it easy for me to walk away rather than risk disappointing you."

"You didn't even bother to ask what I wanted."

The muscle in his jaw twitched, and she held her hands up in surrender. He continued, "You shoved my key in my hand. That said a lot."

He reached for her hand and stroked his thumb across her knuckles. "I'm asking you for another chance. I haven't been able to get you out of my head since I left."

She quietly slid her hand from is grasp. "I appreciate this."

"But?"

The kettle whistled, and Griffin turned and filled her mug before Indy could move. She accepted the steaming cup.

"Everything I said earlier stands. My life is a huge, stinking mess. I can't add anything else to my life right now."

Griffin broke the string on the bakery box and lifted the brownie. He set it in front of her, still wrapped in wax paper. "I don't want to add anything. I'm suggesting we take the time to get to know each other and explore what we have."

Indy stood and gathered the pages she'd spread across the kitchen. She stacked them neatly beside her laptop. Her silence was excruciating. He stuffed his hands in his pockets to prevent himself from shaking her.

"No sex," she finally said. "It'll muddy everything."

No sex? He'd never been with any woman without sex. For how long?

She chuckled. "Now who's spooked?"

He leveled his eyes on hers. "Not spooked. Thinking. How about kissing? Touching?"

"I don't think so. It all leads to sex." She fidgeted with everything within reach.

"Any other demands?"

"No demands at all. This is all new territory for me. I do have a question. You said you couldn't marry me. Why?"

"You want to get married?"

"I didn't say that. You're dodging the question. You didn't say you didn't want to get married, you said you couldn't."

Damn. She would pick up on that. His muscles tensed and he sought the words to explain. The wrong tactic would shut him out again. He paced. "The simple answer is my father. He married my mother but constantly cheated. I don't want to make promises I can't keep."

"That's bullshit. Cheating is a choice."

Griffin shrugged. "I think he loved my mom. She believed he did, so she kept taking him back."

"What does that have to do with you getting married?"

He knew his fear was irrational. He'd never tried to explain it to anyone before. "I've got a lot of him in me. I swore to myself that I would never do what he did. I'd ruin a marriage."

"How do you know if you've never tried?"

"Marriage isn't something you try on for size." He believed marriage was a lifelong commitment. Maybe he had more of his mother in him than he thought.

Indy closed in, and he smelled her perfume, enticing and inviting. She stroked his cheek. "You're already a better man than him."

"Thanks." He didn't buy it, but he felt better hearing it.

"Come and share this brownie with me."

The thought of her moaning and licking chocolate off her lips made his blood race again. "No, thanks. I'm going home. See you tomorrow?"

She pointed to the papers. "Yeah. I should have this put in some semblance of order." She flipped through the corners of the pages. "I need to find an apartment soon. Quinn is going to get tired of me taking over her kitchen for work."

"When do you plan to move?"

"Whenever I find something I like and can afford. My search has slowed because I'm busy with school and work."

"Let me know if I can help." He already had ideas. She wouldn't ask for help, but she'd probably take it if it stared her in the face.

He thought of the kids in his program. None of them asked for help either, but when he offered a way out, they grabbed on.

Indy walked him to the door. Knowing he was pushing his luck, he pressed a quick kiss to her lips. "This might kill me. You know that, right?"

"No man has ever died from lack of sex. Besides, I said *I* wouldn't have sex with you. I'm sure someone else can help."

He growled out of frustration as much as need. She didn't get it. He pulled her close again, letting her feel his need, his desire. "No one else can help me."

Exiting the house, he inhaled the below-freezing air. It worked better than a cold shower. He couldn't marry Indy, he couldn't take the chance on screwing it up, but she'd be a definite part of his life.

He knew he wasn't his father any more than Indy was her mother. But they were the products of the parenting they received. No one could escape it.

If Indy wanted to know him, she'd have to see all of him.

That meant meeting the kids and understanding the vision he had for the foundation.

It scared the shit out of him.

He'd never shared the foundation on a personal level with anyone. He cared what Indy thought. Her opinion mattered.

She mattered.

She'd be spending so much time at his house that she'd have to get used to the idea of the kids being there.

The kids would have to get used to her too.

What if they didn't like her?

He shook his head. What's not to like? Indy was bright, beautiful, and funny. And pregnant. Unmarried and pregnant.

He'd bring the kids to her.

INDY PRIED OPEN the lid on the paint for Griffin's bedroom. She'd chosen a shade deeper than maroon, with a tinge of brown. She smeared a patch onto the wall to check it. She'd hired a couple of college kids to help with the painting, but today she worked alone in order to stay on schedule. The doctor said to limit her exposure to the paint; so as long as the windows were open and she wore the respirator, she and the baby would be okay.

While she worked, she thought about Griffin. She didn't know what to make of him. He'd wanted to go out to dinner to talk about decorating, but he'd spent all of five minutes looking at the proposal for each room before signing. Then he'd spent the rest of the time talking about his charitable foundation.

His excitement shone with every word. The charity was obviously the most important thing in his life. It explained a lot.

Now she understood why he'd been upset over the bad publicity for *Night Beasts*. It also explained why he couldn't marry her.

Her pregnancy could easily become a scandal. Especially given his past. He hadn't said it, but she knew.

She'd enjoyed learning more about him, and he'd been downright explosive with information over the last two weeks, but they couldn't continue to go out. He appeared in the paper too often, and their relationship would quickly be misconstrued.

She stepped back and admired the paint job. The warm color accentuated the dark wood, creating a romantic atmosphere. *Stop thinking like that.* The reminder did nothing to lift her mood.

Griffin insisted she come to the house today, yet he wasn't here. She removed the mask she wore and gathered her brushes and roller to clean. She wanted to spend some time in the workroom and computer lab. It remained the only room for which she hadn't created a proposal because he hadn't told her what he wanted.

After wrapping the brushes and roller in plastic until she could find a spot to clean them, she wandered downstairs. The silence startled her. The construction noise had become so much a part of her experience that the quiet felt weird. Carpenters had been finishing trim when she arrived, but they were gone. A peek out the window confirmed it. Not a truck in sight.

She sighed and went to the computer lab. Griffin hadn't indicated what the layout would be, but the outlets dictated the workstations. He'd said he'd been working with a small group of teens and wanted to grow the program. The room was huge. How many kids did he plan to have here?

Loud noise outside pulled her attention. Before she could move to explore, the door flung open and Griffin came in followed by a group of teens. When their eyes met, his face lit up with a smile, creased dimple and all. She loved that smile.

"Good, you're here." He moved toward her. Kids poured past them and began commenting on the size of the house.

"Yeah, but I'm the only one. The rest of the guys took off," she said over the din of the kids.

"I know. I told them to wrap up early today because I wanted the kids to see the house."

"Oh." She looked away. "I'll get out of your way."

"No." He grabbed her hand. "I want you to meet them."

Meet them? The kids in his program? Probably not a good idea. No one jumped to conclusions quicker than teenagers.

When she tried to pull away, his fingers tightened on hers. "They don't bite." Still holding her, he turned and called, "Okay. Everyone in here, then we'll do the official tour."

Kids came from upstairs, around corners, and down the hall. She counted twelve.

"What's up, Mr. Griffin? This really your house?"

"Yes."

"Then why isn't your furniture and stuff here?"

"The house was run-down when I bought it. It needed a lot of work, but I'll be moving in soon. This is the room you guys need to see." He hitched a thumb over his shoulder, and they all filed into the empty lab.

Their comments echoed in the huge space. "It's big."

"There's nothing here either."

"What's it supposed to be?"

Griffin released her hand and moved to the center of the room. "This is our computer lab. Behind you will be individual workstations, extending around this side." He backed up and swung his arm to the other side of the room. "Over there will be the repair center. I've already got five companies donating broken computers for you to fix."

They all stood in awe. Griffin continued to rattle on about how he expected them to work, and Indy told herself to pay attention, that she'd probably need the information for decorating, but her focus was riveted on the kids. They looked at Griffin like he was a god. But more.

He wasn't just a suit with deep pockets. They liked him. He connected with them.

She had no idea what they talked about. She tuned out the conversation and watched the interaction. When they stared at her with open curiosity, she snapped to.

"Everyone, this is Indy. She found this house for me and now she's decorating it."

She waved from the doorway.

A tall, thin black guy stepped forward with one eyebrow cocked. "Are you his girlfriend?"

"No," she answered at the same time Griffin said, "Yes."

The conflicting responses elicited snickers from the group.

"Nice to meet you, Indy. I'm Duane." He reached her with his hand extended.

She shook his hand and he held tight, adding, "If you were my woman, there wouldn't be no confusion."

She couldn't help but smile. She looked around him and pulled her hand free. "Giving charm lessons, now?" she asked Griffin.

"Hell, no," Duane said. "I'm teaching him."

Griffin closed in and put his arm around Indy's shoulder. The casual gesture made her knees wobble. She'd been careful to restrict all physical contact between them. Her heart leaped. How could he tell them she was his girlfriend?

"Let's give them a grand tour."

He didn't give her much choice. He pulled her along, prompting her to tell the kids about her plans. At first she thought the details would bore them, but they listened intently.

They wanted to know about the work Griffin had done himself, and they looked for things to criticize. She enjoyed the kids and their enthusiasm. They were rough around the edges and they let enough slip that she could tell they came from hard lives. She totally understood Griffin's dedication to them.

Listening to them talk and joke, inspiration struck, and her fingers itched for a pencil to sketch her ideas for the lab. The computer lab was their space. She wanted it to reflect them.

After the tour, Griffin promised to take them all for pizza. Pizza with rowdy teens? He was definitely a brave man.

"You coming with us, Miss Indy?" a bright-eyed girl asked.

Indy searched for her name. Marisol. "No, I don't think so. I still have some work to do here."

She looked disappointed, but turned to Griffin. "I think she needs to eat, Mr. Griffin. She's kinda skinny."

Indy resisted the urge to rub her protruding belly. Her baggy shirt didn't hide the pregnancy.

"I think you're right, Marisol."

Indy clenched her jaw. Hadn't she decided to limit her exposure with Griffin? He always acted like everyone should bend to his will. "Sorry to disappoint you, Marisol, but I really do have work to do. Then I have homework to finish."

"You're still in school?"

"Yes."

"But you need to eat. We know the best pizza place."

Indy's stomach growled. She'd already skipped her morning snack and lunch was late.

"You guys go get in the van. We'll be right out," Griffin said. He moved against the current of kids to reach her. "I think Marisol likes having another female around. Usually Caitlyn would be here, too, but she's sick. Marisol's feeling outnumbered."

"So am I."

"Have pizza with us and I'll help you with your homework. I have something to show you anyway." He bent and kissed her cheek.

Why that made her feel like a schoolgirl, she didn't know. Her cheek warmed and something fluttered in her chest. "Fine. I'll eat with you, but then I have to do my homework."

He held her coat open for her to slide in. A huge fifteen-passenger van was parked at the curb. The kids had their faces pressed to the windows like expectant puppies. They hooted while Griffin locked up, but attempted to straighten their faces before he got to the van.

If anyone could keep Griffin on his toes, these kids could.

CHAPTER 17

Griffin was glad he'd convinced Indy to join them. When he came into the house with twelve teens, she'd been startled but eased into comfortable conversation with them. Over pizza they joked and had a good time. She seemed to have genuinely enjoyed the time with the kids. He didn't like having her with them while driving the kids home, though. He'd been into these neighborhoods plenty while visiting the kids. Although he'd never had any problems, it didn't mean some wouldn't pop up. Indy didn't seem bothered by where he drove. Instead she watched with open fascination.

Four of the boys all lived in one of the few remaining projects in the city. The buildings were slated for demolition within the next two years. In the meantime, these boys spent their days dodging bullets and flashing gang signs to survive.

Duane was the last to be dropped off. He lived in a modest bungalow with his grandparents. He never mentioned his parents. Griffin suspected they were either dead or in jail.

As he exited the van, Duane paused and tapped Indy on the shoulder. She twisted in her seat.

"Remember what I said about being my girlfriend. I'm all good."

She flashed him a friendly, flirtatious smile. "Thanks, Duane. I'll keep it in mind, but I'm off the market for now."

"Too bad. See you around." He slid the side door open and jumped out. Before closing it, he asked, "When you figure we'll be back in class?"

"A few weeks. Maybe a month. All of the equipment is on order." Griffin knew Duane needed the influences outside his neighborhood. "I'll see if I can find you something to do before then."

"'Kay. Thanks." The door slammed with a boom. Duane's grandmother waved from behind gray curtains.

"You weren't blowing smoke were you?"

"About what?" he asked, pulling away from the house and the miserable neighborhood.

"Finding something for him to do."

"No. He needs something to keep him involved or he'll drop off the map. He's the kind of kid this neighborhood will swallow."

"And spit out."

"No. They'll realize how smart he is and he'll run the shit. Once he gets a taste of that power, I won't get him back." Griffin hit the highway toward his office. Anticipating her question, he added, "I need to drop off the van and get my car."

"I have my old desktop."

"What?"

She twisted slightly so she faced him. "I got my laptop because my desktop kept freezing and stuff. It probably won't take long, but cleaning and upgrading it would be a small project."

He glanced over but couldn't keep his eyes on her. "Thank you. I might take you up on it."

"I think I finally understand Quinn now. For years, she's been teaching at Jones and she loves her job, but she keeps feeling burned out. I understand why she hasn't left." She paused and added, "You know he totally respects you."

"What?"

"Duane. Sure, he was hitting on me, but it was a test. If I had given him any hint that he had a chance, he'd be calling you and telling you to get rid of me."

"What makes you say that?"

"Just a feeling, I guess."

"Loyalty means a lot to them." He briefly wondered how many people were loyal to her besides Quinn and Kate. Griffin parked the van and pointed her toward his car. "I know you said you have homework to do, but I have something important to show you."

"What is it?"

His muscles tensed in his shoulders. He hated not being able to tell how she would react. "It's a surprise."

Her smile was broad and bright. "You know I love a good surprise. If it's a bad one, I'd rather skip it."

"This one's definitely good." He rounded the corner in front of his condo.

"I've seen your condo," Indy said. "That's not a surprise."

"The surprise is inside." He parked and led her upstairs. Her smile faded and her pace slowed. Fear struck him. What if she didn't like it? He opened the condo and flipped on the lights. "Come on. I told you it's a good surprise."

He pulled her toward the spare room that he'd used for storage until a week ago. Seeing her try to run her new business and complete her schoolwork at Quinn's kitchen table spurred him into action. He wanted Indy to use the wasted space. He turned on the light in the new office and waited for her reaction.

She entered the room and shrugged. "Nice room. I don't think I ever took a tour before."

He sighed and shook his head. Forgetting to explain himself was becoming a habit with her. "Welcome to your new office."

Indy spun quickly to face him. "My what?"

"Your new office. You can't continue to try to run a business and do homework at a cramped kitchen table."

"I won't. I'm looking for a new apartment, which will have at least two bedrooms, one of which will be my office."

"Don't you mean three bedrooms? Or is the baby going to share space with your office?"

"I don't know. Maybe the baby will share my bedroom. Maybe I'll have three bedrooms. I don't know, seeing as how I haven't found the place yet." Her voice rose in anger as she rattled on. "The point is, I'm not one of your charity cases. I don't need you to create an office in your home for me."

The muscles around his eyes twitched and he took an audible breath. "I don't think of you as charity. I'm trying to help you."

"I didn't ask for help!" She flung the words at him and collapsed into the recliner. She rubbed her stomach in small circles.

He rushed to her, not knowing what to do. "Are you okay? Do you need a doctor?"

Her breath was heavy, but she shook her head. After a moment, she sat back. "I told you he doesn't like it when I get upset." She continued the rhythmic circles on her stomach.

Griffin knelt beside her. "I didn't mean to upset you. I don't use this room. I thought you'd like to have a real office. You're juggling a lot right now. This would take one thing off your shoulders."

"I'm not your burden to carry. I can do this on my own."

He touched his palm to her cheek. "I don't doubt you can. But you don't have to."

She pushed to her feet and away from him. "We can't do this."

"Do what?"

"Any of it. First you hire me to decorate your new house, then you're telling your kids I'm your girlfriend, which I'm not, and now you want me to practically move in here supposedly so I have a place to work." She walked toward the window.

She saw right through him. He did want her here. Her resistance made no sense. The sparks were still there between them. He was trying to nudge them along. "You're right on most of that. I hired you to help you out, sure, but I had my own motives. You're good and I trust you. That's why I hired you. I turned this room into an office for you so I could have a chance to spend more time with you. You keep pulling away from me and it's making me crazy. As far as introducing you to the kids, I had to tell them something. Calling you my girlfriend is something they can relate to."

"We're not dating. I'm not your girlfriend. It's wrong to mislead them."

"I wasn't misleading them. I have every intention of keeping you in my life."

Her shoulders sagged and she turned slightly but didn't face him. Her voice, barely above a whisper, croaked, "Don't do this. Not again."

"I can't help it. I want you. You broke up with me. I thought you needed space."

"Three months is a shitload of space."

"I came back."

She shrugged and turned. "I know. Like you said, I'm juggling a lot right now. I appreciate the effort, but you have to stop trying to run my life. We can work together. I'd love to be friends with you, but that's where it has to end."

"Why?"

Her eyes shone with determination. "Because my priorities have shifted. In truth, for the first time in my life I have priorities beyond having a good time. I need to put my energy there."

He plunged his hands into his pockets to stop himself from reaching out and touching her. She'd never looked as sexy as she did right now, turning him away. Again. Any doubts he might've had about what kind of mother she'd be dissolved. He saw the struggle going on behind her eyes, but her determination won. "Okay."

She flinched. "That's it?"

He had no intention of backing down and walking away, but if he admitted it, she'd leave and cut him out altogether. "You don't need any more pressure right now. I get it."

She looked deflated, like she'd expected more of a fight. Damn, he couldn't win with this woman.

"Thank you. Can you take me back to my car now?"

"No. I'm not done negotiating."

Her eyes narrowed. "Negotiating?"

"I'll leave you alone—for now—if you'll use this for your office." He removed his hands from his pockets, now having the upper hand, and closed the distance between them.

"I didn't say anything could be negotiated. Other than the decorating proposals, we have no contract."

"That's where you're wrong. We have a connection. Deeper than attraction or lust. You want me to back off, you have to give me something in return." He reached out and pulled her hair free from the rubberband. He liked it flowing over her shoulders, but he stopped short of running his fingers through it.

To her credit she didn't shy away from his touch.

She tilted her head and looked straight into his eyes. "I'll use this office until I find an apartment. I'll also give you a ten percent discount on the decorating to cover expenses. Finally, there is no 'for now.' Move on with your life and the next woman in your bed." She held out her hand to seal the deal.

"There hasn't been anyone else in my bed."

"I didn't ask."

No, she hadn't, but he wanted her to know. "I don't want anyone else." He noted that she hadn't offered up information about herself during his absence. Could she have moved on to another man?

She didn't respond to his admission, but her hand wavered slightly.

He took her hand, fighting the burn in his gut. "You have a reprieve."

He'd let her settle in comfortably as a business partner, friend, or whatever label she added. Then he'd go in for the kill, so to speak. He'd become so irresistible she wouldn't be able to walk away.

THREE WEEKS HAD PASSED since they'd made their agreement. Indy had moved into the office immediately. It was a mega-cool office, one she'd never be able to afford on her own. She spent more time there than anywhere else.

Somehow she felt like she'd lost a battle with Griffin. He treated everything like a business deal. He held her heart but acted like they were hammering out points of a contract. She'd failed at protecting herself.

She wished she had Kate's intelligence. Kate would've used her lawyer skills to make sure Griffin hadn't taken advantage of the situation. He found every loophole.

She'd agreed to take the office because she truly believed their paths wouldn't cross more than usual. After all, he had a company to run, a charity to organize, and a house to renovate. But he showed up every day, usually for lunch. He brought her food and they'd share a meal in her office.

The house was almost finished. After he found her painting the master bedroom, he hired an army of painters, citing the negative effects on her and the baby for inhaling fumes. She tried to discount the decorating, but he said he'd hired her to plan, not paint.

The man was so damn frustrating. His most disturbing action was trying to communicate with the baby. At first, he'd asked if he could feel the baby kick. The baby, of course, refused to cooperate. No matter how much the baby kicked, elbowed, and somersaulted, as soon as Griffin's voice coasted through the room or his hand palmed her belly, the baby stilled.

Griffin had made it his mission to get a reaction. Daily he would rub, pat, or poke at the baby, waiting for a response. Every day she willed the baby to move, give Griffin something so he could claim victory and move away from the intimate interaction. She loved the feel of his hands on her body but knew it was a mistake.

His caring and kindness would be her downfall. She loved him, and no matter how she tried to ignore it, her heart swelled more with each moment they shared.

Indy wandered around her office, studied the boards of design ideas, fingered swatches of fabric. Time was up. Time to move on and out. Time to uphold her end of the agreement. She removed the boards and packed up the books and files in the desk.

Always be prepared for a hasty retreat.

She changed into her O'Leary's shirt so she'd be ready for work. The third trimester of pregnancy had brought easy exhaustion with it. She relaxed in the recliner for a nap, knowing it would be the last one in her fine office.

~

SILENCE MET Griffin when he entered the condo. No music blared from Indy's office.

He'd become accustomed to the noise while she worked. And he enjoyed startling her over the sound of the music and her intense concentration. He moved silently through the condo, not wanting to disturb her. Only a small lamp lit the office, and the afternoon sun streaked through the windows. The room was different.

He scanned the space. Her work boards were gone. No chaos cluttered the desktop. She couldn't have found an apartment yet. If she broke their agreement, he wouldn't have to honor his end any longer. He'd been dying to kiss her for weeks, but he'd promised to back off. He'd been regretting the move ever since.

But she was gone. The familiar burn in his gut had him pacing. Every time he made some headway with her, she took off. He pulled out his phone but paused in front of the door. On the mirror in the hall he saw the pink sticky note.

At the house checking on final touches. Indy

He needed to handle this face-to-face. He had too much invested for her to think she would sneak out again. He sped all the way to Oak Park. Her car still sat at the curb. No one else was around.

He swung the front door open and froze. Indy sat curled up on the bottom step. "Indy?"

She looked up from under wet lashes. "It's the baby," she whispered. "Something's wrong."

"I'll call an ambulance."

Relief washed over her face and he watched her rebuild

her confidence. "No. Can you drive me to the hospital? I already called my doctor. I was taking a break before going to my car."

"You were going to drive yourself?"

"Do you see anyone else around?" She stood, and he saw that she wore her O'Leary's shirt. She was going to the bar again.

He hooked his arm around her waist.

She pushed at him. "I can walk. I'm just a little queasy."

He held her coat open to wrap around her. "I came from the condo. Why is all of your stuff gone?"

She pulled her hair from under her coat collar. "The job is over. Your house is ready. I honored our agreement."

"Fuck that. We're well past an agreement." He held her elbow and navigated their way to his car. "Every time I get close, you run away."

She snorted. "I obviously didn't run too far. You found me at your house."

"You know what I mean. For as long as we've been together, you've been running away."

"I have not." She buckled up and settled her hands on her stomach.

He noticed how pale she looked. "You have. The first night we slept together, you snuck out of the condo. You dodged me all night at Ryan's wedding. You ran all the way to Hooperville. Now things are clicking between us, and you're doing it again."

She closed her eyes and rested her head against the window as he hit the highway. "There can't be an us. I'm pregnant with another man's baby. You're trying to build some crazy empire. We don't belong together. I'll ruin everything you're doing."

"No, you won't." He reached across the seat and held her hand.

~

SHE'D NEVER BEEN MORE afraid in her life. Not when she'd moved to Chicago alone. Not when her mom died. Not even when she first found out she was pregnant.

What if she lost the baby?

Her mother had miscarried. She had miscarried. What if she couldn't carry a baby?

Her chest tightened, and she forced a hard breath into her lungs. Griffin had practically carried her into the emergency room. Now a nurse buzzed around attaching leads and monitors to her. She couldn't talk. Griffin didn't try to make conversation.

He'd asked if he should call Quinn. Indy didn't want to worry her. She'd just gotten off bed rest herself. No, she'd do this alone. She'd call Kate later, after she knew something.

Griffin continued to pace the room.

"You can go now. I'll be fine."

He spun and looked at her like she'd grown a second head. He raised an eyebrow and with a slight shake of his head continued his circuit of pacing.

Moments later, Dr. Rollins strode in. She glanced at Griffin, who said, "I'm going to get a cup of coffee."

Once the door closed, she patted Indy's leg. "How are you?"

"Scared," she croaked. Why couldn't she at least sound strong?

"The baby's okay. A little distressed, but the ultrasound shows he's okay."

"Why was I bleeding?"

"We're not sure yet. It's stopped, which is good. I'm putting you on bed rest. You need to stay off your feet and take it easy for a while."

Indy swallowed hard. How was she going to do that? She

didn't even have an apartment of her own. She imagined her savings dwindling to nothing before she even got to the delivery room. She said nothing, but nodded.

~

GRIFFIN COULDN'T MAKE Indy accept his help, but she and her baby were entitled to Richard's money. Besides, Richard had a right to know there was a problem. Griffin knew better than to interfere, but he couldn't let this go. Pushing his own ego aside, he had to trust Indy wouldn't want to go back to Richard. Long ago, he'd researched Richard Burke to understand his competition.

Now seemed like the perfect time to pay him a visit.

Griffin strolled into the offices of Burke and Hester, financial consultants. The young secretary gave him a quick once-over and said, "Hi, may I help you?"

"I'm here to see Mr. Burke."

"Do you have an appointment?" she asked, opening a planner.

"No. I've been out of town. I'm sure if he's not with another client, he'll make time to see me. I'm Griffin Walker of Walker Industries.

If the name meant anything to her, she didn't let it show. She quickly walked to the office on the right and went inside, closing the door softly behind her. Griffin waited, knowing it would only take minutes.

The door reopened and the secretary emerged, pink cheeks revealing her boss had been unhappy with her.

"Mr. Burke will see you now. Can I get you coffee or water?" She stood stiffly, waiting for a response.

"No, thank you. I won't be long." He followed her to the office.

The office exceeded his expectations. Walnut bookcases

lined the walls, an oval conference table sat in the corner, and a private bathroom was off to the side. Burke was an adequate advisor, made decent money for his investors, but he tried to appear big league.

Griffin didn't know what he expected when he laid eyes on Burke. He'd seen his photo, known he was older, but knowing didn't prepare him for the shock. He looked older than Malcolm.

Burke stood behind his desk. "Mr. Walker, it's nice to meet you. What can I help you with today?"

Griffin moved to stand in front of the desk. "I thought you should know that Indy's in the hospital."

Burke's mouth pressed into a firm line.

"You do know Indy Adams, right?"

"Yes."

"She's had some complications with the baby."

"Excuse me for asking, but why should I care?"

Griffin sneered. "I thought that being the father, you had a right to know. That maybe you'd man up and help her."

He snickered. "I'm not the father."

The silence in the room weighed heavily. Air locked in Griffin's chest. He didn't know what to say.

Another snicker and Griffin flinched, wanting to launch himself at the man. Instead every muscle in his body tightened and froze.

"She showed me the ultrasound with a date of conception after she left me. The baby belongs to whomever she moved on to. Judging from the look on your face, that would be you."

Griffin turned stiffly and left the room. He rushed outside to get air into his lungs. The baby was his? She'd said she hadn't slept with anyone else besides Burke.

Why wouldn't she have told me?

He went back to the hospital, determined to confront her.

Anger boiled in his chest and betrayal hung on his back. He'd never trusted a woman as much as he'd trusted her, and she'd lied. The nasty little voice in his head nagged, "Just like Selena."

Back at the hospital, he caught the doctor at the nurse's station. "Excuse me, Doctor, do you have an update on Indy Adams?"

The woman turned to him. "And you are?"

"The baby's father." The words bubbled like acid through his throat.

"She'll be released tomorrow. Don't upset her. She needs to stay calm and rest."

"Thank you." Don't upset her? Upset was the least of her worries. He pushed open the door to the room. Indy sat in bed, eyes closed.

She was pale and hooked up to monitors. He remembered seeing his mom in the same spot. Anger began to fade.

Her eyes fluttered open, and she smiled.

It was a punch to his chest. "Hi," he croaked.

"Hi yourself. You didn't have to come back."

When would she stop pushing him away? "Yeah, I did. What did the doctor say?"

"I'm fine. The baby's fine. I have to be on bed rest for a while. Take it easy."

He unclenched his jaw. "Isn't that what I've been saying for weeks?"

"Yeah, yeah. And I'll start listening to you when you have MD after your name."

No, she'd start listening to him now. His muscles tensed and he fought to relax them. She needed to stay calm. For his baby. "I want you to move into my house."

"What?" She bolted up in bed.

He gently pushed her back. "Take it easy, remember? You don't have anywhere else to go. What are you going to do, stay with Quinn? She just got back on her feet. You're not going to want to stress her out. You can't move right now. I have a huge house. You'll have time to recuperate."

She hitched her chin up. "I don't need your charity."

"Where are you going to go?"

"Back to Hooperville. Lydia can help me."

"You'll let Lydia help you but not me? She has her hands full with your dad. And no matter how smoothly your last visit with him went, I don't see staying with your dad being stress-free. This isn't charity." He paused, wanting to tell her that he'd do anything for his baby, but that conversation would surely upset her. "Let me help."

Tears streamed down her face. Christ, so much for not upsetting her.

"Don't cry. It's not that bad."

"Yes, it is. For months now, I've been working, trying to be responsible, make it on my own, and here I am, having to lean on someone else." She swiped her palm against her cheek.

"You don't have to do it alone."

"Yes, I do. I'd rather die than let Richard into this baby's life."

The mention of the lie curdled in his stomach. It took all of his restraint to stop himself from lashing out. "Don't you think the father has a right to know what's happening with his baby?"

"In theory, sure. But I don't want him in this baby's life. Or in mine. He manipulated the situation to try to keep me. I can't prove it, but I'm pretty sure he's the reason I lost my job at the real estate agency. He'll try to control everything until he tires of us. My baby deserves better."

Is that what she thought of him? That he'd try to control everything? That he'd manipulate things?

He had. Consistently. She had no reason to think he was

any better than Burke. Only he would never tire of her and their child, and he'd prove it. "I care about you. I want to help."

She sighed and wiped at fresh tears. "I'll move in and pay you rent. We're roommates, nothing more."

"No rent. I don't want your money."

"You said I'm not a charity case."

"We'll talk about it later. When you're back to normal. I'll have your stuff moved in within a day. Get some rest." The need to touch her consumed him, even though anger pulsed through his body. "Roommates, huh?"

Her tongue flicked out and wet her lips. "It's better that way. We've been getting along pretty well as friends, right?"

Friends? He'd thought he'd been romancing her, taking his time, being patient, and she thought they were friends? "Yeah. You're making the right move."

"Let's hope we both don't end up regretting it."

He left the room before he could do something he'd regret. When she was back on her feet, she'd have plenty of explaining to do. In the meantime, he'd have the chance to get to know his child.

CHAPTER 18

Indy sat on the bed, watching as Kate hung clothes in the closet. Kate said, "This is kind of a sudden move."

Indy stared at her friend. "I needed to. I have a month of bed rest and I can't expect Quinn to worry about trying to take care of me. I needed somewhere to go, and Griffin offered. It's temporary, like everything else in my life."

"What do you mean?" Kate pulled a pile of T-shirts from the suitcase and placed them in a drawer.

"My whole life, I've never expected anything to last. Richard was a fling, someone to have fun with, and he went and proposed. Griffin was my rebound guy. I moved home temporarily to figure out my life, I stayed with Quinn to help her, now I'm here until I'm back on my feet. Sometimes I feel like I'm floating." She spread her hand across the fluffy blanket on the new bed Griffin had insisted on buying. She'd planned on moving her bed in, but since this would be a guest room, he thought a king-size bed would be better.

"Are you sure this is temporary?"

"What else can it be? Griffin and I are not forever kind of

people. He said so himself. He's not looking for a family. Certainly not one he didn't plan on."

"I've seen him look at you. You're not a practice run for playing house. He loves you."

She rolled her eyes. No matter what her heart wanted, she couldn't believe it. "Those words have never been spoken. It's a moot point anyway. This is Griffin's home. I need to build one for the baby and me. A real home, not something temporary."

"Where does this one go?"

Indy turned to see Griffin standing in the doorway. She could read nothing on his face to let her know if he'd been listening. She gave herself a mental shake and read the side of the box. "Put it in the corner. I'll deal with it later."

"That's the last of the boxes you wanted from storage. Are you sure you don't need anything else? There are still a lot of boxes left there." He moved to the corner and set the box down.

"I brought what I'll need for the next month. Most of what's left is probably junk. I'll sort through it later and decide what to keep."

Kate touched her arm. Indy had forgotten she was in the room. She looked at Indy and said, "I'm going to go make some coffee. Holler if you need anything."

Griffin continued after Kate left, "You can move that stuff in here. Then you can go through it whenever you have time."

Time always stood still when they were alone. "No, it's fine where it is. I don't need to take up any more space here."

She moved to the dresser and closed the drawer Kate had been working in. Moving in a slow circle, she surveyed the room. "I think I'm done unpacking. Or I should say Kate's done unpacking my stuff. Do you need any help?"

"You should be in bed. You look tired. Why don't you take a nap?"

"I'm fine." If the man started telling her to eat her vegetables, she'd scream. "I have a midterm project to work on for a while. I have to talk to my teacher and see what I can do about class. If I'm out for a full month, there's no way I can pass."

He walked toward her, forcing her back to the bed. "Don't worry about that now. Get some rest."

She swallowed hard, afraid he would kiss her. The air around them remained thick with tension, sexual and emotional. It swelled with words unspoken.

"I'll be down the hall if you need anything."

"I'm good." And she'd continue to be good as long as he wasn't in her bedroom. When she'd packed her suitcases and brought them to the house, she thought she'd have a few days before he moved in. When he made the offer, he still hadn't bought any furniture. Yet today, he moved in. It eerily felt like a happy couple moving into their first home together.

It's not our house. This is Griffin's house.

She moved back to the bay window and peered out. Another delivery truck from a furniture store arrived. Griffin had hustled to get deliveries and probably paid extra to make this happen. She lay back on the bed and opened her notebook of design ideas. Her eyes fluttered closed and she forced them open. She had a lot of work to do, but the softness of the pillow called her.

INDY ROLLED over and realized she had fallen asleep. When the doctor said bed rest, Indy hadn't actually planned on staying in bed. She stretched and admitted the nap had been necessary. Leaving her room, she peered up and down the hall and then snuck down the back stairs leading into the kitchen. This room was empty of people, and she looked for a coffee cup.

She found one in the cabinet and stared at the coffeemaker that had more buttons than a TV remote. Glad Kate had already brewed a pot, she poured her one and only cup for the day and walked out the back door. Spring had broken through: birds chirped in the trees and the sun warmed her skin. A slight chill in the air warned that winter might fight back, but she wanted this small reprieve. A chance to bask in warmth.

Voices carried from the front veranda, and footsteps followed. Indy glanced back at the door and wondered if she could run in without being seen, but Dr. Rollins's words pounded her brain. *Take it easy. Don't push anything.*

Griffin turned the corner of the wraparound porch and caught sight of her. The woman next to him continued to talk, but his smile sucked Indy in like a black hole. His gaze assessed her as if he'd been expecting to see her here.

"Indy, this is Kendra, my publicist. Kendra, Indy."

The short blonde extended a hand. "You're the real estate agent-slash-decorator."

It wasn't a question, so Indy knew Griffin had told this woman about her. Kendra's eyes scanned the length of Indy and stopped on her belly.

Indy set her coffee cup on the ledge of the rail. "Hi. It's nice to meet you."

"Yes." Kendra brought her gaze back to Indy's face. They shook politely, but Kendra's eyes were far from friendly. She looked like she'd just uncovered an ugly secret.

Indy nodded and backed away. She retrieved her cup and headed inside. "Excuse me. I'm going back in. It's a little chilly out here."

Kendra obviously wanted to be alone with Griffin.

Before Indy even made it to the stairs, she heard Kendra's angry whisper. She couldn't make out the words, but the tone was unmistakable. Slipping quietly back to the open door, Indy leaned forward to eavesdrop.

"I've spent months cultivating your image. This matters."

Griffin's low voice rumbled, but Indy couldn't hear and she couldn't get closer without giving herself away.

"I don't care what the reality is, it's all about perception."

Indy turned and tiptoed away. She climbed the stairs feeling like she'd managed to screw up again.

In her room she napped again for a short time, but it didn't break her out of her funk. A brief look out the window told her everyone had left. She opened her door to a quiet house. No moving, scraping, banging, yelling. It was too quiet now.

She turned back to her desk, tucked her earphones into her ears, and blasted her iPod. Music filled her head and soothed her heart. She began to sing along with Melissa Etheridge, letting the rhythm of the music take her away. Ideas began to rush into her brain. She knew how to complete her project for school.

Sitting on the bed, she pulled out her colored pencils, rulers, and her notebook. Music always helped her productivity.

When he hadn't seen Indy for hours, Griffin became worried she'd heard Kendra. Kendra's bottom-line concern was always how he appeared to the public. He'd hired her for that reason, but sometimes she neglected to remember that he was a person, not a company.

He went to search for Indy. Her voice floated from her room. He knocked on the door before pushing it open. Her back faced him. She sang while pinning pieces of cloth to a board, her voice smooth and full of emotion. The songs she chose always said more about how she felt than her words did. She was hurting, but he had no idea why or how to fix it. He'd give anything to see her smile and laugh uncontrollably. She carried a weight on her. She wasn't the same Indy he'd left in front of the hospital months ago.

He'd cared about her then; he loved her now.

The realization stabbed his chest. He needed her in a way he'd never needed anyone, in a way he'd never wanted to need anyone. She turned and clutched her chest.

Tugging the earbud, she yelled, "What the hell are you doing? You scared the shit out me."

"Sorry. I knocked, but you didn't answer." He stood awkwardly for a moment, allowing his mind to catch up with his heart. "I ordered dinner. I thought you'd be hungry."

Her shoulders relaxed, and she tilted her head as if inspecting him. She shook her head once and smiled. "I'm starved."

He led the way down to the kitchen. The emotions rolling through his system battered his senses. Indy always pushed him into new territory. Speaking about his feelings had never been his strong suit.

"Oooh. I love the way this turned out. Great choice for the living room."

She detoured into the living room, and he followed. "You should like it. You picked it all out."

She winked. "I guess I have really good taste then."

Her fingers trailed along the fabric of the couch, and her toes curled into the plush area rug. He envisioned her lying naked in front of the fireplace on that rug.

Turning abruptly he said, "Let's eat."

In the kitchen he flipped open the pizza box. "I have no

idea where the dishes are. I came down earlier and Kate had already unpacked."

"She does that." Indy walked over to the cabinets and opened doors. She found the dishes on her second try. She pulled two down and froze, staring at her collection of cows. "I didn't mark this box to be brought here."

He joined her at the counter, took the plates from her, and set them down. "I know. I saw the box in storage and thought you'd like to have them."

She picked one up and turned to face him with tears in her eyes. Shit. He'd done it again. His hands moved to rest on her hips, and he kissed her forehead. "I thought they would make this feel more like home for you."

"You're making this more complicated than it's supposed to be." She put the cow down and pushed past him.

"Not complicated. This is your home too." How could he tell her without scaring her that he'd envisioned her living in his house every time he walked through the door? *Just tell her.*

She shook her head. "No. It's your home and I'm a long-term visitor. We agreed to be roommates."

Telling her he loved her would make her run. Words didn't mean much to her, so he offered the words he thought she'd accept. "I want this to be your home, Indy. No expectations."

"You always say no expectations, but you don't mean it. You mean *I* shouldn't have any expectations. You have them and you want me to conform to them." She grabbed her plate and walked over to the pizza box.

He had no argument. Right now, he did have expectations: he expected her to admit the baby was his; he expected her to admit she loved him; he expected that by having her move in, they'd pick up where they'd left off; he expected they'd sleep together. Celibacy didn't sit well with him.

"What? No argument?"

He shrugged. "Let me kiss you once and then tell me you still just want to be roommates."

"No." A half smile rose to her lips. "We have chemistry. I don't deny it. But you're like chocolate cake for me—once I get started, I can't refuse, then I spend three days cursing the scale for my stupidity."

Her admission was all he needed to hear. She wanted him. And he'd thought ahead and ordered dessert.

He picked up her plate and tilted his head. "Come on. Let's go relax in the living room in front of a fire."

She stood and smirked. "If you're trying to seduce me, it won't work."

"Trust me, when I'm seducing you, you'll know it."

~

THAT'S WHAT WORRIED HER. Not if, but when. "I have a steel resolve."

And knees of jelly.

She was still being selfish, but she didn't care. They were together, and if she could have another month with him, she'd take it. If he kissed her, though, she would melt and want to have sex with him. He was worse than chocolate cake. And the doctor said no sex for at least a month.

They sat together on the couch in front of the fire, flames licking at the silence and warming the air. Indy devoured her pizza and wondered how long it would take to lose all the weight she'd put on during the pregnancy.

She stretched her legs out until her ankles rested on the table next to her plate. "Aah."

"Sore feet?"

"Swollen ankles."

He wiped his face on a napkin and tossed it on his plate. "Let me see."

She inched her feet away. "No. I look like Shrek. They go down overnight."

He pushed their plates over and sat on the edge of the table. Lifting one heavy ankle, he peeled away her sock. She cringed. It was worse than usual.

"Is this normal?"

"One of the many perks of pregnancy. It's right up there with crazy hormones that make me cry for no reason."

Keeping her left foot in his lap, he reached across to grab a pillow from the couch. He placed the pillow under her right ankle and began massaging her left foot. She wanted to stop him, she really did, but it felt so damn good. She leaned her head back and closed her eyes. A moan formed in her throat, threatening escape, and then he stopped.

"Do you want some tea? I bought a kettle because I didn't think you brought yours."

"Thanks. That would be great." He bought a kettle and was making her tea. Moving in began to feel like a mistake, but one she was enjoying. Her stomach flipped at the thought of sleeping under the same roof with Griffin but not in the same bed.

From the comfort of the couch, she heard the kettle whistle. It dawned on her that she'd never had a man bring her tea before. She didn't get cozy moments like Quinn did. She remembered Quinn telling her about Ryan making her breakfast. Not for a special occasion—just because. How great it must feel to have a man love you like that.

"Here you go."

She opened her eyes to see Griffin holding a cup of tea and a plate with chocolate cake. She straightened on the couch, shifting into the corner, and reached out, not sure which she wanted more. No contest. Cake always won. She took the plate from him, and he placed the tea on the table beside the couch but still within her reach. "You better watch out. I could get used to someone waiting on me."

"Any time. I'm no cake connoisseur, but I have it on good authority that this is the best cake around." He sat on the opposite end of the couch and pulled her feet into his lap.

"Aren't you having any?"

"No. I get my pleasure from watching you eat it." His fingers caressed slow circles on the ball of her foot.

She placed the first bite of cake into her mouth, and he moved his fingers to the arch of her foot. The low, wanton moan crawled from her throat. Very little could top a foot massage while eating chocolate cake. She licked the frosting from the fork. "Who's your authority?"

"Moira. She insisted I wouldn't find better cake. Was she right?"

"It's a tough call. Quinn's has always been the best, but this one would definitely give hers a run for the money." She closed her eyes and swirled another thick piece onto her tongue. The frosting melted and squished with the moist cake. Her toes curled in satisfaction, and Griffin shifted.

After two more bites, she leaned over and put her cake plate on the table. "Sure you don't want some? I'm full."

"I might try a taste."

She leaned back, and he closed in. He lips touched hers gently and coaxed hers open. His tongue slipped inside. The moment was too brief before he pulled away.

"You're right. Delicious."

She reopened her eyes and their gazes locked. Desire clouded his irises, and a lustful pull formed low in her belly. It had been so long since she'd been touched. She missed being touched. She wanted more and didn't care about her resolve of steel melting into a pool.

The punch of her belly stopped her. "Oooh."

Griffin moved closer. Their faces remained within inches of each other. "What?"

She paced a finger on his lips to keep him quiet and raised her shirt. The baby somersaulted. Bumps rose and moved against her taut skin. Griffin's large hands covered her stomach, and the baby continued to toss around.

"Wow."

She laughed quietly. "Pretty cool, huh?"

"What the hell was that? It looked like an alien moving around getting ready to burst out." His hands slid across her belly, feeling for more.

"I think it was an elbow, but it might've been a foot."

"He stopped." Griffin moved his hands, sounding disappointed.

"He always does at the sound of your voice. It doesn't matter how far away you are or how fidgety the baby is. Your voice calms and soothes him." She pulled her shirt back into place. "Or scares him."

"Scares him?" Worry etched his voice.

"Kidding. I don't think babies can get scared in the womb."

Griffin still sat close enough that she felt the heat of his body. Her breath came in short pants. This man was chocolate cake. Definitely bad for her, but he tasted so good. How could she walk away? She never got the hang of deferred gratification.

He stood abruptly. "I have some work to do in my office. Do you need anything else?"

She blinked twice before answering. *He* was stopping? They'd both be better off if they kept their hands off each other, so she should be grateful. "I'm fine."

Taking all of the dirty dishes with him, he left the room. Indy leaned back into the couch with her cup of tea. Maybe the sight of the alien in her tummy quashed his desire. She did resemble a beached whale at this point. A whale with fat ankles. She sipped at her tea. She'd seen something in Griffin's eyes when he'd rubbed her belly. He might not want to have sex with her, but he cared about her baby. She could probably live with that. Learning to live without sex would do her good.

~

TWO DAYS LATER, Indy lay in bed, trying to follow doctor's orders. Left with little more than her own thoughts, misery set in. Griffin tiptoed around her, and it freaked her out. He decided to work from home to keep an eye on her.

Nothing she said changed his mind. So now, not only did she live in the same house with Griffin, worrying about spending nights with him, but she also saw him all day. His attentiveness made her nervous.

Man, she wished she could leave.

In a half hour, class would start without her. One more thing she wouldn't finish. Seemed like every time she attempted to make a plan, she failed. How was she supposed to run a business? Follow-through didn't come naturally.

Griffin knocked at her door. "Ready for some company? I brought a snack and some water."

"You don't need to wait on me. I talked to the doctor, remember? When she said bed rest, she meant I shouldn't spend hours on my feet. I already quit working at the bar. I think I can get food when I'm hungry."

He put a bottle of water and a plate of fruit on the nightstand. "You need to fuel up. Class starts soon."

She grabbed the bottle and chugged. "Ha-ha. No class, remember?"

"Ah, ye of little faith. Class starts in twenty."

"What are you talking about?"

He left the room and returned with a laptop and a rolling tray like they have at the hospital. He booted up the computer.

"I have a laptop. Stop buying me stuff."

"I only brought this in because I didn't know if yours would work." He spun the screen to face her.

"What is that?"

"A video link to your class so you don't fall behind. No need to drop out."

She felt like a fool again as a tear streaked down her cheek. "You did this? Thank you."

He shrugged. "Have a good class."

She wiped her face and straightened in the bed. She reached across to the nightstand and grabbed her notebook and pen. Griffin managed to save her the headache of trying to get a refund, and she wouldn't lose the time she'd already invested in the class.

He was like her own personal superhero.

CLASS HADN'T BEEN EXCITING, but she'd been able to participate. Her classmates liked that not only was she able to video chat but that she had a personal stand-in to operate the computer. Griffin had sent someone to sit there and run the computer to make sure she didn't miss anything. She'd talk to one of her classmates to get them to do it instead. She couldn't rely on Griffin to pay one of his employees to sit in her class.

She pushed the computer away and climbed out of bed. Her muscles were stiff. Lying around all day wasn't just boring, it added to the loss of shape of her body. The beach ball under her shirt itched. She rubbed the taut skin. She'd never be herself again.

Hadn't that always been her fear?

She'd lose her body and her personality. She'd have to become someone else. What if she didn't like that someone else?

She sighed. This was why bed rest sucked. Too much time to think. If she could plow through her life without thinking about it, she'd be better off.

Downstairs, silence greeted her. Griffin must've gone out. She loved this house. Where quiet usually made her bat-shit crazy, here it gave her calm. The colors on the walls and the soft fabrics of the furniture made her cozy. She had done a great job. This alone told her she had a chance to be successful.

"Fuck!"

She whirled at the sudden noise. Quietly, she moved toward Griffin's home office. She didn't want to interrupt his work, but she peeked in the open door. He sat at his desk, running his hands through his hair.

Mussed and sexy.

But very unlike him. She knocked to get his attention. "Problem?"

His face blanked out whatever he'd been feeling. "No. Work shit. How was class?"

"Good. Thanks. You didn't have to do that, but I appreciate it. I'll pay whomever you sent today and I'll have a classmate take over next week." She shook her head. "I can't believe you sent one of your employees to sit in my class."

"I did what was necessary to remove some stress from your life. You're supposed to stay calm."

"It's hard to stay calm when you're stuck in bed doing nothing all day. There's only so much TV you can watch."

He stood and walked around the desk. "What do you want? Name it."

"I don't want anything. No, what I want is to have my life

back. To go to work and school and be a regular person. So unless you can wave a magic wand, there's nothing you can do." She pushed her hair away from her face. "Sorry. You keep being nice to me and I'm being a bitch. A whiny one at that. I'm just restless."

He tugged her hand. "It's fine. Are you ready for dinner?"

She shrugged. "It's pretty sad that the highlight of my day revolves around meals. I used to be a fun person. I was the girl everyone called when they wanted to have a good time."

CHAPTER 19

*A*fter dinner, Griffin invited her to join him in his media room. Fancy description for a man cave. He used this room often, more than any other room as far as she could tell.

Reddish-brown mahogany trim accented dark hunter green walls. With the blinds and drapes drawn, it really felt like a cave. He plopped crookedly on one of the leather recliners, dangling his legs over one arm.

"Come on, this'll be fun." He pointed to the chair beside him.

She opted for the chaise lounge on the other side. The room was definitely designed for comfort.

"What do you like to play?"

"Huh?"

"What type of video game? RPG, first-person shooter . . ."

His sentence trailed off as if he expected her to jump in with a response. The problem was, she had no clue what he'd asked.

"Haven't you ever played video games?"

"No. It's more a of a teenage boy thing."

He clutched his chest like she'd shot him. "I'm neither a teenager nor a boy. Didn't you even play at the arcade as a kid? I have some of the classics if you want to go old school."

"I lived in Hooperville. We didn't have an arcade. The pizza place had a couple of games, but I really only liked pinball."

He began pressing buttons on the remote. The TV lit up and a game system hummed. "Pinball is so primitive."

She laughed at how offended he seemed. "That's what's great about pinball. Its simplicity. It's all timing and rhythm. Then, when you get it right, there are lights and bells telling everyone you're a winner. Instant gratification."

"I get instant gratification when I blow the enemy's head off." He responded while staring at the TV, scrolling and clicking. "What do you want your name to be?"

She hesitated. "I'm good with Indy."

He shook his head. "You need a screen name. Something kick-ass."

"Hmm . . . Lara Croft."

Griffin stared at her and then shot a dazzling smile at her, the one she loved, deep dimples creasing his cheeks. "Perfect."

After creating profiles, Griffin gave her a quick rundown of the game. She itched to get her hands on the controller; blowing shit up sounded like fun.

But he kept telling her the story of characters in the game.

"Wait a minute," she interrupted. "There's a storyline like in a book or movie? I have to keep track of who these people are?"

He nodded. "It makes the whole experience better. What did you think?"

"I thought a bunch of gamers all sat around in their boxers killing each other."

Griffin handed her a controller. "I'll wait if you want to change into some boxers."

"Ha-ha." She snatched the controller from him. X Y A B buttons. How the hell could she keep it all straight and watch the screen?

"We'll start offline to give you some experience and get used to how to play."

Five minutes later, she mourned her own death. She tossed the controller down. "This is such a guy thing. You said it would be fun. Dying? Not fun."

He sighed his poor-Indy-doesn't-get-it sigh and stood up. "Scoot over. I'll show you how to have fun."

Oh, yeah, he could show her fun. Hormones flooded her system. She slid across the lounge to make room for him.

He sat against the back, angling himself with long legs spread wide.

Her mouth went dry.

"Come here." He patted the space between his legs.

She answered with a raised eyebrow because she couldn't speak.

"Get your mind out of the gutter. No funny business. I'm going to help you with the game."

His quick dismissal of his innuendo stung, but she held in her grimace. She needed some fun and she'd take it any way she could.

She nestled between his thighs and prayed her hormones wouldn't give her away. His body heat radiated through her shirt and kicked her temperature up a notch.

Griffin's arms encircled her. He held the controller out. Once she took it, his hands cradled hers and directed her fingers to the correct buttons.

For the next couple of hours, she sat with Griffin and fought her hormones like they were enemies on the battlefield.

But she had a hell of a good time.

INDY WALKED past his office wearing nothing but some long T-shirt thing for sleep. He used to prefer sexy lingerie, but seeing her in comfortable cotton turned him on more than imaginable. They'd been living together for weeks and he didn't know if he would make it. He'd agreed to be nothing more than roommates, but he didn't think he could keep up his end of the deal. She was so damn sexy. And he couldn't touch her, not the way he wanted to, because that would be far from bed rest. He wouldn't chance hurting the baby. His baby.

Refraining from sex with Indy was the hardest thing he'd done. Every day he wanted her. From their first night when he practically ran from her chocolate moans to spending an evening playing video games, he was sick of trying to hide his near-constant hard-on.

He needed to focus on taking care of her. Sex had to wait. When she was better, they'd have it out and make up. They didn't have a choice. They were tied together forever now. It would be easier to take if he could understand why she lied.

Admittedly, he hadn't been keen on the idea. He'd kept telling her no expectations. That he couldn't marry her. That he wasn't meant to be a father.

My big mouth.

No wonder why she didn't want him to be the father. He'd have to prove her wrong.

He stared at the projections for the second quarter for Walker Industries. The spreadsheet blurred. How could he focus on numbers when his baby was down the hall? What if there were more complications? Maybe he should check into getting her the best doctor in the city.

Scale it back. She's not going to let me run her life. She won't even admit I'm the father.

He closed the file and opened Kendra's notes. Press releases and plans for a party. She was still nagging him about Indy. She thought Indy's pregnancy would be bad for his image. It would bring his history with Selena out. Part of him didn't give a fuck anymore. He'd moved on, gotten past his mistakes. And he'd made a bunch of them with Selena. He wouldn't make the same mistakes with Indy.

Knowing he was too distracted to get any work done, he planned on holing up in his media room. Unfortunately, when he got there, Indy sat in his favorite chair. He'd known she'd been playing a lot since that first night. She didn't have much else to occupy her days, but he needed to escape her and his need for her.

She turned and caught sight of him. Her cheeks were ruddy from crying. His heart plummeted. "What's wrong?"

He prayed the baby was fine.

"You didn't tell me he was going to die."

"Who?"

"Shepard."

Pent-up air seeped from his lungs. She was talking about the damn game.

"You could've warned me. But no, instead you have me invest all these hours getting to know these guys as people and then he dies. There's no way around it. I played the same mission more times than I care to count trying for a different outcome."

"It's war. People die."

"But not *people* people. Not the main characters you get to know."

"I'm sorry. It didn't occur to me to tell you. Plus, I didn't think you would stick with the game until you reached the conclusion. You didn't seem into it."

"You suckered me in. This is why I like pinball. No one dies in pinball." She stormed out of the room.

If having blue balls didn't kill him, her mood swings might.

But before he even got to his recliner, he knew the first thing on his agenda tomorrow would be to find a pinball machine for her. The room was big enough to house one without cramping his space. He wanted her to be happy. If lights and bells would work, he'd make it happen.

The doorbell rang, startling him from his thoughts. He wasn't expecting anyone and Indy never had guests. He stood and then made his way down the hall, but the person impatiently rang again.

Indy yelled from the bottom of the stairs, "Got it."

She was supposed to be in bed, and he wanted to make sure she headed in that direction. When he got to the stairs, the sight in front of him stole his breath.

Malcolm.

Indy stood smiling up at him, looking so much like Selena had ten years ago. He shook his head to remove the image. Indy was not Selena.

"How are you doing, son?" Malcolm asked him.

Indy spun and with wide eyes said, "Oh, shit."

Griffin's jaw muscles clenched and he ground out, "Give us a moment, please, Indy."

"Sorry," she mumbled, and turned to go upstairs.

He jammed his hands in his pockets and said to Malcolm, "I told you never to call me that."

Malcolm hovered in the doorway. "So you did. Can I come in?"

"How did you find me?"

"You're not difficult to track down. I followed you from the office yesterday when you didn't answer at your condo." He gestured to the interior of the house again.

Griffin stepped back from the door and closed it quietly once his father entered. He didn't even pretend to be hospitable. No offer of drinks or a seat. Griffin just wanted him gone. "Why are you here? I made it clear months ago that you wouldn't be getting any more money from me."

"I know that's what you said, but I thought you might change your mind."

"I haven't."

Malcolm smirked. "Haven't learned much in ten years, have you? Another one knocked up. You're not parading this one in front of the cameras. Are you sure it's yours?"

He grabbed a fistful of Malcolm's shirt and shoved. "Get the fuck out of my house and don't ever show your face here again."

Malcolm smacked against the door before fumbling for the handle.

"You're making a mistake, treating me this way. You'll regret it." The man slipped through the door.

"I doubt it." Griffin slammed the door and bolted it. What the hell was he supposed to do now? He should probably call Kendra. And say what? He'd never told her about his father. It was one of the few secrets he'd kept.

He wanted a stiff drink, but he heard soft footsteps and knew it should wait. What could he say to Indy?

"Are you okay?"

"I'm fine." Rage trembled through every muscle. He couldn't do this. He'd never talked about his father with anyone. The burn of whiskey called to him. He walked down the long, dark hall to his office and pulled the bottle from the side cabinet. Unfortunately, Indy followed.

"I thought you didn't know your father."

"I wish I didn't." He slugged a shot, keeping his back to the door, to Indy, blocking her out.

"Want to talk about it?"

"No." It came out sharper than he'd intended, but he couldn't muster the energy to care.

A sigh slipped out, but she didn't leave. He felt her staring at him.

"I—"

Without turning, he said, "I want to be alone."

If he looked at her he'd want her comfort, and he couldn't afford that. He feared taking this out on her. Dragging her into his mess.

"Okay." Hurt sounded through her quiet voice.

He heard her shuffling away. "Indy."

"It's fine, Griffin. You don't owe me any explanations. I thought that since you do so much for me, I could at least offer to listen. Good night."

Wasn't that a punch in the gut? Guilt tugged at already strained nerves. He should probably go after her, but he couldn't trust himself. The anger would come out, and she didn't deserve it. She needed to stay calm. Nothing having to do with his father reflected calm. He gulped another shot of whiskey. The less Indy knew, the better off she'd be.

INDY WAS ecstatic to get her life back. The doctor had finally cleared her. She could go back to school and run basic errands, as long as she didn't overdo it, which meant no going back to O'Leary's.

She needed to find a job, something that wouldn't require hours of standing, and she also needed to find a place to live. Griffin hadn't asked her to go—just the opposite, in fact. He'd done everything he could to make her feel like this gorgeous house was her home. *In my dreams.*

She checked the time. The kids would be here soon. This would be an awesome surprise for Griffin. She hoped.

The computer lab hadn't been touched since construction had been completed. Griffin said equipment would arrive later in the week. He wanted to keep it utilitarian, but this bordered on ridiculous.

The slate-gray walls would bore even the simplest of office drones. He wanted to inspire these kids to create and learn. They'd be stifled in this room. She remembered the notes she'd sketched out after meeting the teens. She needed to finish this room before moving out. Griffin wouldn't take any money from her, and she wanted to show her gratitude. Including the kids would give them a chance to say thanks as well.

The doorbell rang, and Indy opened the door to twelve eager faces. Who knew teens would get so excited about keeping a secret? She'd asked for Ryan's help in reaching out to the kids, and she'd been in touch with them for over a week know, making plans to redecorate and celebrate with the kids and Griffin.

As the teens poured into the lab, she tried to describe her plan. She'd already sketched on the walls and the kids laughed.

Marisol stepped forward from the crowd. "Are you sure about this? Mr. Griffin is okay with it?"

"He'll love it." She hoped. His words echoed in her head about how he'd hate someone changing his space without permission. But this felt right.

Indy showed the kids what to do. She opened the windows to the cool evening breeze and handed each kid a can of spray paint. Once they got the idea, the kids got to work and she sat on a chair in the middle of the room wearing her dreaded respirator. She supervised color choice and eavesdropped on their conversations.

Thick bubble letters took shape into words, ideas, messages. Around the room, bold graffiti-style letters screamed the mission statement for Griffin's foundation: Power, Respect, Learning, Self-Confidence, Strength, Resilience. In smaller block letters, scattered throughout the room, she'd written every computer-related term she could think of. The room became magical.

Hours later, the doorbell rang again and she knew the pizza arrived, which meant Griffin wouldn't be far behind. She swung the door open and stared at Griffin, who held a stack of pizza boxes.

"I know you're pregnant and all, but why did you order so many pizzas?"

"Hey, you're early." She stepped toward him, which forced him back onto the porch. "Don't be mad. It was all my idea."

He got an *oh, shit* look on his face. "What?"

"The kids are here."

"What kids?"

"Your kids. The program kids. Marisol, Duane, all of them." She took a deep breath. "We wanted to surprise you. So even if you hate it, pretend for them, okay? They worked really hard."

"What's going on, Indy?" His voice took on a serious tone.

"Trust me," she whispered. She took the pizzas from him and led the way back into the house. "Hey, everyone. Pizza's here and so is Griffin."

The teens all froze in place. They'd completed the room and started cleaning up the empty cans and brushes. Indy put the pizza down on a table and waited for Griffin's response. She watched and wondered if she'd be able to tell if he was upset.

He greeted the kids and looked at the walls. "So, you guys decided to vandalize my home, huh?"

The kids looked stricken and turned on her with mouths open. How could he do this to them? She saw the glimmer in his eye and heard the humor in his voice, but they didn't get it.

Indy smacked his arm. "Stop messing with them. What do you really think?"

"It looks great."

The crowd in front of her released a collective sigh. They were so afraid of disappointing him.

Duane, in his usual swagger, sauntered forward. "I knew you were playin'. I'm starving. Are we gonna eat or what?"

Indy tilted her head toward the pizza. "Dig in."

While the kids converged on the food, she took Griffin's elbow. "Do you really like it?"

"Yes. It fits who they are, yet it's positive. How did you manage this? You're supposed to be in bed." He slid his arm around her shoulder in a move that was beginning to feel natural.

"First, the doctor gave me the all clear today. I'm free to get back to my life as long as I don't overdo it. Second, the kids did most of the work here. I laid it out and got them started. Then I did what I've gotten so good at: I sat on my ass."

His gaze roamed the walls as he read the words and message. "You didn't have to do this."

"Yes, I did. You're always doing things for me. I wanted to repay you."

"No one's keeping score. I'm glad the doctor cleared you." He paused and looked like he was going to say something else, but Duane bumped him.

"Better get some food before it's gone."

Griffin smiled. "We're coming." He spun them both, his arm still around her, and headed into the fray of a dozen noisy teens.

Indy knew she'd miss this. Seeing Griffin at ease and laughing, part of a family. An odd-looking family, but they were his. She swallowed past the lump in her throat and bit into a piece of pizza. Tomorrow would be soon enough to deal with it.

THE FOLLOWING AFTERNOON, Indy set her focus on finding a new place to live. She felt like such a sponge living in Griffin's house and contributing nothing. She had enough money for a down payment on a house, and as tempting as that was, she knew she couldn't get a loan without a job. Plus, she'd need the money for hospital bills and baby stuff. The weight of everything pulled at her. Afternoon passed into evening, and she heard the front door open and then slam.

Griffin came into the living room looking pissed off. She never knew how to handle angry Griffin. He looked like he needed a good fight, but he continuously backed away from any confrontation with her. He wasn't himself.

"Bad day?"

"Yes."

"Want to talk about it?" She straightened in her seat on the couch.

He sat next to her and rubbed his temples. "A reporter called today for an interview. Kendra cleared it, and then I was blindsided when . . ."

"When what?"

He shoved off the couch and paced. "I thought it was over, that I could keep this from touching you."

A worried ball of anxiety sank in her stomach. Her hands rested protectively across her belly. "What?"

"Malcolm is still fucking up my life." He returned to the couch. "Remember when I told you a woman once told me she was pregnant?"

Indy nodded but didn't speak, not wanting to stop him. He was finally opening up.

"Her name was Selena. When I accused her of lying about the baby being mine, she killed herself."

"I know."

He looked into her face for the first time. "How?"

"When I took that woman Michelle for a tour of the city while you tried to hire her husband, she mentioned it. Why is this a big deal?"

"Because I'm going public with the foundation and the program in a month."

Debating her reaction, Indy reached out and softly touched his hair. "You had to know it would probably happen. How is it news anyway?"

"Selena's father is a former senator. It made the news when it happened. He resigned shortly after her death, so the connection between us hasn't been made. With enough digging, anything can be found. The reporter wanted to know why people should trust me with their children when I had so adamantly denied Selena's child and she was a woman I supposedly loved." He scrubbed at his head.

"How can you be the bad guy? You didn't kill her. And I know you. You wouldn't have denied the baby unless you had reason to believe she lied."

He calmed, but she still saw the anger simmering. He pointed to her laptop and narrowed his eyes. "What's that?"

The rapid change of subject caught her off guard. "The doctor cleared me, so I'm looking for a part-time job and a new place to live."

"What?" The simmer blazed to boil.

"It's not that I'm ungrateful. I've loved living here, but it was supposed to be temporary." She closed her laptop and stood. She'd known he wouldn't like her leaving. But it was time for her to stop being selfish.

"The fuck it is. You're not leaving with my baby."

Her heart seized with panic. "This isn't your baby."

"You want to talk about lies? How about you finally tell me why you lied about the baby being mine?"

"What are you talking about? I've never lied to you about this baby."

"I went to see Burke."

Her heart jumped into her throat and threatened to choke her. "What? When?"

"When you were in the hospital. You refused to ask for help. I thought he had a right to know there were complications with his baby. He also had a responsibility to help you."

Her blood raced and her stomach sank. Oh, God. She wanted to be angry. She wanted to yell, but the fear overtook her.

"You have nothing to say? Not even another lie?"

She sat on the edge of the couch. Tears streamed down her cheeks. She'd never felt such desperation. Richard would come for her baby. "I didn't lie to you. I lied to Richard."

"Show me the ultrasound." His voice was a low growl.

"Why? I can tell you what it says. According to the doctor, I managed to conceive during the time I didn't sleep with anyone. The date is after I broke up with Richard, and I used it to my advantage. I don't want him near my baby. But the date is before we slept together. I didn't lie to you."

"But you've known for months the baby might be mine."

She stood and stared at him. "Richard poked holes in condoms to get me pregnant. You brought your own condoms with you."

"I usually used my own condoms. Remember that morning in your kitchen? On your table?" He stood still, deceptively calm.

Lord, did she ever. It had been a fabulous way to start her day.

"I used one of your condoms."

So many questions flooded her brain. New concerns piled on old.

She swallowed hard. The thought had never crossed her mind. "I didn't know. I had no reason to think . . . Besides, when I got the ultrasound, you were already gone. What was I supposed to do?"

"Answer any one of my calls and tell me. I had a right to know."

"If I had told you, you'd accuse me of trying to trap you again. I thought it best for me and the baby to take care of everything myself. He's not yours." She pushed around him to get to the stairs.

"So now you're telling me you lied for me? Bullshit. You lied for yourself. We've been working together—hell, living together—and you never said anything. It's all been about you."

She froze. He was right, of course. She had been selfish. She wanted to enjoy this time with him, have this chance to feel cared for.

"You're not leaving. I want to make sure my child is taken care of. You need to be where I can watch you."

Acid burned in her gut. "I don't need you to watch me. *My* baby is fine."

"But I don't know that. It's not like I can trust your word."

His distrust shot through her, but she didn't want to back down. She didn't need to be taken care of, regardless of how much she enjoyed it. "The chances of this baby being yours are beyond slim. That hasn't changed. Even if he is, you have no rights until he's born."

"You'll live here until he's born. Then if he's not mine, you can go on your way." He stood, relaxed yet rigid, like he had no idea he was tearing her world apart. "And you have to tell Burke. He has the right to know the truth."

She cocked an eyebrow. "If I refuse?"

He closed in again. "Then I'll tell him myself."

A nasty chuckle battled the fear curdled in her throat and caught. "You wouldn't . . ." But the look in his eyes told her he would. Empty, unfeeling muddy brown eyes stared her down.

"You son of a bitch. And here I thought Richard would be bad for my baby. You're no different. No wonder Selena offed herself. She probably couldn't wait to get away from you." The verbal slap had the desired effect. Grief stole across his face. She hiccupped and tried to compose herself.

He'd cornered her and she had no options. Except one. The words came out on a shaky breath. "I'll have the test now."

"What test?"

"The paternity test."

His eyes narrowed.

"There's a test they can do now."

"Then why haven't you already done it?"

"I didn't think I needed it, and there are risks involved. They go in with a needle and withdraw fluid . . ." Just saying the words made her fear more real.

He shifted and crossed his arms.

"I was afraid to have it done because my mother miscarried her first pregnancy, I miscarried, and Quinn had problems. I'll make the appointment tomorrow. After we get the results, we can address your demands." She held her shoulders straight and pressed her lips together to prevent the quivering, but she wanted to curl into a ball and cry.

What little strength she had left oozed from every pore. Her fight left. She sidestepped Griffin to avoid contact. She needed air. Every breath barely hitched enough oxygen into her lungs.

"Wait."

She kept moving.

"Please." The one, simple, raw word froze her feet.

"I can't fight anymore, Griffin. Let me go."

He tugged on her arm, forcing her to turn. If only she could steal away some of his strength.

"You don't have to have the test now."

"I won't have you dictate my life. You can't control me."

"Take the night to sleep on it. We'll talk tomorrow after we've both had a break. This isn't about you, Indy, it's all about the baby now." He released her arm and walked down the dark hallway.

Didn't he think she knew that? Everything she did was for the baby. Except her time with Griffin. That had been selfishly about her. The way he'd looked at her and wanted her even though she was pregnant. The way he'd make her laugh by trying to provoke the baby. The way he could wrap her in warmth with a kind gesture. Yes, her love for him had been selfish.

Well, I totally fucked that up. Things had been going so well for them. Indy had been accepting him in her life. They were building something together. At least that's what it had felt like.

He went to the kitchen and poured a whiskey. After downing it in one gulp, he poured another. Trying to keep Indy in his life had been a mistake. He'd known it when he gave her office space in the condo. He knew it every day as she became comfortable in his house and in his life.

This was never supposed to be his life. But he'd never considered meeting a woman like Indy either.

Being bashed because of his history with Selena, regardless of the baseless assumptions, and then finding Indy searching for a new place to live was too much. Panic struck him so deep, he didn't know what else to do but lash out. He paced with his whiskey in his hand. He could let her go. It made sense. Everything would be easier if they went their separate ways.

But then he truly would be like his father. He couldn't do to a child what had been done to him.

And then there was Indy. He loved her in a way he never imagined.

The need to fix his relationship with her scared the shit out of him. He didn't want to lose her any more than he wanted to lose his baby. The only thing he could think of was to give her what he'd been asking for: the truth.

Whiskey in hand to bolster his courage, he went upstairs and knocked on her door. She didn't answer, so he tried the knob. Locked. Further proof that he'd screwed up. It was like an extra slap. She'd never locked her door before. "Indy, can we talk?"

No answer. He knocked louder in case she had her iPod on. Still nothing. "Look, you don't have to do anything but listen, but I need to know you can hear me."

"What do you want?"

He could still hear the tremble in her voice.

"I fucked up. I shouldn't have attacked you. I've been carrying around this knowledge for a month now, giving you every opportunity to tell me the truth."

He didn't hear any movement behind the door. He'd hope at some point she'd open the door so he could look at her, but it was probably better she hadn't. The devastation in her eyes cut right through him. His fingers itched to knock again, get a response, but he fought the urge.

He waited for an argument but got none, so he forged on. "I thought I was prepared to be questioned about Selena. That's how I run my life. I don't enter into a business deal unless I'm aware of all of the contingencies and can control the outcome.

"You throw me every time I look at you because I never know what to expect, and I sure as hell can't control you. I panicked with the thought of you leaving. I don't want you to go. I should've just said that.

"I'm sorry."

The door suddenly swung open. Although he'd thought he was used to her tears—she'd cried a lot throughout this pregnancy—he wasn't prepared for the dull indifference on her face. The light in her eyes had been snuffed out, and he'd do anything to change that.

"I'm not a liar—at least not to people I care about. I lied to Richard because he would try to take the baby from me in order to keep me. He doesn't even care about the kids he already has, but I can't fight him. I don't have a home or a job."

"I wouldn't let him take your baby."

"I've never lied to you, and you of all people have a lot of nerve calling me a liar." She swiped at her ruddy cheeks.

Her emotion wasn't so far from the surface after all. "What's that supposed to mean?"

"Everyone thinks you don't know who your father is, that you haven't seen him since you were a little kid. Why not tell the truth? You like the 'poor Griffin' effect?"

She was in rare form. Anger zinged through his muscles and tightened what the two shots of alcohol had loosened. "You want to know about Malcolm? I'll tell you who my father is."

He pointed into her room, and she returned to the bed while he placed his glass on her dresser among all her girly bottles and sprays. When he turned to face her, her arms were crossed, bracing herself for lies.

"Ten years ago, Selena and I were dating, getting serious. Then one day, I walked into my condo and heard her laughing. There, in my living room, she laughed with Malcolm. She used her father's connections and called in favors to find my dad. Thought it would be important to me. I wanted to know him, why he left, get some answers, I don't know. Anyway, he was there and no DNA test required. You saw. He blew into my life full of promises and regrets. Within a month, Selena told me she was pregnant and I realized my father was a two-bit con artist.

"He saw the return to my life as a means to fill his bank account. When I refused to give him money, he sprang his surprise. He'd known Selena longer than either of them let on. He said the baby Selena carried might not be mine."

Indy's arms uncrossed and she covered her mouth with her hand.

"That's right. Dear old Dad informed me the baby might be his. I flew into a rage and accused Selena of all kinds of things. Meanwhile, Dad decided a paternity test would ruin me as well as Selena's family, so paying him made sense. Then Selena killed herself."

He sipped from his glass, even though the alcohol-induced comfort no longer interested him. "After her death, I didn't see the point in telling her family. Surprisingly, they didn't blame me; they knew Selena had issues. Things no one ever mentioned to me until after her death. They didn't need the attention my accusations would bring."

"So you don't know if she lied."

He shook his head. Words could never convey the guilt he carried.

"Occasionally, Malcolm would pop back into my life. He used my mother to get to me. Threatened to pay her a visit, knowing she'd take him back. I knew it would kill her if he left her again, so I continued to pay. I hadn't seen him for three years, and when he showed six months ago, I told him my mother died and cut him one last check."

"Why did he come back?"

"I'm not sure, other than money. But he saw you and I knew he'd tried to ruin everything agnain."

She snickered. "I can one hundred percent guarantee this baby isn't his. I might've fucked up a lot, but I never slept with your father."

"He burns everything he comes in contact with. That's why I lied about him." Swallowing the last of his whiskey, he turned to leave. Spilling his guts to Indy didn't fix anything. Whoever said talking makes you feel better was full of shit. He still felt like his entire world was about to crumble.

He left Indy sitting in her room to digest the information he'd shared. Tomorrow would be filled with gossip from the article. The online version was probably already live. He wondered what Malcolm had cost him this time.

After another shot, he made the call he should've made a long time ago.

"Hello?"

"Hey, Moira, it's Griffin."

"Hi. What's up? You sound funny."

He twirled the whiskey glass in front of him. The O'Learys always said, if you have a big family, you might as well use them. He was so used to being the one called on for favors that asking for one grated on his nerves. "I need a favor."

"For you, anything. I think for all you've done for me, I probably owe you my first born."

"I have an exclusive for you. You write the article and sell it to the highest bidder. Wherever you'll have the biggest audience."

"Oooh. Sounds good."

"It will be."

"What's the article about?"

"Me."

INDY FELT LIKE CRAP. She'd barely slept. She'd never been so confused in her life. Griffin being the father had never entered her mind as a reality. Lying to him had been unintentional. She didn't like his demands, but after his apology and a whole lot of time to think, she realized she'd been wrong to lie to Richard. She didn't want the baby to be his, and maybe, just maybe, Griffin was the father. That small nugget of hope gave her the strength to meet Griffin's demand that she tell Richard she'd lied. He wanted Richard to know, so she'd be an adult and come clean.

Painting on her best smile, despite the way she felt, she strode through the doors of Richard's office. At the reception desk, she spoke quietly to the secretary. "Hi, I don't have an appointment, but if he's not busy, could you tell Mr. Burke that Indy Adams is here? I won't take much of his time."

Indy paced the reception area, hoping she could go through with this. She hadn't seen Richard in months, since before she left for Hooperville.

"He said you can go right in."

Indy turned and walked to Richard's office. She'd never been in his office before. All the time they'd dated, she hadn't been in this part of his life. The furnishings were too big, imposing, like Richard. She closed the door behind her. "Hi."

He already moved from behind his desk to come toward her, a smile beaming on his face. "Indy, I knew you'd be back. Wow, you've gotten big. How are you feeling?"

She opened her mouth to answer, but he kept going, talking in his excited tone. "I guess the story broke, huh? I knew that once you saw Walker's ugly side, you'd see I'm not so bad."

"What? What are you talking about?" She had that same sinking feeling she got when he told her he'd ruined the condoms.

"I have to admit, this is much faster than I thought."

She shook her head. The man made no sense. "What are you saying?"

"After Walker paid me a visit, I figured he took you away

from me. It took some time and a lot of digging, but I found his skeleton. He's not a family man like I am, Indy. Even if the baby's not mine, I'll raise it. We can still be a family." He ran his hands up and down her arms.

When had he gotten so close? Trying to focus on what he'd said, she took a step back and hit the door. "No, we can't. This was a mistake. I can't believe you would try to ruin a man's reputation to try to get me back." Her voice shook as much as her hands.

She fumbled behind her for the doorknob.

"Don't go. Let's talk. We can fix this."

Pushing him away from her bulging stomach, she pulled at the door. "This is exactly why I didn't want you to know the baby might be yours. But Griffin insisted you had a right to know. Well, know this. I will never speak to you again. Even if the baby is yours, I will fight with everything I have to keep him from you."

Moving as quickly as her bloated body would allow, she ran from the office. Richard continued to call her, but she kept going. Not until she sat behind the wheel of her car could she breathe.

Everything was all her fault. The anger bubbling in Griffin last night. The frustration over the damage to his reputation with the foundation's launch being so close. It was all on her. She drove to Griffin's office. She might as well get all of her confrontations done at once. No more lies.

God, she hated driving downtown. She drove in circles looking for a metered parking spot, practicing what she would say to Griffin. That was of course assuming he'd even speak to her. It's not like she'd met him halfway last night.

She swung into a spot and paid the meter. Walking down the block to his building, she called him.

"Hello?"

"Hi. It's me."

"Indy? Where are you?"

"I'm outside your building. Can you come down and talk for a few minutes?"

"You're here? Come up."

"No. I need to tell you something and it's nothing I want to say in front of an audience. And it's probably not a good idea for people to see me in your office."

Moments later, he pushed through the glass doors of the building. "Where's your jacket? It's cold out here."

He stood in his suit, looking sleek and polished, so different from last night. He stole her breath every time she looked at him, even when he nagged her.

"Stop mothering me. I'm fine. I'm a walking incubator."

"Come inside." He gently pulled at her elbow.

Her elbow, she noticed, not her hand. Not an arm over her shoulder. She tugged free. "No. People will talk." She drew a deep breath. "I need to tell you . . . I went to see Richard."

"What did he say when you told him?"

"He was too excited to see me." She watched the muscle in his jaw twitch. "He'd been expecting me."

"Why?" he asked through clenched teeth.

"The reporter, the story, the interview, it was all Richard, not your father." She crossed her arms and waited.

"What?"

"Your relationship with Selena was brought out because of me. Richard dug into your past to get me back. He wanted you to look bad so he would look better. I'm sorry." Her muscles were tight and a rock sat on her chest. She'd never been more sorry. She didn't know what she'd do if his work was ruined because of her.

He turned away and ran his hands over his head, a sure sign of frustration for the normally cool Griffin Walker. But she didn't feel afraid. The sudden jolt of fight or flight didn't strike her even though she had a feeling Griffin had the capability of exploding. She stepped forward and placed her hand on his shoulder. "I really am sorry. I'll be out by tomorrow. I won't cause any more problems for you."

He spun so quickly their bodies were nearly touching. "What?"

"I'll be out of your house by tomorrow. It'll be like I was never there."

"What I said yesterday stands. I don't want you to leave."

Her throat constricted. "Don't you get it? I'm ruining you. I make you look bad. If we weren't together . . ." But they weren't together, were they? She swallowed again.

"You don't make me look bad. My own behavior caused this mess."

"But it wouldn't have happened—"

"Stop." He pulled her into his arms, and she froze. It felt so good having him hold her. She wanted to crawl onto his lap and stay in his warmth. "Let's go home. We need to talk."

"It's the middle of the day."

He looked down at her and smirked. "Boss, remember?" He pulled his phone from his pocket. "Cancel the rest of my day. Something came up. E-mail whatever I need and I'll work from home."

Slipping the phone into his pocket, he turned back to her. "Where's your car?"

"Down the block." She turned to walk, and he grabbed her hand.

"Nothing is your fault. You couldn't possibly ruin me."

She wished she could believe him.

GRIFFIN SPENT the next week attempting to make Indy believe she wasn't some kind of poison and trying to make up for calling her a liar. The story about Selena broke and barely made a ripple. No one seemed to care what happened in his social life ten years ago.

Of course it probably helped that Moira wrote her version, which included an interview with Selena's family as well as his side. No one else had his side of the story, so it gave Moira the byline she'd always been looking for.

Indy had stopped talking about leaving, so he'd made at least some progress. They'd fallen into a comfortable routine of living with each other. Comfortable for him as long as he kept taking cold showers anyway. He paced the length of the hallway, waiting for Indy to come home. She was on her way *home*. It had a nice ring to it. He hadn't put much thought into having a family or having someone to come home to until now.

The front door swung open and Indy came in carrying two big bags. "Okay, what's the emergency requiring me to come home now?"

It sounded even better coming from her mouth. "Drop your bags and come with me."

Her brow furrowed, and he half expected an argument. He took the bags from her and added, "I have a surprise."

Her eyes lit up like a kid on Christmas morning. He knew the surprise factor would get her. After dropping the bags at their feet, he pulled her through the house to the back door. "Okay. Close your eyes."

"I can't close my eyes. I'll waddle the wrong way and fall."

"I'm holding on to you. I won't let you fall." Not ever.

She sighed but closed her eyes.

"No peeking." He led her down the stairs into the side yard. When they stood in front of the willow, he said, "You can open them now."

"Oh, my God." Her voice lifted with excitement. "This is so cool."

They stared at the tire swing he'd hung hours ago. He'd had a hell of a time finding an actual tire instead of some hard plastic shaped like a tire. He wanted her to have the real thing. "You did say tire swing, right?"

"Yeah. It's just like I pictured it."

He nudged her with his elbow. "Go ahead and give it a try."

"My butt is way too big to fit."

"Your butt is fine." He gave it a swat. "It held me. It'll hold you."

Her teeth sank into her lower lip and her smile broadened. "Really?"

"I'll push."

She climbed onto the tire, and he grabbed the ropes and swung her. Her hair whipped around her face and into his as he shoved the swing. She smelled of springtime. The momentum of the swing increased, and he heard what he'd been waiting for. A giggle started and grew into a full-blown laugh, unrestrained. It echoed across the lawn. He knew he couldn't live without hearing that sound for the rest of his life.

"You better stop me now before I puke."

"Too fast?" he asked, grabbing the ropes to stop her.

"If I wasn't pregnant, it wouldn't have been fast enough. Junior's getting jumpy."

Griffin helped her off the tire and swung her into his arms. "God, I love your laugh. It's been too long since I've heard it."

She stiffened in his arms. He couldn't let the moment slip by. Whatever he'd said wrong, he'd make her forget. "Junior, huh? Is that the best name you've got?"

The smile eased back onto her face. Her sinful mouth drove him insane. To add to the torture, her tongue darted out and licked her lips. "I haven't thought about names yet at all."

"Why not?" With his arm still around her, he guided her back to the house.

Her arm slid around his waist and paused as she caught herself. He pulled her closer and she held the band of his pants. More progress.

"What if I pick out a name that doesn't fit the baby? I don't want to fall in love with a name, take one look at my baby, and discover it's wrong."

He enjoyed the feel of her holding on to him, but they both couldn't squeeze through the door at the same time, so he stepped aside to let her go first. "You have nothing picked out at all?"

"No. When I see my baby, then I'll think about it."

Back inside she gathered her bags from the floor where he'd tossed them. He reached to take them from her. "I thought you were still supposed to be taking it easy."

"I needed to get supplies for my last class project. Then I stopped at the baby store and bought a few things." She tugged the bags away from him. "I can carry my own stuff."

"Can I see?"

"The baby clothes?"

"Sure, why not?"

She shook her head but went into the living room and swung a bag onto the table. "Since Quinn knows she's having a boy, I bought a couple of boy things for her shower." Pulling them from the bag, she laid them across the arm of the couch. "For me, I bought clothes in green because they'll work for a boy or a girl."

The items she produced appeared incredibly small. He tried to imagine the little person who could wear them and he couldn't. He could, however, imagine Indy snuggling a small bundle wrapped in the light green she held.

"See? Nothing too exciting."

"If you think it's exciting, I can at least pretend." He touched an outfit and found the fabric so soft, he might want to find something in her size. No wonder women enjoyed cuddling babies if this is what they wore.

"You don't fake anything, remember?"

He moved her hair off her shoulder and nuzzled her neck. "For you, I'd try."

"You've already failed. The clothes are in front of me, not wrapped around my neck." She skirted away and shoved her purchases back into the bag.

"When's your shower?"

She shrugged. "I don't think I'll have one."

"Why not? Isn't it a typical girl thing?"

"Quinn is due before me, so hers is first. I don't want to take anything from her. Besides, her pregnancy is more traditional and easier to throw a party for. It's more awkward for me. Like 'Hey, I screwed up, but give me a party anyway.' I don't want to listen to the questions about who the father is and why I'm not married yet. It'll be bad enough when Quinn is the center of attention."

Tension balled in his stomach when she referred to the baby as a screwup. But it was, wasn't it? Neither of them planned on becoming parents. "I'll throw you a party."

"No, thanks. I don't need a party. I'm not that desperate for gifts." She picked up her bags. "I have homework to finish. Are you going back to work?"

"No. I'm done for the day. I'll figure out dinner." In fact, he hadn't put in any long days in more than a week. He wanted to be at home with Indy. She swooshed out of the room with the bags crinkling at her side.

She'd get a baby shower. He'd make sure of it. He'd grown tired of her feeling like she deserved less. He'd call Kate and have her make the arrangements. She would know who to invite. It would be the best damn celebration Indy had ever seen. Their baby was no mistake.

Their baby.

When had it gone from being her baby to theirs? His heart thumped against his ribs. He sat heavily on the edge of the coffee table. Once he regained the ability to breathe normally, he had his answer.

The moment he realized he loved Indy, the baby became theirs. Indy would fight him. She kept insisting the baby wasn't his, regardless of what the doctor said.

The baby was his regardless of where he got his genes. The baby responded to his voice, his touch, not Burke's.

He knew what he needed to do to convince Indy and it wouldn't be easy.

CHAPTER 21

Indy sat on her bed surrounded by fabric: swatches for school and cute, little baby pajamas. The clothes made it hard to focus on schoolwork. Four weeks left of school, six until she had the baby, maybe less if her calculations held true. Luckily both classes met only once a week and had no finals, only projects.

A knock at the door brought her head up and stilled her fingers fondling material.

Griffin opened the door without waiting for her to respond. She wanted to admonish him for the act, but she felt she had no place doing so. It was his house. *But he's trying to make it mine,* she thought, remembering her cows in the kitchen, the pinball down the hall, and the tire swing in the yard.

He stood in the doorway. "I'm disappointed. I thought I'd catch you changing."

"You're not missing much, trust me. Or I should say, you're missing a whole lot." She rubbed her belly for emphasis. "What'd you need?"

"I forgot I had dinner plans."

She shrugged. "Okay."

"I want you to come with me. It's dinner with Eileen O'Leary."

"A real home-cooked meal? Sounds good. When do I need to be ready?" The thought of something, anything, home-made had her mouth watering. She'd missed that part of living with Quinn. Eileen visited a lot and always brought dinner.

"An hour?"

"Cool. I'll be ready."

Getting ready entailed napping for thirty minutes. Even without working at the bar, she was exhausted. The baby liked to kick and punch as soon as she settled in for the night.

When Griffin knocked again, she was ready. At least she'd freshened up in the bathroom. The fabric remained piled at the foot of the bed. Given the baby's propensity for keeping her awake, she'd have plenty of time to work.

On the ride to Eileen's, Griffin was unusually chatty. First he told her about some extravaganza Kendra planned for the foundation because she wanted a big reveal.

Griffin didn't seem too keen on it.

"I've been thinking about hiring a cook," he said, switching the subject.

Indy offered a noncommittal hum.

"What do you think?"

"About you getting a cook?"

"Yeah. I figured we're both home a lot more, and I'm getting tired of takeout."

"We could take turns cooking."

The look he shot her was one of pure amusement. "You cook?"

"I can make some simple stuff. Kind of." In truth, Quinn

had always been the one to want to learn from their mother. "I make a mean salad."

"Well, I don't. Do you think we should go with someone who's just a cook or someone who'd cook and help with the baby?" He stared straight ahead through the windshield. No smile tugged at his lips. His knuckles were white on the steering wheel.

He's serious. He's thinking long term.

He must've felt her stare. He glanced out of the corner of his eyes and then filled the empty air. "I thought if we had someone who was part nanny, part cook, you'd have help as your business takes off. But if you think we should get a full-time nanny and part-time cook, like for dinner, we'll do that."

He'd been thinking, planning. This wasn't something off the cuff for him. She couldn't quite wrap her head around it. This man, whose life's motto was "no expectations," expected her to continue to live with him after she had the baby. As roommates? Partners? Lovers?

"Are you okay? It's not like you to be so quiet."

"I'm . . . I'm fine. Just thinking."

"Let me now what you come up with. We should have someone hired before the baby comes." He parked on a quiet, residential street.

A few kids ran down the block screaming. Their jackets flapped open, and their cheeks were pink as they celebrated the beginning of spring. Griffin stood beside her door and helped her out.

They walked up the concrete front steps in silence, Indy's head still reeling with information. Griffin opened the door the way she imagined Ryan did, like family. When they entered the living room, Eileen emerged from the back of the house.

"Hi." Griffin bent and kissed Eileen's cheek. He straightened and turned to face Indy. "This is Indy."

Indy smacked his arm. "We've met. Her son, my sister, big wedding, remember?" She laughed quietly and gave Eileen a soft hug. "How have you been?"

"Good, good. Dinner will be on the table in a minute." She stepped away from Indy and her gaze darted between Indy and Griffin. As she scooted back toward the kitchen, the realization hit Indy.

Dinner at Eileen's. Griffin's nervous introduction. Her skin warmed, and she grasped Griffin's forearm. "My God. This is your version of meet the parents, isn't it?"

"What?" He tried to shrug it off, but she saw the truth in his eyes.

"Are you kidding? She's going to think, to assume . . ." Indy pointed to her stomach with her free hand.

"She already knows."

"Oh, shit." Her grip on his arm tightened. "Then she thinks I'm a total slut. And we're living together. Isn't that a sin or something?"

Panic rose where it shouldn't have. She shouldn't care about Eileen O'Leary's opinion. It mattered to Griffin, though, so it mattered to her.

He peeled her fingers from his arm. "Relax. Eileen's not that bad. She'll love you."

"You should've told me." Told her what? What did this mean?

"You look pale. Are you sure you're okay?" He rubbed a hand across her shoulders and then pulled her into a warm embrace.

She inhaled his scent and felt his heartbeat, steady and sure. His expectations were growing exponentially and she wasn't prepared.

"It's dinner. Like you said, you've met Eileen before. Let's enjoy a good, home-cooked meal."

He moved to pull away, but she held tight. She wasn't

quite ready to leave the safe comfort of his arms. After one last deep breath she released him. "Payback, Walker, you have payback coming."

He chuckled. "I already sat through your uncomfortable family dinner. I had to meet your dad before I even got to sleep with you."

"You were there for Ryan, not me." She took a seat at the table.

"I still suffered through it." He kissed the top of her head. "I'll be right back."

He returned minutes later carrying a platter of turkey breast with Eileen trailing behind. The smells wafted across the room, and her stomach danced hopefully. Indy pushed back from the table. "Can I help?"

"No. We've got it," Griffin answered.

AFTER A COMPLETELY PAINLESS and delicious meal, Griffin stood and picked up Indy's plate.

"I can take care of my own plate."

"I have dish duty."

"I'll help."

He leaned over and kissed her cheek. "Give your swollen ankles a rest. I've got it."

Eileen followed him into the kitchen and returned with a pot of coffee and a plate of cookies. Indy straightened in her seat and forced a smile. "Is this where you grill me and ask what my intentions are?"

Eileen laughed a delicate, ladylike, graceful laugh. "No, I won't be doing any grilling."

Indy relaxed a hair and helped herself to a cookie.

"Griffin is special, but I think you already know that."

"I do. Can I ask a question?"

Eileen nodded.

"Why did he bring me here?"

"Because you're important to him. He loves you, and he wanted you to meet his family."

Love? Even after all this time, they still hadn't spoken the word.

Eileen continued. "I told him you must've been important because he never spoke to me about any woman." She paused to take a sip of coffee. "He's never brought anyone to meet me."

Indy's heart beat double time. Was Eileen supposed to reveal all of this?

Eileen sank her teeth into a cookie and eyed Indy. "I think Colleen would've liked you."

"Colleen?"

"His mother."

"He never talks about her except in abstract terms of how hard her life was as a single mom." Indy planned to soak up every bit of information Eileen offered.

"He still hurts. It's only been a couple of years. She died not long after my Patrick. Griffin had been working so hard to give her a better life."

Indy's heart broke for the man who had tried to care for his mother. "Were you close to Colleen?"

Eileen gave a slight shake of her head. "Not very. I don't think she wanted too many people close. One time she came here after her husband had gone again. She cried and said she wanted to thank us for being good to Griffin."

Indy's head swam. Too much information crowded her mind. Too many emotions pressed against her heart.

"Is it safe to come in?" Griffin asked from the doorway.

Indy spread her lips into a wide smile. "Sure. Eileen was sharing all of your embarrassing childhood moments."

The look on his face was priceless. Her flip comment shot

fear into his eyes before he covered it with a charming smile. "Not possible. I've never done anything embarrassing."

"Of course." Now she wanted to dig, but she stood instead, because Eileen did. Turning to Eileen she said, "Thank you for a fabulous dinner and interesting conversation."

Eileen blushed. "I miss having the family to cook for. You come back any time."

"I will." Indy leaned forward and brushed a kiss on her soft, wrinkled cheek.

The older woman pulled her closer and whispered, "Let him take care of you. It's what he needs."

A lump stuck in Indy's throat, so she nodded and pulled away. So that's what the big parent talk boiled down to—learning what Griffin needed. After months of working to be responsible for herself, the nagging question for her became whether she could give Griffin what he needed without losing all she'd gained.

THE DAYS BEGAN to drag for Indy. Her nights involved walking through the dark, silent house. She blamed the baby's restlessness, but she had plenty of her own.

For the last week, since their dinner with Eileen, Indy hadn't been able to sleep much. Oh, her afternoon naps were restful and complete, but as soon as she settled beneath the blanket at night, the baby stomped, punched, and elbowed her.

Quinn told her it was nature's way of preparing her for sleepless nights with a newborn who would require multiple feedings overnight.

Nature sucked.

Indy worried it wasn't just the baby keeping her up. It

hadn't been her imagination that Griffin was home more. No late nights in the office. No business trips. Every night he came home for dinner. On her school nights he arrived early so they had time before class.

They were more than roommates, but not lovers. He hadn't even attempted more than a kiss. Steamy, set-me-humming kisses, but still just kisses.

She couldn't blame him. She was completely unsexy right now, but most men wouldn't show such restraint. Unless he wasn't.

Flipping the covers from her body, she stood to take her nightly stroll. The baby tap-danced on her bladder. After relieving herself, she walked down the hall.

Her stomach continued to flip without the aid of the baby. Why should it bother her if Griffin was having sex with someone else? She'd said no sex, and he'd respected that. He came home to her every night. He wanted to care for her and the baby.

She still felt like she was selling herself short.

As she shuffled past Griffin's room, the door opened. Her heart leapt into her throat.

"What are you doing up?" he asked, his voice groggy with sleep. Wearing nothing but a pair of boxers and tousled hair, he looked yummy.

"Sorry. I didn't mean to wake you." Her voice came out a husky whisper as if someone else was asleep.

"Something wrong?" He left the doorway and closed the distance between them.

"No. For the last week or so the baby's decided to dance all night while I try to sleep. Walking calms him."

Griffin scrubbed a hand over his face. "That's why you've looked so tired. Why didn't you say something?"

She chuckled, and the baby flipped. "There's nothing you

can do about it. I saw no reason for both of us to miss out on sleep."

"Ah. You've forgotten my magic touch."

Her heart fluttered and hormones surged at the memory of his magic touch.

His fingers closed over hers. "Come on."

Oh, God. He wanted to have sex now? She scanned her memory for the last time she shaved her legs.

He led her to his bed. "Get in."

She climbed on the cotton sheets, which were still warm from his body. The logistics of pregnant sex wasn't something she'd thought about. She didn't know what to do or what to expect.

Griffin crawled in beside her and pulled the blanket up around them. The hair on his chest bristled softly against her arm, and she lay stiffly on her back. The baby turned, doing his alien impression again.

Griffin snaked his hand up her nightgown. Her nerves tingled in anticipation.

He kissed her ear and his hand landed on her bulging belly. His gentle caress immediately soothed the baby. "Get some sleep, love."

Not sex, sleep.

He wasn't going to touch her, other than to rub her enormous belly. The disappointment stung, if only for a moment.

His breath fluttered her hair as he snuggled close and anchored her body to his. He'd called her "love."

It seemed completely out of character for him, but she basked in the feeling and the knowledge that for right now, she was his.

After loving him for months and dismissing it as wasteful longing, she tried to imagine a life where Griffin loved her back.

~

KENDRA PACED THE LIVING ROOM, and Griffin was glad Indy had class.

"I don't get it. Why now? You've been doing great at keeping out of the spotlight."

He shook his head. She didn't get it. "It's not about being in the spotlight. I love Indy."

Even now, after accepting the idea in his own head, it felt strange to admit it to someone other than Indy. That would change soon enough.

"God, why her? Do you think she's your redemption for Selena?"

"No," he answered quickly, but the thought stuck with him. Something to ponder later. "I don't need redemption, but I'm determined to do this right, if she'll have me. I'm only telling you now so you can be prepared when the story breaks. The baby is due in a little over a month. That's a shit-load of news for the gossip hounds."

"It will probably overshadow the foundation and your program." She stopped pacing, but her toes tapped.

"Not for the people who matter. We were both so worried about Selena's story coming out, and it made nowhere near the stir *Night Beasts* did. I guess I'm not as interesting as you thought." He got off the couch, anxious to plan his evening. "Figure out what to do for the reception. Make all the plans you want, but be aware that Indy's in my life and she's not going anywhere."

Kendra gave him a curt nod and left.

~

HE WAS WINNING INDY OVER. He just needed to find a balance

of persuasion and coercion. She no longer dodged his physical affection, so it was time to bring it home.

Marrying Indy seemed to be the best way to keep her. Surprises. She loved surprises, and he'd planned the best one yet.

He heard her key in the door, and he stood in the entryway to the dining room and waited. Nervousness assaulted every ounce of his being.

She kicked the door shut and her hair swung wildly over her shoulder. Great. Starting with a pissed-off Indy wasn't going to make things easy.

"What?" she shot at him when she found him staring.

"Bad day?"

"Yes."

"Tell me." He neared her and took her bag.

"My final project. After I spent hours scouring stores to find the perfect fabric to use for the central motif for a room, our teacher decided it would be more fun if we didn't get to choose." She snatched her bag back and rummaged through it.

Shoving a piece of yellow and green material at him, she continued, "This. That raging lunatic put all the fabric we bought and turned it into grab bag. I'm stuck with this hideous piece of crap."

She rambled, and he didn't care about fabric. He did the only thing he knew would shut her up: he kissed her. When he closed in, the furrow between her eyes deepened. He cupped her jaw, and his tongue probed her lips. On a sigh, she opened for him. The sweetness of her mouth tempted him to take her right there, but he needed to stick to the plan.

He pulled away and her eyes fluttered open. "Better?"

"Much." Her eyes were darker, filled with desire.

"Forget school for now. I have a surprise." The single

word had her eyes brightening. He hoped their child would have the same attribute.

He wrapped an arm around her shoulders and pulled her into the dining room. Candlelight flickered across the room, and the scent of roses filled the air.

"What's this?"

"Dessert." He pulled a chair from the table for her. "It seems I've chosen the perfect day for this surprise. Chocolate cake fixes everything, right?"

He placed a thick piece of cake in front of her.

She stopped with her fork poised above the plate while he sat beside her. "Aren't you having any?"

He shook his head and waited for her to start.

Her fork sank in and she placed a bite in her mouth, leaving a drip of frosting on her lower lip. How did she manage to do that with every piece of cake?

"Mmm." The low moan shot straight to his groin. Her narrowed gaze locked on his. "What's going on? This is Quinn's cake."

"I asked her to make one because it's your favorite."

Her tongue dipped out and swiped away the errant frosting. Her eyebrows furrowed in suspicion and nervousness entered her eyes. "Why?"

"I wanted to surprise you." He poured her a cup of tea and wished for a shot of whiskey for himself. He'd practiced what to say in order for this to be perfect. Maybe clichéd, but flawless.

Another bite of cake made its way into her mouth without her eyes leaving his. She washed it down with a drink of tea.

He held her hand and his plan dissolved. "Marry me."

The fork clanged to the plate and her mouth dropped open. Okay, maybe he should've stuck with the plan. "Indy?"

"Did I hear you right?"

"I asked you to marry me." So it wasn't really a question.

She tugged away from him and stood. He'd imagined this differently. She was supposed to be in his arms kissing him wildly.

He stood and joined her. She touched his cheek. "Thank you for offering, but I can't marry you."

The pain began in his chest and burrowed deep in his stomach. "Why not?"

"It's too complicated. Right now, you look at me and you're picturing a family. What happens when you find out the baby's not yours?"

"If we're married, he's born with my last name."

"Legally, yes, but when you look into his eyes and know he's not yours?"

He jammed his hands in his pockets. He wanted to touch her, to prove to her this was real. "I don't care. I love you."

She leaned heavily against the wall behind her and closed her eyes. When she reopened them, they were filled with tears. "What happened to not trusting yourself to get married? Am I your trial run?"

The first tear slipped down her cheek, and he brushed it away with the pad of his thumb. "My father taught me that another woman could lure a man from his family, offer something better. It's how I've lived my life."

She blinked and two more tears rolled.

"He was wrong. When you find the right woman, there is no one else. I can't look at anyone and think she's better than what I have right here."

"I wish I could believe that, trust in that. Being pregnant isn't a reason to get married."

"I didn't say—"

"Marriage never entered your mind until you thought this baby might be yours. If I wasn't pregnant, would you be proposing now?" She folded her hands over her belly.

He didn't have an answer, but he suspected she was right. But he loved her; he would've gotten to this point eventually. "I love you. I can't live without you."

Wrapping her arms around his neck she leaned into him. "I'm not asking you to."

He bent and kissed her tear-streaked cheeks, tasting the salt. Her head turned until her mouth found his. She tasted of chocolate—sweet, dark, and smooth. His hands moved up her body until they reached the sides of her breasts, and his thumbs sought her nipples. They were already hardened into stiff peaks. Knowing his kiss made her this hot caused his blood to race, and his dick became rock-hard.

He fought for control. "We should stop."

"Why? It's okay." Her watery eyes opened and searched his. "Unless you don't want . . . to."

How could she think even for a minute that he didn't want her? He took her hand and rubbed it against his crotch, proving his desire. "I definitely want you. But you said no sex."

"You said you love me."

"I do."

"Then show me."

His hands reached around and caressed her ass. "My sources tell me sex is good for a pregnant woman. From what I understand, if mommy's happy, baby's happy."

She ran her fingers through his hair and laughed. God, how he loved her laugh.

"I don't think I want to know who your sources are, but I like the way they think."

He turned and blew out the candles. He held her hand to make sure she didn't go anywhere. "Let's go make mommy happy."

$\mathcal{I}$ndy stretched in the bed. Griffin had gone into work hours ago, but she'd slept in. She'd needed the recovery time. Never in her life had she had such slow, tortuous, glorious sex. No, they'd made love. Griffin had made love to every inch of her body. Not a cell or nerve went untouched.

They'd had fun, pure and simple. Laughter had overtaken them when a position didn't work and they'd needed to rearrange themselves. They'd said so much with their bodies, deepening their connection. It felt good to hear him laugh. Afterward, Griffin stayed close with his hand on her belly to keep the baby calm so she could sleep. But with her sleeping naked, he awoke twice with a hard-on, ready for another round. She had no idea how he functioned at work.

As she flipped back the covers, a glint in the sunlight caught her eye. *Holy shit.* A diamond ring circled her finger. The setting itself was simple and beautiful, the diamond gorgeous. Her heart crashed against her ribs.

Griffin had proposed. He'd thought about it, planned. It

wasn't the spur-of-the-moment thing she'd assumed. *I told him no. We can't get married.*

Her phone rang. Griffin must've brought it into the bedroom. "Hello?"

"Good morning, beautiful. What are you up to?" Griffin sounded happy.

"I'm sitting in bed staring at a huge-ass diamond on my right hand."

"If you don't like it, we can pick out something else."

"I said no."

"I'm banking on changing your mind, and until you say yes, your finger is a better place to keep the ring than my pocket."

The man was impossible. "What if I never say yes?"

He laughed as if the idea had no merit. "Then I guess you get to keep said big-ass diamond."

Indy dropped into silence. She didn't know how to respond.

"Are you going to be home today?"

"Yeah."

"Good. Kendra needs to come by to plan for the party. Can you show her whatever she needs?"

Party? Oh, yeah, the big extravaganza. "Sure."

"While you're there, move your clothes into my closet."

"What?"

"I've finally got you back into my bed. I'm not about to let you out again. Move whatever you need to make space."

Her heart hopped like a bunny on speed. "Are you sure?"

"I have no doubts. I'll talk to you later. Love you."

He clicked off without waiting for her to say anything. She loved him so much it scared her.

Being responsible interfered with her instincts.

If Griffin proposed before she'd gotten pregnant, they'd

have been on a plane to Vegas. She'd never want to leave here. Hell, she was living in the Barbie Dream Mansion.

What more could a girl want?

Her instincts failed her here. She didn't get why she held back. He loved her. He'd said so. Why not believe him?

Tired of her brain running in circles, she rose from the bed and felt awkward strolling around naked with her big boobs and belly sticking out. The trip down the hall to her room felt weird. She'd been sleeping in Griffin's bed, but her stuff remained in her room. He'd asked her to move her things, to make whatever space she needed.

After a shower, she planned to do that. They were a couple. They were in love. She should be happy. Part of her held back, though. The same part that refused his proposal. She had no doubt he'd take care of the baby no matter what, but she wanted more for her child.

She needed to know Griffin loved her baby. She had no way of knowing for sure until the baby was born. Waiting was the smart thing, the responsible thing.

Being responsible sucked.

BY THE TIME she'd managed to move her small wardrobe into Griffin's room, she was starving. In the kitchen, Griffin had left a note on a stack of papers. She flipped through to see he'd placed an ad for a part-time cook and full-time nanny. The pile contained the first batch of applicants. He wanted her to go through them and choose some to interview.

Life suddenly seemed too real. He'd pushed her into a committed relationship whether or not she wanted it. He was creating a family where there shouldn't be one.

The microwave beeped with her leftover pasta, and the doorbell buzzed. Her stomach growled, so she took the plate with her to answer the door. Swallowing her first bite, she opened the door.

Kendra strode in looking peeved.

"Hi, Kendra. Nice to see you again."

"Thank you." Her heels clicked on the hardwood floor. She moved straight to the computer lab.

Indy followed, shoving more pasta in her mouth. "Did you need me for anything?"

"No. I can take care of everything."

Indy shrugged and went back to the kitchen to finish her lunch. The woman obviously didn't like her, so Indy didn't need to waste energy trying to make small talk.

In the kitchen, she read the first couple of applications and decided she had no idea what to look for. She'd never hired anyone for anything. A piece of paper could never tell her enough about an applicant. She needed to look someone in the eye to form an opinion.

She shoved the papers back in a pile and cleaned her dishes. Before heading upstairs to work on her project with the hideous fabric, she went to check on Kendra.

From the hall she heard Kendra comment, "I don't know what Griffin was thinking when he allowed her to do this. I feel like I'm standing in the ghetto."

Anger propelled Indy into the lab. When Kendra saw her, she quickly said good-bye and closed her phone.

"Griffin and the kids love the lab." Indy fought to keep her voice calm.

"Of course *they* like it. This program is supposed to take them out of the trash and into the business world."

"They get that from what Griffin teaches them. The program is about the kids—and they are still kids."

Kendra strode across the room, heels clicking, until they were nearly toe-to-toe. Even without her heels, Indy stood a head taller.

Disdain shot from the woman's eyes. "I don't know how deep you think you have your teeth in him because of this." She pointed at Indy's stomach. "But I will not let you ruin all of the work I've done."

"Me? I'm not looking to ruin anything. I created a room I thought the kids would enjoy working in."

Kendra hitched up her chin. "I know he's been looking at jewelry, but it won't last. You're not the first gold-digging piece of white trash to come his way."

Indy shoved her right hand behind her back to hide the evidence. If Kendra noticed, she didn't comment, which led Indy to believe she hadn't seen the ring.

"You will drag him down. The scandal of you being knocked up and seen with him will ruin his credibility. Playing house with you will not make his history with Selena go away."

The words were more effective than a slap. Indy straightened her shoulders and stiffened her back despite the shot to her heart. "Griffin is a big boy who makes his own decisions. He hired you for PR, not to be his mother." Indy turned and said over her shoulder, "Don't let the door hit you on the way out."

The lame parting shot didn't say much, but Indy didn't have enough venom to fight the truth. She'd known it. In her heart, it was part of her refusal to marry him.

Once reporters got a picture of her, questions would be raised. She'd be labeled a slut or he'd be pegged as irresponsible. Then Selena would be brought up again. Either way, who would want to expose their children to that?

Back in her room, Indy turned the radio up and began work on her project. Kendra's opinion didn't matter. She'd meant what she'd said about Griffin making his own choices, but she also wouldn't bring bad publicity to the foundation and the kids.

She loved Griffin too much.

She'd hide out for a few weeks, and the baby would be born. They would have their answers and deal with it then.

Dodging Griffin's proposal shouldn't be too difficult. If she told him to give her time, he'd have to respect it.

Within the walls of the house they'd be a couple, but no one else would know. His reputation would be safe.

She'd have time to build her business and prove herself.

FOR THE NEXT FEW WEEKS, the house became a hive of activity. Party planners and caterers moved through, finalizing everything for the launch. They all traveled with Kendra, so Indy kept her presence minimal.

Griffin pressured her to interview chefs but made no mention of marriage. She'd read through the applications to appease him, but no one jumped out at her. It would help if he'd told her what he wanted.

They slept together every night. They'd lie together in the dark and discuss their days. She'd never felt as safe and secure and whole as she did in his arms in the middle of the night. That knowledge made her days with Kendra livable.

Three days before the party, Griffin came home carrying a garment bag and thrust it at her. "Here."

"What's this?"

"The reception is formal and you haven't gone shopping. The saleswoman assured me it would fit."

Indy unzipped the bag. Inside, a glittery, copper-colored gown shimmered in the evening light.

"It's sleeveless," Griffin continued. "You're always hot these days and there's going to be a lot of people here, so I think you'll be comfortable."

"It's beautiful." She zipped up the bag and kissed him. She

didn't have the guts to tell him she wouldn't be attending the party.

Kendra's words rang in her head. Reporters would have a field day, especially since she'd already been pictured with him months ago, looking thin and available. She had a plan in place: she was tired and needed to work on her project. But now, seeing this beautiful dress and the look of excitement on his face . . . maybe she could show up at the very beginning of the party before too many people arrived and then duck out, claiming to be too tired.

If he knew her real reason, he'd be angry and probably buy the front page to declare them a couple.

He pulled away and studied her face. "Something wrong?"

"No. I'm tired."

"Everything go okay with Kendra today?"

"I guess. Why? Did she say something?"

His eyes narrowed. "No. She's suspiciously closed-mouthed except for laying out specific details for the party."

"Well, I try to stay out of the way, so we don't interact much."

"Did she say something to you?"

"Like?" Indy knew where he was going, and she couldn't let him know. She scrambled for something to throw at him.

He shrugged.

"Have you slept with her?"

"What?" His face fell in alarm. "Did she tell you that?"

Good. She grabbed it and ran. Let the crazy pregnancy hormones do their job. "No. Just a feeling. She seems a little possessive of you."

He stepped forward, wrapped his arms around her, and kissed her head. "There is absolutely nothing going on, and nothing ever has."

"I didn't ask if you were sleeping with her now," Indy

added. She kept enough question in her voice to sound jealous and insecure. She hoped she could sell it.

"I've never been involved with Kendra, and I've never even gotten the hint she'd want to. She works for me and we keep it professional." His lips moved down the side of her neck.

Her pulse kicked up a notch. She had no lingering doubts about his attraction to her. Regardless of how fat and Shrek-like she felt, Griffin made her feel like her former self. Even when they weren't having sex, he touched her. Often. "I remember what happened when I tried to keep it professional between us."

"You're different. What's on the agenda for tonight?"

"Mmm . . ." She tried to pull her focus from his lips on her earlobe. "Homework."

He grunted. "When are you done with school?"

"Summer."

His hand rubbed her belly. He whispered in her ear, "Then we'll have a newborn to contend with. Can I talk you into dropping out of school?"

"No." She shoved his shoulder. "This is important to me."

"I was kidding. I miss you when you're in school or holed up in your room working." He tugged her close. "What's for dinner?"

She shrugged. "Leftovers."

They walked to the kitchen, and she wondered if this would be the rest of her life. She'd accused Kate of living in Leave It to Beaver–land. Would it be enough for her?

GRIFFIN THOUGHT OF INDY. For the last few days she'd been distant. No matter how he'd tried to pull the problem from her, she glossed over it. She claimed fatigue. Although she appeared genuinely tired, something else that he couldn't quite read stirred.

She hadn't mentioned marriage or his proposal, so he hadn't either, but she wore his ring. He wanted to make it real and permanent. Looking at her, he knew they could build a life and have a family like the O'Learys.

He moved among the catering staff and around ice sculptures. His home didn't feel much like his tonight. After dressing in his tuxedo, he looked for Indy. The thought of her in the dress he bought gave him an instant hard-on. Mostly he pictured the flimsy material pooled at her feet.

When he found her sitting at her desk in sweats and sketching in her notebook, it surprised him. "Shouldn't you be getting ready? Guests will arriving start soon."

She rose from behind the desk. "I'm trying to get this project done and I finally got something working here. I totally lost track of time."

"But you are coming, right?" She had to come. She had to know how important she was.

She fidgeted under his gaze. "It's not like you need me there. Kendra will keep you busy shaking hands all night."

Kendra. He'd known something had happened between them. "This is important to me. I want you at my side."

"I don't want to go because I know how vital this is."

Her words snapped out and he could almost see her try to reach out and grab them back.

"What do you mean? The two most important things in my life are you and the foundation. We're officially unveiling the program tonight. I need you there. What did Kendra say to scare you off?"

Her eyes shifted. "She didn't say anything."

"You're lying."

She tilted her head up. "I must need practice. She didn't

say anything surprising. She accused me of being after your money. And of you using me to erase the memory of Selena."

His muscles flinched. Indy reached out and smoothed her palm against his cheek.

"It didn't bother me. Everyone will think I'm after your money. What people say about me is meaningless."

He wished she believed her own words. Then he understood her full meaning. She worried about what people would say about him. "I'm not using you to fix what I did with Selena. I'm not ashamed to be seen with you."

"I know you're not. But right now is not the time to piss off people who could be supporters of your program by flaunting your disregard for morality. Living in sin with a woman who's knocked up with a bastard. We both look incredibly irresponsible. Not the picture of someone most people want to entrust their children to."

He cupped her face in his hands. He had to learn to never underestimate the woman's instincts and intelligence. He saw no sadness or regret in her eyes, only honesty. "I don't care what they say. I love you."

She smiled a gentle smile that hinted at something more. A smile that made him want to devour her mouth. He kissed her.

She pulled away and said softly, "I love you too."

His heart swelled. He'd known she loved him. He saw it every time she looked at him, every time she responded to his touch, every time she spoke his name. Hearing her say it created a renewed need in him. A need to make her his. He pulled the ring from her right hand and slid it on the left. "Our baby is not a bastard."

He kissed her cheek and turned to go. "Get ready. I'll be waiting downstairs."

"Hey," she called.

When he faced her, he saw her twist the ring on her finger.

"Are you going to tell me the name of this program or is it always going to be called *the program?*"

"It's named Project Independence." He closed her door behind him and headed downstairs. Indy's acceptance of his ring loosened every taut nerve in his body.

If he had his choice, they'd be married within a week.

INDY PACED HER ROOM. Her project had taken the one successful turn she'd needed and was almost complete. The music from the party floated up the stairs. From her window, she'd watched guests arrive by limo or town car. Having the party in a residential neighborhood must've caused a stir, because very few people drove and parked their own cars.

Unless that was the norm for Griffin. Maybe he only knew the superrich.

Then she thought of the O'Learys and KD's Diner. No, he never got too far from his roots. She twirled the ring on her left hand again. He expected her to marry him. He called the baby "our baby."

Nerves fluttered in her stomach, and she rubbed the huge protrusion that had become her body. The dress that Griffin bought looked better on her than she had imagined. She glanced in the mirror one last time and headed for the door.

When she reached the top of the stairs, she saw people milling around and Griffin standing near the front door greeting guests as they entered. Then he turned to face her as if he'd known she was there. The serious expression on his face faded and a broad, dimpled smile replaced it. His eyes scanned the length of her, and she took the steps toward him. His gaze heated her from scalp to toe.

At the bottom of the stairs, he reached for her hand and leaned in to kiss her cheek. "Thank you for coming. You look gorgeous."

Flustered by his words, she had no quick comeback. "Thanks."

"Come on. I want to introduce you to some people."

Her grip on his hand tightened. So much for her quick appearance and departure.

Griffin called out to a man, "Ron, I want you to meet my fiancée, Indy."

Indy froze. She didn't hear the rest of the introduction and had no idea who the man was who stood in front of her. She pasted on her friendly smile, but she felt Kendra's scorching stare poke at her from next to Ron.

Indy tried not to fidget or hide her left hand. This was *not* going to go well.

"So Griffin tells me that you decorated the house."

"Yes, I did," Indy answered.

"Care to give me a tour?"

She released Griffin's hand. "Certainly." She squeezed between Griffin and Kendra to take Ron's offered elbow.

Indy became comfortable as she talked about the design. During their tour, she discovered that Ron was a lawyer and politician who wanted to donate to Griffin's foundation. She tried to be as charming as possible.

With the tour complete, they headed back into the living room, and Indy was surprised to see Kate standing with a glass of champagne in hand. Kate smiled at Indy and then looked at Ron.

"Kate?" he asked. "I didn't know you'd be here. How have you been?"

Kate leaned her cheek forward for a kiss. "Good, and you?"

Indy's gaze darted back and forth.

Kate said, "Ron and I worked together for a few years."

"Oh, I'll let you catch up then." She turned to leave and nearly bumped into Kendra. Not surprising, since she nearly bumped into everything these days.

Indy nodded her head and said simply, "Kendra."

But Kendra tugged her arm. "I'd like a word."

Indy yanked discreetly from the woman's grasp but followed her lead.

"How dare you show up to try to steal this night from him?"

"I'm here because Griffin wants me here. I'm not stealing anything." Indy walked away, hoping Kendra wouldn't follow.

Her stomach muscles tightened. She hadn't felt like that in a while, since she hadn't been upset about much lately. She caressed her belly and tried to soothe the baby. She walked the room again, hoping the motion would relax him. The room was filling rapidly and the warm stuffiness was getting to her.

Although she wouldn't let Kendra drive her from the party, Indy really wasn't feeling well. She scanned the room for Griffin but couldn't find him in the crowd.

Then suddenly he was at her back, wrapping his arms around her. "How are you?"

She placed her hands over his on her belly. "Actually, not too good. I'm tired and icky."

His laugh rumbled against her back. "Icky? Is that an official description?"

"I don't know about official, but it works. Would you be okay if I went to bed?"

He walked around to study her face. "You're really not looking good. Are you sure you're okay?"

She patted his chest. "Yeah. Nothing a little more sleep won't fix."

"Good night." He kissed her cheek.

"Take good notes and wake me when the party's over. I want all the details."

He smiled, and she went upstairs without anyone taking notice. She took the stairs slowly, the muscles in her stomach tight and uncomfortable.

She paced for another ten minutes, but her muscles hadn't loosened and now her back ached. She stopped pacing and went to the bathroom and stripped. Maybe a warm shower would help.

After lingering in the shower, she still felt like crap. She redressed in her sweats and lay on the bed. Sharp pain started in her lower back and shot around her pelvic bone. She sucked in a sharp breath and eased onto her side. She finally thought she'd found a comfortable position. Then it happened again.

The pain arrowed through her and she gripped the bedspread.

Something's wrong.

Panic seized her heart while cramps clamped her abdomen. Sounds from the party filtered through the pain. She couldn't go back downstairs. Hell, she wasn't sure she'd make it if she tried.

Kate. Kate was at the party. She fumbled with her phone to call Kate.

"Hey, where are you? You're missing a great party."

"Come upstairs. Something's wrong." Indy gritted her teeth against the pain.

"I'm coming."

Moments later, Kate stood beside the bed and pressed her cool hand against Indy's forehead. "What's wrong?"

"It hurts, Kate. God, it hurts so bad."

"You might be in labor."

"No. It's too early. I expected you to come up here and tell me it's in my head. That it's false labor." God, this can't be happening. Not now. Not tonight.

"I've never had false labor. Only the real deal. We need to get you to the hospital. Do you want me to call an ambulance?"

She thought of the party. Of Griffin's foundation. Even without being there, she managed to screw it up. Tears gathered on her lashes. "No. But get Griffin."

CHAPTER 23

Fingers grabbed his elbow, and Griffin turned to see who needed his attention now. As he turned, Kate took the drink from his hand. She leaned close to his ear. "Indy's in labor. She needs to go to the hospital."

If Kate hadn't taken the glass from his hand, it would've shattered on the floor. He suddenly felt boneless. It was too early. They had weeks to prepare.

They weren't ready.

He wasn't ready.

Kate pulled on his elbow. "Don't make a scene. Go to the kitchen. I'll get her down the back stairs."

He moved at her direction. Plastering a smile on his face, he wove through the crowd and fought the panic clawing at him.

When he entered the kitchen he walked straight to the back stairs. Kate had an arm around Indy as they eased down the steps. Indy was pale, and her eyes were filled with fear.

"Shouldn't we call an ambulance?"

Indy smiled. "No. Kate will get me to the hospital. This is

probably a trial run. I'll get there and they'll tell me I have gas."

Kate shook her head.

"Let's go." He reached for her.

"Kate will take me. Finish—"

"Shut up. If you think I'm sending you to the hospital alone, you're crazy." He took her hand, and she squeezed tightly. The fear in her eyes eased a little. Had she thought he'd stay at a party instead of taking care of her?

Indy walked incredibly slow. They had to stop once on the trek to the car because she nearly doubled over in pain. Fear gripped him. Sweat trickled down his back, and he wiped his palms on his pants.

Labor was natural. Women did this all the time.

Why didn't anyone tell him how scary it was to watch the woman you love in pain?

They raced to the hospital in silence, except for Indy's pants and grunts. He tried to focus and come up with something soothing to tell her, but he had nothing. Driving without crashing took every bit of his attention.

Once at the hospital, everything blurred.

If the moments in the kitchen were slow motion, the hospital was all fast forward.

He felt totally helpless. Her doctor arrived shortly after they stuck Indy in a room. He remembered her from the last time Indy had complications.

"What's wrong?" Indy demanded. "What's wrong with the baby?"

"Shh." She patted Indy's leg. "The baby seems fine. Heartbeat is strong."

"It's too early."

"We're giving you some medication to try to stop the labor. But if the baby's ready, he or she is coming. You've said all along my dates were wrong."

Tears ran down Indy's cheeks. Griffin didn't know what to do. What to say. He held her hand.

Her breath hitched. "Get Kate."

Kate had said she'd follow in her car, but he didn't know if she'd arrived. "Do you want me to call Quinn?"

"No. This will freak her out. I need Kate." She pulled her hand free and turned away.

She was shutting him out. He'd heard stories of women screaming and cursing at their husbands during labor. No one ever said she might not want him.

In the hall, he found Kate.

"How is she?"

He shook his head. "I don't know. Scared. They're trying to stop the labor, but the doctor said it might be time. She wants you."

Kate left him, and he paced the hall. He removed the tux jacket and shoved his tie in the pocket. He failed at blocking out the sounds of the hospital. The quiet that wasn't quiet. He remembered the nights sitting by his mother's bed. He shut out the thoughts as sounds returned him to the present. Machines beeped, wheels on carts squeaked, women screamed.

Babies cried.

No other men, no fathers, wandered the hall. If they left the room, they had a purpose. They were doing something for the mothers. He stood useless.

An eternity passed before the door opened and Kate came out.

"The drugs seem to be working. The contractions have stopped." She ran her hand down his arm. "She said you should go home."

"No." They'd gotten past these bullshit games. "What happened?"

Kate sighed and shook her head. "When the doctor told

her the baby might be ready, Indy realized she was right all along. The baby is Richard's."

He sank to a chair and held his face. Which was worse—that the baby be born healthy but not be his, or be his and born prematurely? It didn't matter. He shoved up from the chair. "Bullshit."

Pushing past Kate, he entered the room. The anger that propelled him past the door sank in his stomach when he saw Indy. She looked frail, lying on the hospital bed. He'd been successful in blocking out the smell of the hospital that would remind him of his mother's last days, but this overwhelmed him.

She turned to face him. "Go home."

"No." He forced his feet forward. He slid the tray away from the bed. On it stood a cup of melting ice chips.

When he reached the bed he took her hand. It was cold, and he covered it with his other hand, offering his warmth. "I told you earlier tonight that our child would not be born a bastard. If I have to go hunt down a priest right now to marry us in order to prove it to you, I will. You will not push me away."

Her lips trembled, and she pressed them into control. "The baby's not yours. No matter what you hoped, or thought, it's not yours. Do the math."

"I've done the math every which way. Me minus you is zero."

"You're not making sense." She squeezed her eyes shut, and a tear leaked from the corner.

He never made sense when he needed to for her. Not letting go of her hand, he sat on the edge of the bed. "I wish you'd gotten the chance to meet Patrick O'Leary. He was a great man. An amazing father. He always treated me like one of his own kids, whether it was buying me ice cream from the truck on a summer day or slapping the back of my head for being an ass."

Indy's eyes opened to slits. Puffy from crying, the green shone through more than the gold.

"When I left town, I never stopped thinking about you, but fatherhood wasn't in the cards for me. I didn't think I could handle it. After I came back, I talked to Eileen. She gave me the proverbial head slap. I was Patrick's son, regardless of my last name."

He leaned forward and kissed her lips. They were cold from the ice. He rested his forehead against hers, and their breath mingled. "I love you and the baby inside you. This child is mine regardless of genetics."

INDY STARED bleary-eyed at the baby in her arms.

A little girl.

A little girl who still had no name. She'd been sure that inspiration would strike when she saw her baby's face for the first time.

All she felt was scared and tired.

The contractions had started again in the middle of the night and her water had broken. The flurry of activity of extra doctors and nurses confused her.

But Griffin had been there the entire time.

When she was sweaty and gross, he wiped her forehead with a cloth. When she didn't think she had it in her to push again, he talked her through.

When panic gave way to hysterics as they took her baby to a warming table, he held Indy's hand while watching over the shoulders of doctors to count fingers and toes.

It had taken forty-five excruciating minutes before they declared the baby okay. Forty-five minutes of lying in bed, feet in stirrups, feeling empty and scared. Forty-five minutes for the experts to decide that her six-pound infant was healthy and that she could hold her.

Only Griffin's reassuring words had kept her sane.

He sat beside her now, sleeping in an uncomfortable chair. He'd refused to go home to sleep, and he looked like crap. Blood smeared on his tux shirt from when he'd cut the umbilical cord, he desperately needed to shave, and his hair stood up in odd patches.

And he was beautiful.

He was a good man. His mother would've been proud. His eyes popped open. They reflected the love she felt in her heart.

"What's wrong?" His voice was rough.

"Nothing. I'm watching my two favorite people sleep."

He leaned closer and kissed the baby's head. "Do you think I can finally hold my daughter?"

"You hoped for a boy, didn't you?"

He shrugged. "All I wanted was for her to be okay. She's perfect."

Indy scooped the baby and reached her out to Griffin. His broad hands cradled her small body. When he brought her close to his chest, Indy knew she'd never see a more perfect sight. Then she knew. The most fitting name flashed, and she knew.

"She needs a name," he said, stroking the baby's head. "I feel bad enough that we called her a him for all this time."

"She has one."

Griffin's gaze swooped up to meet hers. "My daughter will not go through life being named Freedom."

The laughter poured from Indy's heart. "Her name is Colleen Alice. It gives her a lot to live up to."

His eyes became misty. "Colleen Alice what?" He asked as if he feared her answer.

"Walker." She stroked the top of Colleen's head. "It doesn't make sense to complicate her life with a name that's not her father's."

"So you'll finally marry me?"

"Yes."

Griffin leaned forward and kissed her with Colleen snug and safe between them. Indy didn't know how she could've questioned her happiness with him. Yes, family would definitely be enough.

Thank you so much for taking time to read my book. I hope you enjoyed hanging out with the O'Learys in Chicago. Keep reading for an excerpt of the next book in the series, *Something to Prove*, where Colin O'Leary works to prove to his family that he's back for good. And if he falls in love with his new partner, that's even better.

If you could spare a moment, I would appreciate you leaving a review of this book.

If you'd like to stay up-to-date on my releases and have the chance to win some prizes, click here to join my newsletter.

SOMETHING TO PROVE - EXCERPT

*E*lizabeth drove up and down Addison, west, then east again, watching the addresses. No matter which way she went, the gray slab of a building had to be the right place. She parked and climbed out of the rental car. Motorcycles leaned against the building—not at the curb, but on the sidewalk actually touching the building.

Why the hell would Dad own a biker bar?

She glanced up at the rusty sign, The Irish Pub. It didn't look much like anything Irish. She pushed through the door and a cloud of smoke smacked into her lungs. Chicago was supposed to be smoke-free. Didn't the manager know this? That alone was fine-worthy. Trying to keep her breaths shallow to avoid inhaling too much smoke, she walked toward the bar, hoping to find someone in charge. The room, what she could see of it, was dark and tables were scattered haphazardly.

"Excuse me, I'm looking for the manager," she called out.

"Are you the health inspector?" a grizzled man asked while drying a glass with a dirty cloth. His pasty skin reminded her of a vampire's, but she doubted he'd sparkle if she took him into the sunlight.

"No, I'm the owner."

He laughed and the men sitting on stools at the opposite end of the bar joined him. She stiffened. It wasn't like this was the first time she'd been laughed at, and it undoubtedly wouldn't be the last. She produced a card from her suit coat pocket and slapped it on the bar. "Elizabeth Brannigan. My father has owned this bar for more than ten years. Feel free to call the office to check."

She prayed her bluff would work. If he made the call, she'd be caught.

The man sobered and took the card. He brushed his stringy salt-and-pepper hair from his eyes. "So you're here to finally sell?"

"No. I'm here to save it." Until the words left her mouth, she didn't even know that was her plan. She had arrived in Chicago thinking she wanted to know more about this property, but now she knew it would be her mission. Her chance to prove her worth to her father.

Her statement set off another round of laughter.

"Then, when it's turning a profit, I'll sell."

The man leaned forward and extended his hand. "Mitch, your manager. I was hired on about ten years ago and have seen many men come through from your daddy's company talking about change. It ain't happened yet."

She shook his hand, trying to ignore whatever diseases she was accepting in the action. "Maybe that was the problem."

"What?"

"They were all men." She paused. "I'll need to see the books and any other pertinent information. I'll be back tomorrow morning at nine a.m."

"We don't close until two. I won't be here at nine." His

eyes were already bloodshot, so she couldn't imagine him more sleep-deprived.

"Then give me a copy of the key and leave the information in the office. I assume there is an office?"

"You got ID on you? It'd be just my luck to give keys to someone who isn't the owner."

Elizabeth reached into her wallet and slipped out her driver's license. Mitch took it from her hand and tilted it in the light, glancing from the card to her face. Satisfied, he tossed it on the sticky bar for her to retrieve.

"Hold on." He walked to the end of the bar and flipped up a piece of the counter. He disappeared into the back and returned a few moments later with a ring of keys. He tossed them on the bar.

"Thank you." She slipped the keys into her pocket and walked back outside. Within a few minutes she had already learned more about the bar than the audit of her father's properties had taught her.

From behind the wheel of the rented Mercedes, she stared at the building. It must've meant something to her dad. He'd never done any work on it, but never sold it either. If she could turn this place around, prove to him that she could handle this task, he would have to hand the reins of the business over to her instead of Keith.

She'd never taken the lead like this before. They tended to treat her more like the clean-up crew. Dad didn't even know she was here. He'd been keeping this place a secret. This was her moment to shine. If she fixed this, he'd have to see that she could handle doing it all.

And if he didn't?

She shook her head. She'd cross that bridge later. Right now, she needed to do some research, starting with finding a place to live.

While allowing her GPS to guide her to a hotel, she called the office. "Hi, Meg."

"How was the flight?"

"Fine. Listen, I need you to get some information for me about a property." She heard some rustling and knew Meg was getting her notepad out.

"Shoot."

"My dad owns a bar called The Irish Pub here in Chicago. It's part of his personal holdings, not Brannigan Enterprises."

"I don't have access to his personal information," Meg said, uncharacteristically nervous.

"I want you to talk to Claire. She's been with my dad forever. Talk to her, assistant to assistant. Tell her that I need whatever information she has."

"Can I ask what's going on?"

"I'm not sure. I'm going to call my dad, but I have a feeling he won't give me all the details, so I'm making a preemptive strike. I also need everything you can get me on the codes for bar ownership in Chicago."

"Anything else?"

"Not yet. I'm sure that once I hit the ground on this, I'll need some more support."

"I could do my job from Chicago. I've never been there."

Elizabeth smiled. "I'll let you know if I need you. In the meantime, if Keith asks, play dumb. I don't want him following me here trying to help."

"Okay."

They clicked off, and Elizabeth pulled into the lot of a chain hotel. No five stars here, but it would have to do. Her mother would choke if she knew. At the reception desk, she negotiated a month's stay for a decent price and went to her room to set up her office away from home.

She tossed her suitcase on the brown paisley bedspread and

pulled her laptop from her shoulder bag. While the computer booted up, she hung her suits in the minuscule closet and placed the remaining clothes in the dresser. From the front pocket of her suitcase, she pulled the frogs. For this trip, she had four.

She set the frogs beside her computer: two plastic, one stuffed, and one metal. It was her niece's way of making her feel at home. Before every business trip, Melissa snuck some frogs into the suitcase. It had started when Mel was little more than a toddler and offered Elizabeth her stuffed frog to keep her company. She'd just moved into Keith's carriage house, and her relationship with Mel was nonexistent. What did she know about kids?

But they'd bonded over frogs.

Over the years, it had bloomed into a collection. Her family now gave Elizabeth frogs for gifts. It became a competition to see who could find the ugliest one.

Smiling at her family of frogs, she set to work. Her first order of business would be to check out the competition. Returning to the computer, she Googled Irish bars in Chicago and then narrowed her search for the neighborhood.

The results stared at her, a mass of red pushpins on the screen. "How can there be so many damn Irish bars in one area?"

She expanded the map and looked closely. In a ten-mile radius, she counted twenty-three Irish pubs. She'd bet she wouldn't find that many in the entire state of Florida. Zooming in on the map, she copied the addresses of the five closest to The Irish Pub and sent the information to the GPS on her phone.

The Irish Pub.

What a dumb name. The total lack of creativity or originality grated on her nerves. She checked the time. Six o'clock. After-work hours for most. Tucking a notepad into her purse, she headed out to the first bar, figuring she'd get dinner along the way. The research and reconnaissance was the worst part of the job. Keith usually handled it. He was good at reading people.

She was better with the finances, which was why Brannigan Enterprises should be hers. The CEO didn't need to be a people person. The job required an understanding and ability to wrangle the bottom line. Definitely her forte.

Pulling into the lot alongside a bar called Duffy's, her stomach growled and her eyes felt dry. It promised to be a long night, and she planned to be back at the bar at nine. She climbed out of her car and pushed on. The sooner she got started, the sooner she'd be done.

For a Monday night, she hadn't expected to find crowds at any of the bars she'd chosen to investigate. She pushed through the glass doors of the bar and was met with chaotic noise. The crowd wasn't huge and the patrons were mostly young, early twenties. Two TVs blared in competition with the jukebox that played some kind of rock. As she moved toward the bar, her feet squeaked in the stickiness of the floor, and she cringed.

The lighting wasn't bright enough for her to see what made the floor gross or for her to make sure there wasn't anything stuck to the stool as she took a seat. The bar itself was made from a nice dark wood, walnut, if she had to guess, but puddles of some indeterminate liquid lingered across the surface.

Not very inviting.

She slung her purse over the back of the stool and waited. Within moments the bartender asked what she wanted.

"Do you have a menu?"

He slapped a laminated sheet of paper down in front of her. The menu consisted of the usual bar food: hot wings, burgers, nachos. "I'll have a burger, everything. Do you have a drink menu?"

"Huh?" His eyebrows rose with the question.

"A drink menu? So I can decide what to drink?"

"Uh, no."

Huh. How was a customer supposed to know what to order if choices weren't presented? "Can I have a wine spritzer?"

"Coming right up."

While she waited, she took in the atmosphere. Tuning out the noise, she focused on what she saw. Young people, dressed casually, congregated in clusters at tables. Waitresses circulated around, but the only thing that distinguished them from the customers were the aprons tied around their waists. No uniforms, no name tags. Cardboard decorations hung drunkenly from the soffit above the bar. Beer promotions and green-clad leprechauns dangled lopsided, and their discoloration told her they'd been hanging there far too long.

Her drink was delivered. She only took a small sip to find it relatively tasteless. When her burger arrived, it wasn't much better. She tossed money on the bar beside her half-eaten food. Regardless of location, when she was done, Duffy's wouldn't be much competition.

FOUR HOURS and three bars later, Elizabeth was ready to call it quits. She was tired of drinking cheap alcohol and being hit on. Her last stop for the night was O'Leary's. She'd almost decided against it, but after checking out their Web site on her phone, it looked too promising to pass up. Cars filled most of the lot, but spots were still available. She tugged the heavy oak door open and walked through, pleasantly surprised. No cigarette smoke and the noise level was tolerable. She eased her way toward the bar, scanning the crowd as she moved.

The main bar area had a variety of seating from booths to tables and in the back area she saw high-top tables and dart-boards. All of the waitresses wore O'Leary's Pub T-shirts with jeans and they each had a name tag. She took a seat at the end of the bar. On a small stand was a menu for both food and drinks.

This bar was doing something right.

The bartender came over as she was reading the menu. "Hi. What can I get you tonight?"

She looked up and swallowed hard. The man in front of her was mouthwateringly gorgeous. His mussed black hair framed a face dominated by a happy-go-lucky smile. She lost her ability to form coherent sentences. "Uh…"

He tilted his head and studied her face. "You look beat. Tough day?"

She nodded. What was wrong with her? She didn't do this around men. She'd had no fewer than eight different men try to pick her up tonight. This one was just doing his job, and she had to fight for focus.

"How about an Irish coffee?" Dark brows arched over navy eyes.

She cleared her throat. "Sounds good."

He walked away. She studied the menu. It wasn't fancy. Like the rest of the bars, it offered burgers and hot wings, but they had more traditional pub fare, like fish and chips and shepherd's pie. Her mouth watered at the thought of real food. The drink menu was plain as well, but at least displayed a list of drinks with the basic ingredients. Pictures and descriptions would've been better, but this bar had already exceeded the competition from the other Chicago neighbor-hood pubs she'd visited.

The bartender returned with her Irish coffee. She sipped

and found it perfect. The whipped cream puffed and floated on top and she used her straw to scoop some up. She ran her tongue over the cream-laden straw and heard a groan.

She looked up to find the bartender looking at her. Replacing the straw, she waited for an explanation.

His mouth quirked up at the corner. "Sorry. I couldn't help it. That was downright sinful."

Her cheeks flamed. She was blushing? No. The alcohol from earlier in the evening was catching up with her and colliding with her exhaustion. He broke eye contact and mumbled, "Give me a holler if you need anything else."

He walked away and picked up a conversation with other customers. She tried not to be obvious in studying him and the way he interacted with people. This was something the other bars had been missing as well. A personal touch.

She finished her drink, tossed cash on the bar, and took a few moments to wander toward the back of the bar. There was a small stage, a jukebox, and dartboards. Down a dimly lit hallway were the bathrooms. Too tired to think, she opted to leave. Part of her wanted to talk to some of the patrons, get their perspective as to why they came here, but it would have to wait.

By morning, hopefully Meg would have information about The Irish Pub and, with any luck, the books wouldn't be as bad as she imagined. As she wound her way back toward the front, raucous laughter exploded at the bar. The sexy bartender was enjoying something.

He caught her eye as she passed. His laughter made his eyes twinkle with mischief, his smile lighting his face, like he had the best life in the world. She wondered what it would be like to feel that even for a night. It wasn't that she was unhappy; she liked her life very much, in fact, but it had been too long since she'd experienced a laugh that shook her whole body.

~

COLIN O'LEARY BOUNDED down the back steps that led from his apartment to the bar. As he moved through the bar flipping on lights and prepping for the lunch crowd, he whistled a tune. As much as he enjoyed the crowds and the noise of the lively bar, this was his favorite part of the day. This was his time to be Colin O'Leary, bar owner. It didn't matter that the bar wasn't really his. Morning prep allowed him the time to pretend it was, that his father had left the bar to him. As if he hadn't screwed up everything.

Then the back door swung open and his bubble burst. He could tell by the sound of Ryan's steps that his brother was in a bad mood. Again.

"What's up?" Colin asked as he took chairs down and reset them where they belonged at each table.

"Don't ask. Did you get the inventory done?"

"Just about. I—"

Ryan spun from where he was making coffee. "What do you mean, just about? I told you I needed to get orders in today."

Colin let out a heavy breath. "As I tried to say, I got most of it done, but then we got slammed last night. By the time we got the crowd down to a manageable size, I was tired and didn't want to miscount."

Ryan shook his head. "Sorry I jumped on you. Things are a little crazy."

"Everything okay with Quinn? Any more problems?"

"Nothing more than usual. She's ready to pop and won't take it easy. You'd think that after spending most of the winter in bed, she'd know better. At this point, she just wants to have the baby. It doesn't help that Indy went into labor early. Indy's due date was a couple of weeks after Quinn's, so now she's really impatient."

Colin continued to work his way around the room. "Send her over to the house. Mom's so excited about the baby, she'll do nothing but fuss over her."

Ryan smiled. "I already tried. Quinn wouldn't fall for it."

"You look like shit. Aren't you sleeping?"

"Not much."

"Then take off. I can handle this."

Ryan raised a single eyebrow and Colin's shoulders tensed. After all these months, hadn't he proven enough yet? "It's inventory, not rocket science."

"How many times have you ordered?"

He shrugged. "Mary walked me through it while you were out of town. The distributors' numbers are in the Rolodex."

Ryan scrubbed a hand over his head. "No, I should check the numbers. I want to make sure we don't over-order."

Colin slammed a chair down harder than he'd intended. "When are you going to stop treating me like a fuckup? I've been here for a year, every day, doing exactly what you've asked. When are you going to stop punishing me for leaving?"

Ryan crossed his arms and stared at his feet. "You're right."

Silence.

At first Colin thought he'd imagined it. "What was that?"

A tired grin crossed Ryan's face. "You heard me. I said you're right. Something had to give. I thought I could keep doing it all with both bars even after getting married and having a baby."

"I told you I'm not going anywhere. You can depend on me. Let me take on more. Between Quinn and the baby and running Twilight, your hands are full. I'll ask if I have questions about anything before I make a move."

Ryan still didn't look sold on the idea.

"I'm ready for this."

"Fine." The acquiescence came quietly, but Ryan followed with a finger pointed at him. "But if you fuck up this time, Mom won't be able to save your ass."

"Like I'm afraid of you?" Maybe Ryan had forgotten who was the older brother.

As if he'd read Colin's mind, Ryan continued, "We're adults now, age is meaningless, except for the fact that your body has already taken an extra year of beating that mine hasn't, so I'm faster and stronger."

"Only in your dreams."

Ryan left on that note, and Colin felt the most at ease with his position in the family since his return. When their father died, Colin had taken off for three years. Everyone thought he'd done it out of anger because Dad gave O'Leary's to Ryan. He let them believe it because the truth was so much worse.

Now he finally had the chance to redeem himself. He no longer had to be the irresponsible, lazy O'Leary. He could finally become the man his father had expected him to be.

QUINN'S IRRESISTIBLE CHOCOLATE CAKE

2 c flour
   2 c sugar
   1 c cocoa powder
   2 tsp baking soda
   2 tsp baking powder
   2 eggs
   ¾ c vegetable oil
   1 tsp vanilla
   1 c milk
   1 c hot water

Preheat oven to 375 degrees. Grease and flour two 8- or 9-inch cake pans.

Combine all dry ingredients in a large bowl. Add eggs, oil, vanilla, and milk, and mix on low until well blended. Slowly add hot water while mixing. Batter will be runny.

Pour batter evenly into prepared cake pans and bake for 30

minutes or until a toothpick inserted in the center comes out clean.

Cool in pans for a few minutes, and then remove to cool completely.

Frost when cool.

Chocolate frosting

2 sticks soft butter
1 c cocoa powder
5 c powdered sugar
½ + c milk

Mix butter, cocoa, and powdered sugar until combined. Add ½ cup of milk and mix completely. Add more milk to desired consistency. Frost bottom layer of cake. Add top layer and frost.

ALSO BY SHANNYN SCHROEDER

<u>O'Learys</u>

More Than This

A Good Time

Something to Prove

Catch Your Breath

Just a Taste

Hold Me Close

<u>For Your Love</u>

Under Your Skin

In Your Arms

Through Your Eyes

From Your Heart

<u>Stand Alones</u>

Between Love and Loyalty

Meeting His Match

<u>Daring Divorcees</u>

One Night with a Millionaire

My Best Friend's Ex